CHAPTER 1

Mayfair District, London
April 1818

"JASPER, YE BOLLIX! No!"

Lily Farthingale had just passed through the front gate of her family's fashionable townhouse to turn onto Chipping Way when she heard a deep, rumbling bark, followed closely by a repeat of the man's frantic shout. In the next moment, she was knocked to the ground by the biggest, hairiest excuse for a dog she'd ever set eyes upon, more of a muddy brown carpet with legs and a playfully wagging tail.

"Ugh! Get off me!" Lily cried, but the dog paid no heed, too excited and happy to contain his joy. He stared down at her as though she were his favorite person in the world, even though she was now flat on her back in one of the many puddles left by the morning's rain, her spectacles dangling off her nose. "I said, get—*ew!*"

The slobbering beast had begun licking her face, his tongue leaving a trail of drool across her cheek, her chin, and even more disgustingly, on her mouth.

She was still spitting his drool from her lips when the owner reached her side and unceremoniously lifted Jasper out of the way. "Och, lass! Are ye hurt?"

Only my pride. "I don't think so. But I've lost my book." More precisely, she'd lost the book she had borrowed from her elderly neighbor, Lady Eloise Dayne, and was on her way to return when attacked by the playful beast. It had flown out of her hands, and she had no idea where it might have landed.

"I'm that sorry, lass. My fault entirely." The burly Scotsman knelt beside her, looming quite large, or so he seemed to her slightly dazed eyes— for he was broad in the shoulders and almost as shaggy as his dog. His reddish-brown hair was as thick and unkempt as his companion's. His bushy growth of beard made him appear as daunting as a pirate.

"I'll pay for the damage, of course." He tried to straighten the spectacles on her nose, but then simply removed them when he couldn't. "Ewan Cameron's the name, and I'm in residence at... och, I'm not sure o' that yet, but you can contact me through Eloise Dayne."

"You know Lady Dayne?" Lily gazed at him in surprise, wondering how and where a man such as he might have met her respectable neighbor.

"That I do, lass," he said with an engaging smile.

His lips were nicely shaped, and so was his jaw, what Lily could see of it beneath his beard. She ought to have been more than a little intimidated, perhaps afraid of this rugged stranger, but he'd mentioned Eloise, which meant he was no ruffian, though he quite looked the part.

He took gentle hold of her hand. "Can ye move?"

She nodded. "I'm sure I can."

"Good. Be careful now. Put your arms about my neck, and I'll help ye out of this puddle." He spoke in a deep, rumbling brogue that she found surprisingly comforting. "Poor little thing, ye must be soaked to the skin."

Up close, practically nose to nose, Lily could not help but notice his darkly sensual eyes, a deep, forest green with flecks of gray swirling within their depths. *Mercy!* "You mustn't concern yourself, sir." A little "eep" escaped her lips as his rough hands now circled her waist and his keen, assessing gaze locked onto hers. "I'm fine... truly."

"Can't say as much for your frock," he muttered, helping her to her unsteady feet, which must have been the reason he held on to her a moment longer than was necessary. He released her when she regained her footing, then retrieved his handkerchief, and was about to use it to dab the mud off her gown when he suddenly stopped and let out a short, strangled laugh. "Ah...er...och, lass," he said, his hands hovering precariously over her breasts, "ye'd better... I can't... no, I definitely can't—"

Lily followed his gaze as it swept the front of her gown.

Jasper's muddy paws had left a perfect imprint on each of her lightly heaving breasts—like an officious clerk with his itchy fingers on a new ink stamp. *Stamp! Stamp!* The delicate lemon silk just delivered yesterday, which she had worn for all of ten minutes, was ruined.

Oh, crumpets!

The noticeable paw prints on her front were bad enough, but there were also splotches of mud along the length of the expensive fabric, and cold, murky water from the puddle in which she'd landed now seeped down her back.

Jasper, obviously feeling contrite, whimpered as he came forward and rubbed his head against her knees. Tufts of his hair ground into the ruined fabric, leaving it not only wet and muddy but now adorned with dog hairs.

Oh, perfect! What more can go wrong today?

And where were her spectacles? She recalled Ewan Cameron had taken them off her nose before he put his arms around her...and then she'd gazed into his eyes and simply forgotten about everything.

"Can ye walk on your own, lass? Shall I help ye into the house?"

"Thank you, Mr. Cameron. I can manage the rest of the way." She couldn't very well say it had been a pleasure to meet him, since it hadn't been. Anyway, they hadn't been properly introduced. "It was a most unusual... well, unexpected... encounter. I don't suppose we shall ever meet again. Goodbye."

She turned to walk back into the house, took a step, and squished. Took another halting step, then another. *Squish, squish.*

Her humiliation was now complete.

"Lass, I had better go with ye," he said, clearing his throat and once again smothering the laughter Lily knew was desperate to burst out of him. "I can explain to your father. It wouldn't sit right with me if ye were punished for something that was entirely my fault."

"It isn't necessary," she insisted, holding her head up proudly even as droplets of water dripped off her nose. She wished he would stop acting kindly and simply go away.

The sooner this embarrassment was forgotten, the better.

Jasper, now standing between her and the Farthingale entry gate, began to whimper again.

"That's right. Ye ought to be ashamed, ye great beastie," his owner muttered. "Look at the mess ye've made of the pretty girl."

As though understanding his every word, the dog gazed at Lily with the softest, most innocent brown eyes. His tail wagged hesitantly, once... twice. Oh, his big chocolate eyes! Too adorable to resist. Lily succumbed with a sigh. "You're forgiven, Jasper. Now, to find my book—"

Jasper was off in a shot and back in a trice with the volume, a work written by the Scottish scientist Colin MacLaurin about sixty years ago on the theory of fluxions. Tail wagging, eyes gleaming with pride, he dropped it at her feet...and into the puddle from which she'd just emerged.

His owner let out an agonized groan. "Lass, I'll pay for that, too."

* * *

"Please don't trouble yourself, Mr. Cameron. It was an accident and nothing more."

Ewan Cameron stared at the girl with the prettiest blue eyes he'd seen in an age while she assured him that he was not responsible for his dog's actions. Of course, he was. However, he held his tongue, preferring to replace the book and stylish gown—a yellow confection that made him think of lemon sweets—as soon as possible, rather than waste time arguing about it with the young thing who was soaking wet and probably shaken from the jolt.

He retrieved the book from the puddle while she busied herself wringing water out of her obviously ruined gown. He also noticed her spectacles on the ground where he'd earlier set them aside, so he reached down and stuck them in his pocket before turning his attention back to her. "Ma... Mac... lau..." he murmured, examining the book's spine for the title. But he found it hard to make out the words, for they were smeared with mud and water stains.

"MacLaurin," she repeated smoothly, casting him an encouraging glance. "There's a symposium exploring his work on elliptic integrals at the Royal Society next week, and I thought to do a little studying on my own ahead of time."

"You're a bluestocking," he said with a chuckle but quickly regretted his words. Though he meant it as a compliment, few females would take it as such. Och, it was a clumsy thing to say—but she didn't seem to take offense.

"Yes, I suppose. I love to read... er, though many people don't and there's certainly nothing wrong with that, not at all. Not being able to read, that is." She cast him another encouraging glance.

"I enjoy it, too. When I have the time." He frowned, thinking of how much work he had and how little time he had to attend to all of it while in London. "Lately, I've had very little."

"Of course. I understand completely." She cast him yet another sympathetic look.

"Ye do?" Suddenly, he realized the girl believed him an ignorant oaf, illiterate and probably unable even to dress himself. And why wouldn't she think the worst? Ten days of hard riding from the Scottish Highlands to London, ten days of choking dust on the roadway, of not shaving and hardly bathing, had left him looking like the basest ruffian.

The clothes he wore, buff pants made of homespun and heavy brown jacket to ward off the Highland chill, were not in the least fashionable London attire. His brown leather boots were scuffed and stained from several years of use and abuse. His hands were rough and calloused, though he'd tried very hard to be gentle when helping the girl to her feet.

To this young innocent, he must look like his heathen warrior ancestors, lacking only blue paint on his face and battle axe in his hand to complete the image. "Lass, may I ask your name?"

She didn't appear ready to give it, but whatever she meant to say was drowned out by the sound of a carriage rumbling toward them. It turned out to be three gleaming black carriages rolling through the townhouse gate from which she'd emerged a short while ago, each led by a pair of high-stepping matched bays.

He let out a long, low whistle, admiring the horses and wondering who had picked them out. They were magnificent, but he didn't bother to ask the girl standing at his side. It wasn't something the pampered daughter of a wealthy household was likely to know. Then again, the young thing was not the typical society debutante. Och, she was pretty enough, but there was a scholarly earnestness about her that he found appealing, though a bit unusual.

A girl who looked remarkably like the one at his side, same black hair and striking blue eyes, popped her head out of the third carriage. "Lily, you're missing Lady Turbott's tea!" she cried as it passed by.

He turned in dismay to the girl he now understood was called Lily. "Lass, it seems I've ruined your entire day."

"Please don't give it another thought, Mr. Cameron. My family will never notice," she assured him with a wistful sigh.

"I can no' believe that." Were she his daughter, gazing up at him with those vibrant eyes and the obvious intelligence behind them, he'd have a hard time forgetting her.

"Oh, they love me," she hastened to explain, obviously noting his darkening expression. "I'm not at all neglected, as you can see by the quality of my new gown... well, no... never mind about that. My sister and I are identical twins, you see. I suppose it's obvious. She'll pretend to be me and no one will be the wiser. That's all I meant by it. The arrangement has worked quite well so far. I've already missed several of these society affairs because of my studies and never been reprimanded for it."

He quirked an eyebrow.

"Not that I'm proud of the deception, mind you," she continued, the momentary downcast of her eyes revealing that she felt some remorse for her wrongdoing. "But the scholarly work is so interesting, and sometimes these affairs can be so deadly dull. Dillie—that's my sister—doesn't mind helping me out at all."

"I'm surprised ye have no' been caught yet. You're not entirely alike," he said with a shake of his head. "Your eyes are a more vivid blue than your sister's, and your features softer, like the soft coat on a newborn lamb."

She blushed. "Oh, that's a lovely thing to say. Thank you. Er, you did mean it as a compliment, didn't you?"

He nodded. "That I did, Lily."

She slipped the book out of his hands. "I had better change my gown. Goodbye, Mr. Cameron. I hope Lady Dayne finds you a nice place to live."

CHAPTER 2

"WHY DIDN'T YOU tell Lily that you're to reside with your grandfather?"

"I did no' wish to involve myself in long explanations," Ewan said, feeling too big for his delicate silk chair. He and Lady Eloise Dayne were sitting in the drawing room of her imposing residence at Number 5 Chipping Way, situated on one of the prettiest streets in the elegant district of Mayfair.

Though Eloise had made him feel quite welcome, Ewan knew he was out of place amid the clamor and clatter of London, with its smoke-filled air, muddy Thames waters, and crowded streets. He couldn't wait to fulfill the damn promise and return to his Highlands home. Indeed, he already missed the dark, soaring crags and windswept valleys as lush and green as the eye could see in summertime. By fall, those valleys took on a soft, purple hue, and by winter they were a rugged brown, dotted with patches of white snow.

The crystal loch waters remained eternally blue, as deep and bright a blue as Lily's sparkling eyes, he realized, but dismissed the thought as quickly as it had come to mind. "Besides, I have no' been to Lotheil Court yet and do no' know where it is."

As Eloise leaned forward in her chair, the gray silk of her gown rustled like wind through one of those Highland valleys. "Then you are the only man in this fair city who doesn't know that the London residence of the Duke of Lotheil is located off Knightsbridge in Belgravia. You could have asked Lily, she would have told you."

"And reveal to her that I'm the duke's grandson? Och, no. There'll be none of that for me. The lass might get ideas."

"About what?"

"Marriage. Isn't that the only thing these English girls are taught to think about? How to sink their claws into the first unsuspecting bachelor who stumbles their way? I can assure ye, no weepy-eyed, drippy-nosed English girl will trap me. I'll be off for Scotland the moment I've fulfilled my promise."

Eloise's jaw dropped. "It is obvious you know nothing about Lily. Honestly, Ewan! Did you lie to Lily? What name did you give her?"

"Ewan Cameron, which is my own. I'm Laird Carnach in my own right, and have no need to grovel before my grandfather in the hope he'll restore me as his heir. The bastard can stuff his dukedom up his noble arse."

"Ewan!"

"My apologies," he said, running a hand through his hair in frustration, "but 'tis this damnable deathbed promise I gave to my father. What can I accomplish in three months that he and my grandfather failed to do over the course of thirty years?"

Eloise sighed. "They were always like two oak trees standing tall and proud against the wind—each too proud to bow, and suffering the consequences for it. Had they been less alike in temperament, one of them might have bent a little and saved the family connection."

"Grandfather's to blame," Ewan insisted, not bothering to mask his contempt. "He cut my father out of the line of succession simply because he dared to marry a MacKenzie. He knew nothing of my mother, yet dismissed her out of hand, for she wasn't one of the pale-haired, weak-minded English debutantes he'd selected for his son. He never gave my mother the chance to show her worth. She was the best. Gracious and loving. But the old man had made his devil's pact with the *Sassenach* invaders and was determined that Father should marry one of them."

Ewan paused, struggling to regain his composure as a wave of sadness overcame him. "Father loved her dearly and was never the same after she died."

Eloise leaned forward and patted his hand. "I expect this past year has not been easy for you or Meggie either, first losing your mother to illness and then your father so soon afterward."

"He wasted away of a broken heart. There can be no other explanation for it." That was eight months and two weeks ago, by Ewan's count. And now he was here in London, forced to fulfill the promise to his father. The timing could not have been worse, for it was the height of the London season. Having to deal with his grandfather was bad enough, but dealing with him while all of London society watched and gossiped was going to be intolerable.

Hellfire!

Eloise seemed to soften in the face of his discomfort. "I know these next three months will be hard on you, but you must get through it for Meggie's sake as much as for yours. When is your sister due to arrive?"

"End of the week." He shook his head and sighed. "Meggie's scared out of her wits, thinks our grandfather will eat her alive if she crosses him. That does no' leave me much time to smooth the way."

"It might help if she had female companionship during her stay."

"Why? I'll be here to protect her. But she'll need a lady's maid. I'll select a suitable girl from my grandfather's staff, or hire one if I don't like the look of them."

Eloise rolled her eyes. "Meggie will need much more than a maid, unless you intend to keep her locked in her bedchamber for the duration of her stay. Oh, I know you have no such plan," she added before he could protest. "So you must allow me to guide her. First, I'll arrange a fitting for her with my dressmaker. She'll require suitable gowns for the season."

"I have no intention of putting my sister on the marriage mart. She's no head of prime Scottish beef."

"Indeed, not! And as for gaining entrance into society, it wouldn't be proper at all just now. You've both just come out of mourning for your parents. But what harm can there be in a few quiet enjoyments, perhaps an occasional party to lighten her grief? She's young and merry. These next few months will be impossible for her without these small distractions. Does she dance?"

"Aye."

"Highland reels, I suppose. I'll hire a dance instructor."

Ewan frowned.

"Dear boy, you must stop fretting. I promise you that I won't turn her into a proper English lady. Indeed, if she's as strong-willed as you, I'm sure she'll bite the head off any English gentleman who dares approach her," she said with a mock shudder.

"Och, that's the problem. She isn't. Quite the opposite, she's as sweet-tempered as my mother was." He gave a wistful shake of his head. "I'm already regretting my agreement to bring her to town."

"It isn't a mere agreement," Eloise reminded him. "You made a sacred promise to your father that the pair of you will reside with your grandfather these next three months. That your grandfather accepted the arrangement can only mean he bitterly regrets his actions toward your parents and seeks to make amends."

Ewan doubted it. The old bastard's agreement merely signified that he sought to control Ewan and his sister now that their father was out of the way to prevent it. However, Eloise meant well, and he was glad to call her a friend. Not wishing to overset her further, he allowed her to return their conversation to descriptions of those insipid society functions.

"Though your months here will be on the quieter side, it surely cannot hurt to attend an occasional soiree or musicale. There are several fine Scots families in town at the moment. Why, even my grandson is here with his wife. You remember Graelem, don't you?"

He nodded. "A decent chap."

"He's married to Lily's sister, Laurel."

"Is she as... er, unusual as Lily?"

Eloise frowned. "There is nothing wrong with Lily. She's a dear girl, and has been a good friend to me these past five years since they moved next door."

"You mistake my meaning, Eloise. I meant to compliment the girl. She's different, that's all." Ewan realized that the well-meaning old dowager was probably quite bored living alone in this grand home and eager for young company. He was glad that Lily often visited her. He hoped Meggie would make her as good a companion as that pretty bluestocking.

"I shall accept a few engagements on your behalf," she continued, "but only those I think will best distract Meggie and allow for quiet amusement."

"Very well." His hatred for his grandfather had blinded him to the practical implications of their visit. How would he and Meggie endure all that time under the old man's roof? Eloise's suggestions had merit. "I'll rely on you to guide my sister. Spare no cost to make her happy."

"What of you?"

He laughed. "I'll leave you ladies to the business of going about the shops. I'll find other ways to pass the time."

Eloise cast him another stern glance. "And abandon your sister? It is important for Meggie to have you close at hand. She can't attend any of these social engagements alone."

"She'll have you."

"As much as I adore her, I'm not family."

Ewan scowled. "This isn't some trick of yours to turn me into a proper English gentleman, is it?"

"Heavens, no. Even if I wished to, you're far too stubborn for me to succeed. No, I quite like you as you are. You're a handsome man, or rather, you will be pleasing to look at once you've properly cleaned up. At the moment, you look shaggier than Jasper."

Ewan eased back, laughing softly. "Very well, but don't you dare take your matchmaking aim at me. I will not have an English bride."

Eloise's butler walked in just then carrying a tray laden with cakes, a teapot, and the makings for a proper tea. Assuming the role of hostess with elegance and obvious ease, Eloise poured Ewan a cup of tea before resuming the conversation he preferred she would forget. "Well, you're almost twenty-nine years old and have never been married."

He dropped two cubes of sugar and a lemon slice into his cup. "Never found the right girl."

She handed him a slice of plum cake. "What harm can there be in searching for one here? There are many young ladies who come down from Scotland at this time of year. Any one of them will make an excellent wife. And not all English girls are detestable. Take Lily, for example."

"Her again." Ewan let out another rumble of laughter. "She's a pretty lass, but also very young. I do no' rob from the cradle."

"She's almost nineteen."

In truth, he'd noticed her womanly curves. How could any man miss the way she was put together? Slender waist, long neck… soft shoulders. Even softer lips. Nor could he overlook her nicely shaped breasts, not with Jasper's paw prints clearly stamped atop them.

He shook out of his wayward thoughts. "She seems a very clever girl and a decent sort. I would have been ranting had someone—or someone's dog," he added, casting a scowl in Jasper's direction, "dropped me into a puddle. But she did no' get in the least ruffled and said it was no' necessary to rectify the damage. I will, of course. So I'll be needing the name of her dressmaker."

"That would be the same as mine, Madame de Bressard. She runs the busiest fashion establishment in town."

He pursed his lips. "Busy, you say? Then it will take a bit of doing to have Lily's gown replaced by tomorrow."

"Quite a bit," Eloise said with a grin, obviously referring to the coin he'd have to spend to achieve the intended result. "Her prices are little more than sanctioned thievery."

"I'll no' pinch pennies when it comes to setting things right with the lass. There's also the matter of the book she intended to return to you today."

"That might be a little harder to replace," Eloise said, handing him another slice of plum cake. "You see, it was a first edition acquired by my husband shortly before his death. You know how he loved shopping for these little finds."

Ewan's heart twisted into a knot, understanding the sentiment attached to the book above and beyond the financial outlay. "I'm truly sorry. A greater loss than I imagined, for I can never replace the memory of his joy in its acquisition."

"No, no, dear boy. He would not have blamed you, nor do I. In truth, I've never read the book and don't intend to. My taste runs to gossip sheets and scandalous novels, but Lily gets such pleasure from my husband's library. She'll feel responsible for failing to return it to me in its proper condition, but I'll assure her—"

"No." He lifted his teacup as though it were a tankard of ale and gulped down the last of the liquid, which had now cooled. "I'll set that right tomorrow, as well."

"Nonsense, dear boy. I'll stop by the antiquarian shops on Charing Cross Road sometime next week and see what they have available. It isn't all that rare a book. I'm certain I will lay my hands on two or three copies in no time."

Next week? Though he did not know Lily at all, he sensed she was the sort who would silently agonize until all was properly put back in place. He resolved to browse the bookshops as soon as he finished with Madame de Bressard tomorrow morning. Perhaps squeeze both chores in between his other responsibilities this afternoon.

Having devised a plan in his own mind, Ewan spent another few minutes reminiscing with his hostess and polishing off the last of the outrageously tasty plum cake. As he rose to leave, he wondered whether the duke's kitchen staff at Lotheil Court was as talented as Eloise's cook. He'd find out soon enough. "Eloise, I've enjoyed your company, but there's too much left to be done before nightfall."

"Of course, but here's one last matter before you go." She rang for Watling and instructed the man to bring in certain papers she'd left on her desk.

"What are these for?" Ewan asked as the butler returned and handed them over.

"The first sheets are letters of introduction to your father's London solicitors, Dumbley and Sons, and bankers, Lord Guinn and Mr. Ashfield at the Royal Bank. I can vouch for both since my late husband and I have used their services for years. They still represent my interests."

"And these others?"

Eloise took a deep breath. "I suspected that you were too caught up in your duties to think of these small matters, so I took the liberty of making lists of the best men's clubs, tailors, employment agencies. You'll need to acquire a valet. Obviously, you're in dire need of one to dress you properly."

"I do no' need some *Sassenach* wanker—"

"Ewan! Your language!"

"Och, Eloise, I'm sorry. You know I do no' belong here, dressing like a peacock and sipping tea with my little finger daintily pointed into the air. I can no' tiptoe around, for I'm a big oaf. I'm already struggling to be on my best behavior, and even my best is abysmal. No matter, though. I'll have work enough to keep me busy and out of trouble sorting out the last details of Father's estate."

She cast him an indulgent glance. "Of course. And I'll busy myself entertaining Meggie. But I'll have to make some tactical changes if you will not always be at her side. Would you mind if I introduced her to Lily? Encouraged a friendship between the two girls?"

He arched an eyebrow and laughed. "Do I have a choice in the matter?"

"I suppose, as her brother," she said, but the determined gleam in her eyes warned that he didn't really.

He nodded. "She's about Meggie's age and seems to be a steady lass."

"She is. I'm sure Meggie will like all the Farthingale girls."

"Are there more than just Laurel, Lily, and her twin?"

Eloise nodded. "Five of them. The twins, Lily and Daffodil."

"Daffodil?"

"Everyone calls her Dillie." Eloise shook her head and sighed. "Goodness, what were her parents thinking when they named her? Anyway, the twins are the youngest daughters and still unmarried. There's Rose Farthingale, the eldest, who is married to Julian Emory, the present Viscount Chatham. Laurel is married to my grandson, Graelem Dayne, who is next in line to the baronial estates of Moray. Daisy recently married my other grandson, Gabriel Dayne, who was made Earl of Blackthorne as reward for his bravery in battle."

A lot of fancy titles, Ewan thought, but are they decent in their hearts? He was acquainted with Graelem, liked and admired him. "Do what you think best, Eloise. I trust your judgment."

He leaned over and gave her a peck on the cheek before heading for the door. "I'm grateful for all you've done for me and my sister. I do no' know how we can ever repay your kindness."

A blush crept up her lightly wrinkled cheeks. "Nonsense, dear boy. That's what old friends are for, and I do mean old." she said with a chuckle. "Our families have known each other for decades. I shudder to think how many!"

He bussed her cheek again and left.

Papers in hand, he descended the front steps in a hurry, for he had much to do before the day was through. Eloise had arranged for her carriage to take him to his grandfather's residence, Lotheil Court, and even allowed Jasper into the gleaming conveyance for the ride.

"You'd better no' piss on the fine leather," he warned his happily slobbering companion as they drove away. Jasper ignored him, instead poking his head out of the window and whimpering as they turned through the gate onto Chipping Way. "What now, ye big looby?"

Ewan glanced out and saw Lily, now wearing a simple white gown with a peach shawl over it, searching for something by the puddle into which she'd fallen. She looked as tempting as a peach ice on a hot summer's day.

"Bollix. Her spectacles," he suddenly realized, reaching into his breast pocket and starting to instruct the driver to bring the carriage to a halt so he might return them. But a lens popped out as he withdrew the spectacles, and so did the tiny screws attaching the nose piece.

"Jasper, ye looby." He'd have to replace those too.

CHAPTER 3

EWAN'S GRANDFATHER summoned him into his library shortly after Ewan had settled into the quarters assigned to him. "How do you like your rooms?" the old man asked, not bothering to rise from his chair. The blasted monstrosity was as big as a throne and situated behind a large mahogany desk in the center of the imposing library. A silver candelabra with scented candles sat atop the desk, gleaming as though new and never used, although Ewan knew it had been acquired by an ancestor centuries ago.

Mahogany shelves filled with books ran from floor to soaring ceiling and covered all four walls. An exquisite burgundy carpet of oriental design covered much of the polished wood floor. The library and the man seated squarely in the center of it exuded wealth and power.

"Does it matter what I think?" It did not escape Ewan's notice that the old man had failed to give him permission to sit in either of the two chairs placed in front of the desk. He considered taking a seat anyway, but decided against it. He wasn't planning on staying in his grandfather's company a moment longer than was necessary. No point in getting comfortable. When he challenged his grandfather, it would be over something more important than the offer of a seat he didn't want in the first place.

"I suppose not. But this was your father's home, and can be yours if you'll allow it. You may not like me, but I'm your grandfather, and there's no denying the family resemblance."

To Ewan's disappointment, the old man did bear a striking resemblance to Ewan's father... as did Ewan. The duke was not as broad in the shoulders as he was, or as his father had been. However, the old man must have been formidable in his earlier days. Ewan noticed the portrait of the duke as a young man hanging over the fireplace mantel and inwardly shuddered. Damn. He could have been gazing into a mirror.

He studied his grandfather. The duke still had a full head of hair, though now a snowy white. His stern lips had yet to crack a smile.

In truth, Ewan wasn't smiling either.

"I put you in your father's bedchamber. Thought it might please you. Margaret will have the rooms next to yours. You'll both join me in the summer salon for breakfast each morning at eight. Promptly. Do as you wish the rest of the day." He rose and stepped around the desk to approach Ewan, his movements showing none of the frailty often associated with old age. "Is there anything you need?"

"No," Ewan said.

"Let me know if I've overlooked anything for Margaret's comforts."

"I'll provide *Meggie* with whatever she needs." Ewan tried to recall the last time anyone who truly knew his sister had called her by that given name.

"Ewan, I—"

"Will that be all, Your Grace?"

The old man sighed. "Yes, I suppose. For now. Breakfast is at eight o'clock sharp."

*   *   *

Ewan arose at daybreak the next morning, annoyed to find his clothes cleaned and pressed, and boots polished to a perfect shine despite the fact that he had come in late the night before and not left them out for the duke's servants to tend.

Someone must have come into his quarters during the night and taken them.

Jasper, his trusted watchdog, was stretched out like a lump on the cool marble tiles in front of the hearth, sound asleep and snoring in that rheumy, whining way that only Jasper could manage.

"Wake up, ye looby. Did I no' teach you to bark when a stranger enters?"

Jasper forced one eye open and shot him a look.

"Right, we're the strangers. Is that what you're trying to tell me? Still, you could have warned me." In truth, Ewan was just as irritated with himself. He'd been pleasantly surprised to encounter a friend down from Scotland, a hard-drinking companion who happened to be passing through London on his way to Dover. Before Ewan knew it, he was stumbling back to Lotheil Court in the wee hours of the morning. He barely remembered taking off his clothes before his head hit the pillow.

Most comfortable bed he'd ever slept in.

Best sleep he'd had in months.

Then again, he was piss drunk and would have felt as comfortable collapsing into a coal bin.

His throat was parched and his head pounded louder than a war drum. Not even the hot bath he'd taken before joining his friend for the evening had worked to soothe the tension in his muscles.

"Stuffy in here, isn't it, Jasper?" Ewan strode across the room, drew aside the drapes, and opened a window. The hazy glare of sunlight and a hot breeze assaulted his senses. "Bollix! Wind's blowing off the Thames." He shut the window and sighed. "Three months o' this? Don't know if I can take even one more day."

Someone rapped lightly at his door.

"Go away," Ewan said at the same time a thin, impeccably groomed gentleman a few years younger than his grandfather opened the door and stepped in.

He stifled an oath and quickly donned his pants. "I told you to go away."

"I'm Jergens," the gentleman replied, "your valet while you're here. May I assist you with your clothing?"

Ewan let out a soft growl. "Put a hand on me and that's the last you'll ever see of it."

The man took a step back. "My lord, you appear to be out of sorts this morning. I took the liberty of preparing a... er, remedy for the headache I expected you to have upon awakening. The glass is sitting on the table beside your bed."

"What's in it?" He followed the direction of his valet's gaze.

"It's best you don't know," Jergens replied without so much as a blink.

Ewan stepped to the table and lifted the glass to his nose. His eyes instantly began to tear and he let out a gagging cough. "What the hell is this? Smells worse than a horse's arse!"

"An old Scottish remedy," Jergens said. "I gave the same to your father whenever he came home a little worse for wear."

"You knew my father?" Ewan glanced at the man in surprise. "How long have you been working here?"

"Oh, well over forty years. I started as a lad of sixteen." He paused the length of a heartbeat. "Yes, I knew your father. I was his valet, too."

"And now my grandfather's ordered you to spy on me."

"Yes, my lord. I'm required to provide details of your every movement."

Ewan, still holding the glass and its vile contents, arched an eyebrow.

"He ordered me to spy on you, not lie to you," Jergens said smoothly. "Is there anything else you wish, my lord? Shall I take Jasper for his morning walk?"

Jasper wagged his tail.

"I'll walk him." Ewan drained the contents of his glass. If Jasper trusted Jergens, then he might as well give the man a chance. Surely his grandfather had the entire household staff under orders to watch him and Meggie and report their every movement. Probably had Bow Street runners watching him as well. "Bollix, that stinks."

Had they seen him enter Madame de Bressard's dress shop to order the replacement gown for the lass, Lily? And purchase the MacLaurin book on Charing Cross Road? He intended to visit his father's London bankers and solicitors today.

The duke probably had them in his pocket as well.

*　*　*

Lily was about to change out of her morning dress and into her new riding habit for a jaunt in Hyde Park to take advantage of the fine April afternoon when her maid dashed into the room, quite breathless and excited. "What is it, Gladys?"

The girl paused but a moment to adjust her pert white cap. "Two boxes just arrived for you, Miss Lily! And there's a letter with them!"

"From the Royal Society?" she asked, her heart rushing into her throat. Was it possible they'd had a change of heart and accepted her research paper for publication?

Gladys shook her head, her blonde curls bobbing like corks upon a stormy sea. "No 'um. Lady Sophie recognized the crest on the messenger's livery and claims the boxes are from the Duke of Lotheil!"

Lily frowned lightly and resumed changing into her riding habit. "There must be some mistake. The duke and I are not acquainted." Still, he was on the board of directors of the Royal Society. Could it be? No, she decided with sinking heart. He'd spoken out loudest against her admission into that male bastion.

"I don't know, yer mother's rarely wrong about such matters. It must be 'im for sure. Yer Aunt Julia agrees."

She groaned, suddenly realizing the effect correspondence from a duke would have on her boisterous and extremely meddlesome family. "Who else knows about the packages?"

"Everyone. They're all waiting for you downstairs."

"Good gracious. All this fuss over one of Dillie's tricks."

"My tricks are never that subtle," her sister said, choosing that moment to enter the room they shared. She proceeded to poke about the enormous armoire that spanned the length of one wall, searching for her own riding clothes. She tossed several gowns across their neatly made beds, messing the cream satin counterpanes. "Putting honey in your shoes, a toad in your bed, sewing up your sleeve cuffs, that's more my style. Who is E.C.?"

"I haven't a notion. Why do you ask?" Lily helped Gladys to pick up the gowns and put them back in order. Then she finished fastening her black velvet skirt and riding jacket, donned her polished boots, and looked closely into the mirror to inspect herself. Her eyesight wasn't all that bad, nor was it very good. Too much reading, her mother had insisted, was to blame.

She could see clearly when squinting, but that wouldn't do. One could not go about in society looking like a mole just come out of its burrow.

Drat. She had to find her spectacles.

"Mother said something about an E.C."

Lily shook her head. "Doesn't sound familiar."

"Aha! Here's my riding habit. Wait for me. We can march downstairs together."

She watched as Dillie quickly changed into her riding attire. The two sisters then turned to each other with matching sardonic grins, for they were mirror images, both dressed in black velvet skirt and jacket, and polished black boots.

"You look nice, Miss Lily. The black velvet brings out the shine in your dark hair and deepens the blue of your eyes. Why, they almost look violet. And I like how you've styled your hair."

"Thank you, Gladys." She'd pulled it back in a fashionable French braid. Nothing too fancy or complicated. She peered into the mirror once more while she pinched some pink into her cheeks and lightly nipped at her lips to add a little flush and fullness to them.

Dillie nudged her out of the way. "My turn. Are you sure you don't know what an E.C. is?"

"I'm certain. Why do you keep asking?"

"Because the envelope is addressed to Miss Lily Farthingale from E.C."

"Not a *what*, but a *who*," Lily corrected her sister. A thought crossed her mind, but she quickly shook it off. No, it couldn't be Mr. Cameron. Surely, he had no money. And what was his name? Alexander? Malcolm? Angus? Perhaps, James? "An E.C. with a duke's crest?"

Dillie and Gladys nodded.

"Right, time to solve the mystery." She descended the stairs, ready to face the horde of aunts, uncles, and cousins, ranging in age from six to sixty, who were gathered in the entry hall for the sole purpose of finding out why the duke had sent her those boxes.

It was to be expected. Farthingales were notorious for prying into everyone's business but their own, which they tended to leave in shocking disarray. Though the Farthingale townhouse was a large, gray stone affair with equally large and impressive rooms, right now it felt quite small and oppressive.

Her mother stepped forward. "Here they are... er, Lily?"

"Yes, Mother. It's me."

"Good. Are you certain you're not Dillie?"

"I ought to know myself." She breezed past her relatives, scooped up the boxes, and made for the stairs.

Dillie blocked her path. "We do not keep secrets in this family."

More precisely, one tried to keep secrets but never succeeded in this household.

She heard the word "duke" whispered several times. Finally, her uncle George folded his arms across his chest and said, "You're not going to win this battle, Lily."

"Even you, Uncle George?" All was lost if her most reliable ally had deserted to the enemy. Not that her family was that...no, she loved them all dearly...most days.

Sighing, Lily opened the smallest box. "My spectacles! Wherever did he find them? You see, I lost them yesterday," she started to explain, but quickly saw that no one cared.

A collective rumble of disappointment resounded through the entry hall. Had they expected diamonds?

"Open the other box," her mother urged.

Lily smothered a smile. Having established three daughters in brilliant matches, the matriarch of the Farthingale family obviously believed a fourth was at hand. "I've never met the duke, and he's only aware of my existence because he wishes to keep me out of the Royal Society," Lily said while unwrapping the second, a slightly bigger and heavier box. "The MacLaurin book!"

"A book!" Her mother turned away in disgust. The other relatives soon lost interest, too, leaving only Dillie and her uncle George at her side.

"Open the letter," Dillie urged. "Is it from the duke?"

"No, it's from Mr. Cameron. Ewan Cameron."

"Of course! I saw you with him... the man with the overly friendly dog." Dillie grinned wickedly. "Large fellow. Nice looking. How did he get hold of the duke's stationery?"

"Or the duke's messenger." Lily nibbled her lip with concern. The letter contained little more than another apology and no indication of where he had settled. "He knows Eloise. I'll show her this note and ask her to speak to Mr. Cameron. He's a Scot, a Highlander judging from his dress and demeanor, and may not understand about... er, borrowing writing paper from a duke."

Her uncle began to stroke his chin. "When did you happen to meet this Mr. Cameron?"

"Yesterday when I—" She stopped in mid-sentence, realizing no one but Dillie knew she had missed Lady Turbott's function. "Just before we all left for the tea."

He pinned her with a stern glare. "Which you obviously missed, though you would have your family believe otherwise. Dillie pretended to be you."

She nodded. "Let me explain about—"

"No need. Your little secret is safe with me for now."

Lily threw her arms about his neck and gave him a quick hug. "Thank you, Uncle George."

Her uncle, sharp as a tack and dogged as a bull terrier, shook his head soberly. "Girls, your parents have gone to great expense to introduce the two of you into society. They believe you're both attending the many functions held, meeting eligible gentleman, the finest London has to offer."

Lily glanced down at her feet, feeling a little ashamed, for her parents had indeed expended great effort on her behalf. "I know. I never meant to trick them."

"You've been spending too much time in Eloise's library, poring over musty science chronicles while Dillie, your partner in crime, has been covering for you."

"I promise not to let it happen again. Truly."

"You had better remain true to your word, Lily. I don't hold to deception, particularly when it involves your parents. You know they love you dearly." His frown faded into a grin. "Even though they can't seem to tell you apart."

"Too bad you still can," Dillie muttered.

"It's in the eyes. Gives you girls away immediately."

Lily glanced up in surprise. "How odd. Mr. Cameron said the same thing."

"Did he?" Her uncle took her by the arm, his large hand taking gentle grasp of her elbow. "Tell me more about this Mr. Cameron."

He led Lily and her sister into the more private summer salon. She and Dillie settled on an aquamarine silk ottoman, a hideous piece of furniture acquired by her mother on impulse—though what could have possessed her mother to purchase that tasseled monstrosity—well, it wasn't important at the moment.

"About Mr. Cameron." Her uncle reached out and tucked a finger under her chin to turn her to face him. He must have thought her mind had wandered, as it often did.

"There isn't much to tell. His dog, Jasper, accidently knocked me down while I was on my way to Eloise's to return a book I had borrowed. I lost my spectacles, ruined the book, and soiled my new gown. Mr. Cameron took it upon himself to replace all but the gown."

"I see."

"No, you don't," she responded, growing more concerned as she pondered Mr. Cameron's fate. "He doesn't have a place to live yet and now he's spent all his money on me."

"Obviously, he has settled in with the Duke of Lotheil."

"He can't possibly have." She felt heat creep up her neck and cheeks. "Uncle George, I must speak to Eloise as soon as possible. I'll need her help to pull Mr. Cameron out of this scrape."

He slipped the letter out of her hands and into his pocket. "Lily, let me handle the matter. I think it best that I speak to Eloise and Mr. Cameron."

"You won't have him put in prison, will you?"

Her uncle shook his head and cast her a wry grin. "Neither he nor his dog will be clapped in irons. You have my word on it. Now, run along and enjoy your ride. It's too beautiful a day to waste indoors."

* * *

"A spectacular day," Lily decided as she, Dillie, and their cousin, William Farthingale, rode out of the stable and turned onto Rotten Row. William was George's son and all of twenty-two. He'd been assigned by the family elders to serve as their chaperon during the season, a foolish choice in Lily's opinion. Her cousin fancied himself a rake and, in true rakehell fashion, had his eyes on every female in Hyde Park but them.

Neither she nor Dillie protested when he rode ahead to greet several young gentlemen of his acquaintance. They purposely lagged behind, neither one of them keen on his circle of friends.

"First blue sky we've seen in months, but we have many such days in Coniston," Lily said with a sigh, thinking wistfully of their quiet country home, though no house was ever very quiet with Farthingales about. "I wish we were there now."

"So do I."

"Truly? I thought you were enjoying London?" Lily closed her eyes and turned her face toward the sun, enjoying the warm breeze and clean scent that tickled her nose. London air was rarely this fresh, and she sought to take advantage while it lasted.

"There's nothing so fine as a day spent fishing at Yewtree Tarn."

Lily opened her eyes and turned to her sister, a gleam in her eye. "Or reading on the bank beneath the giant yew tree by the tarn."

"Or picnicking in the valley or hiking up Coniston Old Man. But those days are gone, mere faded memories."

"Why sound so gloomy, Dillie? The season will be over in a few months, and we'll return home to enjoy the August heat and October chill."

"And the Christmas snowfall." Dillie cast her an odd look. "I'll miss it without you."

"Something's addled your brain. Where do you think I'll be, if not with our family?"

"Surely, it hasn't escaped your notice."

"I haven't a clue what you're talking about."

"Your encounter with E.C., in front of our townhouse... on Chipping Way."

"No, no, no!" Lily burst into laughter. "The Chipping Way bachelor's curse is all stuff and nonsense. Besides, Mr. Cameron didn't run into me. His dog did. And I doubt Father would consent to my marrying his dog."

"You're purposely being obtuse."

"Who taught you that fancy word? Obtuse? I'm not. Really, Dillie. This is too much!"

"You can't explain away what happened to Rose, Laurel, or Daisy."

"More precisely, what happened to the unsuspecting bachelors who met their doom upon encountering them on our street. They were gentlemen. *Gentlemen.* Not clumsy heathens passing through town."

"Mr. Cameron is obviously not a heathen. He took the trouble to replace your spectacles and the MacLaurin book."

"He probably stole the book." She was uncertain what to do about that.

"He knows Eloise, and she doesn't invite just anyone into her home."

"You must put Mr. Cameron out of your mind. He isn't at all the sort of man I'd consider suitable husband material. No, indeed. Though I would be glad to have him along if I were off on an exotic adventure. He seems quite capable. Strong."

"Handsome."

"Very, if one looks beyond his beard and shaggy hair," Lily admitted, though it wasn't as much of an admission as a fact. "He seems to be the no-nonsense sort. And he's big and brutish, the sort of man no ruffian would dare trifle with. But enough about him. As I said, put him out of your mind."

Dillie glanced over her head and down the bridle path. "I don't think I can."

"Why not?"

"Because he's walking toward us. He's seen us."

Lily's heart began to beat a little faster. "Oh, no."

"Oh, yes." Dillie chuckled.

Lily muffled an anguished groan as Mr. Cameron, with Jasper bounding at his side, approached. He had on the same clothes he'd worn yesterday and appeared just as unkempt. Well, not quite as ungroomed as yesterday. His beard was neatly trimmed and boots polished to a shine. She noticed that his clothes had been washed and ironed, and even from this distance she could see that he'd bathed, for his hair gleamed only as clean hair would in sunlight, now appearing more red than brown. A rich shade of chestnut. Quite nice, really.

"Not bad," Dillie murmured.

"For a heathen." She hated to admit that he might be the handsomest man she'd ever encountered, even if he did resemble a rugged Highland rogue. "Not at all like Lord Mortimer's son, Ashton."

"Oh, him." Dillie scrunched her nose.

"What's wrong with Ashton? He's a nice young man." And a good match for her, if she were ready to settle down and marry. He was tall, blond, and decent looking. More important, he was a thoughtful gentleman who enjoyed scholarly pursuits.

"Nice? Is that the best you can come up with? Does he make your heart sing? Your legs buckle?"

"Love is not the same as animal attraction. Attraction is a physical response, a hot jolt as you just described, something necessary for procreation, which is why rams, stags, and stallions roam about during mating season with their male parts ever in readiness and why females of the respective species emit a scent that—"

"Lily!"

"The point is, attraction fades as quickly as it appears. Love is something that lasts over decades. Love grows slowly, develops deep roots over time."

"Over a season?"

"Much longer." Because it was taking her longer than expected to develop feelings for Ashton. She wasn't certain why. He was a perfect match for her, and it didn't matter that his hair lay a little flat and thin around his face, or that he wasn't nearly so handsome as Mr. Cameron. He was thoughtful, intelligent, and the youngest man admitted to the Royal Society. That counted far more than good looks.

"Good day, Lily," Mr. Cameron called out to her.

She cringed at the appalling familiarity.

Dillie smirked. "Let's have some fun with him." She nudged her mount forward and held out her hand, expecting him to politely bow over it. "Good afternoon, Mr. Cameron. Thank you so much for replacing my spectacles and book."

"Pleased to meet ye, Dillie." He shook her hand brusquely, as though they were two farmers completing a sale of crops.

Lily couldn't help but laugh at her sister's comeuppance. "How did you know it was Dillie and not me?"

"First, she's no' squinting. Second, Jasper's panting and wagging his tail at you." He let out a deep, gentle chuckle as he fixed his gaze on her. "He's quite taken with you, lass."

Lily dismounted to pet Jasper, who was looking at her as though he were in love. Just her luck to be adored by a dog. She glanced from hound to owner. While Jasper's eyes were as sweet as pools of melted chocolate, Mr. Cameron's were emerald-dark and decidedly dangerous.

Curiously, she felt an odd tingle in her bones.

He smiled.

The tingle spread throughout her body.

"I like Jasper, too," she hastily admitted, kneeling to hug the hairy beast before her legs turned to butter and gave way.

Jasper responded by nuzzling his head against her chest and shedding hair all over her new riding habit. She didn't mind. He was her anchor in a sea of turmoil. The hairs would easily brush out later.

Mr. Cameron knelt beside her and began to tickle Jasper under his chin, something the dog obviously enjoyed because he emitted a low rumble of contentment. "Why are you no' wearing your spectacles, Lily? Did they no' fit right?"

"They're fine," she admitted after a moment's hesitation. "Just perfect... but I've asked my uncle to return them."

He looked surprised and disappointed.

"Mr. Cameron." She sighed at the unpleasant task before her, made more unpleasant by the fact that she liked the man who was a hair's breadth away from going to prison.

"Yes, lass."

"About the MacLaurin book. I really can't accept it either."

He arched one dark eyebrow and frowned. "Why no'?"

"It must have cost you a tidy sum," she whispered, heat creeping into her cheeks. She'd learned early on that true ladies did not discuss matters of wealth or one's lack of it. But it couldn't be helped. How else was she to keep him out of trouble?

"Och, lass. Dinna worry about the bodles and bawbees."

"The what?"

"My finances. There's plenty more where that came from."

"That's the problem," she said, sounding harsher than intended, a mark of her frustration. She rose abruptly, startling Jasper and his owner, both of whom jumped to their feet along with her. "My uncle George intends to speak to you, but he isn't here now and you are. The problem is... what I mean to say... I just don't know how to say it politely."

Mr. Cameron folded his arms across his chest and regarded her with obvious confusion. "It's best if you just say it."

She nodded. Goodness, he was big. Handsomely big. "I know you mean well. And I do appreciate the lengths to which you've gone in order to make amends for the damage. But imposing upon the Duke of Lotheil, no matter how wealthy he is... well, I don't wish to see you go to prison."

"What are you talking about?"

"Just because he may not be aware of what you've done... oh, dear. Let's take this one step at a time. Mr. Cameron, did you pay for the book and spectacles with your own funds?"

"Aye, lass. How else would I acquire them?"

She let out a sigh of relief. "Good. Very good. Now, about using the duke's stationery to write your letter."

He frowned. "Oh, that."

"Yes, that. In future, you must use your own paper. And for pity's sake, how did you get the duke's messenger to do your bidding?"

"I asked him."

"And he obliged? Just like that?"

He finally seemed to understand. "Of course, next time I'll deliver the package myself. I still owe you a new frock."

Perhaps he didn't understand at all. Goodness, the man was dense. "No... no... never mind. Just promise me you'll not use the duke's supplies, or messengers, or... his purse, any more."

He let out a soft, rumbling laugh. "Och, Lily."

"And you mustn't call me Lily or lass. It implies an intimacy we do not share. How much of it do you have left?"

"The letter paper? Lots."

She began to nibble her lower lip. "Oh, that's not good. Indeed, that's very bad. We must return it to him, somehow."

"Him?"

"The Duke of Lotheil, of course. Well, not directly to him. I doubt he'd grant us an audience, but to his man of affairs. I think it best that I return it, let him think it was delivered to me by mistake."

"He'll know it was no' so."

She shook her head sadly, wondering how this poor man was going to survive in London. He had no sense of etiquette and an impossibly casual regard for property rights. No doubt he was still homeless. "Did Lady Dayne find you a place to stay?"

His lips began to twitch, tugging upward in a smile. "Och, lass. You've a good heart, but you're obviously misguided."

"Me, misguided? It's you who needs to be taken firmly in hand."

His eyes glistened with mirth and he cast her a wickedly attractive grin. "Lass, you ought to lift your pretty nose out of your books on occasion. You know shockingly little about men. And I wouldn't offer to take a man *firmly in hand* if I were you. It will get you into a lot of trouble."

"I haven't a clue what you're talking about."

He sighed. "Didn't think so. No matter. The point is, you have no need to save me. I happen to be staying at Lotheil Court."

"Are you visiting a relative who works there? A butler? A groomsman? Perhaps the duke's man of affairs, which would explain how you got your hands on the duke's stationery. Mr. Cameron, was the duke's man the one who introduced you to Lady Dayne?"

"Lily, there's something you should know."

She refused to pay attention, her mind too busy concocting a plan to keep him safe, though why she should worry about him or his friendly lump of a beast was beyond her.

"—Duke of Lotheil," was all she heard as he grabbed her by the shoulders and shook her lightly.

"What?"

"I'm the duke's grandson."

"Oh, dear. Mr. Cameron…"

"And the present Laird Carnach."

"I…" Her voice trailed off. This was worse than she'd thought. Next he'd claim to be Robert the Bruce.

"Lass, why are you looking at me like that? I'm no' mad."

Yes, he was. Mad as a hatter.

"Well, it was delightful to see you again, Mr. Cameron. Oh, look at the time. We really must be going." Which she might have done if she hadn't tripped over Jasper's big, lumpy body just then, losing her balance and falling flat on her back onto the riding trail's soft earth… soft, muddy earth still damp from this morning's brief rain.

Lick, lick. Jasper was over her in a trice and running his tongue along her face, no doubt intending to be friendly, but did his tongue have to be so… wet?

"Lily…" Ewan Cameron murmured with a soft, strangled laugh, gently pushing Jasper aside. He knelt beside her, putting his big hands on her body as he carefully helped her to her feet. "We must stop meeting like this."

Lily rarely was at a loss for words, but she couldn't seem to put two words together at the moment. Bits of Jasper's drool were slipping off her chin, her clothes were stained and wet, and her cheeks were on fire. In truth, her entire body was on fire. The pulse at the base of her throat was racing as fast as a horse cart barreling down a steep hill.

Nothing to do with Mr. Cameron. Or the fact that his hands were still settled on each side of her waist. Or that her own hands were on his rock-hard arms, clinging to them for support… goodness they were hard.

"You're covered in dog hair," Dillie added unhelpfully.

"Och, lass. I've done it again, ruined your new clothes."

She finally found her voice. "It doesn't matter."

"It does to me," he said in a husky brogue that sent her bodily organs into happy spasms. "I'll replace your riding habit too."

CHAPTER 4

ANOTHER BOX ARRIVED for Lily the following morning.

"Aren't you going to open it?" Dillie asked, hastily closing their bedroom door and presenting the package to her.

"No. I know what's inside." She turned away and began to fuss about the room, straightening drawers and pulling aside the cream lace curtains to allow in the sunshine. Despite an earlier rain, it seemed another beautiful day in the making.

"If you won't look inside, then I will."

"Don't!"

But it was too late, for Dillie had lifted the cover and was digging into the box. "Oh, my! Madame de Bressard must have charged him a fortune." She shook out an exact replica of the tea gown Jasper had ruined the other day.

Lily glanced at the shimmering yellow silk. Goodness, it was beautiful. However, she wasn't going to admit it to her sister, especially since Dillie was taking his side just to irk her. "Obviously, he can afford it."

Dillie grinned. "You're still angry with him."

She stuffed her arms into the bare sleeves of an apricot-colored pelisse and buttoned it over her white frock. "Not at all. Why would I be angry with *Ewan*? Just because it turns out he really is the duke's grandson? To think, I fretted over him!"

"Needlessly, as it turns out."

"Nonetheless, I fretted! He might have been tossed into a dungeon, locked up in chains, and left there to rot."

"But there was no danger of it."

"He ought to have advised me of that fact sooner."

"He did, or at least he tried to. Does it matter who he is? He used his own funds and he's got his own Scottish title... Laird something-or-other."

"Laird Carnach."

"Right, Laird whatever-you-said. And he's a bachelor," Dillie continued in that slow, pensive way their mother often used when contemplating her daughters and marriage. "If someone were to polish his rough edges, he'd make quite the suitable catch."

Lily glowered at her sister. "It certainly won't be me. He laughed at me!"

"He did not."

In truth, he'd appeared quite confused as she'd rambled on about her concerns, merely grinning in that infuriatingly charming way that set her internal organs tingling, as he listened to her declare that she'd spent a sleepless night worrying about him and whether he'd found a place to stay. He could have said something to stop her, but did he? No. Not a word. Instead, he burst out laughing when she offered to help him escape back to Scotland. That he'd just stared at her, seeming to devour her with that confident gaze of his while she made a fool of herself, still rankled.

"*Mo creach!*" he'd finally said, once more laughing out loud. "You thought I was a card short of a full deck?"

Yes! She had. But a lady did not show it, even when the man she considered daft, unhinged as an old gate, thanked her for her good intentions by taking her face in his big hands and kissing her on the nose. In public, no less!

"There's a note in the box."

"Rip it up."

Dillie rolled her eyes. "I will not." She ripped the seal off the envelope instead. "Oh, you'll never guess what he wishes of you now."

"Not funny."

"I'm serious."

Lily took the parchment out of her sister's hands, read it, and gasped. "He wishes to know where we purchased our horses. What sort of man asks a lady such a question?"

"I'd say, a man who wishes to know where we purchased our horses."

She crumpled the note. "Dillie, you know what I mean."

"Were you expecting a flowery apology from Ewan, Laird Something Unpronounceable with Lots of Rolling Rs?"

"No. And it's Laird Carnach. It isn't that hard to remember. Ewan, Laird Carnach, grandson of the Duke of Lotheil, and holder of probably a dozen unpronounceable titles. Did you know most Scots titles originated in the time of the Druids, before the Roman, Dane, and Norman invasions? Obviously, he's the sort who speaks plainly, revealing only what he considers important to know. He also speaks directly. If he's curious about something, he simply asks. If he thinks something is funny, he laughs. If something strikes him as ridiculous, he promptly says so."

"You're right. The man is an utter fiend."

"He has neither tact nor diplomacy. Just brutal honesty."

"Since when is honesty to be frowned upon?"

Lily blushed. "It isn't. But that isn't my point."

"Then what is? Oh, never mind. Tattersalls is running an auction next week. Uncle George plans to attend with Laurel. We can ask her to help Ewan pick out a suitable mount."

"Go ahead," Lily said, her chin shooting upward as she huffed. "Ask her, for I won't."

"Fine. I will. She knows all there is to know about horses. Her Brutus is one of the finest stallions in England. Ewan's eyes will pop wide when he sees him."

"Stop calling him Ewan. He isn't our friend."

Dillie wiggled her eyebrows. "Though you'd like him to be."

Lily ignored the comment. "He probably ate in the stable with the duke's grooms last night. Not that there's anything wrong with the notion, though society certainly frowns upon it."

"We used to spend many a lovely afternoon helping Mrs. Mayhew bake pies and enjoyed the spoils afterward, didn't we?" Dillie sighed. "I don't regret a bit of the time spent in the kitchen."

"Nor do I. However, Mother would be horrified if she ever found out. I suppose I sounded like her just now when complaining of Mr. Cameron."

"A lady's place," Dillie started in a high-pitched voice, a wicked imitation of their beloved, but slightly scatterbrained, mother, "is not in a stifling kitchen. She'll wilt under the heat of those bubbling pots and blazing fires, and then no gentleman will have her."

Lily's frown faded into a chuckle as she joined in. "Don't forget her remark about our hands. They must remain as delicate and unblemished as a baby's bottom," she mimicked. "Perfect hands are the true mark of a lady."

"Of course, we'll overlook the dreadful rash that afflicted Cousin Harry's little bottom last spring. Or Mother's horror when you sprained your thumb sneaking that oversized Druid fertility god into our room." Dillie placed a hand over her brow and pretended to swoon. "Oh, the shame! The disgrace! Girls, fetch me my smelling salts!"

Lily burst into laughter. It was impossible to remain irritated with Dillie. She always knew how to tease her out of ill humor. "Do you think Mother knows how many relatives are floating about this house? Or that Uncle Ernest and Aunt Mary left for Bath yesterday with only three of their five children?"

"More important," Dillie continued with a nod, "do Uncle Ernest and Aunt Mary realize they are missing two of their children?"

"About those horses for Mr. Cameron," Lily said, now restored to better humor, "I'll stop by Laurel's this afternoon on my way home from the Royal Society meeting and ask her to assist him."

"Och, ye're a braw, bonnie lass, and I'm that sorry m'beastie shed his fur all over yer new riding frock!" Dillie, ever irritating, took Lily's face into her hands and kissed her on the nose just as Mr. Cameron had done yesterday. Then she released Lily and marched out of their bedchamber pretending to play bagpipes while dancing a jig.

Lily sighed.

Sometimes, she hated being a twin.

* * *

Lily spent the rest of the morning corresponding with friends and playing Duck, Duck, Goose with her cousins. When the little ones were sent up for their naps, she decided to pay a call on Eloise, hoping to learn a bit more about Ewan Cameron. Clearly, he had not been raised to assume the dukedom, for he had little knowledge of polite society and little desire to learn. He had a gruff manner and the rough hands of a man used to hard labor. He also had the brawny good looks of a warrior.

On him, a very nice combination.

Oh, how had that thought slipped in? She cleared her throat and paused at Eloise's front door to ring the bell.

"Lady Dayne is not at home," her butler informed Lily. "Shall I leave word that you stopped by?"

"No, Watling. It isn't important."

She returned to the Farthingale residence and prepared for the Royal Society meeting. Today's lecture was to be on geological formations. For that staid affair, she chose a midnight blue pelisse over a light gray frock, selected a midnight blue reticule and pair of gray lace gloves, and then completed the outfit with a stylish hat topped with a gray feather.

Finally, she nudged her new spectacles firmly onto the bridge of her nose, framed a few playful curls at the nape of her neck, and marched downstairs to join her uncle, also an admirer of the Royal Society and the lectures offered to the public.

"I haven't had the chance to speak to Eloise or this Mr. Cameron yet," her uncle George said as they climbed into one of the Farthingale carriages.

"Don't trouble yourself." She settled against the black leather squabs. "There's something you ought to know. Something I ought to have mentioned last night."

Her uncle leaned forward.

She proceeded to tell him of Mr. Cameron's connection to the Duke of Lotheil.

"I suspected as much."

"You did?"

He nodded. "Gossip and such, but didn't wish to say anything before I was certain."

"I wish you had told me. I made an utter fool of myself in front of him."

He patted her hand. "I'm sure he finds you as charming and clever as we all do."

"Jasper might, but I doubt his owner feels the same way."

*　　*　　*

Ewan stood in the back corner of the lecture hall watching the crowd. The men looked quite distinguished in their afternoon grays, and the few ladies in attendance were finely turned out. Lily arrived, as he expected she would, escorted by a tall gentleman whose dark hair was sprinkled with gray. The man had a commanding presence and appeared old enough to be her father... possibly was her father.

Ewan decided not to approach, but Lily saw him out of the corner of her eye. Turning to her companion, she began to tug on the gentleman's sleeve to draw him toward the back of the hall. "Good afternoon, Mr. Cameron," she said, reaching his side.

He nodded. "Hello, lass." She looked adorable with those wire-rimmed spectacles perched on her nose. Prettiest scholar he'd ever encountered.

"May I present my uncle, Dr. George Farthingale?"

"A pleasure to meet you, sir."

Lily's uncle responded cordially, but Ewan knew the man was wary of him and obviously protective of his niece. He wouldn't hesitate to confront Ewan—duke's grandson or no—if he were ever to hurt Lily. Ewan understood and respected the man for it. He would be just as wary of any man sniffing about his own sister, Meggie.

Not that he was sniffing about Lily, though she did smell nice. Like pink roses in the evening dew, sweet, warm, and subtly intoxicating.

Bollix.

"My niece tells me that you're looking to purchase a horse for yourself."

He glanced at Lily and then turned back to her uncle. "That I am."

"I may be able to help."

"I'd appreciate it." He glanced at Lily again and grinned. "And just so we're clear on the matter, cost is no object."

Lily rolled her eyes. "Gentlemen do not discuss their finances in public."

"I know, lass. Couldn't resist teasing you. Not that I'm much of a gentleman, but rest assured that I am usually cautious with my blunt. In truth, I am as tight-fisted a Scot as you'll ever meet."

The shadow of a smile fell across her lips. "Then I would advise you to keep your hands in your pockets, Mr. Cameron. Lord Squeers is coming toward you to hit you up for a donation, no doubt. He may tell you it's for a worthy cause, but I hardly think acquiring a case of whiskey for his cellar counts as such. Oh, dear. Lady Marchmain has just seen you, as well. She's desperate to marry off her widowed sister and will be impossible to shake once she starts talking."

Her uncle frowned. "Lily, that's not a kind thing to say."

"But it's the truth."

"Even so."

A blush ran up her cheeks. "Forgive me. I have an awful habit of... I merely thought to be helpful... obviously, I'm not... being helpful, that is. I must sound quite petty and insulting. I don't know why I felt the need to warn you about them, Mr. Cameron. I'm sure you can take care of yourself."

"No harm done. I appreciate your candor. 'Tis hard to know whom to trust," he said quietly.

"About the request in your note," she continued, "my sister, Laurel, is the expert on horses."

"She's promised to help me select top bloodstock at next week's auction at Tattersalls," her uncle added. "Join us there, won't you? I'm certain Laurel will be glad to give you advice."

"I'd appreciate it. Thank you, I will."

"Can you ride?" Lily asked.

Ewan realized that she'd never seen him on horseback, only out walking with Jasper. "A little."

She shook her head as she studied him. "Are you being honest or modest?"

Ewan chuckled. "Modest."

"You must have been born in the saddle, probably took to it like a duck takes to water." She let out a delightful sigh. "I'm a fair rider at best. I understand the motion of a horse, its loping rhythm and the need for one's body to attune itself to the animal so that both move as one, but I fear I'm hopeless. My body insists on bouncing one way while the horse trots another way, so we always seem to be moving at cross purposes."

"You'll have to show me. I may be able to teach you a few tricks."

Her eyes brightened and she cast him a radiant smile. He drew in a breath, cautioning himself. The girl was like a smooth, aged scotch, easy to drink until the force of it hit you like a cannonball and dropped you to your knees. "The lecture's starting."

Lily's uncle took her arm. "We had better find our seats. Will you join us, Mr. Cameron?"

"I'll stand back here." Though Ewan tried not to stare at Lily or notice the gentle sway of her hips as she walked to the front of the hall, he couldn't help himself. The girl was a fascinating mix of innocence and sensual appeal. Not that she knew it. He watched her take a seat. So did most of the men in the hall.

The innocent was completely unaware.

Having intended to remain only a short while, he decided to change his plans. There was no need to rush off now. He could wait until later to tend to his business affairs. And would wait until next week to acquire his horses. He looked forward to the auction and meeting Lily's sister, Laurel. She was the one who'd married Graelem Dayne—tamed him, if the rumors were true—but not before she'd almost killed him.

Lily seemed gentle enough.

Probably didn't take after her sister.

Ewan enjoyed the lecture, listening with interest as the elderly Lord Guilfoil finished his speech on James Hutton's theories on geological formation of the earth and took questions from the floor. Lily attempted to ask a question, probably several if he knew the girl, but was ignored. She finally stood up and tried to speak but was immediately cut off. "Miss Farthingale, sit down!"

She tipped her pretty chin into the air. "Lord Guilfoil, I will not."

"Of all the impertinence! I will not have you making a mockery of this lecture!"

"I have no such intention," she tried to assure. "All I wish to ask is—"

Others in the audience began to call out, not to defend Lily but to shout her down. Ewan was shocked. The very men who had smiled and ogled her before the start of the meeting were acting like insufferable boors. Was he missing something? She'd done nothing wrong. The floor had been opened up to questions, and she had as much right as any man present to have her say.

"Sit down!" Lord Guilfoil said, his face now red and eyes blazing. "We do not wish to hear yet another comparison of our noble English society to your savage jungle baboons."

"My monograph is on *swamp* baboons, much of it based on research published by Sir William Maitland, a man greatly admired by all of us in this hall."

As the crowd began to grow restless, Ewan noticed Lily gazing at a young gentleman who was seated with other Fellows of the Royal Society on the stage behind Lord Guilfoil's podium. Did she expect the young man to come to her defense? Clearly, he wasn't about to do so. At first, he purposely looked down, but when he glanced up again, he seemed noticeably angry, and all that anger was trained on Lily.

Suddenly, the lecture did not seem so enjoyable to Ewan. He clenched his hands into fists at the disdainful manner in which all of them were responding to Lily, remarking on her obvious ignorance and lack of understanding before she had even asked a question. *Bloody wankers.* The lass had more intelligence in her little finger than the pretentious blighters had in their entire bodies.

Ewan started toward Lily, expecting a feisty retort from the girl and wanting to be at her side to protect her if things got uglier. Instead she sat down as though whipped into submission. After a moment, she whispered something to her uncle and quietly slipped from the hall. Ewan followed her out, catching up to her on the street just outside the Royal Society hall. "Lily, are you all right?"

"Do I look all right? Honestly, I could scream." She began to pace back and forth in front of him, looking proud and determined, yet at the same time heartbreakingly fragile. "Lord Guilfoil is an utter dolt. They're all dolts, and they hate me for my heinous crime."

He arched an eyebrow in question. "I never took you for a criminal. What did you do?"

"Applied for membership in their Royal Society." She stopped pacing to pin him with a glare. "Don't tell me you agree with those wooly mammoths."

He raised his hands in surrender. "Not I. Did I give you that impression? Were I a member, I'd cast my vote for you."

"Seriously?"

He nodded. "We're not as stodgy up in Scotland. In fact, we have many female members in our historical and scientific societies. Several also serve as directors on our society boards."

"They do?" She gazed at him with longing. "I wish it were the same here."

He wanted to reach out and swallow her in his arms, but knew she'd resent it. Lily was the sort of girl determined to stand on her own.

He liked her all the more for it. "It will be in time. Soon, I'm sure. And you'll be the one to lead the way."

"Thank you, Mr. Cameron. I appreciate your attempt to cheer me, but I don't think anything will work just now. I'm so angry I could spit. I have only myself to blame. I knew it would happen, but I couldn't help myself. That's my failing... one of my many. I can't seem to keep my mouth shut."

"Nor should you, lass."

She cast him the softest smile. "That isn't what my family says. Well, most of them. Not my father or Uncle George. They're not afraid of my brain. Everyone else is. My mother thinks I'll die an old maid, that any man who spends more than a few minutes in my company will run off screaming."

"I haven't."

She shook her head and laughed. "What does that say about you?"

He wasn't certain. Hadn't really given it much thought. In truth, he'd been worried for her safety in that hall, a slip of a girl standing alone and defiant, surrounded by a crowd of men who somehow felt their masculinity threatened by this innocent.

"By the way, where's Jasper? I half expected to find him out here waiting for you."

"I left him at Lotheil Court. He must have chewed the legs off several priceless chairs by now." He called over a flower girl who happened to be strolling by with a basket of violets and purchased a bouquet. "Here, Lily. I know they're just flowers, but I can't think of anything better to cheer you. Well, that isn't quite true. I considered slamming my fist into that idiot Guilfoil's nose." He would have pounded his fists into any man who attempted to touch her.

"So did I. It wouldn't have helped. We would have been tossed out and banned from ever stepping foot inside there again."

"Who cares?"

"I do," she said quietly, her pretty lips quivering as she struggled to hold back tears. "I love the lectures. The science and discovery. I wish they'd allow me to be a part of it. This isn't the first time I've been shouted down at the Royal Society."

Once again, he was struck by the urge to take her into his arms. Of course, he couldn't act on it. Wouldn't act on it. "Still doesn't make it right, lass."

"I suppose not. Thank you for these." She held up the bouquet of violets and graced him with a smile as spectacular as a smooth, well-aged scotch. Ewan felt that cannonball shoot straight to his heart, the force of her sweet innocence almost dropping him to his knees. "No one's ever given me flowers before."

He was glad to be the first and felt surprisingly possessive about it. About her. No, not her. He wasn't interested in women... rather, he wasn't interested in *nice* women, at the moment. He was in London because of the damn promise he'd made to his father. Once he'd fulfilled his duty, he'd head back to Scotland.

That's where he belonged. Not here. Not losing his mind and handing this lovely slip of a girl a handful of violets. Bloody hell, what was wrong with him? In time, the girl would forget the gesture. Despite what she thought, he knew she would have a steady stream of admirers through her parlor.

He shifted uncomfortably. The notion troubled him. He couldn't understand why. It just did.

Lily gazed at him with those soft, blue eyes of hers. "Mr. Cameron, you may not look the part of a proper gentleman, but you are one. Thank you for making me feel... no longer miserable."

He reached out and tucked a finger under her chin. "Lass, if anyone ever insults you, well you just let me know and I'll set the bounder straight."

"With your beefy fists?" She tipped her head toward him and laughed again in that gentle, unaffected manner that had the power to bring grown men to their knees. "I'll consider it."

"You do that." He ran a thumb along her cheek to wipe away a stray tear, still overwhelmed by the need to protect her. She felt soft as a lamb, her skin silken smooth beneath his rough palm, and he wished he could take her into his arms and hold her until the pain she so obviously felt went away.

After a moment, she stepped away and fumbled through her reticule. "Oh, dear. I seem to have misplaced my handkerchief." She glanced up and then shook her head and sighed. "I've been doing that a lot lately. Losing small items here and there. I never did that before."

"I'm sure your handkerchief will turn up. Do you wish to return to the lecture hall?"

"Yes, but I think I'll wait out here anyway. The speaker ought to be finished by now, and the crowd will soon pour through these doors. I'll wait here for my uncle."

As she predicted, the attendees began to file out. It wasn't long before Lily's uncle stepped outside and scanned the ladies and gentlemen milling about the street. "There you are," he called out and soon joined them. "What have you there?"

"Flowers, Uncle George." She inhaled their scent and smiled. "They're from Mr. Cameron."

Her uncle eyed him curiously, then smiled.

Oh, bollix.

He'd given Lily violets, not a betrothal ring.

CHAPTER 5

LILY ENTERED Eloise's salon the following morning clutching the note her butler had delivered earlier. She saw Eloise seated at her writing desk. "You wanted to see me?"

"I have a favor to ask of you, child," she said, setting down her quill pen and placing the stopper back on her inkpot before rising to greet Lily. "My dear, the Duke of Lotheil has invited me to tea. I'd like you to join me."

Lily shook her head. "But he hasn't invited me."

"Nonsense, he knows a woman my age can't make her way about London on her own. He expects me to bring a companion."

"Is this the only reason you want me to go?"

Eloise laughed lightly as she motioned for Lily to take a seat beside her on the divan. "Ewan will be there, of course. So will his sister, Meggie. She's due to arrive at Lotheil Court today and I'm concerned she'll be quite overwhelmed by the grandeur. Not to mention that her grandfather can be an ogre."

Lily rolled her eyes and plopped into the seat beside her. "I know. He's the one thwarting my dream to be admitted into the Royal Society. I'm not violent by nature, but I've wanted to poke him in the nose more than a time or two this past year."

"I know, dear." She patted Lily's hand. "Perhaps he'll soften once he gets to know you better."

"I doubt it."

"One can always hope. He's asked me to help him plan his seventy-fifth birthday celebration, and I would love your help. You're so capable and efficient. He intends to hold it in the new wing of the Royal Society, sort of a double celebration of his birthday and the grand opening of the new geographical hall. He wishes it to be a splendid affair - a full orchestra, the best champagne, fireworks."

Lily rolled her eyes again. "The duke refers to me as *that baboon girl* and cringes at the mention of my name. He'll never allow me to participate in planning his party."

Eloise cast her an indulgent smile. "We won't know for certain unless we try. In the meanwhile, you'll have a reason to be at Lotheil Court quite often. I count on you to befriend Meggie. She's a timid girl, and I'll need your assistance to make her London visit a little less frightening for her."

"Timid? Then she's nothing like her brother."

Eloise sighed. "Ewan can be a bit headstrong, but he's a good man. What do you think of him?"

Lily pursed her lips as she gave the question some thought. "I don't know. He's blunt, unimpressed by society. Clearly hasn't spent any time going about in society. But he's kind to his dog and was very kind to me yesterday. He bought me a bouquet of violets."

Eloise's ears perked. "Did he?"

"Ah, your eyes have lit up like fireflies on a summer's eve. Please don't make too much of it. He saw that I had been treated cruelly by certain members of the Royal Society and took pity on me. That's all. It was a small bouquet. Tell me more about his sister."

"I haven't seen her in a while, so I don't know much more than I've already told you. I'm certain you and Meggie will become fast friends."

"I look forward to meeting her."

"Good. Then it's settled. You'll join me at Lotheil Court. Did you know the duke has one of the finest libraries in England?"

She nodded. "I'm eager to see it. Do you think he'll allow me a view of it?"

"Ewan will give you a tour if his grandfather won't. Run along and ready yourself, child. We haven't much time."

Within the hour, she and Eloise were in the Dayne carriage on their way to the duke's imposing residence. Lily had known the place would be impressive, but she wasn't prepared for its palatial size or splendor. Built in the style of a Grecian temple, Lotheil Court had soaring marble columns and an enormous fountain in the center of the circular drive. The duke stood at the top of the porticoed steps, staring down at them with arms folded across his chest.

His thick head of white hair matched the color of those soaring portico columns, and he looked every bit as grand as his home. So did Ewan, who stole Lily's breath away as she gazed at him standing at the foot of the steps, his arms folded across his broad chest and his brow furrowed in that same look of determination his grandfather had on his face.

She imagined the two men would be appalled to realize how closely they resembled each other. They looked like a matched pair of fire irons—stiff, unbendable—and both had the same, stubborn set to their jaws.

A young woman stood beside Ewan. Her long hair was a shade redder than her brother's. Her eyes were a lighter green than his, more of a sea green, and showed signs of crying recently.

"That's Meggie," Eloise told Lily. "She's a sweet-looking girl. Poor thing, she looks as out of place here as a donkey in a henhouse."

Lily agreed.

The footmen lining the steps were more finely dressed than either Ewan or Meggie, she noted. Indeed, even the duke's gardener went about his work in more stylish clothes.

Ewan strode toward the carriage to greet Eloise and help her down.

He smiled as he turned to Lily. "Glad ye made it, lass. What do ye think of the place? A braw paffle, is it no'?" He took her by the waist and lifted her into the air as though she weighed no more than a feather.

She grabbed his shoulders for support, not surprised to find them hard and muscled. "Oh, yes. Quite braw and extremely paffled."

Chuckling, he set her down beside him but didn't release her.

She had to admit, this was an excellent way to descend from a carriage.

"Come, Lily. I'd like you to meet Meggie." His warm breath tickled her ear and his fingers lingered at her waist, his touch light and at the same time possessive. Little tingles of heat ran up her body and shot down to her toes before racing upward again. A delightful flutter began deep in her stomach, as though it housed a thousand dancing butterflies.

She took a deep breath to steady herself and inhaled Ewan's scent, an earthy scent of pine forest, clean and pure and rugged. "Meggie's been crying since she arrived," he said in a whisper. "I can no' make her stop."

Lily's gaze darted to his sister. Poor thing. But what could she do? "I'll try my best to cheer her."

Ewan tossed her a lopsided smile. "Och, lass. That would be grand."

Oh, his smile! The butterflies in her stomach were now dancing themselves into a frenzy.

When he made quick introductions, Meggie graced her with a hesitant smile and Lily returned it warmly. She noted that the duke had not deigned to descend the few steps to greet them but was waiting for them to climb the steps to reach him.

Eloise walked up them assisted by Meggie, who had a hand on her arm. Ewan had tried to offer, but she'd dismissed him with some nonsense about not seeing Meggie for ages and wanting to catch up with all that had happened since Eloise's last visit north.

Ewan was left with his arm sticking out conspicuously, so he offered it to Lily. "By the way, what's a paffle?" she asked as they approached the duke, who had escorted Eloise and Meggie into the entry hall.

He chuckled. "A bit o' land."

She looked about, her gaze once more falling upon the ducal residence in all its white marble splendor. "Indeed, it's quite a paffle." The gleaming entry hall was two stories high and full of light from an elevated row of windows. The light reflected off the black and white marble tile floor. One wall of the sparsely furnished hall contained an enormous mirror edged in gold leaf and, under it, a mosaic table of Arabian design.

"May I present my companion, Miss Lily Farthingale," Eloise said.

The duke regarded her with the same, dark emerald eyes as his grandson's. "I know you. You're that baboon girl, the Farthingale chit everyone at the Royal Society is in a fuss about. You don't look like much."

A soft growl emanated from the back of Ewan's throat, and his hands curled into fists. "Insult her again and I'll—"

Lily put a hand on his fist. "I am the very one, Your Grace. I'm glad to hear I've made you all take notice. Rest assured, you haven't heard the last of me."

"Is that a threat?"

"Against your male bastion?" She nodded. "And a promise. I'll have your ancient walls crumbling before the year is out."

"Gel, you're fortunate you came here with my dear friend. Otherwise, I'd have tossed you out on your impertinent ear."

"Lotheil! Really!"

"I beg your pardon, Eloise. Your young friend here ought to be taken to the woodshed and soundly thrashed."

Ewan's sister burst into tears.

Ewan groaned. "Och, Meggie. Will ye no' stop crying?"

So much for introductions. Lily put an arm about Meggie's shoulders. "Don't you fret. You and I shall be great friends. Your grandfather and I are just amiably sparring. It's all the rage in London to... er... engage in witty repartee. Do you like to ride?"

She sniffled. "I'm no' very good at it. My brother is, though."

Lily nodded. "So I've heard. Do you enjoy lectures? There's a fascinating one tomorrow on Charlemagne."

"Who?"

Lily exchanged perplexed glances with Ewan. "Never mind."

The duke led them into his conservatory, where a table overlooking his impressive garden was set for five. Ferns in decorative pots stood at measured intervals around the room, except in one spot where there seemed to be a pot missing.

"Jasper broke it this morning," Ewan whispered. "The big looby slid on his belly across the polished floor and next thing ye know, there's a great crash followed by a whimper."

She let out a laughing groan. "Poor Jasper." The adorable beast did not walk or trot. He bounded, sprang, leapt. "Where is he now?"

"My chamber. Safest to keep him up there for now. There's so much shine and polish in this house, poor creature's been sliding into walls all day." He held out a chair for Lily, then turned to his sister and held one out for her. "Meggie, you and I can take him for a walk later."

The poor girl looked as though she were going to burst into tears again. She cast Ewan a look that clearly revealed her desire to return to Scotland *now* and never come back.

Ewan had the same expression on his face.

If they hated being here, then why had they come? Lily glanced at Eloise, who was engaged in conversation with the duke. She recalled the little bits of information Eloise had revealed in the carriage on their way over, something about a family bitterness that had lasted thirty years.

She'd have to pry more details out of her companion as soon as they were on their way back to Chipping Way. She couldn't understand such feuds. Her family always talked through their differences, compromised, put love above all else. That's what the duke and his grandchildren ought to have done years ago.

For the remainder of the afternoon, the duke spoke mostly to Eloise about plans for his birthday party.

He ignored Lily.

Endured Meggie.

Surprisingly, Lily caught him glancing at Ewan in admiration. Not once, but twice, and only when Ewan had turned away.

Near the end of the afternoon, the duke surprised Lily by offering her a tour of the house. "Might as well show it to you and my granddaughter, since she hasn't let go of your arm since you arrived."

Eloise remained behind in the conservatory, shooing Ewan away when he offered to remain with her. "Nonsense, join the ladies," she insisted. "You'll be grinding your teeth and fretting until they return. Quite an annoying habit. Can't abide it."

The duke led them through his summer salon and winter salon, the summer dining room and winter dining room, the ballroom, music room, a smaller conservatory, portrait gallery, and finally his library.

Lily gasped as she entered. "I've never seen anything so fine!" She walked from bookshelf to bookshelf, trailing her hand along the spines of the assorted volumes. There were so many! "I could spend years in here," she said, more to herself.

"Spend as long as you wish," the duke replied. "Come over whenever you wish."

Meggie broke into a smile for the first time since they'd met. "Oh, Lily! Please do."

Lily glanced at Ewan, but he had his gaze fixed on the duke, eyeing him warily. Lily was wary, too. "Very kind of you," she answered cautiously, wondering at his sudden generosity and how she fit into his schemes.

The old man was plotting something beyond a mere request to provide companionship for Meggie. Lily knew he detested her, though after their first encounter had alarmed Meggie, he'd strained to be more civil to her. Hadn't actually spoken to her, for that was too much to ask. But he hadn't shot daggers at her either.

They returned to the conservatory. The remnants of the tea had been cleared from the table, which was set anew with a tablecloth of embroidered linen, delicate china, and brilliant sterling silver. "A fortnight ago, I was roasting rabbit over a campfire," Ewan muttered. "Right now, I feel like the rabbit roasting on a spit."

Lily nodded sympathetically.

Ewan had reason not to trust his grandfather.

He was a mean old man.

Had anyone else given her an open invitation to use a magnificent library, she would have considered the gesture quite charitable.

But to use Lotheil Court's library?

The duke was a cold, proud man.

He did nothing out of charity.

"Will you be holding a ball in honor of your grandchildren?" Eloise asked.

Ewan regarded her with horror. "I'd sooner invite wolves to chew off m'leg! I told ye, Eloise. I'm not one for society. His Grace may do as he pleases, just leave me and Meggie out of it."

Lily glanced at Meggie.

"Margaret," the duke said, jolting the poor girl to attention. "Do you feel as your brother does about a party?"

She clutched Lily's arm and nodded.

"Well, that answers your question," he said to Eloise. "My grandchildren want nothing to do with me."

The tea, about as pleasant as the Spanish Inquisition, ended a few minutes later.

Ewan and Meggie assisted Eloise into the carriage, but the duke held Lily back, mentioning something about a book he thought might interest her. "Come with me," he commanded, leading her briskly into the library and offering her a seat beside his desk, which she declined. "I'll come straight to the point. My grandchildren like you. They obviously detest me," he said, and Lily noted a surprising tinge of sadness in his voice.

"Can you blame them?" She ought to have kept her mouth shut, but couldn't help it. "You weren't very kind to their parents, cut off all relations for the past thirty years."

He looked her sternly up and down. "That is none of your concern."

"Your Grace, is there a reason you wished to speak to me alone?"

He looked her up and down again. "You want admission into the Royal Society, don't you?"

She glowered at him.

"I'll get you in... on one condition."

"And what would that be?"

"Restore my relations with Ewan and Margaret. They'll be leaving London in three months' time. I'll never see them again, unless the improbable happens and we reconcile. Miss Farthingale," he said, taking her hand in a firm grip, "if you make us a family again, I'll make you the Royal Society's first female member. What do you say? Do we have a bargain?"

"How can I restore affections that never existed?"

"Do we have a bargain? Will you deliver my family back to me?"

"I'll think about it." She slipped her hand out of his cold fingers, not sure why she felt so unsettled about doing a good deed. Families ought to be together, but to accept such a bribe for something she would have gladly taken on simply for the asking?

He threw his head back and laughed. "I knew you had larceny in you, gel! I'll see you tomorrow."

She walked away.

Had she just made a deal with the devil?

*   *   *

The next afternoon, Lily was summoned to Eloise's home. "I've invited you here today for Meggie's sake," her friend explained. "She needs more help than I imagined. Though she won't be formally introduced into society this year, I'd still like to take her out, show her a bit of London, and introduce her to my friends. The clothes she's brought with her simply won't do. She'll need an entirely new wardrobe. Her brother will undertake the costs, of course."

Lily grinned. "Of course. And since at least three or four gowns must be ready within the week, Madame de Bressard will likely triple her fees. She'll be dancing a jig by the time she's finished draining Mr. Cameron of his hard-earned blunt."

"Now, Lily. It isn't polite to speak of finances."

"I was merely making an observation about the economics of the transaction. The greater the demand for a particular good—"

"Yes, yes, but I would appreciate your help in solving this particular problem. Ewan refuses to attend any society functions. Not a one. I can't convince him otherwise."

"These affairs can be dreadfully dull." She often thought so herself. "He doesn't strike me as the sort of man to put up with idle chatter. As for Meggie, even though almost a year has passed since their father's death, she still appears to be in mourning."

Eloise nodded. "Meggie's miserable here and afraid of her grandfather. She needs companionship and more than a little distraction."

"Of course, I'll help. I'll enlist all the Farthingales. What would you like us to do?"

"Include her in some of your activities," Eloise said as they settled down to further discussion over a hearty lunch of sausage cobbler and assorted meat pies.

* * *

Lily thought they made great progress in their plans during the course of the meal. She hoped Ewan and Meggie would be as pleased with the results. "Have we overlooked anything? You know them far better than I do. Anything special we can do for Meggie?"

"I'll give it some thought. She does need a good bit of cheering. As for the rest of it, I think we've been quite thorough. Just some minor details left to discuss."

"Such as?" Lily set down her fork and drew the napkin to her lips to dab at a crumb or two that clung to her lips after devouring the tastiest chicken and leek pie she'd ever had. Eloise's cook had mastered the art of making pastry dough, exceeding even the impressive talents of Mrs. Mayhew, who was practically perfect as far as Lily was concerned. Indeed, Mrs. Mayhew was a saint to put up with the thoroughly disorganized Farthingale clan, who had a habit of showing up unannounced at all hours. Her father and uncle George were the only sensible Farthingales, and if not for their good business sense and generosity, most of the family would likely be out begging on the streets.

She was brought back to attention as Eloise responded to her question by counting on her fingers. "Well, Meggie will need a French lady's maid to style her hair, tame those wild Highlands curls."

Lily nodded, sympathetic to the struggles since she (and Dillie, of course) had similar thick hair that seemed to have a life of its own, always ready to break free of its pins and spill over her shoulders, though hers was much darker than Meggie's.

"Meggie will have to learn some of the more popular dances. Ewan as well, though I expect he's more polished than he'll let on."

"Are you certain?" He was so obviously rough around the edges and had made no secret of his determination to remain that way.

Eloise nodded. "Not about the dances, for he isn't one for genteel entertainments. You won't find him fitting a dance instructor into his busy day. But he has a natural, manly grace about him, don't you think? And he's a fast learner. He's always been that way. Even as a child he was wise beyond his years." She paused a moment and pursed her lips. "He's never worn a beard before. He's usually clean shaven and keeps himself well clothed and groomed."

Lily felt her heart take a little leap.

"I'm sure he's kept his beard and rustic clothes simply to irk his grandfather. Well, he's had his bit of fun, and it's time he made himself presentable. He'll never dress like these young London dandies, but he knows how to carry off a stylish look. He's a handsome man, or would be if he ever decided to fit in with the London crowd."

Lily imagined he would look magnificent even if he were dressed in a burlap sack. The thought of running her hand along Ewan's clean-shaven cheek, feeling the warmth of his skin beneath her palm, and the light roughness of his stubble after a morning's shave... oh, dear! The room had suddenly grown unbearably hot.

Eloise arched an eyebrow as Lily poured herself another glass of lemonade and gulped it down. "The pie was very salty," she mumbled, pouring herself a second glass of the tart liquid and finishing that one off as well, though it did little to keep the heat from crawling up her cheeks. "Delicious pie... but salty." Ewan would taste that good, she simply knew it, and could prove it if she ever got to lick his skin. Not that she would. Ever.

Eloise rang for more lemonade and then turned to Lily and smirked. "You look like you could use another pitcher full."

"As I said, the salt." She silently apologized to Eloise's cook for the lie and drank some more. Good thing it was only lemonade and not wine or that insipid ratafia that proper young ladies were permitted to drink at Almack's. Otherwise she'd be passed out on the floor, drooling and making a general spectacle of herself. "So, Meggie will have to learn to dance. What else?"

"Meggie ought to learn the more popular card games and should have lessons on the order of precedence among the nobility. I would not like her to make a *faux pas* when introduced to some of my more elegant friends, though most would never pass an unkind remark. Will you teach her, Lily? She won't be so scared if the lessons come from you."

"I'll do my best, but do you think she can learn all of it in so short a time?"

"I don't know. We'll soon find out. Ewan and Meggie are to pay a call on me this afternoon. You'll stay, of course."

So Lily stayed, and tried to ignore the rampant butterfly flutters that sprang into her stomach the moment Ewan strode into the salon. And tried to brace herself when Jasper trotted in behind him, noticed her, and with a lovesick *wroolf, wrooolf,* leapt straight for her, knocking over Eloise's precious teacups that—thank goodness—happened to be empty, for Watling had yet to bring in the afternoon tea and cakes. "Jasper, sit!" she cried at the same time Ewan called him a *hairy wanker* and lunged for him to keep his woolly beast from knocking her over yet again.

But Jasper surprised them all by obeying her command, which caused a different sort of chaos when he stopped himself in mid-leap, his paws clawing the air to slow himself down, and landed with a gentle thud at her feet, his head held high with obedient pride. Ewan, who was himself in mid lunge, arms extended, and hands now aimed straight for her breasts, tripped over the beast.

"Bollix," he said in a choked breath, immediately drawing his hands in and twisting his shoulders to alter his trajectory so that he'd hit the floor and not her, obviously preferring to land badly rather than take her down with him.

Lily watched in horror as Newton's laws on bodies in motion and forces of gravity unfolded before her. She cringed at the outcome. It would not be pretty. "Ewan, look out!" she cried, fascinated by the glorious motion of his big, male body crashing against the stiff arm of the sofa, then rolling off the overstuffed sofa cushions onto the floor where his body wedged between her legs and the tea table.

"Bloody looby," he muttered, the breath clearly knocked out of him.

"Are you all right?" Lily reached out to help him up, but as she bent down, Jasper mistook it for a game and gently pushed her. "Jasper!" She fell atop Ewan, her knees landing squarely on his stomach and her hands on his chest. Big, solid chest. "Oh, dear! I'm so sorry."

Ewan caught her by the waist to steady her atop him, which seemed a Ewan thing to do, for he was always protectively considerate of her. His grip was firm, yet gentle, as she tried to slide off him, actually tried to slide *down* his body. She didn't get very far because Jasper was still at their feet, his enormous, shaggy body blocking her way as he sat obediently, refusing to budge.

Ewan let out a sharp, laughing gasp as she started to move back up his body. "Better no', lass. That isn't going to work."

"Well, I... I could—"

He began to laugh in earnest, a glorious, deep rumble that she found irresistible. No longer able to stifle the urge bubbling inside of her, she simply gave in and began to laugh as well. They were well and truly wedged, and had no delicate way out of this situation.

She was practically atop Ewan.

Meggie and Eloise were gaping at them, seemingly unable to move, or afraid to move for fear of worsening the situation.

Then Jasper pushed her, and suddenly, she *was* atop Ewan.

Her legs tangled between his thighs.

Her breasts intimately pressed against his chest. *And loving it.* Not that her breasts had a mind of their own. They didn't. Though if breasts could ever be happy, hers were.

Jasper, enjoying what he thought was a game, jumped atop her.

Ewan let out a groan that seemed to rise from the depths of his soul. "Lass, I'm... och, Jasper, ye looby! Ye're killing me."

Lily knew she'd struck his ribs with her sharp elbow and struck other parts of him that should not be mentioned. "I'm so sorry. Are you hurt?"

He seemed to have trouble breathing. Oh, dear! Was he in that much pain? No, he was laughing. Why was he still laughing? He enveloped her in his magnificently muscled arms and used his booted foot to gently shove Jasper off her. "No, lass. Are you?"

She wasn't feeling any discomfort. Quite the opposite, she felt quite light and deliciously boneless. "I feel perfect."

"Lass... I'm... bollix." He lifted her off him with the speed of a hummingbird's wings and half tossed, half deposited her on the soft sofa cushions. Then he grunted to his feet beside her, still breathing unsteadily as he ran a hand through his hair. He gazed at her with an odd expression on his face. She couldn't quite decipher it. Perhaps confusion. Or was it unbridled horror?

"No harm done, Mr. Cameron. My gown may be a bit rumpled, but it remains intact."

"It isn't the frock I was worried about." He stared down at her, his eyes dark and roiling with sensations she still didn't understand.

She smiled and slowly rose to face him. "It strikes me, Mr. Cameron, that you and I must work on our introductions. Every time we meet, someone ends up flat on their back. Usually me. Fortunately, this time it was you. I think it would have been a lot messier had you fallen atop me, your weight on my body."

Your glorious, crushing weight.

As she thought about it, her cheeks began to flame. Discomfort always made her sputter and ramble. "And speaking of weights and bodies," she said, pausing to sputter and let out a nervous titter. *Stop talking!* Of course, she couldn't. Another titter. Another sputter. "It brings to mind one of Galileo's experiments. Quite fascinating. Did you know he climbed to the top of the Tower of Pisa with a pair of heavy balls, and when he reached the top he dropped his balls—"

"Lily!" Eloise let out a burst of laughter, reminding her that she and Ewan were not alone. "Child, how you do go on!"

Of course. She was rambling and making a fool of herself, something that couldn't be helped while Ewan held her in his arms. How did she get back in his arms? No matter. She wasn't complaining. He was silently laughing. About to explode with laughter. She could feel his shoulders shake beneath her palms. "Well, you get the point. No need for me to go on."

There was nothing funny about Galileo's experiment. It proved an important point about the laws of gravity, but it was no use continuing the explanation. "Obviously, no one appreciates Galileo's balls."

Ewan opened his mouth to say something, glanced at Eloise, and then changed his mind and snapped it shut. He removed his hands from her waist and took a step back, this time careful to avoid Jasper, who was still underfoot, his tail wagging and tongue hanging out of his mouth as he joyfully panted, so proud that he'd obeyed her command to sit. "Your days are numbered," Ewan said, scowling at the dog.

Jasper scrambled to his feet, scurried over to Ewan, and began to lick his hand. Ewan sighed and patted him affectionately on the head.

"Well, that was most extraordinary," Eloise said. She turned to Ewan's stricken sister. "See, Meggie, even your perfect brother can make a complete ass of himself. You will notice that the sky hasn't fallen. The walls haven't crumbled down around us."

Meggie, her lips now quivering, glanced at Eloise and promptly burst into tears.

Lily sighed. She had her work cut out with the girl.

*   *   *

After calming Meggie and righting Eloise's elegant tea cups—which had been tipped over but not chipped or broken in the debacle—Ewan managed to settle down with the ladies to afternoon tea and a discussion about what was needed to make Meggie's stay in London pleasant. He didn't think anything would help, but Eloise and Lily were game to try and he was grateful for their assistance.

Conversation flowed smoothly, though he participated very little. His thoughts were still on Lily and the way she'd fit so perfectly against his hard frame. She'd been atop him. Soft, warm, the look in her eyes warning that she'd be willing to let him do anything to her that he wished. He'd wanted to kiss her beautiful lips for starters, then kiss his way down to her lush, perfect breasts... and further down to taste the heat between her thighs.

Bollix!

Eloise would bludgeon him with that cake knife now in her hands if she knew the manner of his thoughts. Damn. The wily old dowager probably knew exactly what he was thinking. He braced himself for the private conversation between them that was sure to follow, Eloise eager to lecture him about his marital status and the need to find himself a proper wife.

He wasn't looking for a wife. Wasn't going to happen. Not while he was in London fulfilling that damnable promise to his father. He needed to pay full attention to his malicious, manipulative grandfather, and he didn't need a female to distract him.

Especially one as distracting as Lily.

Problem was, almost an hour had passed since he and Lily had been lying on the elegantly carpeted floor with their bodies plastered to each other and their limbs entwined. He had yet to calm his body down. Damned traitorous thing was a man's body.

Eloise interrupted his thoughts by calling for her writing paper and pen. "Now, let's get down to business," she said, dipping her quill into the ink pot also provided by the ever-efficient Watling. "Meggie, can you sing?"

"No."

"Play an instrument?"

"The flute."

Eloise nodded. "That'll have to do. Can you sew? Knit? Embroider? Paint?"

"No, no, no, and no."

Ewan saw the panic in Meggie's eyes and knew by the quiver in her lips that she was about to cry again. He didn't know what to say or do, but in the next moment he realized he didn't have to say or do anything. Lily had all under control. "Neither can I, Meggie," she said with genuine warmth. "In truth, I'm sorely lacking in almost every talent. I sing like a bullfrog and dance with the grace of a walrus."

"I doubt that," Ewan said softly, which caused her to blush. Damn, had he said that aloud?

Meggie glanced at him, then at Lily, and smiled.

Eloise saved his sorry self by moving on to topics of more general interest while desserts were served. "Mr. Cameron," Lily started, but he cut her short.

"About that, lass. I'm Ewan. Plain and simple. Ye needn't be so formal."

"Yes, but what I meant to say is that you're a lord and I should actually be calling you by your proper title, Lord Carnach, and not—"

"A title's just a title. What's important is the man who fills it."

"Precisely my point. You fill it quite well," she said with a blush, certainly revealing more than she intended through her innocent blue eyes, "yet you've never corrected my mistake. In truth, you don't seem to like your title."

He sighed. "It's being in London that I dislike. In Scotland I'm Lord Carnach... or Laird Carnach to most Highlanders, and I don't mind at all. But here it all sounds so pompous, so condescending to those who are not as fortunate in the circumstances of their birth. That's all it is, the luck of the bloodstock. No valor or brilliance on my part. So call me Ewan, lass. Or Mr. Cameron. But I prefer Ewan with you. Especially since we have so much in common."

She tipped her head and studied him. "What do we have in common?"

He glanced at Jasper. The great, foolish beastie instantly perked up and wagged his tail. "We've both landed on our backs thanks to him."

She laughed, a gentle laugh that reminded him of warm summers and lush, green meadows. "Of course. That dangerous fiend who tries to slather my face with his ridiculously wet tongue each time we meet. How is it possible for a dog to generate so much liquid?"

Ewan couldn't answer, for his brain had frozen at the mention of slathering and tongue and all he could think of was licking his tongue down Lily's body and making her ridiculously wet... and hot... for him.

He was as big a looby as his dog. A bigger looby, if that were possible. Jasper's affection for Lily was pure and innocent. His was just hot and wicked.

Lily pursed her lips adorably, unaware of the depraved thoughts rolling around in the mind he'd obviously lost. "Ewan," she said with a nod, gracing him with a smile that set him on fire. The lass was dangerous, had a way of turning him inside out with a mere glance of her warm and vibrant eyes.

"Dogs have wet tongues. Particularly Jasper's breed." His voice was little more than a strangled rasp as he struggled to fashion a response, though none of the ladies appeared to notice the extent of his discomfort. Eloise was busily scribbling something on her paper, and Meggie was busy looking down at her toes as she'd done for most of this hour.

Lily noticed his sister's shyness as well. "Meggie, have you any other relations in town?" she cheerfully blurted, unaware of what she had just asked. "Cousins? Uncles? Family who will receive you and Ewan?"

Meggie's gaze shot up and exchanged tense glances with him. "We do have some."

"Hush, Meg. They'll no' be helpful."

Lily frowned. "What makes you think they won't cooperate?"

"I just know. Leave it at that." He was no longer smiling, for the last thing he wished to discuss was the Cameron family animosities.

"Surely, once they meet Meggie—"

"Leave it alone, lass," he said more sternly, though he understood the reason for Lily's persistence. She came from a big, loving family. He came from a pit of vipers.

"Would you kindly explain why?"

"I'd rather no'."

He could practically hear her teeth grind in frustration, her agile mind attempting to get at the truth, wanting to help overcome Meggie's fear and shyness, turn her into the engaging young lady Ewan knew she could be, one with the confidence to handle those unfriendly relatives if they chose to poison her time in London. "Ewan, what's going on? I need to know."

"No, you do no'."

Unfortunately, Meggie thought otherwise. "They want Ewan dead."

CHAPTER 6

"WHY DOES EWAN'S FAMILY want him dead?" Lily asked Eloise, once more alone with her now that Ewan and Meggie had departed. Eloise, who usually adored gossip, chose precisely that moment to repent her ways and embrace discretion. Imagine! Lily's trusted informant regarding all things scandalous declined to discuss the reason, advising that it wasn't her place to say and Lily should ask Ewan. Had the world just been tipped on its end?

Honestly, discretion was highly overrated.

And she *had* asked Ewan, tried in every way to pry the information out of him. He was like the granite rock on a cliff face. Hard, sharp. Impenetrable. She wouldn't get anything out of him. Not ever. She'd seen his dark expression and practically felt that wall of privacy build around him, stone by stone. Well, if he wouldn't talk to her, that left only Meggie, assuming her brother hadn't forced her to take a blood oath of silence.

Of course, she knew that he had.

Or if he hadn't yet, he would before her next outing with Meggie.

Which was why Lily was still a little peeved when another box arrived for her the following morning. A very large box.

Lily had no intention of accepting it, but Dillie grabbed it out of their butler's hands as he was about to set it on the entry hall table and raced off with it before Lily could refuse the delivery.

Pruitt, their stoic butler, arched a bored eyebrow. He'd been with the family too long to be surprised by Dillie's antics. "Seems your sister has left you with no choice."

Lily nodded. "Does anyone else know about the box?"

"Not yet. I suggest you find your sister before she lets the cat out of the bag."

"Of course. You're right. Please don't tell anyone yet, Pruitt."

His eyes twinkled. "Tell anyone about what?

She gave him a quick hug. "Thank you."

She hurried upstairs, knowing she'd find her sister waiting in their shared quarters. As expected, Dillie was sitting on her bed, the box beside her. She was strumming her fingers impatiently across the top.

Lily shut their door and turned to scowl at her sister.

"Took you long enough," Dillie muttered. "Go ahead, open it."

"No. I know what's inside."

"Come on. You know you want to. Well, I'm going to have a look."

"Don't you dare! It's my—"

But she was too late. Dillie had already lifted the cover. "Oh, my!" She shook out an exact replica of the riding habit Jasper had ruined. "Madame de Bressard must have charged him a king's ransom. Oh, Lily," she said with a bubble of laughter, "you're going to bankrupt the poor man."

"I'll do nothing of the sort. He can afford it." Still, she couldn't take her gaze off the shimmering black velvet.

"You're frowning. Why are you still angry with him?"

"I'm not... not really... not anymore. He's definitely holding back about his family, but on the whole he's been incredibly noble. It's Meggie I worry about. I think of her as an unpainted canvas with all these lovely colors to be applied to create a masterpiece. But how can I paint a proper portrait if important colors are missing?"

"And Eloise won't tell," Dillie said, having already heard that complaint from Lily.

Lily rolled her eyes. "Can you believe it?"

"Then you'll just have to work on Meggie."

"I don't think she knows the entire story."

"So we're back to Ewan. And that will only make you angry again."

She slumped her shoulders and let out a sigh. "No, it won't. I like him."

Dillie grinned. "A little more than you'd care to admit."

Lily nodded. "He melted my heart the other day, buying me flowers and offering encouragement, something I sorely needed after the humiliating set-down I received at the Royal Society." She paused to glance at Dillie. "Not even Ashton stood up for me, though I wouldn't have expected him to since he's their newest member. I would never ask him to anger his colleagues, especially within a month of his admission. I'm sure he'll say something in my defense at one of their private meetings. After all, I'm helping him with his latest monograph on the impact of earthquakes and other catastrophic events on the evolution of lemurs on the island of Madagascar."

Dillie rolled her eyes. "I'm all agog. Can't wait to read about his monkeys."

"Lemurs aren't monkeys, but I can't either," she said with enthusiasm, then realized her sister was merely being sarcastic. "Oh, but it is interesting. I've been helping him gather information on the various lemur populations in Madagascar. Never realized there were so many distinct offshoots, and—"

Dillie jutted her jaw, pounced on the bed, and began to make monkey sounds just as their mother swung open their door and dashed into their bed chamber. Sophie Farthingale came to an abrupt halt. "Lily, I warned you all that studying would damage your constitution," she said, staring at Dillie, who had frozen in mid monkey grunt. "I do wish you'd take the season more seriously. Why can't you behave like Dillie?" She mistakenly pointed to Lily and flashed her a warm, maternal smile. "Now you've made me forget why I came up here. Oh, yes! Eloise's carriage is at our gate."

"We promised to take Meggie Cameron shopping today," Lily explained, though only she had promised to take Meggie, but to now reveal that she was Lily would only confuse her mother, who seemed to have raised confusion to an art form. Not that she was to blame. Anyone would be attics-to-let trying to manage a household full of Farthingales for the season. They'd descended on Number 3 Chipping Way from all over England. Yorkshire Farthingales. Oxfordshire Farthingales. Devonshire Farthingales. Dozens, possibly hundreds, swarming like bees about John and Sophie Farthingale's London townhouse. Honestly, couldn't they find residences of their own?

Her mother glanced at the box on the bed. "What is your riding habit doing in that box? Never mind. Make sure Sally brushes the dirt off it. Oh, perhaps she has. It looks new, as though it's never been worn. Well, hang it up with your other gowns." She turned on her heels and hurried out.

"Must I go shopping?" Dillie asked when they were once more alone. "I was going to visit Daisy."

"I'll drop you off along the way. Give her a hug for me." Daisy was due to give birth soon, though the newest addition to the family wasn't expected for another month yet. Which meant Lily and her sisters would meet at least once more before the baby was born.

She thoroughly enjoyed their monthly meetings. Laurel was to host the next one this coming Thursday, and Lily looked forward to it. Not only did she miss her sisters, but she also wanted to speak to them about Meggie and ask for their help in easing the shy girl into some of the smaller family gatherings.

She could also ply them for gossip. Laurel's husband, Graelem, was a friend of Ewan's. Perhaps he knew more about the Cameron family bitterness.

After dropping off Dillie, she directed the driver to take her to Lotheil Court. Meggie stood waiting on the steps. She cast Lily a sweet, sincere smile, entered Eloise's carriage, and settled in. "Good morning, Lily. I hope I haven't put you out."

"Not at all. I look forward to shopping with you."

"I'm so glad." She nibbled her lip. "You always look so elegant and I know so little about fashion."

"I'm sure I know even less. My sisters, Rose and Daisy, are far more capable. They helped my mother choose my wardrobe. I asked them to join us, but Rose is busy entertaining her husband's family and Daisy is about to give birth. Laurel knows horses, not clothes, and Dillie promised to visit Daisy today. So, I'm afraid it's just the two of us. I hope you don't mind."

"No, of course not. It's just that—"

"You mustn't fret," Lily insisted when Meggie began to nibble her lip again. "Madame de Bressard knows what she's doing. All you have to do is trust her judgment, and I'll watch her prices."

Madame de Bressard greeted Lily and Meggie with exuberance as they entered her salon, and then with a sharp clap of her hands and some hastily uttered orders in French, she had her staff scrambling for fabric samples. "See, I told you she'd know precisely what to do," Lily said, watching half a dozen shop girls rush to obey those orders with the discipline and precision of the elite King's Guard.

Meggie's eyes brightened and she managed a genuine smile. "Oh, Lily! You're right. This is going to be such fun." Her trepidation now eased, she allowed Madame de Bressard's girls to fuss about her. That freed Lily to listen to Madame's design ideas—shockingly expensive ideas, all requiring exquisite fabrics—all of which were approved by Lily after a good bit of haggling.

After all, she would not allow Ewan to be duped. He was generous with those he loved—or those like her, to whom he felt he owed an obligation—but that didn't mean she could spend him into the poorhouse.

"Lily, I've had such a lovely time," Meggie whispered hours later as she was being fitted for the last of her gowns, an iridescent green silk that brought out the green in Meggie's eyes and the reddish-brown of her hair. "I'm so glad Eloise introduced me to you. I can't wait to meet the rest of your family. Are they as perfect as you?"

Lily cast her a warm smile. "I'm hardly that. As for my family, I think you'll like them all, though the Farthingale clan can be quite overwhelming at times. They're best taken in small doses, so I'll have you meet my twin, Dillie, first. She'll join us tomorrow when we return here to choose fabrics for your riding habit and morning gowns. After that, we'll stop by my sister Daisy's house. I'm hoping Rose and Laurel will be there, so you can meet all my sisters at once. They're simply wonderful."

"I can't wait to meet them. You're so fortunate to have such a loving family. We were that way once, but now both my parents are gone and my brother is doing his best to fulfill his promise to our father. Do you know about the promise?"

"Not really. I've only heard bits and pieces."

"Ewan knows more about the family animosities than I do, but the situation is bad. Really bad, Lily. I wasn't exaggerating when I said that my father's family wishes Ewan dead."

Lily didn't wish Meggie to upset herself, so she quickly returned the topic to her own family. "We have a large family, lots of aunts, uncles, and cousins, and many of them are in London for the season. At times, the house feels more like an army barracks. They're meddlesome and boisterous, but they're all well-meaning, so Dillie and I endure them. Usually we love them, even when we're ready to pull out our hair in frustration. Dillie's much better at handling the family than I am."

"They sound delightful. Do they need handling?"

"Every family does to some extent. Dillie is my savior. She keeps them distracted so that I can tend to my studies. I could never have finished a single research paper had she not... well, no point in discussing how she managed it. Though I'd never admit it to her, I think she ended up with the best qualities of us all—she's smart, funny, caring. But don't you dare tell her I said so! I'll deny it."

Meggie shook her head and laughed. "I promise you, I won't. I feel much the same way about Ewan. He's smart, loyal, and protective, and when he loosens up, he has a brilliant sense of humor." She laughed again. "Don't you dare tell him I said that. I'll deny it, too."

Madame de Bressard bustled in and gave her nod of approval over the green silk now beautifully draped over Meggie's body. As the shop girls helped Meggie to remove the gown, taking extra care so as not to stick her with the pins, Lily made arrangements with Madame for tomorrow's appointment. Everyone seemed pleased with the progress made.

Madame de Bressard left to mark down the appointment in her calendar. The shop girls slipped out of the fitting room to set aside the gowns for the seamstresses to finish. "Are you and Dillie really identical twins?" Meggie asked in the quiet of the moment. "Can anyone tell you apart?"

"Your brother can." He'd proved it when they'd met the other day in the park, though he'd claimed Jasper had given her away. Lily knew his eyes had been trained on her before Jasper had loped to her side. She didn't wish to think that a stranger could know her so well in so short a time. Especially not Ewan. The mere memory of his dark, emerald gaze raking over her body shot heat into her cheeks.

Meggie eyed her curiously. "You're blushing."

"It's a little warm in here." *Blazing hot fires of hell warm.*

"Ewan has that devastating impact on all the ladies," she said with a knowing grin. "Very little gets past him. He's the smartest man I know. He claims that you're smarter. I think he likes you, even though you're a *Sassenach*. I'm glad."

"I'm sure you're mistaken on all counts." She didn't like Ewan in *that* way. He didn't like her in *that* way either. He couldn't possibly. Men always ran from her and her overactive brain. Ran away screaming.

"I hope not. I like you, Lily. You've been wonderful to me from the first moment we met. And you've been beyond patient with today's fittings. I'm glad we're almost done here. I've had a grand time, but I'm getting a bit tired of all the poking and pinning."

Lily waited in the salon while Meggie returned to the dressing room to don her clothes. Feeling quite pleased, Lily was about to compliment herself for a job well done when the little bell over the doorway rang to signal more customers entering the shop.

Lily turned toward the door. An exquisitely dressed young woman strolled in followed by an equally striking young man. Both were tall and golden-haired. "Good day," she said, casting the attractive couple a smile.

They ignored her.

She shrugged in response and waited for Madame de Bressard to appear through the curtain separating the salon from the fitting rooms. The agile woman did so promptly and with a cheerful greeting for her new customers.

"Where is the wretched creature?" the female asked, cutting her short.

"We know she's here," the man snapped.

"My lord, I don't know who you mean." She turned to Lily, obviously seeking help, but Lily was as confused as she.

The man waved his ornate, silver-handled cane in front of her. "Margaret Cameron. The Scottish bitch's offspring!"

Lily gasped. "Sir!"

She'd heard worse language spoken, but rarely so venomously. Her mind began to race, her first concern being for Meggie's safety. She had to sneak Meggie out of the shop at once. Was there a side entrance? Who were these awful strangers, anyway?

Madame de Bressard shrank back against the hats counter, in her distress knocking over several hats and feathers. Her complexion was as ashen as the white satin fabric draped over one of the nearby armchairs.

Lily moved toward her, determined to get between her and this unwholesome pair before they frightened the woman into giving Meggie away. Though Madame de Bressard appeared to be made of sterner stuff, not the sort to toss a customer to the wolves, Lily couldn't be completely sure, so she stepped forward, her chin raised high, and tried a little intimidation of her own. "I've waited months for an appointment with Madame and will not have it interrupted by pretentious commoners—"

The man's lips curled in a snarl. "How dare you! Do you know who I am?"

No, but she hoped to find out. "I'm not in the least interested. You're obviously not quality."

"Wretched girl!" He raised his arm and struck her on the shoulder with his cane. She hadn't seen that coming. He'd actually struck her! "I'm the Duke of Lotheil's grandson! His one and only rightful heir."

"An obvious lie, sir." *Ow, that hurt.* "I doubt anyone secure in his standing would shout such drivel in a ladies' dress shop. Now, I suggest you leave without further fuss or I'll summon my footmen to toss you out."

He raised his cane again, but as Lily turned to grab a hat pin off the counter to defend herself, the man suddenly moved away. Or rather, he was hurled away. Lifted off his feet and sent flying across the room by... Ewan!

The man landed with a crash atop one of the tables beside Madam de Bressard's floral silk sofa. Lily watched in horrified glee (or was it gleeful horror?) as the table groaned and then cracked beneath this villain's flailing weight. His companion rushed toward him.

So did Ewan.

Oh, crumpets! Ewan was going to kill the man unless she stopped him. "Ewan, help me! Please!" She pretended to swoon in that ridiculously theatrical way her mother and Aunt Julia had perfected over the years. She'd never tried it before. She hoped it would work on Ewan as well as it seemed to work on most men.

It didn't.

Crumpets again! She scampered to her feet, determined to get between Ewan and the man before Ewan lifted him again and tossed him through the window onto the street, because she knew, as surely as she knew the orbits of the various planetary objects in Earth's solar system, that Ewan was going to do it.

Fortunately, the man's companion got to him before Ewan did. She leaned over the villain and promptly burst into tears. Loud, wailing, seemingly genuine tears. Lily knew that Ewan wouldn't shove a lady out of the way, even if she wasn't a very nice one. "It's done. I'm fine." Lily placed a trembling hand on his taut arm. "Let's go. Please."

She had to tug on his arm to gain his attention.

Ewan finally turned to her.

She tossed him a weak smile.

He glowered at her, not in anger, but in that man-protecting-his-woman sort of way, that strong, aggressive way a lion might look after chasing away male interlopers who'd wandered too close to the females of his pride. Not that she was one of Ewan's lion pride. "I'm fine," she repeated, her heart leaping into a happy dance at the hot, hungry glances he was giving her.

"Lass—" He stopped, his voice raw and rugged, for he could surely tell by the pain reflected in her eyes that she wasn't fine at all. Her shoulder was throbbing, and the spot where the cane had struck now felt as though it were on fire.

Ewan clenched his hands into fists, obviously deciding that the villain hadn't learned enough of a lesson and really needed to be tossed through the shop window. At that same moment, two burly men marched in. Madame de Bressard quickly identified them as Bow Street runners hired by the local shopkeepers to watch for criminal activity on the street. They were older men, their dark hair mingled with gray, and their dark eyes sharp and assessing. "We'll take care of this unruly pair, sir. Sorry they frightened your pretty wife. Are you hurt, m'lady?"

"I'm not—" Lily was trying to tell them that she wasn't Ewan's wife, but they mistook her protestations.

"Now, don't ye deny it," one of the men said, holding up a large, callused hand. "Just glad yer husband got here in time to prevent something worse. Now ye just forget this bit of nastiness and let him take care of ye."

She sighed. "Of course." And burrowed against Ewan so that he had no choice but to put his arm around her. *Oh, he felt good.* Warm and solid and good. But that wasn't her true purpose in burying her body against his... *crumpets*, she had to concentrate on anything but that animal heat radiating off his body. Right, concentrate on her true purpose, which was to keep him from doing permanent bodily harm to this villainous stranger.

At first, she didn't think her plan was working, for Ewan's body grew tenser the closer she burrowed against him. However, when he finally spoke, he managed to speak calmly. First he thanked the Bow Street runners, and then he turned to the young couple. "Stop crying, Evangeline. I won't kill your brother. Not this time."

Evangeline? He knew this beautiful young woman? Not that she cared. Not that it was her business. But Evangeline's brother had attacked her. Well, that made it her business.

Ewan turned to stare at the young man who was shakily rising to his feet. "Desmond, you bloody bastard. Set a hand on Lily again, and I'll kill you. Come near Meggie, and I'll kill you."

Evangeline glowered at him. "Who are you to speak that way to my brother? You're not good enough to polish his boots. Do you think you can come here and turn Grandfather away from us? You disgusting heathen. We all know you're only after his wealth and title. You're nothing but a filthy, Highlands pig. Grandfather couldn't stand the sight of your mother and he can't stand the sight of you, so go back to your Scottish hovel before you humiliate yourself. You have no place here among your betters."

Lily's fingers dug into Ewan's hand with enough force to leave the imprint of her nails on his flesh. She was bracing herself to hold him back, for Evangeline was goading him. Especially the remark about his mother. She'd felt Ewan's heart leap into his throat at that cruel snipe, but he'd surprised her by controlling his anger. He turned to the Bow Street runners. "Take them away."

"With pleasure, m'lord," they replied in unison and promptly did as ordered.

No one moved until the shop door closed, and then it seemed everyone was moving and speaking at once. Madame de Bressard was going on in an agitated mix of English and French about those horrid people, and how that well-dressed brute wearing an exquisite blue silk foulard (she was in the fashion trade, after all) had struck Lily, and how Lily had been so brave.

"I wonder how they knew Meggie was here," Lily mused.

"Desmond must have bribed someone at Lotheil to keep track of my sister's whereabouts," Ewan said. "No doubt my whereabouts as well. Where's Meggie?" His gaze never left Lily as he made sure she wasn't hurt worse than she was letting on.

"She's in the dressing room. I'll fetch her."

"I'll go," Madame de Bressard insisted and hurried off.

Lily knew that she was the one who should have gone, for Meggie was certainly hiding in a corner, shivering in her undergarments. But her legs suddenly seemed wobbly, and the room began to spin. Ewan's arms folded around her. "I'm not going to faint," she assured, though it might have been a lie. She was cold and suddenly shaking. She closed her eyes and leaned her head against his shoulder. "Just give me a moment."

"Take all the time you need, lass." He ran his thumb across her cheek in a gentle, easy motion. Oh, that felt good! Scary, how good.

"I could have defended myself," she began to ramble because she didn't trust herself at the moment. She wanted to reach up and kiss him on the mouth. His warm, nicely shaped mouth. "I was about to grab a hat pin and press it to his throat. It was the only weapon I could think of. Handy things they are, too. But I wasn't trying to draw blood or pierce his jugular vein. Do you know where the jugular vein is located? It's the line that runs right here along the neck." She was about to reach up and stroke his neck, then thought better of it. She eased out of his arms, not far, just a step or two away, and tilted her head to better expose her skin while she slowly ran her fingers down her own neck. "There. See? If you look closely, you can see it throbbing."

He suddenly looked as though he'd stopped breathing. He was doing that a lot around her lately. No doubt the musty London air, which was nowhere near as pure as the clean mountain air he was used to breathing in. His emerald eyes turned hot and dark. "Lily... lass..." His voice was little more than a whispered groan as he dipped his head and—

"Ewan! Thank goodness!" Meggie tore out of the dressing room and threw herself into her brother's arms, her red curls bobbing frantically as she hugged him. "I don't know what we would have done without you. You saved the day. Oh, Ewan! I hate it here. Not Lily, of course. I adore her. She's perfect. I want to go home. Scotland is where we belong. Evangeline is right. We don't fit in here."

"Now, Meggie—"

"No!" Those red curls bobbed again. "You see, Lily. See what I mean? Those people were our cousins. They really do want Ewan dead. They want me dead, too!"

She began to wail again.

* * *

"Is she feeling any better?" Lily asked Ewan, rising from her chair in the duke's library where she had been left to wait for him. After departing Madame de Bressard's shop, they had climbed into Eloise's carriage—the one loaned to her and Meggie for their shopping outing—and gone straight to Lotheil Court. The carriage was still waiting outside. She could have used it to return home, but she wanted to stay close at hand until Ewan assured her that Meggie was settled in her bedchamber and moderately calmed down.

He ran a hand through his hair and sighed. "She's a little better. I'll take you home now, lass. I ought to have done it first."

"No, Meggie was hysterical and it was important to take care of her right away." She had been happy to wait in the library, at first thinking to skim through the duke's vast array of books. Ewan had also ordered refreshments for her, but she hadn't touched them. Nor could she concentrate. So while he was upstairs with his sister, she settled in one of the overstuffed chairs beside the massive hearth and did nothing but stare into the fire. She'd needed the warmth of the flames to chase the cold that had set into her bones after the incident with his cousins.

"You don't look all that well yourself, Lily." He knelt beside her, offering the glass of warm milk still sitting on the silver tray beside her. "Drink this. It's laced with a smooth, aged whiskey to help calm your nerves. Have you ever had spirits before?"

"Of course," she said, though she hadn't really. Nothing more than a mild champagne was all that had ever touched her lips. She took the glass from his hand with a muttered thanks and managed a sip. *Ugh!* It was vile.

He let out a pained laugh. "Och, Lily. Drink it slowly."

She nodded and took another, more careful sip.

"Better?"

She nodded again, for he was kneeling beside her and gently stroking his thumb along the palm of her hand. She took another sip. More of a gulp. Actually three gulps. She gagged, then let out a strangled cough.

Sighing, Ewan removed the glass from her hand and set it on a nearby table. "Excellent, lass. I think you've had enough. Let me take that from you." He remained beside her, his expression tense and worried. "How is your shoulder?"

Painful. Throbbing. "It's just fine."

"I'll take you home now."

"No need. Eloise's carriage is just outside."

"Lass, if ye think I'm going to let ye ride back alone, well, think again. And I'll stay with ye until I'm sure your uncle has tended to yer injuries and confirmed no broken bones." His face was close to hers, his brow furrowed, and his brogue thick and husky, those deep, melodic tones as soothing to her insides as that vile concoction of warm milk and whiskey that now had her entire body buzzing. Like a little bee. A little drunk bee.

A very drunk bee.

Which explained her next inexplicable actions. And had she been sober (alas, she wasn't, for the whiskey had roared through her bloodstream like a raging current), she never would have closed her eyes, leaned forward, and kissed him squarely on the mouth, that beautifully shaped mouth almost hidden by the auburn bristles of his beard. But she did close her eyes, pucker her lips, and let out that breathy moan as her lips touched his. There was no taking it back. Not that she wanted to. Goodness, no. His mouth felt exquisitely warm against hers, and the soft, bristled hairs of his beard tickled her nose.

A delightful heat welled within her as Ewan deepened the kiss. Or was she the one doing all the kissing? Then something less delightful welled within her... rather, it heaved upward from the bowels of her stomach. She heaved again.

Ewan unlocked his lips from hers. "Och, lass." He reached for one of the duke's priceless Chinese urns that stood beside the hearth and stuck it under her chin at the same instant she gave a third and final heave that thrust everything she'd eaten since the day she was born— nineteen years worth of digested food and stomach juices—in a perfect arc into that urn.

CHAPTER 7

"**HOW IS SHE?**" Ewan rose as Lily's uncle George entered the Farthingale salon where Ewan had been waiting—mostly pacing for the better part of an hour—and quietly shut the door behind him.

"She'll recover. Her shoulder's bruised, and she's still feeling a bit queasy, but that's all."

Ewan ran a hand roughly through his hair. "All? Isn't it enough?"

"I don't know. Why don't you tell me what happened?"

"It's all my fault," Ewan started to say, but George cut him off with a short, rumbling laugh.

"Lily warned me you'd say that, but she claims you had nothing to do with it. She insists you happened to be passing by the dress shop in time to save her and Meggie. She likes your sister, by the way. Says she's quite delightful, but cries a lot. Not that Lily blames her. She says that she would cry too if her cousins were that odious." George motioned to several crystal decanters filled with liquids in varying shades of scarlet and amber standing atop an ornate bureau. "Care for a drink? Make yourself comfortable while we talk."

Comfortable was not possible, for Ewan was still as angry as a wild boar.

"What's your poison? Whiskey? Sherry? This one's a delightful Madeira."

He nodded to the Madeira, though his throat was so parched, he could drain every one of those bottles in a single gulp. Lord, the girl had given him a scare. "Thank you."

While George raised a glass and poured, Ewan thought about Lily. Not only that his cousin had attacked her, injured her badly enough to make her ill. No, he was thinking about the kiss they'd shared, the sweet caress of her lips against his own, the mere touch rousing such a hot ache in him that he'd almost lost control.

When had he ever been driven mindless by a simple kiss? Never. And the girl was an innocent—her kiss hadn't even qualified as a real kiss, more of a give-your-aunt-a-peck-on-the-cheek-goodbye sort of kiss. Soft, tentative, closed mouth, yet every damned organ in his body had exploded with the force of a hundred cannons going off at once. All aimed straight at his heart. Their aim, dead on.

Had she not been busy tossing the contents of her stomach into his grandfather's treasured urn, she would have noticed the wild heat in his eyes and the painful hardness of his rod straining against his trousers.

He was more or less under control now, though he couldn't be sure how his treacherous body would respond the next time he saw Lily. Great, just great. First the little bluestocking claimed Jasper's heart, and now she was threatening to claim his.

No, his heart wasn't at risk.

It sure as hell had better not be. Lily was a *Sassenach*. He meant to marry a Scottish girl, just as his father had. No English girls for him.

He drained his drink, finished his discussion with Lily's uncle, and returned to Lotheil Court to look in on Meggie. Fortunately, she was sleeping. He descended the stairs and headed for the library, wondering whether Jergens had taken care of Lily's... er, little mishap.

Apparently he had.

He must have also reported it to his grandfather, for the old man walked in shortly after him, closed the door, and took a seat behind his enormous writing desk. "Well, Ewan, are you going to tell me what happened?"

"What for? Haven't your spies told you all you need to know?"

"I want to hear it from you. Is it true? Did Desmond strike that girl?"

Ewan nodded. "She was protecting Meggie. And *that girl* is called Lily."

His grandfather dismissed his rebuke. "But you arrived in time to save her. Isn't that convenient. Who knows what Desmond would have done had you not been there?"

Ewan ignored the dry remark, instead stemming his anger by folding his arms across his chest. He'd known where Meggie was to spend the afternoon and had stopped by to look in on her before meeting with his father's solicitors. Thank goodness he had. He'd send his apologies and reschedule the solicitors for another day. "Fortunately, we didn't have to find out."

"This time. What's to stop him from succeeding next time?"

"Nothing, other than he knows I'll kill him if he dares come near Meggie or Lily again."

"My boy, I think you're serious." He cast him an approving nod.

"I am. Deadly serious."

"Would you have told me about the incident if I hadn't learned about it from... my other sources?"

"No. Meggie is my concern, not yours."

The old man gripped the sides of his desk as he rose to face Ewan. "She's my granddaughter as well as your sister. She's my concern, too."

"Granddaughter in name only. She wants nothing to do with you."

"Is that the way it's to be? You and me at odds for the next three months? I won't have it. My blood runs through you, Ewan. We're family, whether or not you like it. We're more alike than you'll ever admit, though you try to hide it in every way possible."

"I'm not a bit like you."

"Aren't you? Why do you think Desmond is trembling in his boots? He's afraid we'll reconcile. He thinks I will restore you as my heir." He stood up and opened his arms to encompass the grandeur of the library. "Do you want it? You can have the dukedom of Lotheil and all its benefits. Here it is. I'm offering it to you."

"In exchange for what? My soul?"

"Desmond would gladly sell his to me. But I don't want him," he said, and Ewan shuddered at the casual dismissal of his other grandson. Though he detested Desmond, they were blood relations, for their fathers were brothers. Desmond's father had died young. No wonder Desmond had turned out weak and lacking in honor. He'd only known coldness and manipulation from this old man. "I want you, Ewan. Your loyalty. Your affections."

"Sorry, those aren't for sale."

His grandfather threw back his head and let out a long, hard laugh. The malicious sound resonated off the soaring, beamed ceiling, crawled into Ewan's skin, and penetrated his bones. He felt as though he'd just stepped in a stinking pile of manure.

"Everyone has a price. Even you, my boy. Even that Farthingale girl who seems to have blinded you to her true nature. Mark my words. She can be bought, and cheap, too."

Ewan wanted to leap across the desk and pound the old man's face until it was unrecognizable, but he wouldn't give the old man the satisfaction of knowing he'd struck a raw nerve. Not that he cared what the old bastard said about him, but he did care what was said about Lily. She was a rare gem, sparkling in her kindness, her honesty, and her refreshing innocence.

That he was tainted by Cameron blood couldn't be helped, but he'd never let his odious family taint her. Which meant he couldn't see her again. Not ever. Not him. Not Meggie. Eloise would have to find another companion for Meggie.

For her own protection, Lily could have no further contact with him or his family.

*   *   *

The only problem with Ewan's decision was that none of the women would agree to it. Not Meggie, who burst into tears the moment he dared broach the subject with her the next morning. Not Eloise, who later that afternoon yanked the heavenly plum cake off his plate, rose indignantly, and asked him to leave her home and not return until he'd regained his senses.

And not Lily, who gazed at him as though he'd grown three heads... no, make that four heads... when he'd intercepted her on the way into the duke's library two days after her incident with Desmond. "You mean I can't use the library? How am I to help Ashton Mortimer finish his monograph on the evolution of lemur colonies in Madagascar if I can't use your grandfather's books? You see, as the continental plates shifted and land masses broke apart to form islands, the animal populations on those islands became quite insular—"

Bloody hell. "Lily, that's all well and good, but I'm only thinking of your safety."

"Nonsense. The evolutionary development of these lemurs is far more important. So is your sister's new wardrobe. We had to reschedule our appointment with Madame de Bressard until tomorrow. Dillie and I will take her there. Our cousin William has agreed to come along, but you may join us if you're still concerned. I doubt your cousins will dare threaten us again, not with Dillie and William with us. Oh, and I had Madame de Bressard send the invoice for the broken table to your grandfather."

As she leaned into him, he caught the scent of her warm skin, roses delicately kissed by the evening dew. "He won't dare ignore it," she continued. "After all, it was your grandfather who instigated the whole affair, and everyone knows it. Now, are you going to let me get back to Ashton's lemurs?"

She gave him a smug, adorable smile that left him momentarily speechless. It suddenly occurred to him that she'd said nothing about the kiss they'd shared. Had she forgotten it? Found him lacking? Bollix, what did the girl know about such things?

She was the one lacking in that particular regard. He'd only held back to protect her honor. That, and the fact that she was a sickly green and nauseated at the time. She looked healthy now. Dark, silken hair. Pink cheeks, creamy complexion. Dazzling blue eyes, as exquisitely blue as the loch waters on a gentle summer's day. He dared not glance lower. It wouldn't do to be caught gawking at her breasts, which were achingly perfect, if she wanted his opinion, though she didn't seem to be asking anything of him other than to leave her the hell alone and let her get back to those blasted lemurs.

She placed her hands on his chest. Och, her hands felt good. Warm and gentle against his heart. "Did you ever think of that?"

He shook out of his thoughts. "What?"

"Haven't you been listening to me?"

Apparently not. "Sorry, I was distracted."

She nodded knowingly. "The upcoming sale at Tattersalls. I know how you must feel. Laurel can't contain herself either. All she's been talking about these past few weeks is the horse auction. Oh, Uncle George said to tell you that he'll come around Saturday at half past ten to pick you up. He'll stop at Laurel's first. I can't wait for you to meet her. I wish I could go with you. It's going to be such fun."

"Why can't you?" Not that he wanted to spend more time in her company than was necessary.

Her eyes rounded in surprise. "May I? I'd love to, but I don't wish to be in the way. I'm almost finished with the lemur research, and the Royal Society is threatening to burn my monograph on African swamp baboons, so there's no point in my continuing that line of research. Too bad Sir William Maitland isn't in London. He'd set those old fossils straight. Did you know that baboons are a monarchical society, their king constantly keeping vigil against usurpers to his crown? Much like the turmoil in England's early years when William the Conqueror defeated the Saxons and the Danes. The battle of Hastings was—"

"Fascinating, lass. About Tattersalls, it isn't up to me to decide. I have no objection to bringing you along, assuming Laurel and your uncle don't mind."

"I'll ask their permission." She was about to say something more, but they were both distracted by a crash, then the patter of heavy dog paws running along the upstairs hall.

Ewan heard Jergens' frantic cries. Another crash as Jasper knocked into one of the delicate hall tables, no doubt breaking a valuable vase.

"Miss Lily, look out!" Jergens cried as he followed Jasper into the library.

Wrooolf! Wroooolf!

"Jasper! My sweetheart, I've missed you." Lily stuffed the lemur papers in Ewan's hands and turned to invite Jasper into her open arms. A mistake, Ewan realized at once, for the impact of the lumpy beast against Lily's slight—but delightfully curved—body would not resolve pleasantly. Ewan set himself behind her to prevent her from falling when the dog leaped on her. Which is how Eloise happened to come upon them, Jasper in Lily's arms and Lily laughing in Ewan's arms, her back unmistakably plastered to his chest. That his arms were solidly around her body was of no moment. He was simply trying to shield her from Jasper's dangling tongue and enormous paws, but he doubted Eloise or her companion would see it that way.

Bollix.

Who was the lady with Eloise? What were they doing here at Lotheil Court? Oh, right, they were here to plan his grandfather's blasted birthday party. Lily had been helping with those arrangements, even though the old man had yet to show her any courtesy. Lily, the sweet-natured girl, hadn't uttered a word of complaint.

"Oh, crumpets. It's Lady Withnall," Lily whispered, still laughing and making matters worse by turning in his arms to face him. Which meant that Jasper would knock Lily's perfect breasts into his chest with that hairy beast's next leap. Which is precisely what happened.

"Jasper!" Lily cried, making absolutely no attempt to draw back. Not that Jasper would have let her, but the lass could have at least tried to feign shock, horror. Indignation. She looked and felt too comfortable in his arms. Achingly perfect in his arms.

Wroooolf! Jasper's ungainly paws were now atop Lily's head, knocking the pins out of her magnificent, dark curls so that they spilled over Ewan's arms and continued in a glorious cascade down Lily's back.

Wrooolf, wrooooolf!

Yes, he was going to murder that great, loping beast and turn him into a hairy rug to set before the fireplace. Especially after he found out who Lady Withnall was and why everyone in London feared her, even though she was a tiny woman who stood about eye level to his waist and had a disconcerting way of staring at his groin.

She was London's most prolific gossip.

His grandfather strode in just then and found Eloise and Lady Withnall gawking at him and Lily. "Ladies, I think we had better move the planning of my birthday festivities from the library to the conservatory. I think we'll be more comfortable settled there."

"An excellent idea," said Lady Withnall, shooting her long, pointed nose in the air and letting out an indignant sniff. "Seems we have quite the fireworks going on in here."

Eloise smiled. "Isn't it delightful? Lotheil, I think we should plan on more fireworks for your birthday celebration. Everyone loves to see sparks flying."

Ewan didn't hear his grandfather' reply, for Jasper was still jumping on Lily, his tongue all over her face and licking down her delectable body... something Ewan would have willingly braved the fires of eternal damnation to do... blast, the dog was lucky.

As for fireworks, he was as hot as any of those rockets. Hot and about to explode, though it wouldn't be as pretty or delicate as those shimmering points of light. It would be hot and messy. "Miss Farthingale," he said softly, Jasper still jumping and Jergens doing his best to drag the beast away, "you are a menace to this household."

She smiled up at him, her hair a wild mess and her cheeks flushed pink as she wriggled against his body to shield herself from Jasper's exuberance. "Thank you, Laird Carnach. I'll take that as a compliment."

CHAPTER 8

LILY WAS NOT SURPRISED when Ewan avoided her for the next few days, but he'd given her permission to join him, Laurel, and Uncle George at Tattersalls today—that permission bestowed despite Lady Withnall having seen them in what she'd called "a compromising position" and blabbed it about town with the efficiency of Napoleon's army on the march—so Lily planned to be on her best behavior all day.

No controversy whatsoever.

She caught one look at Ewan's frowning expression and realized he was still displeased about what had happened in front of Lady Withnall. Perhaps she ought to have begged out, but she had nothing to be ashamed of, and it seemed to her that hiding at home would only confirm to the London gossips that she did have reason to be ashamed. "It isn't my fault that *your* dog jumps on me whenever he sees me."

"Ye shouldn't encourage the big looby." His brogue was thick again, a sign of his vexation.

"Me? I didn't... oh, what's the use. You're overset because everyone now believes we're an item and the gossips have spread the news throughout London."

"Throughout England," he corrected, "and the outer reaches of the Antipodes."

"You and I know it isn't true." She glanced up to smile at him, but the sun was in her eyes so she couldn't see whether or not his expression had mellowed. Probably not. He wasn't engaging her in conversation other than to blame her for his dog's behavior.

The sun was a big, yellow ball in the sky, and the sky was one of those rare, cloudless blue skies to be savored while it lasted. Despite the sunshine, there was a distinct chill to the air having nothing to do with Ewan's ill humor. A stiff breeze blew across the stalls and crowded footpaths of the auction grounds, carrying the scent of horses and horse manure along with the various perfumed scents presently favored by the gentlemen of fashion who sauntered along these paths looking for the perfect pair of matched bays to hitch to their sleek carriages and stylish phaetons.

Spiced cinnamon and an exotic fruity scent that someone had described as Chinese orange were the current rage among the younger gentlemen. The overpowering French perfumes were a favorite among the older men. Despite the years of war, those fragrances reliably managed to reach England's shores.

Fortunately, the war was over and done for good now that Napoleon had been defeated at Waterloo. Lily's sister Daisy, and Daisy's brave and handsome husband Gabriel, had been involved in saving the day. Gabriel had been awarded an earldom for almost singlehandedly defeating Napoleon's army. That Daisy had also played a role in the victory made Lily very proud.

Ewan nudged her along when she became distracted by her own thoughts. Ewan, of course, smelled of clean, rugged Highlands, a blend of clear mountain water and pine woods. He looked good, too. Whenever did he not? His clothes were simple but finely tailored, buff trousers, dark brown jacket, and a pine green cravat of finest silk that did not make him look at all like a dandy. He wore no cloak, obviously comfortable in the cold weather.

Lily wasn't nearly as comfortable. Her ears and the tip of her nose were growing numb. "Did you know that horses were originally the size of dogs? And that they are closely related to zebras, though anyone looking at the zebras in the royal menagerie would have a hard time believing it. They're both equines, but horses have long been domesticated while zebras remain wild and unpredictable. There's also a creature known in ancient times to be part zebra and part giraffe."

"What?"

"I'm not jesting. The animal is a mix of giraffe and zebra. I wonder how it happened. And why it happened. Perhaps a necessary adaptation to survive in the wild. That's why I'm so keen on Ashton's research on lemur populations in Madagascar. There are so many offshoots from the original lemur ancestor, it will make your head spin."

He grinned. "Fascinating."

"Rumor has it that the zebra-giraffe creature has been seen on the grass plains of central Africa. I saw a drawing of it in one of the books in your grandfather's library, an ancient Egyptian hieroglyphic text depicting that very animal. I wish I could go to Africa one day to see all these odd forms of life in their natural surroundings. Don't you?"

He paused a long moment, eyeing her warily and with great doubt. "Eloise warned me about you."

"She did not. She adores me. She thinks I'm the cleverest girl she's ever met."

He arched an eyebrow and then shook his head and grinned again. "I suppose you are. But let's concentrate on horses for the moment, just the breeds on display here today, and no more talk of zebras, giraffes, or other oddities." He held up a hand when she opened her mouth to speak. "And no lectures on the baboon colonies of Madagascar either."

She snapped her mouth shut. Tried not to respond. Counted to three, then spoke. "The baboons have established colonies in continental Africa. The lemur colonies populate Madagascar and have thrived on that island since the great rift that split it off from Africa. They've thrived because of the lack of natural enemies, but that's changed recently as humans have settled in."

He let out a laughing groan. "Lily, I think I'm going to miss you when I'm back in Scotland."

Her heart sank into her toes. He'd only been here a week, and he was already itching to return home. He *thought* he might miss her once his time in London was over. She *knew* she would miss him terribly— not lightly or sometimes, but always. Of course, she could never tell him that. She'd already made a fool of herself by kissing him. Once. Briefly. He'd obviously put it out of his mind. She must have done an awful job of it.

She quietly followed her uncle, sister, and Ewan as they walked from stall to stall and browsed the pens inspecting prime stallions and gentle mares. Ewan pointed to an enormous, sinewed beast, a black giant that its owner called Hades, a brute that appeared capable of breathing fire out of its nostrils. Laurel stepped forward and ran her hands along the horse's chest and withers. She inspected his teeth, felt along his forelegs, and inspected his hooves. Hades allowed her to touch him without so much as a whinny of protest. "You have a good eye, Ewan. He's magnificent."

He nodded and turned to Lily. "What do you think, lass?"

Her eyes rounded in alarm. "Why ask me? I only know what's written in books. You're the experts."

"Still, I value your opinion."

"You do?"

"Aye." He shook his head and laughed. "Why no'? You seem to know about everything else."

Not everything. She had no idea how to kiss a man and make him like it. She was a scholar, not a temptress.

"Well," Uncle George said, eyeing her in that discerning way of his, somehow knowing what was on her mind, "we seem to be in agreement that Hades is for you. Let's find a gentle mare for your sister." He took Lily's arm and strode ahead with her, leaving Laurel and Ewan behind to finalize their registration to bid on the magnificent specimen. "You've taken a liking to him, Lily."

She knew her uncle was talking about Ewan, not Hades. "There's nothing between us. You mustn't pay attention to those silly rumors."

"I never do. I hope you don't either." He gazed at her, his eyes filled with kindness and love, for he was quite protective of his nieces and not about to let anyone hurt her or her sisters. "He seems to be a decent fellow, but it's obvious he won't remain in London any longer than is necessary. He isn't here to find himself a bride."

She nodded. "I know."

"Just making certain you haven't taken the whisperings of these bored gossips to heart. I don't want you hoping for something more from the fellow. You have a way of looking at him, as though he makes the sun shine and stars glow brighter. I don't see him looking at you the same way. Just be careful, Lily."

She glanced back to watch Ewan and Laurel approach. They were smiling, both seeming at ease with each other, and engrossed in conversation. She overheard portions of their discussion as they approached and knew they were reviewing the quality of the horseflesh on display at the auction house. Her uncle joined in, and Lily felt a bit like a duck out of water, her knowledge gleaned only from books and not at all from life experience.

As the others walked ahead, she held back and strolled along a quieter pathway that housed the older, less desirable horses. She paused by one stall, drawn to it by the soft neighs of its occupant, a dappled gray mare. "Hello, girl. What's your name? Mine's Lily. You seem lonely."

The mare approached and nuzzled her cheek.

"At the moment, I'm feeling a little lonely too. I wish I'd thought to bring an apple for you." She stroked the mare's nose and received a thick lick on the cheek in return. *Ugh.* "You must be related to Jasper."

She heard a deep, rumbling chuckle from behind her. Ewan stepped forward and leaned his big shoulder against the stall, his gaze never leaving hers as he withdrew his handkerchief and wiped it gently against her cheek. "What is it with you and animals, lass? They can't resist you."

Just her luck, she was devastating to animals. Not to men.

"There's something about this sweet mare that drew me to her. Look how gentle she is. Do you think Meggie will like her?"

He tossed her a careless smile. "I think she'll be perfect. Let me find her owner and I'll sign us up for the bidding. Seems we've had a productive day. The auction will begin soon. Are you interested in watching?"

"Yes, I've never seen an auction before. Have you?"

"Sure, lots of times. I think you'll enjoy it. The bidding moves along quickly, especially under the direction of these experienced auctioneers. There's an art to the process."

"Tell me about it." This was what she loved about being out in the world, the nuances of everyday life. What appeared simple and straightforward on the surface was actually a complicated mix of past events and experiences leading up to a single moment.

"It isn't merely about selling horseflesh, but about desire and temptation."

Lily laughed. "You make it sound like one of those scandalous novels Eloise loves to read."

"It's similar. We think we've come here merely to purchase horses, but it's the auctioneer's job to rouse our passions, to make us desire that horse so badly, we'll throw caution—and our budgets—to the wind to possess the object of our bidding. And if more than one party is aroused, then a bidding war starts. The auctioneer has accomplished his goal."

"Will he start with the best horses first?"

"No. Here's where the art of the process comes in. He starts slowly, perhaps with an attractive mare or high-stepping filly, something to pique one's interest. Then he'll raise the stakes a bit with a promising colt that is likely to attract several bidders. If that colt lands his owner a nice price, then the auctioneer knows he'll have a successful auction, for the losing bidders will be that much more eager for the next promising colt on the roster. But he won't put him up right away."

"Why not? I'd think the bidders would grow impatient."

"They will, and that's precisely what the auctioneer hopes for. He doesn't want them easily gratified."

"Oh, I see. He wants that slow build, that teasing promise of fulfillment. Like the romantic hero's chase for the heroine in Eloise's novels. There's no fun if the heroine easily falls into the hero's arms. He must be tempted, then thwarted and made to suffer before his ultimate triumph."

She tucked her arm in his and allowed him to lead the way to the auction area. "This is all so fascinating. So exciting."

"Better than your books?"

"Much better. My heart's racing in anticipation, and I'm not even bidding. How do you feel? What if someone bids against you on Hades? I doubt anyone will fight for the sweet little mare though. You ought to buy her at a good price. But how high are you willing to bid for Hades? Do you think you'll be swept up in the heat of the moment?"

"I know what he's worth, but I'll let him go if the price is too high."

She nodded, smiling up at him. "I thought as much. You don't seem the sort to lose control. Ever."

"I try not to." He gazed at her, his expression thoughtful.

She shrugged and looked away as the auctioneer pounded his gavel to signal the start of the auction. She felt Ewan's gaze still on her and felt her body respond with hot tingles up and down her spine. Her blood heated, and those little butterflies in her stomach began to flutter about in their usual Ewan-spurred frenzy.

She was glad not to be bidding. She obviously lacked the ability to control her own feelings. Indeed, had she participated, she would have been one of those dupes whose desires were so easily manipulated. Goodness, if Ewan were on the auction block, she would have offered her entire fortune to have him. Quite pitiful really, considering he would not have bid on her were she on the block. He was only interested in Scottish ponies.

Though the auction proceeded quickly, it still took almost an hour for Hades to come up. The little mare had come up early on and only Ewan had bid on her. Still, Lily had been in agony until the auctioneer banged his gavel to signal the end of the bidding.

But Hades was the sort of horse to rouse a man's desire, and she expected several well-heeled gentlemen would try to buy him. The auctioneer signaled the start of bidding. Lily found herself gasping and squealing and clutching Ewan's arm each time the stakes were raised. Ewan's attention was on the prize and not even her childish enthusiasm could distract him. Good thing. Several men were passionate about that horse, but Ewan's cool control won out.

While Laurel and her uncle went with Ewan to secure his purchases, Lily went back to the little mare's stall to tell her the good news. Not that she had the ability to speak to horses, but Lily was bursting with excitement and wished to share it with that gentle creature.

She was still smiling and petting the gray mare's nose when someone came up from behind her and not so gently shoved her into the stall. "What the—" She fell beneath the mare's hooves, startling the old girl, who did her best to avoid hurting Lily. But she was just a horse and didn't understand what was happening. The assailant moved toward Lily, obviously not intending to stop with just a shove. He picked her up and pushed her against the hard, wooden boards of the wall before she had the chance to catch her breath and scream.

Lily expected to recognize her assailant, believing it was Desmond once again releasing his fear and frustration on her, but when she turned, she saw a large, unkempt ruffian with a knife in his dirty hand and an evil gleam in his bloodshot eyes. "Is it my purse you want? Here. Take it."

"I'll have it an' ye as well. Think ye can get the better of m'master. This'll teach ye."

Lily had to think quickly. She pretended to surrender, and then at the precise moment brought her knee to his privates with all the force she could muster. As he bent over with an angry yelp, she grabbed the pin from her hat and stabbed it into the hand that was holding the knife. He shrieked and dropped his knife. Lily used his momentary distraction to race from the stall.

She darted out and fell against another hard wall. Ewan. He tightened his arms around her. "What's the matter?"

Laurel was two steps behind him. "She's afraid of mice. Did you see one in the stall?"

Lily was too frightened to answer.

Ewan took a closer look at her. "Bollix," he muttered, handing her over to Laurel and heading into the stall before she could stop him. "Bloody bastard. Who are you working for?" Ewan growled, then she heard the thud of fists against bodies. To Lily's frustration, she couldn't make out the rest, for Laurel was tugging her away.

A group of men heard the commotion and began to gather by the stall, further shutting her out. Men being men, they were quick to take bets on who would come out the winner, though she could have told them the blackguard stood no chance against Ewan. As the fight spilled out into the pathway, she saw Ewan knock the man to the ground with two swift punches. He hauled the dazed man to his feet, obviously searching for a Tattersalls official to take him into proper custody.

Lily could see he was angry, his dark eyes blazing as he scanned the bloodthirsty crowd. And angrier as his gaze fell upon someone else of interest. He released the man and shouldered his way through the crowd, grabbing his cousin. "Desmond," Lily muttered, drawing Laurel toward the pair.

"Who's Desmond?"

"His despicable cousin. The one who threatened me and Meggie at Madame de Bressard's shop. We'd better stop Ewan before he kills him."

Laurel held her back. "Are you serious? You can't get between those two. It's too dangerous."

As if to prove her point, Ewan drew his fist back to begin pummeling his cousin. At the same time, the blackguard he'd released a moment earlier and three of his friends ran forward, quickly surrounding him. "What are you waiting for? Get him," Desmond ordered, sneering as the assailants obeyed him and attacked Ewan.

Desmond hurried off, leaving Ewan alone to defend himself against the unsavory foursome. Though there were dozens of bystanders nearby, not one man stepped forward to help Ewan. He was in trouble, clearly outnumbered, and he stood no chance of escaping unharmed, especially if those men carried weapons. "Laurel, find Uncle George."

Laurel nodded. "Stay out of it, Lily. Promise me."

"I can't. Someone has to even the odds until help arrives." Lily grabbed a wooden board that lay near her feet. Ewan had shattered it over one of the brigands a few moments ago. She avoided Laurel and rushed forward with careful purpose, holding her breath in order to remain calm as she entered the melee. She struck two of the assailants with precision, catching them at the back of the knees. Their ungainly bodies responded as she knew they would, the precise blows causing their legs to buckle. They lost their balance and fell to their knees.

She swung the board at each man's head, each time striking with a resounding *thwack!*

"Lily, by all that's holy!" Her uncle grabbed her and lifted her out of harm's way.

"No! I have to help him."

"I'll do it." George unceremoniously dumped her beside Laurel, quickly removed his jacket, and rushed forward to haul the other assailants off Ewan.

The crowd cheered. Big bodies flew into the makeshift stalls, splintering wood and frightening horses. Several horses broke loose and galloped across the auction grounds, chased by their owners... angry owners, for no one wanted to lose a precious source of income. Buckets were overturned, bystanders splattered by more big bodies falling into water troughs.

Though it seemed to Lily as though years had gone by, the fight actually ended almost as quickly as it had erupted. Ewan and her uncle were the only ones left standing. Lily let out the breath she had been holding. "Thank goodness."

She rushed to Ewan. "Are you hurt?"

He didn't have time to respond before the Tattersalls officials arrived and promptly ejected them. Lily was surprised and indignant. "Us? You're tossing *us* out? We're the victims here. Where were you when that ruffian shoved me into the stall and tried to steal my purse? And when his companions attacked Lord Carnach and my uncle? I'm appalled. Your directors will hear about this, mark my words. I won't let the matter—*arghh!*"

Ewan picked her up by the waist, scooped her over his shoulder, and hauled her to their waiting carriage. "Och, lass, you're wasting your breath. They don't care. Leave it alone. Your uncle and I will deal with the matter privately."

"When? After everyone hears your cousin's lies and believes them? They'll never listen to the truth, no matter what you or Uncle George say."

Ewan nudged her into the carriage. Laurel and her uncle scrambled in after her. Ewan stepped in last, settling his brawny frame beside her. He cast her a warning glower when she opened her mouth to utter more protest. "Enough, lass. M'head's still spinning."

She stopped complaining. Ewan was the victim in all this and he'd already heard her righteous indignation. "What about Hades and the little mare? We ought to have picked them up."

"They'll be delivered to my stables," Laurel assured. "What shall we name the little mare?"

Lily knew that her sister was trying to distract her from the incident. "We should leave it to Meggie." She sighed, knowing nothing could be done until Ewan and her uncle spoke to the authorities. She glanced at Ewan. He was rubbing his jaw with his left hand and resting his swollen right hand on his thigh. Though his expression was stoic, there was a glint in his eyes that revealed he was in pain. "Oh, dear. Is your hand broken?"

"No."

She turned to her uncle. "How are you? Any bruises? Cuts? Broken bones?"

"I'm sure I'll be full of aches and pains tomorrow, but no serious harm." He grinned. "Felt good to throw a few punches, but I think this afternoon's bout will satisfy me for the next forty years."

Laurel leaned forward. "Lily, how did you fell those two brutes? You hardly swung that wood board but they tumbled to their knees so fast, I'm sure they had no idea what struck them. And come to think of it, how did you escape that ruffian who had you pinned in the stall?"

"What she lacks in brawn," her uncle explained, "she makes up for in brains. She aimed for the pressure points, the parts of the body that respond in a predictable way to contact. The backs of the knees are exceptionally sensitive."

Lily nodded. "And when the villain drew his knife, I simply stabbed him with my hat pin."

There was a collective gasp from all three companions. Ewan pinned her with his glower. "He drew a knife on you? Why didn't you tell me?"

"You didn't wait long enough for me to say anything. You simply went after the man in that protective animal rage of yours. Anyway, the knife had fallen under the little mare's hooves and she wasn't going to let him get anywhere near her. She probably kicked him for good measure."

"Och, Lily. He might have killed you. I should never have left you on your own."

"You? I'd think Laurel and Uncle George are more responsible for me, they're my family after all. Not that anyone is responsible for me. I can take care of myself. As I said, I got him with my hat pin. I doubt he meant to hurt me, just scare me."

"He drew his knife," Ewan muttered, the quiet menace in his voice sending a chill through her.

"Well, yes. That is a fact." She swallowed hard. "Oh, my goodness! Ewan, is that blood on your shirt? Your blood?" She leaned closer, but it was hard to see in the dim light of the carriage. "Take off your coat. Now. Or does it hurt too much? I'll do it."

Her uncle held her back. "Lily, leave him be."

"But he's hurt!"

"I can see that." He thumped on the carriage roof and ordered the driver to take them straight to the Farthingale residence. "My medical bag is there. Ewan, our footmen will help you into the house."

Lily shook her head. "There isn't a spare bed in the house. And there are too many Farthingales about. Laurel and I will help him next door to Eloise's while you grab whatever supplies you need and meet us there."

Which is what they did, Eloise's footmen assisting Ewan into one of the several available guest quarters, while Lily, Laurel, and Eloise hurried upstairs before them to ready the chamber. Ewan looked pale. Angry, but pale. He was now clutching his side with his swollen right hand. There was a widening crimson stain on his dark brown jacket, but Lily allowed herself a small breath of relief. The stain appeared too far above his liver and other vital organs for the villain's knife to have struck one of them. Still, if he were stabbed, the knife point might have pierced his lung. She studied the rise and fall of his chest to assure herself that he wasn't wheezing or having other difficulty breathing.

"Does Meggie know about this?" Eloise asked.

Laurel shook her head. "No, she wasn't with us."

"The girl must be told. She's fragile and will fall into hysterics when she hears the rumors. And she will. These things have a way of burning through London with the speed of a wind-driven fire. I'm of no use here. I'll fetch her. Lily, why don't you come with me? She won't be so frightened if you're there to calm her."

"No, I want to stay."

Lily kept her gaze on Ewan, expecting him to protest, but he didn't. Her heart lurched. He was more seriously injured than he'd let on. Though she'd only known him for a little more than a week, she understood his nature. Were the injuries minor, he'd be on his feet ordering everyone to stop fussing over him. But he was silent. "Please, Eloise. Laurel will go with you. I need to stay here."

Ewan finally did protest, a weak attempt that quickly died out when he saw the determination on her face. "Och, lass. It won't be a pretty sight."

"I know. That's why I want to be here. I can help my uncle tend to you."

Lily waited until her sister and Eloise left the room and then helped Ewan off with his jacket. "Uncle George will be here soon. Can you raise your left arm?"

"Aye." He surprised her by obeying, which meant he was hurt even worse than she'd thought. "Good, now your right. Can you lift it?"

"Aye, lass. Let me do it myself." A request that she ignored because he was pale and she was now terrified that he might actually die from his injuries.

She set his jacket aside and moved to his shirt, the fine white lawn bearing a fat, crimson stain along the front. She helped him to remove his shirt and used it to apply pressure to the site of the wound that was still spewing blood. *Oh, God!* "Ewan, why didn't you tell me how bad it was?"

* * *

Ewan was worried. He'd been stabbed between his ribs, and though it was not a life-threatening injury, it was serious enough to worry about fatal complications if not properly cleansed and treated. He didn't want Lily here, yet her gentle touch and the no nonsense manner in which she moved around him was incredibly soothing. Her hands trembled as she carefully lifted his shirt to see if the blood had stopped pouring out of him.

"Oh," she said in a choked whisper.

Guess it hadn't stopped yet.

She looked ready to cry, her beautiful blue eyes laden with unshed tears. For him. Just for him.

"Lass, it's just a nick."

She blinked her eyes—still beautiful—and cast him a look of exasperation. "The heroes in Eloise's books are just like you. Strong, ready to suffer in silence so as not to overset the delicate sensibilities of the young lady in question. Their behavior is supposed to be manly, but I think it's idiotic."

He tried not to laugh. Damn, even the smallest chuckle sent pains shooting up his ribs. Hot, intense pains as though someone were jabbing a hot poker in him. "Why idiotic? It seems quite noble to me."

"Noble and foolish in the extreme. How is the young lady in question to know how seriously the man she loves is hurt? And if she doesn't know, then how can she do something about it? The answer is that she can't. She has no choice but to watch the man she loves fall into manly unconsciousness and die in manly silence at her feet."

He arched an eyebrow, wondering whether Lily loved him. She'd mentioned the word twice, but the look on her face was one of frustrated disgust and not wide-eyed adoration. She thought he was an ass. He probably was. "Point taken."

"Here, keep the shirt firmly pressed to the gash while I look at the rest of you." That she thought so little of him did nothing to stem the desire he felt for her. He almost leaped out of his skin when she put her soft hands on his shoulders and began to run them outward down his arms, then across his chest, then downward in a slow, sensual stroking motion to his waist.

A little lower, he silently urged, knowing he would die happy and with a smile on his lips if she unbuttoned the flap of his trousers and took him *firmly in hand.*

He was beginning to like that expression.

Then she did move lower, to the top buttons of his trousers.

His heart exploded and whatever blood had not yet seeped out of him pooled in his groin. "What the hell are you doing?" *Besides torturing me.* He caught her hands in his when she moved between his legs and placed her roving fingers on his thigh. She would be the death of him. The hot, delicious death of him.

"You have the start of some serious bruising at your hip. I need to examine it, as well as take a closer look at your extremities." She grabbed the shirt he should have been pressing against his bleeding wound, caught it as it slid down his chest, and quickly set it back in place. "Your limbs. You know, arms. Legs."

"Not necessary, lass. My hip is just bruised, that's all. And the rest of me is fine."

"Are you certain? Because I don't need you being stupid and dying in manly silence in my arms."

"I'm quite certain, Lily." The lie rolled off his tongue with ease. In truth, none of him felt fine. He was writhing in agony, aching to strip the clothes off Lily, toss her beneath him on the bed, and bury himself deep inside her. It didn't matter that one of his ribs was probably broken, or that his damned wound was still gushing. If it didn't stop soon, he'd bleed to death. All worth it to feel Lily's soft body beneath him.

"Oh, dear. You're hot." Her hands were on him again. All over him, bless her adorably methodical brain. "I hope you aren't developing a fever."

"No, lass. It's simply my body's response to pain."

"Pain makes you hot?"

You do.

She nibbled her lower lip. He really needed to taste her lips, drink in their cherry sweetness.

"How odd? I thought pain left one cold." She shook her head and sighed. "Let me see your wound again. How deeply did the knife penetrate?"

Deep. Really deep. About as deep as I'd like to penetrate you.

Bollix. Now he was just being an idiot male again. A dying, idiot male whose last thoughts were to seduce his ministering angel. Nothing noble or valiant. No. Just hot, baboon male lusting after virginal baboon female.

"Oh, thank goodness. It's small. No bigger than a thimble."

He was not. He was big and hard as a stallion. Hades big and hard. All she had to do was spread her legs and he'd prove it.

"Lily, where are the others?" George's voice was like a splash of cold water, the icy splash Ewan desperately needed, for he was within a hair's breadth of doing something very, very stupid. Why did Lily have to be so pretty? And smell like roses in the evening dew? Why did her hands have to feel so soft and loving on his skin?

"They went to fetch Meggie. What took you so long, Uncle George? I'm worried about him. He's been rambling about baboons and stallions and roses. I couldn't make out any of it. I'm afraid he's delirious. His skin feels hot."

Her uncle frowned at Lily. "You touched him?"

"Of course. How else was I to check for hidden injuries? I'm sure there's more than that one knife wound. There must be. He shot off the bed each time I touched him."

Ewan coughed. *Ow, that hurt like hell.*

George turned his frown on him. "I'll take over from here. Lily, why don't you go downstairs and wait for the ladies?"

"I couldn't. Please don't make me go. *Please,* Uncle George." She cast him the most sadly pathetic gaze she could muster, and Ewan had to admit, were he her uncle, she would have had him in utter surrender.

"Very well. Sit over there and be quiet," her uncle said.

She nodded. "Be very careful when you touch him, Uncle George. He must be developing a fever. That's why his skin is so hot and sensitive. I tried my best to be gentle whenever I touched him, but I only seemed to make matters worse. Was I doing it wrong?"

Ewan coughed again. The girl obviously didn't understand the meaning of quiet, which was fine if she were naked and writhing in ecstasy beneath him, crying out his name between breathy moans. But right now, not so fine.

Her uncle glowered at him.

Indeed, George understood exactly what was going through his depraved Scots mind. Perfect. The one man he depended on to save his life now wanted to pull out his own knife and mercilessly cut him to pieces.

All worth it for Lily.

Too bad he couldn't bed her before he died. Then he wouldn't mind so much when her uncle carved him into little pieces and fed him to the hogs.

"Uncle George, why is he talking about hogs now?"

CHAPTER 9

"EWAN, LISTEN TO THIS," Meggie said three days later, a grin on her face as she bounded into his room, dropped into the armchair beside his bed, and unfolded the London scandal sheet that passed for a newspaper. He was still at Eloise's recovering from the injuries received during his brawl at Tattersalls, and though George Farthingale had ordered a regimen of rest and quiet, the days had been anything but that.

A steady stream of Farthingales had passed through his door. George, of course, who was his doctor and in competent charge of his care, despite concerns that Ewan was lusting after his niece. John Farthingale, Lily's father, apparently unaware that he *was* lusting after Lily, had stopped by to thank him for coming to Lily's rescue. "No thanks necessary," Ewan had muttered, feeling worse because he liked her father.

John Farthingale was tall and in fit condition for a man in his mid to late fifties. His hair was dark but salted with gray, and he appeared remarkably calm for a man saddled with five independent-minded daughters and a houseful of relatives who had no intention of ever leaving—or so Eloise had remarked earlier with a roll of her eyes and a sad shake of her head.

Ewan had made clear to Lily's father that *she* had rescued *him*, probably saved his life with her quick thinking. "That sounds like my daughter," he'd said with a chuckle. "Smarter than the lot of us by the age of three."

Then Lily's sisters had arrived, supposedly to pay a call on Eloise and Meggie (who had moved in at Eloise's for the duration of his recovery), but it came as no surprise to him when all four sisters entered his room at once and began chattering at him, completely ignoring that he was injured and *not dressed*. A circumstance that neither Dillie, Daisy, Laurel, nor Rose found awkward, inappropriate, or embarrassing for him or for them.

Where was Eloise and why hadn't she stopped them?

Fortunately, when the Farthingale sisters had marched in he'd been under his covers and able to hastily don a nightshirt left at the foot of his bed, one that had belonged to Eloise's late husband. Fortunately, Lily's sisters hadn't stayed long. Unfortunately, all had been fascinated by his ability to tell Lily apart from her twin sister. It wasn't hard to do. Where was Lily anyway? Why hadn't she been with them? You'd think he had performed a miracle as grand as the parting of the Red Sea, but all he'd done was recognize Dillie at once.

How could they think he'd ever mistake her for Lily? Lily's eyes were brighter and she always had a slightly dreamy, hopeful look about her that tugged at his heart. Dillie had an alert, clearly attentive look and often smirked. Lily never smirked. She smiled openheartedly.

"Ewan, are you listening to me?"

"Sorry, Meg. My mind drifted. What were you saying?"

"Here it is." She laughed lightly, a distinct improvement from the weepy girl who'd joined him in London. "Lily must have written the item appearing in Lady Hardstocking's 'It Is Rumored' column. Grandfather will be apoplectic. What fun. She's so brave, standing up to him despite his attempts to thwart her."

Ewan sat up. "Go on. What does it say?"

"It is rumored that a certain despicable grandfather —"

"Let me see that." He grabbed the newspaper from Meggie's hands. "A certain despicable grandfather has set his grandsons against each other in a fiendish and maniacal plot to control them. A plot that's doomed to fail and certain to make his grandsons detest him more than they already do. And if he thinks the spineless, cowardly grandson doesn't detest him, he ought to think again. It is suggested that despicable grandfather apologize to spineless, coward grandson as well as to brave, honorable grandson —"

"She means you."

Ewan groaned. "...apologize to them... as soon as possible, or risk dying alone and unloved in that marble mausoleum he calls a home."

Ewan set the paper on his lap. "Is she demented? Grandfather will eat her alive."

"Then you'll have to stop him."

"Och, Meggie. Easier said than done."

She moved to his bed and sat beside him, taking his hand. "She's wonderful, Ewan. Do whatever you must to protect her. I'll help in any way I can, even return to despicable grandfather's residence to fulfill our promise. Not that I want to be there, but it seems wiser to remain close, the better to see what he's scheming."

Ewan nodded thoughtfully. "Aye, Meg. I'm on the mend and should be up and about in another day or two. I'll take care of it."

"I hoped you would." She kissed him lightly on the cheek. "Ugh, scruffy beard. I know you kept it to irk Grandfather, but you're much better looking without it. When are you going to shave it off?"

"I don't know. Maybe today."

*   *   *

"Lily, how could you do such a thing?" Ashton said, shaking his head and *tsking* as Lily joined him in the Farthingale parlor the following Thursday afternoon.

"What thing?" Lily motioned for him to take a seat across from her, which he did, though he remained on the edge of his chair and his lips were pursed in a tight, thin line. "I didn't expect you today, Ashton. Didn't you get my note? It's only been five days since the Tattersalls incident and my parents haven't allowed me to return to my research."

Nor had they allowed her to visit Ewan, though practically her entire family had found their way into his bedchamber over these past few days— even her youngest cousins, Harry and Charles, who'd spent hours yesterday playing marbles with Ewan. What must he think of the Farthingales and their shocking lack of boundaries? Ladies in his bedchamber. He and the boys rolling about on their knees, playing with their cat's-eyes, daws, and agates. The thought of Ewan indulging four-year-old Harry and the adorably earnest seven-year-old Charles turned her insides soft as pudding. "I'm nowhere near finished with the report."

"I don't care about that." Ashton ran a hand through his thinning hair. "I heard about the incident. Are you all right?"

She nodded.

"Good. I was worried about you."

She smiled at him. "So thoughtful of you. Why are you fidgeting? You seem distressed. I'm truly sorry about the delay in finishing your research paper. I've extrapolated a wealth of information on the lemur colonies of Madagascar and how they've developed distinct mutations, even among themselves, on this isolated island. Did you know—"

"Lily, hear me out." His gaze shot to the door, as though worried someone would interrupt their conversation. There was a commotion by the front entry hall, but Lily dismissed it as more Farthingales coming in and out. Pruitt would have announced other callers. She returned her attention to Ashton when he cleared his throat. "The duke sent me to see you."

Her heart beat a little faster. "Does he wish to apologize to me?"

"To you?" Ashton arched an eyebrow and let out a grim laugh. "You called him Despicable Grandfather and now the name has stuck. Simply everyone who's anyone in London is calling him DG. Behind his back, of course. No one would ever dare say it to his face. Gad, Lily! What were you thinking? He's angry and humiliated, and not at all the forgiving sort. He is now insisting that your name be stricken from this research paper that you've been helping me on."

She shot to her feet, her hands trembling and heart lurching into her throat. "But I've worked so hard on it."

"I know. You deserve all the credit, but he won't allow it. He's a mean old blighter, but he controls the board of directors of the Royal Society. They'll do whatever he demands. If he says no further publications are to bear your name, then that's the way it shall be."

"But it isn't just my work that's affected. You're involved, too."

"He doesn't care. He'll let my work sink into oblivion if he thinks you're still working on it."

"He would do that to you? Delay the advancement of science merely to vent his spleen?"

"Obviously."

"But he'd be hurting you most of all. Ashton, this is your life, your career and reputation at stake. If your monograph on the lemurs of Madagascar isn't published, what will happen to you?"

He rose and put his hands on her shoulders, no doubt to quell her agitation. "He knows that we're friends and that my downfall will be a far worse punishment for you than anything he could possibly do to you. He's that sort of man. Cruel and manipulative. You called him on it, and now he's showing you just how cruel and manipulative he can be."

She shook her head, confused. How could she have made such a blunder? She'd poked the snake, expecting it to coil up and spring at her, but he'd gone for Ashton instead. "I ought to have thought of all possibilities. I never considered that he would turn on you. Please believe that I'd never purposely—"

"I know, Lily. I also want you to know that I'll survive with or without the Royal Society."

"How? It means too much to you. I'll make it right. I promise." She felt awful. How could she have done such a thing to a friend? Her dearest friend outside of her own family.

He tightened his grip on her shoulders, still gentle as he shook her lightly. "But making it right would mean striking your name from everything we've done together. I can't ask you to do it."

"And I can't allow you to give up everything we've accomplished. We're a good team, and I always enjoy our scientific collaborations, but I've brought this on myself and must now face the consequences. I alone. Not you."

He sighed. "Hopefully, the situation will improve over time. What if I were to tell you that I have a potential benefactor for my research?"

"You do? Why didn't you let on sooner? That's wonderful."

"Well, the details aren't quite settled. There's a risk my benefactor will back out if my membership in the Royal Society is rescinded. But I'm hopeful that he won't. There are decent men out there who value science and discovery, who respect a man's ability to think, and who look to expand knowledge instead of stifle it for the sake of their own petty jealousies."

Her eyes rounded in surprise. "Ashton, I appreciate the gesture, but this is all the more reason why I can't let you stand against the Royal Society. I won't allow the duke to destroy your life and all our good work. It's the science that matters, the advancement of man's knowledge. I insist that you do as the duke asks. Strike my name from the monograph. Strike my name from all our collaborations."

"Lily, are you certain? It's asking a lot of you."

"Intensifying hostilities will only get other innocent people hurt. It's better this way. I'm certain, Ashton. I don't mind at all. Really, I don't."

He shook his head, but smiled. "Thank you, Lily. In truth, I've been turned inside out by the situation. I would never have forced you to buckle under to his demands, but it does take a great weight off my shoulders. I was hoping you'd agree to this resolution. It's the only way to save all our hard work."

She kept the smile fixed on her face, though she was aching inside. This research wasn't just an assignment for her, it was something she loved. "You may as well report the good news to the duke, let him know he's won."

"I will." Ashton was still holding her, his hands casually resting on her shoulders. "Lily, what are you thinking?"

That she wished Ewan were here. If he'd been in Ashton's situation, he would have confronted his grandfather, faced him like a man and not backed down to his threats. But Ewan was a stubborn Scot, with an even more stubborn protective streak. He would have given up his membership in the Royal Society and told all the old fossils on the board to stuff their demands somewhere unmentionable.

He would have done it for her, even though he didn't love her. He would have done it in his hot-headed, manly splendor, not caring what it meant for his career, for he was confident of his abilities and would not have doubted his ability to find a benefactor to support his research.

But Ashton wasn't like Ewan. He was an Englishman, bred to be polite and to respect those above his station. It wasn't a matter of finances either, for Ashton's father was a lord and a man of comfortable means. Ashton was his heir and would inherit his title and all the benefits that came with it. Though they never discussed finances, she knew his father had been generous and supportive of his endeavors. No, Ashton's concern was scholarly in nature. Their research was important, and not even their friendship could be allowed to stand in the way.

At the moment, she liked the Scottish way better. Proud, stubborn, stand one's ground. No wonder Ewan held little admiration for the English. *Sassenachs* is what he called them, claiming he would never marry one of them. Unfortunately, that's what she was. English born and raised. Not that she was thinking of marriage to Ewan. She wasn't. Even though he made her insides flutter.

Problem was, she didn't make his insides flutter. The lame kiss she'd foisted on him had done nothing to heighten his desire, though it had sent her into raptures. Who would have thought that a slight pressure to his warm lips would have kindled a fire within her?

She studied Ashton's lips. They were a little thin. Quite pinched at the moment. Would he kiss her if she asked him? Did he ever think of marrying her? She had an ample trust fund that would be made available to her once she'd married. They could use it to endow his research. She'd never mentioned it to him. Perhaps she ought to mention it to him now.

Ashton shifted uncomfortably. "Whatever you're thinking, the answer is no."

"You haven't heard the question."

"I don't need to. There's a glint in your eye that frightens me."

"Why are all men so afraid of me?" Ewan wasn't. But he would return to Scotland in a few months, the promise to his dying father fulfilled, and Lily would never see him again. Why was life always complicated? Studying facts in books came much easier to her. Books didn't threaten or scowl. Books were what you wanted them to be.

"I'm not answering that." He dropped his hands from her shoulders. "I must run. The duke is expecting my answer. I can't be late."

She nodded.

"You're a good sport, Lily. In truth, I'm not feeling proud of myself right now. But we've made the right decision. Wait a few days, quietly finish the lemur monograph, and find a way to sneak it to me. The duke will never know." He tucked a finger under her chin and raised her gaze to his. "Everything will work out. You'll see in time."

"Don't keep him waiting." Ewan's grandfather was as dangerous as a wounded boar in a frenzied rage. He would attack anything or anyone that got in his way. She didn't want him to cause Ashton any further difficulty.

She watched him leave, knowing she had made a muddle of things and this was the only way to fix the problem she'd created. Still, her decision made her physically ill. Her stomach roiled and her heart felt as though it were ripping in half. She hadn't let Ashton know just how badly she hurt, but now that he was gone she wanted to have a good cry and let her tears spill out in buckets. Except she couldn't find her handkerchief. She glanced around. Had it dropped from the cuff of her sleeve? She'd had it a moment ago.

No sooner had Ashton left than Ewan appeared. "How long have you been standing there?" she asked, wondering why Pruitt had not announced him. Or perhaps he'd tried to, but she and Ashton were so deeply lost in their discussion that neither had noticed.

"Long enough to hear about my grandfather's latest mischief." His hands clenched into fists at his sides, and his dark eyes burned with an anger that was obviously directed at himself, though it should have been directed at his grandfather, perhaps a little toward Ashton for buckling under without a fight. No, she couldn't blame Ashton for something that was entirely her fault. Still, he'd been awfully quick to accept her offer to make things right.

"Lily, why didn't you speak to me before you sent that article to Lady Hardstocking? I would have talked you out of doing something so foolish."

Her eyes began to tear, and though she tried to blink them away, they simply kept coming. "I wanted to see you, but my parents wouldn't allow me near you. In truth, they won't allow me out of the house until the end of the week, perhaps longer. I'm stuck here. Not quite punished, but not trusted to be let out into the world... or to be unleashed against the world. They think I'm a menace to society."

He shook his head and sighed, and then took her into his arms and swallowed her in his protective warmth. "You are that. But I happen to like blue-eyed menaces. I missed you."

She melted at the soft, heartfelt tone in his voice. "Did you?"

"Yes, you impulsive little baggage. Although I would have talked you out of what you did, I still think it was brilliant. Meggie and I have been laughing about it for days. Still, your actions did have unintended consequences."

She nodded against his chest. "Yes. Ashton."

"I was thinking of you, all your hard work improperly credited. I'll do what I can to fix the situation. I know how badly you're aching, lass."

She cast him a smile, hopeful that he would talk to his grandfather but knowing it would do little good. "Ewan, I was so worried about you. I see now that I needn't have been. You look wonderful." She reached up and touched a hand to his bearded cheek. The bristles felt soft against her skin. "Dillie gave me daily reports about you. She insisted you were on the mend. I didn't know whether or not to believe her. Your hand is no longer swollen. How is your rib?"

"Healing. Still a little sore, but your uncle did a fine job of cleansing the wound."

"Have the authorities caught the blackguards?"

He frowned. "No, and they're not even looking for them."

"They're not? How can it be? I'm sure they'd be easy to find if anyone bothered to look. Those men were obviously in your cousin's employ."

"Forget about Desmond and his alehouse scum for now. Sit down, Lily. There's something else I wish to discuss with you."

He nudged her onto the sofa and drew his chair closer before settling his large frame in it. Ewan had a way of swallowing up a room with his presence. Perhaps it was just the way she perceived him, big and strong and gallant, though he was rough around the edges. Gruff beard, hard muscles, thick hair too long to be considered fashionable, dark and dangerous eyes.

Really hard muscles.

"I'm listening, but forgive me if I appear a little foggy-brained. I'm worried about Ashton. He'll do what your grandfather demands, but how can I be sure it will be enough? Do you think he'll cause Ashton more harm?"

Those glorious muscles of his stiffened, and his frown deepened. "I'll take care of Ashton. I have friends in Scotland who will undertake to finance his explorations if the Royal Society won't."

"Truly? All the way to Madagascar?" She wiped her damp cheeks against the handkerchief Ewan offered since hers appeared to be lost for good, and then looked up and gazed at him in wonder. "His lemur research is vital to—"

Ewan let out a soft growl and shifted closer. "He'll have funds enough to sail the world if he wishes it. Enough to take you with him."

"Oh, he does wish it! He'll be so pleased. With the funds, of course. I don't think he'll want me around, not after the difficult straits I've put him in with your grandfather and the Royal Society."

"Do you want to be around him, lass?"

"We do work well together, but as I said, he's quite miffed about what I did. And I'm more interested in baboons than lemurs, though none of it matters since my parents aren't willing to let me out of the house. I doubt they'd be willing to send me off to the swamp plains of Africa, or to Madagascar, or anywhere in the world."

"Even if you were to marry Ashton?"

Despite her misery, she laughed in surprise. "Why on earth would he wish to marry me? Ewan, I can't thank you enough for helping me out with your grandfather. Not only for Ashton's sake, but for my own. I was feeling beyond awful for what I'd done. Foolishly, carelessly sending off that missive exposing your grandfather as a heartless, old man."

"That's what he is. Everyone knows it."

"Still, it wasn't my place to shout it to the world. Everyone's suffered for it."

"Life isn't perfect, Lily. It's a work in progress. Mistakes are made, but sometimes they turn out for the better. This past week has opened my eyes to my own mistakes."

She tipped her head toward him. "What mistakes?"

"Lass, I'm far from perfect. I've made plenty of them."

She bit the side of her cheek to keep from proclaiming that it wasn't so. He was perfect. Logically, she knew he wasn't. No one was. But her heart thought otherwise.

"I've been giving a lot of thought to my father's wishes lately. Boredom does that to a man, forces him to reflect on matters he'd rather suppress. My father sent me here to patch family relations, not to prolong the bitterness. Yet all I've done since my arrival is to fan the flames of the Cameron feud."

"How so?"

"By resenting the old man, threatening bodily harm to my cousins—"

"They were beastly to you and Meggie."

He folded his arms across his chest, his expression pensive. "They weren't always this way. In truth, we spent some enjoyable summers together in the Highlands when we were young. Their father was alive then, and though he wasn't as strong-willed as my own father, neither was he a man easily pushed around by anyone, not even my grandfather." He paused and grinned at her. "Or as you affectionately call him, DG."

She winced at the remark. Not that she truly felt remorse, for he was a mean old man, but she had been raised to respect her elders and she'd been utterly disrespectful toward him.

"Everything changed when their father died. Desmond and Evangeline were taken into my grandfather's home."

"Where he proceeded to do what he does best, manipulate and control."

Ewan nodded. "Though for the past year at least, they've been living on their own in a townhouse purchased by Desmond. Perhaps he tired of always being under the old man's thumb. After all, a golden cage is still a cage. I think I can patch things with them, Lily. I may not be able to save the old man, but my cousins are young and I might yet sway them."

"Do you think that's what your father had in mind when he asked you and Meggie to come down here? Not only to patch things up with your grandfather, but to rescue your cousins?"

"Aye, lass. I'm sure of it. I just wish I had realized it sooner. He must have regretted doing nothing for them after their father died. Not that there were any outward signs of their ill treatment. Quite the opposite, they were given every material advantage, best clothes, best schools, best society. But he knew the ogre his father was and did nothing to protect them from the more insidious abuses. So, will you help me?"

She nodded. "Of course, but what can I do?" *Other than make rash decisions that create messes.*

"I was hoping you'd help me come up with a plan." He rose with only a hint of discomfort from his injury and drew her up beside him. "Lily, how do I honor my father's wishes and make us a loving family again?"

"I don't know. Why look to me?"

"Because you're the only one I trust to help me. You're clever and honest."

She shook her head. "A little too honest, at times."

"You're gentle and kind, and having been raised in a loving family, you're the best person to teach us about bestowing love on others." He cast her a sloppy grin. "No matter how despicable those others might be."

Her stomach was fluttering again, but when did it not when Ewan was about? She loved the soft way he was now looking at her. "I'll give it thought."

"Thank you, lass. I'm in your hands. I'll do anything you ask."

Kiss me.

But she was an utter coward and would never reveal how she truly felt.

CHAPTER 10

"SHAVE? YOU WANT ME to shave my whiskers?" Ewan ought to have known better than to ask for Lily's help. She was young and bookish, and she must have been speaking to Meggie about his damned beard.

"And you'll need a new wardrobe." And speaking to Eloise about his need for fashionable clothes.

"Anything else?" he asked, not bothering to hide his irritation. No wonder the lass had asked to meet him for a ride in Hyde Park. She'd said it was to see how Hades behaved when saddled, but he now understood the real reason. The little bluestocking wanted him out in the open where *he* would be forced to behave while she spouted her ridiculous advice.

They had started out riding as a group, he and Meggie joined by Lily, her twin sister, and their cousin William, a young man who seemed to find Meggie infinitely delightful and entertaining. He'd have to watch that lad. If he was thinking about Meggie the way Ewan was thinking of Lily, he'd skin the young bounder alive.

Lily cut through his thoughts with her gentle laughter. "Can you blame William for being infatuated with Meggie? She looks beautiful in the green velvet riding habit, which you paid an arm and a leg for, by the way. Worth it, don't you think?"

At the moment, he and Lily were alone on this cool but gloriously sun-filled, afternoon, the others having gone ahead to introduce Meggie to more Farthingales who happened to be out riding in the park. Jasper, as ever, trotted alongside his horse, gazing up at Lily with his tongue hanging out of his mouth and tail feverishly wagging in adoration. Not that he blamed Jasper. Lily had him panting as well.

She looked sinfully innocent in black velvet, the soft fabric hugging her sensual curves and driving him insane with her every casual movement. He had an overpowering itch to run his hands up and down the lush velvet, slowly strip it off her slight frame, and warm her naked body with his tongue and fingers.

Lord! He was going directly to hell, no bloody doubt about it.

"Ewan? Are you listening to me? What do you think of Meggie?"

"You've done a nice job with her, Lily. It isn't just about her new clothes. She's no longer a weepy little thing who's afraid of her own shadow. You've set the example, shown her how to be strong and trust in herself."

She laughed. "Do go on. I'm liking this conversation very much. I didn't know I was quite this fabulous."

You are. "I was complimenting Meggie," he teased, "not you. You're an annoying little bluestocking who's trying to turn me into an English gentleman."

Her eyes rounded in mock horror. "Perish the thought! I don't wish to change you. However, your table manners need a little polish. Your manners in general, in truth. Quite a bit of polish."

"Sounds like you don't care for me as I am."

"I do, very much. But the point is to make others like you. Your cousins, to be precise. They won't listen to you unless they respect you. Remember what Evangeline said about you at Madame de Bressard's? She was wrong, of course. You're not crude or boorish at all."

His fingers tightened on Hades' reins. "Lass, you're swelling my head with such compliments."

She let out another merry laugh. "Don't be angry. I have given your situation serious thought. You won't get anywhere with your cousins unless they think of you as their equal. Having been raised as *Sassenachs,* and therefore shallow, they will not be persuaded unless you become one of their ilk. To do that, you must fit in with the upper crust. Can you dance?"

He thought about the last clan gathering that dissolved into little better than a drunken brawl. All because of that large-breasted wench... Lord, how was he to know that she was married? "Highland reels. Nothing you would deem proper."

"Um, I see."

He certainly hoped she didn't. Lily was too innocent to understand about such things as lust or casual desire. Lily was a deep, abiding love sort of girl. He hoped she wasn't in love with that self-absorbed wanker Ashton.

"And you can't read very well, but that's not your fault. Indeed, you seem to have as much sense as most highly educated men I know. Certainly more sense than most of the men in my family," she muttered more to herself than to him.

"Lily, I can read."

"Not well enough to pass as an educated man." She cast him another one of those sympathetic glances that only served to rankle him. "But as I said, no one faults you for—"

"Lass, you're wrong." He took the reins of her little mare and turned her about.

"What are you doing?"

"Taking you back to Eloise's. She has an excellent library."

"Yes, but—"

"Pick out whatever book you like." He didn't know why her good opinion was so important to him. It just was.

They rode in silence to Chipping Way, and when they reached the Dayne townhouse, he handed their reins to Eloise's stable boy and started for the house. Watling met them at the door. "Good day, Lord Carnach."

However, when he attempted to lead them into the salon, Ewan stopped him. "Library first."

If Watling seemed confused, he didn't show it. "As you wish, my lord. Shall I take Jasper? I think he'll be more comfortable in the garden. No tables or delicate teacups for him to knock over out there."

Ewan grinned. "Aye, good idea."

Once alone with Lily, Ewan took her hand and led her to the well-stocked bookshelves. "Ewan, you don't have to do this."

He turned away abruptly, grabbed a particularly dense-looking text, and selected a page at random. He began to read aloud. In Latin. He then translated the words.

She leaped to his side. "Let me see that."

"Well?"

"I don't understand. That first day, when you fished the MacLaurin book out of the puddle, you had such trouble sounding out the words."

"The title was smudged. I couldn't make it out. That's all."

"Um... I see," she said again, her brow furrowing in an adorably puzzled expression. "I'm so glad. It makes my job that much easier."

"Lass, let me make one thing clear to you. You're not going to turn me into a perfume-drenched society dandy."

"Ewan, let me make one thing clear to you. Perfume aside, I am going to do it. I must. You need to be accepted into society. Your very life depends upon it."

*   *   *

Ewan was glowering at her again.

Lily didn't mind. At least he wasn't storming out of here with rifle in hand, ready to meet his doom at the hands of his cagey cousin, who deemed him a threat to his inheritance and would kill him at first sight. Desmond was scared of him, and men who were scared took desperate actions, those actions encouraged by Despicable Grandfather. The old rotter was treating his grandchildren like pawns on a chessboard. Ewan had to convince his cousins that they had to unite to defeat him. "We'll start tomorrow morning at ten o'clock. Now if you'll excuse me, I think I hear the ladies returning from their ride. Are we done here? Good. I think I'll join them."

She started past him, her head held high and fingers crossed that he wouldn't see through her bluster and bravado. He reached around her and shut the library door, pinning her against it as he set his hands on each side of the door and leaned in close so that their noses... and lips... were almost touching. *Oh, crumpets.* Speaking of noses, she inhaled his scent as she took a deep breath. He smelled nice. Horse and leather and pine trees nice.

"You think I'm a man in need of civilizing?"

She let out a small *eep*. "Yes, a little. Only a little. On the more trivial subjects such as fashion, etiquette, and dance. Not the important ones. You seem to have mastered those. You're awfully close, Ewan."

"I know."

She licked her lips.

He groaned. "And you think you're just the woman capable of civilizing me?"

She wasn't certain, but she relished the opportunity to mold this raw being into a sophisticated man of substance, a man worthy of inheriting his grandfather's title, a respected duke of the realm. It couldn't be very hard to accomplish. He already had the substance. He merely lacked the air of elegance. Well, he was elegant, if one dismissed that gruff, protect-my-woman arrogance about him. Not that she would ever dismiss it. She loved that about him.

Had she thought *loved*?

She meant *like*. She liked that about him.

Love could never factor into the Ewan equation.

She wished he were not standing so close, staring at her with his smoldering, dark eyes.

"You're *eeping* again. I'll take that last *eep* as a yes." His expression was even darker and more dangerous than the smolder in his eyes. "I won't make it easy for you, Lily. I'm not some lump of clay—"

"Of course not." Had he just read her mind? How did he do that? "You're not lumpy at all. Quite the opposite. You're hard and muscled. Goodness, I couldn't get my hands around your biceps if I tried. It's awfully warm in here. Don't you think so?"

"No."

"Hot, actually. May I go now?"

He nodded but didn't move away.

She put her hands on his chest to nudge him away. A mistake. Unbidden, her hands slid up his chest and circled the nape of his neck. "What are you doing, Lily?"

"I'm not sure. I think I'm about to kiss you again."

"Don't let me stop you," he said, drawing her up against his body and closing his mouth over hers before she had the chance to reconsider. His mouth felt warm, delicious. She yielded to his exquisite conquest. He felt her slight surrender and deepened his kiss.

All of her senses exploded at once, as did her bodily organs, every traitorous, last one of them, exploding again and again in volcanic turmoil as his lips explored hers with possessive urgency and his big hands roamed everywhere they shouldn't be. Not that she was complaining. She wasn't at all.

He cupped a hand over her breast and teased her nipple with his thumb.

"Hot, sugared crumpets," she whispered. "What are you doing to me?"

He answered with the hot dip of his tongue between her lips, an exquisite invasion that shattered her resistance... again, not complaining. Not resisting either. No. Not a whit.

She arched into his hand, loving the feel of his fingers teasing her hardened bud against the fabric. She wanted to feel his rough fingers on her skin. "So many damned layers," he murmured, kissing her again, his tongue parting her lips with ease, plunging deep into her mouth, soft and deep, in a rhythmic urgency that annihilated her resistance, what little she'd had to begin with. Assuming she'd ever had any desire to resist him.

Blood rushed to her head in a pounding roar. "Oh, my goodness. Ewan, please. More."

The pounding persisted.

Ewan drew away with a slow, tortured groan. "Damn it," he said under his breath, "someone's at the door." He waited for her to regain her composure, a task made impossible while he stood so close, the male heat radiating off his body and wreaking havoc with her senses. He—the villainous epitome of male perfection—stood beside her, completely unaffected, as though they hadn't been swallowing each other's tongues or pillaging each other's bodies a mere moment ago.

Blessed saints and burnt crumpets. That was far too much fun to be anything but sinful.

"Open up, Lily." She recognized Dillie's voice on the opposite side of the door.

Still a little dazed, she reached for the knob, but Ewan stopped her. "Take a deep breath. A few deep breaths to calm yourself."

"I hate you. You know that, don't you?"

He grinned. A smug, dominant baboon male grin.

"I definitely hate you," she insisted, opening the door.

"Took you long enough," Dillie muttered. "What were you doing in there?" Then she spotted Ewan standing behind her. No doubt still grinning behind her. "Never mind. I don't want to know. I'm far too young and innocent. Not that I wish to remain that way, but I haven't found *my* dominant baboon male yet."

Lily rolled her eyes. "Don't be ridiculous. Why were you pounding on the door?"

"Daisy's having her baby. Come on. We're needed over there."

As Dillie left, Lily turned to Ewan, not sure why she wanted another glance at him before she followed her sister out. His smile turned tender. He raised his hand to her cheek and gave it a light caress. "Go on, lass. Don't keep her waiting."

She nodded.

Did he like the kiss? He seemed to, but he'd regained his control awfully quickly. Perhaps he'd never lost it.

"Lily," he said as she turned to walk away, "the answer is yes."

"I didn't ask a question."

"You did, lass. It's there in the uncertain, blue pools of your eyes. I did like the kiss. Now, for your second question—"

"I haven't asked it either."

"The answer is I liked it a lot. It was a damn great kiss."

She smiled an openhearted smile. "I thought so, too."

"And to answer your last question, no one else."

She laughed. "What? No one else can kiss you into raptures as I did?"

"No, lass." His voice was tender and husky, and his brogue more pronounced as it often was when he was other than calm. "No one else can kiss *you* into raptures as *I* did."

*　*　*

Rose and Laurel were already in Daisy's bedchamber assisting the midwife by the time Lily and her twin arrived. After giving Daisy a hug and a kiss, she and Dillie remained in the background, running whatever errands were requested of them, then quietly returning to the bedchamber. They simply wanted to be close to Daisy, all five sisters together, as though the strength of their love would make everything turn out right.

"Where's Gabriel? How is he holding up?" Daisy asked, obviously worried about her husband as her contractions continued into the evening.

"He's pacing downstairs. Graelem's with him to lend support. So are Mother, Father, and Uncle George. He'll be fine," Laurel said, her words more reassuring for the hell she had survived during her first childbirth last year. Her husband, Graelem, had been mad with fear, as had the entire Farthingale clan. Even now, Lily wanted to reach out and hug Laurel, just to be sure she was alive and well, and not a ghostly vision.

When the midwife stepped out of the room during a quiet moment, Rose turned to Lily. "You've been distracted all evening. Out with it. What's on your mind?"

Lily knew she ought to keep silent, for this was Daisy's moment and nothing should distract them from that. But Farthingales never seemed able to keep quiet on any topic, even ones they knew very little about. It was the family curse. Except for Uncle George, who always knew precisely the right thing to say... or not to say... and at just the right time. But Uncle George wasn't here to stop her, and she wasn't used to being this confused. She simply hated the feeling. Hadn't experienced it since she was a toddler. "Ewan kissed me."

Even Daisy sat up with a start. "He did?"

Lily winced. "I started it, but he took over rather quickly."

Rose and Laurel were grinning. Smug, womanly grins. Obviously, they understood what she was talking about. Good. She needed help to sort this out. Daisy broke the smiling silence with a sharp gasp. All eyes turned to her. "Forget it. Just a contraction. Go on, Lily. Tell us more."

"Tell us *everything*," Rose added.

Well, she wasn't going to do that. Just the confusing details. "He's very good at kissing. He was quite thorough about it."

Ugh, her sisters were all grinning at her again. "And how did it feel to you?" Laurel asked.

Amazing. Breathtaking. "Good."

Laurel persisted. "Just good? Or spectacular-knock-your-stockings-off good?"

Lily felt her face heating. "Yes, the latter choice. Spectacular. Better-get-a-chaperone-into-the-room-fast good. If Dillie hadn't knocked on the library door just then... well, thank goodness she did."

The grins now stretched so broadly across her sisters' faces, one would think they were fillies at a horse auction, waiting to have their teeth inspected by potential bidders. "Oh, Lily! Don't you realize what this means?"

"If I did, Daisy," she said, trying not to sound as irritated as she felt, "I wouldn't be asking all of you."

Rose reached out and hugged her. "You're in love."

Lily shook her head and laughed. "Oh, no. No, no, no. At best I'm infatuated. Interested. Moderately attracted."

"Love," Laurel insisted.

She glanced at her twin. "Dillie, please rescue me. I feel outnumbered."

"What can I do? I'm still young and innocent. But it seems as though our older and wiser sisters know what they're talking about."

"They don't. It isn't the same at all." She placed her hands on each side of her waist and stared at her three married sisters in accusation. They were in love with their husbands and wanted the same for her, no doubt. Being in love was likely a wonderful feeling if the other party reciprocated. "Your husbands love you back. Ewan doesn't love me."

Rose gave her another quick hug. "Are you sure?"

"Unfortunately, yes. He's going to marry a beautiful Scottish woman. No pale-haired, weepy-eyed English girls for him."

Dillie stepped forward. "Might I point out that you are neither pale haired nor weepy eyed. I ought to know. I look like you. And that's another thing. He *never* mistakes me for you. Don't you find that interesting?"

"No," Lily said. "The Duke of Edgeware never mistakes me for you either. Not ever. And he doesn't like me in that way... he... oh, crumpets! Dillie, it's you he's after!"

Dillie's face turned the brightest shade of red she'd ever seen on a person. "He isn't. Don't be ridiculous, Lily. We're speaking of you, anyway. Oh, look what you've done. Now you've got everyone looking at me. Stop it. Concentrate on Lily. She raised the topic. She's the young innocent who was kissed by the big, bad wolf."

"He isn't bad. Well, perhaps bad in a *good* way," Lily admitted. "No man has kissed me like that before. Not ever. I think I ought to run some more tests, make certain my response was unique to him."

Dillie looked at her askance. "More tests? Do you mean that you're going to kiss other men?"

"Why not? He practically challenged me to it. He said that no one else can kiss me into raptures as he did. Awfully smug of him, I thought. What if he's wrong?"

Rose, Laurel, and Daisy groaned. "He isn't wrong," Rose said. "However, I'm not opposed to your plan. But I'd like to suggest some minor modifications."

"Such as?"

"Make certain that Ewan is close by when you decide to let another man kiss you."

"Why?" Lily was trying her best to follow Rose's logic, but it was difficult. It was also a little humbling to see that her other sisters seemed to grasp the advice so easily.

Rose eyed her with infuriating patience and indulgence. "Because it's Ewan's response that matters most, not your response to the clunch you intend to kiss, or that clunch's response to you. For the record, if you and your hapless clunch happen to consummate that kiss, you'll hate it. At best you'll feel indifferent. But it'll never get to that point because Ewan won't let it."

"Are you sure? What if he doesn't step in to stop us?"

Daisy shook her head. "I will admit, that's bad. But he will step in. How could he not? You're wonderful, Lily."

"You're perfect," Rose added.

"You're kind and caring," Laurel chimed in.

Dillie cast her a wicked grin. "You're beautiful. The most beautiful young woman in all of England."

Lily would take that comment— spoken by her identical twin— with a grain of salt.

But that's why she loved her sisters so much. They were blind to her faults, always caring and supportive. They were the best sisters in the world.

"Here now," the midwife said, stepping back into the room and noticing their smiles. "What's this? A party?" She nudged Daisy back into proper birthing position. "You concentrate on getting that little tyke out of you. Stop dawdling and start pushing. Your body's telling me the babe is ready to slip out."

"How can you tell?" Lily asked, and listened with fascination as the knowledgeable midwife explained it to her in gory, intimate detail. Which was why Lily was closest at hand when not a half hour later, Daisy gave birth to a little girl.

Lily was still marveling about the miracle of life as they all left the room to relate the good news to Daisy's husband. Gabriel let out a rafter-shaking whoop and took the stairs three at a time to be with his wife and new daughter. Lily, her sisters, parents, and brother-in-law all remained downstairs and toasted the newborn. While their small group laughed and cried and hugged each other, their father opened a bottle of remarkably good champagne and poured everyone a glass. The champagne bubbles tickled Lily's nose, but it was otherwise delicious and quite easy to drink.

She had three glasses of it.

Which was why she was a little off her stride when Rose's husband, Julian Emory, burst through the door and announced, "Ewan's been arrested."

CHAPTER 11

LILY WAS SO ANGRY she could spit!

"You promised me you wouldn't do anything foolish!" she exclaimed, finally admitted into the duke's library well past ten o'clock the following morning and finding Ewan seated at his grandfather's desk, engrossed in the Carnach ledgers he'd brought down from Scotland as though nothing untoward had happened at White's last night.

Even Jasper thought better of leaping up to greet her. Instead, the coward scampered out of the room as though his tail were on fire. She heard the crash of another pot and *whoosh* of soil scattering across the marble floor as Jasper slipped and slid his ungainly way toward the stairs.

Ewan finally glanced up. "How did you get in here? I thought my grandfather banned you from ever stepping foot in his mausoleum again."

"He has, but I'm not about to let a crusty old man or his hulking footmen stop me from talking to you."

He rose and came to her side, his eyebrow arched. "So you strong-armed your way through their defenses? Impressive."

She glowered up at him. "How could you do what you did last night?"

"Easy. I simply raised my fists—"

"You know that isn't what I meant."

"I made no promises to you, Lily. Never said I'd play by society's rules. That was your idea, not mine."

She shook her head and sighed. "Is this how you make amends with Desmond and Evangeline? By almost killing Desmond?"

"My cousin deserved the beating. I let him off too easy at Madame de Bressard's. The coward sent his villainous underlings to Tattersalls to hurt you. I wasn't about to let him get away with that despicable stunt a second time. It was the proper thing to do. I should have taken care of the matter sooner."

She wanted to insist that he was in the wrong, but couldn't. She was just as angry over that incident and furious that the Tattersalls authorities had done nothing about finding their attackers. Nor had Ewan's grandfather chastised Desmond for his untoward behavior. She sighed in partial surrender. "Did you have to do it in the most exclusive gentleman's establishment in London, in front of the most influential men in England? Couldn't you have waited until he left his club?"

"You mean ambushed him in a dark alley? It isn't my style."

"Yes... no. Uncle George intended to look into the matter. He would have taken care of the insult to me."

"Insult? The bastard struck you when he couldn't get to Meggie at the dress shop, and then tried again at the horse auction. He happens to be my cousin, therefore my problem. Do you think I'd let your relatives risk their lives on a Cameron clan matter?"

She wanted to wrap her hands around his neck and throttle him. "You were very lucky last night that—"

"Desmond was the lucky one. I still may kill him."

"You've played into his hands. Now, everyone believes you to be the madman he claims you are." She glared at the thick-headed Scot, wondering how he was ever going to gain admittance to White's or any gentleman's club for that matter. Worse, how was he going to fulfill his father's wish to reconcile the family? His cousin was doing a very effective job of pushing him away. Ewan was doing all he could to help him.

"Lily, I don't give a damn."

"Spoken like a true Cameron. Oh, yes. I've read up on your clan history and wasn't in the least surprised to learn that you're the most feared fighters among the fierce Scots, the most infuriatingly honorable—"

"Thank ye, lass."

"I didn't mean it as a compliment. You lose your estates to the Crown every few centuries and spend the next few centuries trying to gain them back because of your stubborn, twisted sense of honor and your penchant for spilling blood. You go to war and worry about the consequences later, when you'd be better served thinking first... oh, what's the use? You'll be fortunate if the Prince Regent lets you off with just a warning."

He crossed his arms over his broad chest and planted himself directly in front of her. "Are you quite through blistering me?"

She took a startled step back, suddenly realizing she might have come at him a little too forcefully. He was a laird. A duke's grandson. A very large and muscular one. The proud leader of a warrior clan. "Oh, Ewan. I'm sorry. I spoke out of concern for your well-being and simply forgot myself."

"Ye're forgiven," he said softly, a small smile tugging at the corners of his lips. "I'm sorry, too. And the Prince Regent did come after me."

"What?"

"I still have my lands, but I've been fined by the Crown." He returned to the desk and lifted a parchment from it, handing it over to her.

She took the parchment from his hands and read it. "Outrageous! I'll see what Uncle George can do about reducing it."

"Ye will no', lass."

Oh, his brogue was thick again. "But it's a fortune!"

"It's an expense I can afford. I will no' fight it, nor permit you to interfere—"

"Interfere!"

"Very well, *intercede* on my behalf. However, ye were right about the Cameron nature. We have an uncanny ability to lose fortunes to the Crown because we fight first and worry about the consequences later. I would no' be a very good leader if I endangered the well-being of my clan in this dispute with Desmond."

She held the breath she was about to release. Could it be? A shred of sense from the proud Scot?

"You win. Lily, I'm yours."

*   *   *

Ewan expected that allowing Lily to mold him into a proper gentleman was a mistake, but he'd agreed to it for two reasons. The first was his approach was getting nowhere with his cousins and his grandfather, all of whom believed he was a savage and disdained him for it. He now stood in his grandfather's study at Lotheil Court, pacing a hole in the exquisite oriental carpet while waiting for the old man, Desmond, and Evangeline to arrive. Ewan had asked for a family meeting and wasn't certain any of them would appear.

The second reason for agreeing to Lily's plan was her situation with the Royal Society. Its board's refusal to acknowledge her research, even her very existence, was squarely his fault. Had it not been for his feud with his grandfather, she would have been tolerated by those old fossils enough for the results of her research to be published even if they still wouldn't have accepted her as a member. No doubt most of the credit would have gone to Ashton Mortimer. Still, it would have been published, and that would have made Lily very happy.

Though he was loathe to admit it, there was a third reason for allowing Lily to get her hands on him... simply put, he wanted Lily's hands on him. All over him. As often as possible. That he wanted her close was not surprising. That he *needed* her close, was. He didn't like needing anyone. Certainly not this bookish snip of a girl.

"You aren't carrying weapons, are you?" Ewan's grandfather asked, striding into his study and taking a seat at the head of the small conference table situated near the far wall. It was shortly after three o'clock, and afternoon light streamed in through the row of Palladian windows, enhancing the warm, red tones of the mahogany wood. Otherwise, there was no warmth to be found in the room, certainly none from the duke, who shot daggers at Ewan with his icy gaze. The rest of the furniture—grand mahogany desk and ornately carved chairs, gleaming silver candlesticks and imposing burgundy silk drapes framing the windows—was like the old man himself, ancient, cold, and severe.

"You're mistaking me for your other grandson, the one who likes to use weapons against defenseless young ladies." Ewan folded his arms across his chest to hide that his hands were now clenched into fists. Not that he'd ever use them on his grandfather, no matter how much he disliked him. No, striking the elderly and defenseless was something only English gentlemen did. And he was considered the savage?

"You're referring to that little nuisance—"

"Lily's not a nuisance."

His grandfather waved his hand impatiently. "The girl ought to be thinking of parties and marriage, not conducting research on shifting land masses and their effect on animal populations. That's Mortimer's topic and he should be taking the lead on that work. Have you read her monograph on baboon populations? The chit is actually comparing our civilized culture to that of baboons, as though such creatures have the ability to organize, to think, to develop a political structure. I will not have the nobility of man tarnished by her ridiculous comparisons."

Ewan arched an eyebrow. "You know quite a bit about her research."

"I know everything that goes on at the Royal Society. Particularly about that nineteen-year-old upstart."

"Yet Lord Mortimer's son is working with her, as you've just admitted, and you've granted him membership in your *exalted* Society."

His grandfather was not in the least repentant or ashamed. "She mocks us, compares men to dominant, male baboons. Ashton Mortimer treats his research seriously. His ideas are thoughtful, respectful."

"Dull as dishwater."

"Deliberate, building on the ideas of the great men who came before him."

"Lily's research is based on foundations set out by Sir William Maitland, an internationally recognized scholar."

"Forget the girl, Ewan. Come sit down and do stop glowering at me. She isn't important."

"She is to me."

He pinned Ewan with his calculating stare. "Since when have you developed a taste for English women? Too bad your father didn't. We could have avoided this family nonsense if only your father had behaved."

The old man was simply goading him now. "This isn't about my taste in women. It's about justice and honor, doing the right thing."

"I see. The sex of the victim, her age and beauty, is irrelevant. What matters is defending a wronged party? And it doesn't hurt that the wronged party has ruby lips and deep blue eyes and a lithe body that—"

"Enough, Grandfather. I won't have Lily spoken of that way." Why had he bothered to call the meeting? Desmond and Evangeline were late. So was Meggie. Where was she anyway? And the old man was having far too much fun baiting him.

"What of the way she spoke about me? I won't have her insulting me privately or publicly. How dare she send that piece of libel to Lady Hardstocking! The girl is forbidden to step foot in the Royal Society hall until she crawls to me in abject apology."

Ewan thought it odd that he hadn't banned her from Lotheil Court as well. Supposedly he had, but Lily had managed to visit him anyway. She was a determined little thing, but not even she could have remained at Lotheil Court against the duke's wishes unless the duke had decided to look the other way.

Perhaps his grandfather feared that he and Meggie would leave for good if Lily were no longer permitted to grace this *mausoleum*, as she'd called it in her letter to Lady Hardstocking. That was interesting, perhaps a glimmer of hope that relations might improve among the Camerons.

A commotion at the door distracted Ewan from further thought. In the next moment, Evangeline and Desmond entered the study, Desmond sporting two black eyes and a bandage across his swollen nose, a sign that Ewan had broken it in last evening's fight. Ewan wasn't sorry about that. Desmond, the cowardly wanker, had intended far worse for him and Lily.

"Why are we summoned, Grandfather?" Evangeline asked, settling beside the old man and casting him a well-practiced, feminine pout.

He turned away to shoot Ewan an irritated glance. "Ask your cousin. *He's* the one who called the meeting."

All eyes were now on him. All angry. All impatient and dismissive.

Desmond settled in a chair beside Evangeline. "Why bring us here? To gloat over your handiwork in front of Grandfather? You tried to kill me."

"You'd be dead if that were my intent." Ewan remained standing near the table, unable to bring himself to sit alongside the threesome. Desmond did look awful. Pathetic, really. The white bandage across his nose a stark contrast to the black circles beneath his eyes. "I called the meeting because I want the attacks to stop. I thought I made that clear when I hauled you off Lily and tossed you halfway across the dress shop the other day, Desmond. Apparently you weren't paying attention."

"You're a beast and an ogre," Evangeline shouted, rising from her chair. "My brother hasn't gone near Lily or Meggie since then. But that didn't stop you from assaulting him. A gentleman. In his own club!"

"You've conveniently overlooked the incident at Tattersalls. Your brother's scum drew a knife on Lily. Four of them attacked me, one of them sticking his calling card between my ribs. Your brother is fortunate I didn't pay him back in kind."

"Desmond had nothing to do with it." Both of his cousins slid glances at their grandfather. Curious, Ewan thought. Did they believe the old man had given orders to those blackguards? Couldn't be. Ewan had heard the command to attack out of Desmond's own mouth.

"Your brother was there, Evangeline. He told those men to come at me."

"I didn't!" Now Desmond was on his feet. "I saw those strangers circling you and merely uttered what I felt. I didn't know who they were, but I wanted them to hurt you for all the pain you've caused us."

Ewan shook his head in disgust. "What pain? I haven't seen you in over a decade. I've had nothing to do with any of you. In truth, I never would have contacted you if not for my father's request."

Evangeline tossed back her blonde curls. "His deathbed request. How clever of him. He knew Grandfather would never restore his inheritance, so he schemed to put you between us and him. Well, it didn't work. None of us wants you here. Not even Grandfather. I think his actions have made that perfectly clear."

The old man slowly rose to his feet, his movement graceful and his manner every bit the imposing duke. His eyes appeared to cloud in confusion. "I want to hear the truth from you, Desmond. My boy, look me in the eye and tell me you had nothing to do with the incident at Tattersalls."

Desmond's eyes appeared to cloud in similar confusion. "Of course I had nothing to do with it. I promise you that. I'll take an oath on it. I thought..." His voice trailed away, but his gaze remained fixed on their grandfather.

"You think I had a hand in it? Me? A duke of the realm! Sending wharf rats to hurt my own flesh and blood? Ordering one of those rats to draw a knife on an innocent girl? Is this what you all think of me? That I'm a detestable old man living in a mausoleum, just as that Farthingale girl wrote?"

"The word is *despicable*," said a young female voice at the doorway. "Sorry I'm late. I was out riding and lost track of the time. Grandfather, she called you *despicable*."

"Meggie, he gets the point," Ewan said, nodding for her to approach and join the family meeting. Since all five of them were now standing, their hands balled into fists, it didn't seem like much had been accomplished during their brief conversation—if that's what one could call accusations hurled back and forth. But Ewan suddenly felt as though a great weight had been lifted from his chest.

Meggie wasn't quite so brave as to approach their grandfather. Instead, she stopped beside Ewan, remaining a step behind him and resting a hand lightly on his arm, as though his nearness would somehow protect her from the other three as she spoke to them. "I'm so glad it wasn't any of you," she said, revealing that she had heard the discussion before she entered the room. "I know you hate us, but we don't hate you. That is... we thought we would... but Lily says family shouldn't hate each other. So I don't want to hate you anymore. I want to honor my father's request. I'm glad you didn't do those awful things."

Assuming the duke and the cousins could be believed. Ewan ran a hand through his hair in consternation. He wanted to believe them. In truth, he did believe them. It was something he felt in his gut, and that gut instinct had never been wrong. But if not his own family, then who wanted to hurt him?

His grandfather must have had the same thought. "Seems this meeting was productive, after all. But in answering one question, it raises a host of others. Ewan, who could have done this?"

"My problem," Ewan said. "I'll deal with it." Had he made enemies in the Highlands? Someone who wished him ill? Someone who hated him enough to follow him to London and attempt murder?

"It's a Cameron family problem," his grandfather said, stiffening his spine and casting all a look to remind them that he was the Duke of Lotheil, a man used to giving orders and having them obeyed. "I'm head of this family, and while I live and breathe, no one is going to lay a hand on any blood relation of mine."

Desmond let out a low growl. "I see. That's what you've wanted all along. Any excuse to make up with *that* side of the family. You don't care a whit about Evangeline or me. You never wanted me to succeed you as duke. It's Ewan you want. The Scottish boor. For all your talk of proper *English* bloodlines, you're still a Scot. You've never escaped your Lowlander roots."

Evangeline's lips began to quiver. Lord, she was another one like Meggie, weepy and afraid of her own shadow. A dose of Lily would do her good, Ewan mused. Since Lily had worked wonders on Meggie, she might do the same for his cousin.

"Damn it, Evangeline. Don't cry," Desmond said, his voice surprisingly gentle for a man so enraged.

"I can't help it."

The duke reached out and took her into his arms. It was the first sign of affection Ewan had ever seen spring from the man. Obviously, the old man wasn't used to such displays for he held Evangeline awkwardly and looked lost as he patted her hand. "I'm proud of all my grandchildren."

"You don't even know us," Desmond said, a remark that must have cut the old man deeply coming from the grandchild he knew best.

He suddenly looked twice his years, a weary sadness on display as he glanced from grandson to grandson, then to his granddaughters. "Apparently I don't." He released Evangeline and turned to walk away, but paused in front of Ewan.

Ewan felt Meggie take another small step back. Even when sad, the proud Duke of Lotheil was a daunting force. Ewan stood his ground and waited for the old man to speak, which he did after a long silence. "Tell that girl she's no longer banned from Lotheil Court."

Ewan nodded. Lily had already violated that ban and intended to do so tomorrow as well, so it wasn't much of a concession. "And the Royal Society?"

His grandfather's expression hardened. "No. I understand that she's young and was obviously rattled by the attack upon her person at Tattersalls. But she humiliated me in public, accused me of that crime. Or at the very least, accused me of goading Desmond to commit that crime. I've told you, Ewan. She doesn't step foot in that vaunted hall unless it is to crawl on hands and knees upon the cold marble and apologize to me."

Ewan held his tongue. Much progress had been made in this meeting. But damn it! He'd sooner build a new hall of science for Lily than ever see her crawl before any man.

He sighed inwardly.

The girl was going to bankrupt him. New gowns, new spectacles, new books, and now a new building. Yes, bless her proud heart and love of science, she was going to leave him flat broke by the end of these three months.

All worth it.

Lily was not going to beg for any man. Not even him... unless it was to beg him to take her to bed. That would happen only in his fantasies. That *did* happen in his fantasies. Every aching night.

CHAPTER 12

LILY ARRIVED at Lotheil Court the following morning, uncertain what to expect after receiving Meggie's note the evening before promising something of major importance today. Dillie, who was bored and looking for something to do, decided to come along even though the day was unusually cold and wet.

Lotheil's staid butler opened the door, saw the two, and stared, wide eyed. It took him a moment to realize he wasn't seeing double. "Good morning, Harding," Lily said. "Miss Cameron is expecting us."

He waved them in, taking their damp cloaks and hats, and started toward the visitors' salon. "This way, ladies. I'll ask if Miss Cameron is at home."

"Of course she's at home," Lily whispered to her twin. "Isn't it the most ridiculous expression? Where would she be at this early hour if not here?" She supposed it was more polite to be "not at home" to visitors one didn't wish to see. Nicer than saying "Go away, she has better things to do than see you."

"Harding!" Meggie called in an excited whisper from the top of the stairs. "Let them come up here. Now. Quickly! But do be quiet."

He led them to the stairs and motioned upward, the put-upon look on his face showing his displeasure at having a pair of look-alike strangers meandering through the Lotheil private quarters. Not that Lily blamed him. What was so important to Meggie that she'd had them come over before noon and was now squealing and hopping excitedly like a frog on one leg?

It couldn't be anything sinister, for Meggie was all smiles. She looked delightful in a cream-colored day gown trimmed in dark green velvet to match her gleaming eyes. Her chestnut curls bobbed up and down as she grabbed their hands and led them down the hall. "Quickly. This way."

Lily held her back. "Why so secretive?"

"Be patient. You'll see."

She wasn't one for games at this early hour, but how bad could this adventure be? Meggie wasn't the wild and reckless sort. She was a sweet girl and painfully unsure of herself when out in society. For that reason, Lily decided to follow along even though the little hairs on the back of her neck were standing on end. She didn't wish to undermine Meggie's confidence. Any slip in etiquette could be corrected later.

"This way, and remember to be quiet."

"Why so mysterious?" Dillie asked.

"Ewan's shaving. I wanted Lily to be the first to see him."

Lily came to a dead halt. "That's it? The important event we simply couldn't miss?" Did Meggie intend for them to burst in and catch him in the act? Lily had believed the utter disregard of privacy was an irritating trait unique to the Farthingales. Apparently, the Camerons had no respect for privacy either.

However, the thought of entering Ewan's masculine domain sent tingles coursing through her body. The host of butterflies lying dormant in her stomach instantly awoke and began to flutter their wings in a frenzied whirl. "Oh, no. We can't go in there. It's impossible. Highly inappropriate."

Meggie laughed. "I'm not attics-to-let. We're not going to break into his chamber. We'll wait in my room. He's promised to show me the result once he's done shaving."

"All well and good, but he won't expect to find me and Dillie with you. He won't be pleased."

"Oh, Lily, my brother won't mind seeing you. He likes you, though he'd never admit it even if his life depended on it. He'd rather die at the hands of Napoleon's army. But *we* know he's doing this for you."

He couldn't possibly, Lily decided at once. She didn't affect him in a this-woman-is-important-to-me way. She didn't rouse butterflies in his stomach. Or make his heart beat a little faster with yearning. "I know you mean well, Meggie. I'm going downstairs to the library. Call me when he's decent."

Dillie cast her an impertinent grin. "I'll wait with Meggie."

Lily tipped her nose into the air. "Do as you wish."

Her sister sighed. "Come on, Lily. Stay. It's just innocent fun."

"But he doesn't know we're here. What if he struts into Meggie's room half dressed?"

"We've seen male bodies before. William struts around shirtless half the time and Uncle Rupert often neglects to wear his pants." She gave a mock shudder as she turned to Meggie. "He has the most hideous, hairy legs."

"Precisely my point. A man's privacy ought to be respected." But the thought of seeing Ewan shirtless, those hard muscles on bold display... goodness, that would be fun.

No, it would be wrong.

Hideously and appallingly wrong.

Not fun at all... well yes, it would be fun... great fun, but very wrong.

She felt her cheeks suffuse with heat. "I'll be in the library."

"Coward," Dillie teased, and then followed Meggie into her bedchamber. Lily heard the pair giggling as they closed the door behind them.

She paused a moment in the hall, wondering at the fuss Meggie was making over her brother's beard. Dillie thought it was harmless. Was she supposed to feel excited and want to participate in the silliness as well? She knew she was different. Books excited her.

Baboon colonies excited her.

Losing one's beard did not. In truth, she liked Ewan's beard and regretted having asked him to shave it off. All of it. Off, even though it suited his rugged bearing. But it was a necessary sacrifice. He needed to look like an English gentleman.

His father's family would never accept him as he was.

Lily shook her head and turned toward the stairs, but as she started down the hall, Ewan's door suddenly burst open and Jasper bolted toward her with an ear-piercing *awroooolf!*

"Jasper, not my new gown!"

Awrooolf!

The great woolly beast jumped on her, knocking her off balance. Since he was as big as a horse and clumsily unaware of his size, Lily ended up on the floor, breathless. As usual. Jasper's tongue washed over her face. *Blech!*

Her spectacles fell off her nose, and she could only hope to grab them before the big oaf stepped on them with his furry paws.

"Jasper, ye looby! Off!"

Lily heard Ewan's exasperated shout, but couldn't see him. Jasper was still playfully bouncing beside her, licking her face, and she was drowning in Jasper's drool.

Ewan tried again in that deep, authoritative voice of his. "Sit!"

Jasper obeyed by sitting on her.

Ewan let out a groaning laugh as he tugged at Jasper's collar, hauling him off her and handing him over to his valet. "Jergens, lock him away. Somewhere. Anywhere. Bollix, how did he learn to open doors?"

"At once, my lord."

Then Ewan knelt beside her. "Lass, are you all right?"

Lily felt the exquisite heat of Ewan's hands on her back as he took her into his arms and helped her to her feet. He had a towel slung over one shoulder, but he slipped it off and used it to wipe the sticky mess Jasper had left on her face. "My spectacles," she muttered as he rubbed the towel across her cheek.

"They're safe. I have them in my pocket. Lass, what are you doing here?"

"Visiting Meggie. Dillie's with her in her bedchamber. I was on my way to the library."

"Then I'll not detain you. Let me toss on a shirt and I'll join you downstairs."

"That sounds..." No, wait. Did he say toss on a shirt? He still had his arms around her. His *bare* arms. And *bare* chest. She felt his warm, damp skin beneath her palms and inhaled the fresh scent of lather against his chin, the appealing scent that tended to linger on a man after he'd shaved. This was Ewan's scent, a mix of pine forest, lather, and male.

She drew away as soon as he'd finished wiping her eyes, eager to look at the muscular body she'd been touching all the while. "I—" *Blessed saints and burnt crumpets!* Her mouth dropped open. She tried to close her eyes, but couldn't seem to do it, for she was too busy staring at Ewan's lean and muscled body. His lean and muscled shirtless body.

She heard the door to Meggie's room open. "Good morning, Ewan," Dillie said. "You're looking quite fit this morning."

Burnt, fiery crumpets. Fit didn't begin to describe how good he looked. "Nice to see you, Dillie."

She grinned. "Meggie invited us over."

Meggie winced. "I thought it would be fun to show you off. You look much better without that awful beard."

"But you're missing some clothes," Dillie added unhelpfully. "Not that my sister minds at all."

"Dillie!" Thank goodness Ewan was wearing trousers. Nice trousers. And boots. He was wearing polished black boots, too. And nothing else besides those articles. His chest was bare and skin lightly tanned. A spray of dark hair ran across his broad chest, and he'd casually thrown his towel back over one of his muscled shoulders. His upper torso tapered at his trim waist. The taut muscles across his chest and flat stomach rippled as he moved, marred only by an ugly red gash along his ribs, a reminder of the knife wound he'd received at Tattersalls. The imperfection only made him look more perfect.

She was appalled. Stricken and frozen in place.

The butterflies in her stomach felt no such thing. Those traitorous creatures were glancing heavenward to smile at the angels. *Thank you, thank you!*

Ewan's half-naked body was so close to her she could feel the heat radiating off his golden skin. Oh, he looked sinfully good! His hair was slicked back and still wet from his earlier bath, several wet strands curling about his neck. She glanced up to meet his gaze. Realization struck her just then. He'd shaved!

"Lily, you're staring at me."

He'd shaved for her. At her urging. The first step to turning him into a proper gentleman, and not a heathen to be attacked at horse auctions, then blamed for starting the fight. His family would be surprised. All of London would take notice. She'd thought him handsome before, but this... this was incredible. Nicely firm jaw, well-shaped mouth. All perfectly situated on his ruggedly appealing face. His hard, muscled body was perfection, too.

She let out an *eep!* as he lifted her into his arms and carried her downstairs. She wrapped her arms around his neck to steady herself as he strode toward the library. His skin was deliciously warm, his body delightfully hard. She touched a hand to his clean-shaven cheek. *Angels, did I thank you yet? Let me thank you again. And again.*

"You did this for me," she said in a whisper.

He ignored the comment as well as the palm she was now resting against his cheek. He lightly kicked open the library door with his boot and set her in a chair beside the fireplace. "Wait here."

She nodded.

Meggie and Dillie had followed them down. She heard their smothered giggles.

Ewan paused beside his sister. "Meggie, don't pull another stunt like that again."

He shot all three of them a warning glance and stalked out of the library, firmly shutting the door behind him.

"Lily, are you all right?" Meggie asked. "Your face is the deepest shade of crimson I've ever seen." She paused to study her more closely. "Oh, dear. You're angry with me."

"Meggie, that was so wrong. So scandalous. So improper. So—"

"Worth going straight to hell for it?" Dillie suggested.

Lily burst out laughing. "Yes, you evil twin. He shaved! I'm so pleased."

Dillie swallowed her own laughter. "Wait, that's what has you in raptures? His face? Didn't you look at the rest of him?"

"I couldn't stop looking," Lily admitted. However, she wasn't feeling quite so mirthful as her partners in crime. Skulking beside Ewan's bedchamber had been a stupid prank, but the powerful force of attraction she'd felt when seeing him in his half-dressed state was no laughing matter. Her sister could giggle and ogle and make jests, but she couldn't.

What she'd felt went far beyond mere attraction. Her senses were still reeling. She understood how Jasper must have felt that day at Eloise's when trying to stop himself in mid leap, clawing the air and trying in vain for a soft landing as he fell.

And she was falling hard for Ewan. Painfully hard.

She wasn't certain she could stop herself.

*   *   *

Ewan returned to his quarters after depositing Lily in the library, and then dressed and hurriedly returned downstairs. He was relieved to find Lily alone where he'd left her in the library. "Meggie and Dillie are in the dining room sharing a pot of tea." She set aside the book she had been reading and started to rise. "Shall I call them?"

He saw that she'd been engrossed in a publication of Sir William Maitland's early explorations. She probably knew it by heart. He wondered if there was a chapter on those baboons that seemed to fascinate her so much. "No, lass. It's you I care to see."

Her eyes rounded in surprise, probably in response to the awkward phrasing of his sentence. He did care to see her. Always liked seeing her. Preferably naked, but that wasn't likely ever to happen.

She sank back down in her chair and waited for him to take the seat beside her. "Lily, I expect I know the answer to this question, but still, I must ask it. Do you have any enemies?"

She pursed her lips and frowned, looking quite adorable and earnest. "Other than your grandfather and the entire male membership of the Royal Society? No."

He dismissed those old codgers and their newest Fellow, her friend, Ashton Mortimer. "Think on it. Anyone who's ever been mean to you or wished you ill? Outside of those fossils in the Royal Society."

She shook her head. "No, I'm certain of it. Why do you ask?"

"My cousin's rudeness to you at the dressmaker's can be explained. He was actually there to scare Meggie. But I don't understand why that blackguard came after you at Tattersalls. It troubles me. It doesn't fit into a neat explanation and that puts me on edge."

"In all likelihood, he and his unsavory friends saw me with you and thought to gain your attention by accosting me."

He shook his head and sighed. "Perhaps. It's logical. But I don't have enemies either, none that I know of... outside of my own family." He winced at the dismal state of his family relations. "But neither Desmond nor my grandfather claim to have had a hand in the incident. I believe them."

"Where does that leave us, Ewan? Was it simply a matter of mistaken identity?"

He took her hand in his, liking the feel of her skin against his. She had small, delicate hands. Innocent hands. "I don't know. Lily, don't go off on your own until we've figured it out. Will you promise me that? I need to know you're safe."

She cast him an indulgent smile, obviously doubting she was in any danger. He doubted it as well, but it couldn't hurt to be thorough. "I'll be careful."

"Good." He rose and brought her to her feet beside him. "I want you to remain with Meggie and Dillie today. Don't stay alone anywhere, not even here at Lotheil Court. Not even in this library."

"Not here?" She seemed disappointed, but reluctantly agreed.

After escorting her into the dining room and depositing her with Meggie and Dillie, he made quick excuses to slip away from Lotheil Court. He cast Lily a concerned glance. "Remember what I said, Lily."

"It is seared into my brain," she teased, but he noted a mix of relief and disappointment in her eyes. He understood how she felt. His senses reeled whenever he was around her, and she responded the same way whenever in his presence. He knew it as surely as if she'd spoken the sentiments aloud. All he had to do was look into her beautifully expressive eyes.

He hurried off, forcing his attention to all that needed to be accomplished in the next few hours. Besides the day to day work of putting his father's estate affairs in order, he had an investigation to conduct. He'd questioned Lily, but merely as a formality. Who would want to harm a nineteen-year-old innocent? No, it wasn't her these villains were after. Someone wanted to hurt him, possibly kill him. His first call would be on a reliable Bow Street runner by the name of Homer Barrow, a sharp old-timer who came highly recommended by a friend.

In any event, he was glad to be away from Lily just now, couldn't remain under the same roof with the girl without his senses exploding. He needed distance from her in order to get his mind and body fully under control. The feel of her soft body was still branded on his chest, and her light, rose scent still tickled his nostrils. She'd seen him bare-chested. All he could think about was seeing *her* bare-chested, running his lips and tongue over her soft, white breasts and worshiping their pink tips. He wanted Lily beneath him, crying his name in ecstasy.

Lord! He was in agony.

Over a bookish, bespectacled innocent, no less!

He had about ten hours to get himself back under control. He knew she would be at the Simmington musicale this evening. Since he, Meggie, and their grandfather planned to attend, he expected to see her there. It was to be one of those small society functions that Eloise had deemed suitable for him and Meggie. A quiet gathering of close friends. Yes, he could manage seeing Lily in a crowd.

Lady Simmington's father was a Highlander, a proud member of the MacCorkindale clan, so he expected to find several of his own friends and acquaintances there. It was a good way to ease Meggie into the stream of London parties. It was also a good way to distract his thoughts from Lily's blue eyes and soft, pink lips.

* * *

Ewan attended to his business affairs, retained Homer Barrow to conduct his investigation, and returned late to Lotheil Court. If he hurried, he could make it to the musicale without missing too much of the music.

Meggie and his grandfather, as expected, were nowhere about when he arrived. They'd surely gone ahead without him. He felt a pang of regret for not being by Meggie's side, but she'd likely spent the day with Lily and her sister, and would only have been alone with their grandfather for the short carriage ride to the Simmington residence.

"My lord." Harding met him in the entry hall as he was about to climb the stairs. "Your sister asked that I give this to you." The butler handed him an envelope. Ewan took it with a nod and continued to his bedchamber, where he opened it, read it, and then paused and laughingly shook his head. Lily had invited Meggie and his grandfather to supper with her family before the musicale. Incredibly, his grandfather had accepted.

He read it again, unable to believe that the old man had accepted a hastily sent invitation from a family of no consequence, from the very upstart he'd just banished from the Royal Society. But this was precisely the sort of generous thing Lily would do, extend an invitation to the old curmudgeon who had treated her unfairly. She'd done it for Meggie.

She'd done it for him.

"Jasper," he said, turning to the lumpy beast stretched out beside the hearth, "you have excellent taste in women." He walked over and scratched him behind the ears. "But I can't marry her. It isn't only that she's English. She's very close to her family. How can I take her so far away from her parents and sisters? And she's a delicate thing. She'd never adapt to the harsh Highlands weather."

Jasper didn't seem in the least impressed or convinced.

"And I'm not about to take her into my heart while some unknown enemy is out there trying to kill me. What if he goes after Lily again? I can't let the lass get hurt." Which was why he'd instructed Homer Barrow to hire another of his Bow Street colleagues to watch over Lily.

Still unimpressed.

"Bah, what do you know, anyway? You're just a dog." He rose and walked across the room to dress.

Jasper began to howl at Ewan. *Wroolf, wrooiditoolf.* His dog voice had the oddest inflection. Sounded as though Jasper was calling him an idiot. Perhaps he was, but he wasn't about to let a damn dog tell him so. "Shut up, ye hairy looby."

Wroolf, wrooiditoolf.

Jasper had called him an idiot again. "Enough, Jasper. I need you to behave. And if you're so damned smart, then tell me why this enemy of mine went after Lily? Not Meggie or any other Cameron. Lily. Why her?"

*   *   *

The Italian singer finished his third song to loud applause, and although Lily was enjoying the evening, she wished Ewan were here to enjoy the Simmington's affair with her. Meggie was having a wonderful time, no doubt because Lily's young and dashing cousin, William Farthingale, was paying her particular attention.

Also, Meggie had walked in on her grandfather's arm and been introduced as his granddaughter, and any relative of a duke was certain to dazzle at any society gathering. The crowd mistook Meggie's panic as delightfully sweet shyness. That, along with her pretty features, enhanced her reputation as a newcomer of note.

Lily wasn't certain what to make of the old duke. He was a puzzle to her. Though cold and arrogant, he'd permitted Ewan, Meggie, and Jasper into his home without complaint and he was now showing off Meggie to his friends as though they'd been a close family for years. He'd even permitted Lily to visit Meggie at Lotheil Court (though she was still banned from the Royal Society), and he'd just dined with Eloise and the Farthingales in the Farthingale home.

The duke had said nothing about lifting the Royal Society ban and she hadn't pressed him on the matter. It certainly was not a topic to be discussed at the supper table. Her mother had worked hard to make an elegant presentation, and Lily had possessed the presence not to ruin it by raising the volatile subject.

Everything in its own good time, her mother often said. Lily had to believe that kindness shown toward the duke would eventually be reciprocated. Not that she was expecting to improve her standing with the duke. Not at all. The point of kindness was to bestow it, not to expect or demand gratitude from others. Still, she hoped to mellow the duke by setting a good example. He didn't need to bribe her to help make the Camerons a family. All he needed to do was ask. She was doing it anyway, for Meggie's sake. "Affection has to be earned, not bought."

"Did you say something, Lily?"

"No, Meggie. Just thinking aloud."

"Mr. Giancarlo's about to start singing again. We'd better take our seats. I've saved one for Ewan."

Lily glanced around. "He isn't here yet."

"He will be. He said he'd attend and he always keeps his word."

As if on cue, there was a sudden flurry of excitement by the doorway. Lily didn't need to see Ewan to know that he'd just walked in. The expression on the faces of the females in the room gave it away. Did she look like that? All moon-eyed and breathless whenever he drew near?

He made his way through the crowd toward them. *Oh, crumpets.* He was wearing a kilt. Typical Ewan, making a scene... goodness, he looked handsome... looked better in a frock than she did. Looked more manly and rugged than any other man in the room, even though all the other men were wearing trousers. How did he manage that?

He'd done it on purpose, swaggered in dressed in his Highlander garb to purposely stick his Scottish thumb in his grandfather's eye, as if to say "I'm a Scot and proud of it. I refuse to accept your *Sassenach* ways."

Too bad. His grandfather had been on his best behavior this evening. Ewan was about to ruin it.

"Ewan, thank goodness you're here," Meggie called to him. "Come sit by us. We've saved you a chair."

"Sorry I'm late." He bussed his sister's cheek, and then turned to Lily and grinned. "Och, lass. You're scowling at me. You disapprove?" He glanced down at his kilt.

"Yes. No. You look wonderful, of course."

He grinned again. "Of course."

Lily rolled her eyes. "You could have worn trousers."

"Aye, I could have. I didn't want to." He glanced at Meggie, who'd turned away to speak to some elderly friends of Eloise's. "How's my sister managing? She looks happy. Thank you, lass. I know it's all your doing."

She sighed, unable to remain irritated with Ewan while he gazed at her in that tender manner, as though her meager assistance meant the world to him. He was being polite to her, that was all. He was so sure of himself, so comfortable in his own skin. He had to be, or he'd never have worn the kilt, or managed to carry it off as though every other man in the room was improperly dressed. He fit in everywhere. She felt comfortable only around her family and books. She wasn't all that good with people. "Meggie deserves all the credit."

He was about to say more when someone called to him in a deep, Scottish brogue, the greeting filled with lots of rolling r's. "Och, Ewan. Therrrre ye arrre, laddie."

A big man with bright red hair strode toward him. Ewan seemed genuinely pleased to see the fellow, who appeared to be a few years older than himself. "Archie, I heard you were in town. Come join us."

Archibald MacCorkindale turned out to be one of Ewan's close friends, or at least Lily thought so by the hearty manner in which they pounded each other on the back. "Callie's here, too," Archie said. "She's eager to see you."

They had only moments before the singer resumed his recital, but in those few moments, Lily was introduced to Archie's niece,

Caledonia MacCorkindale, a beautiful blonde with gray-green eyes, a melodic laugh, and a cheerful outlook.

Cheerfulness was overrated, Lily thought.

And somehow, in the rush to take their seats when the bell chimed and the Italian singer began to clear his throat, Lily ended up seated in the front row, wedged between the elderly Duke of Lotheil and the young and rakish Duke of Edgeware, while Ewan ended up two rows back between Meggie and Caledonia, who was sitting unnecessarily close to him. She was all over him, to be precise.

"We hate her, don't we?" Dillie said, leaning across the Duke of Edgeware to pat her hand.

Lily nodded. "Vehemently."

And if Lily hadn't been so distracted by petty jealousy—honestly, books were so much easier—she might have wondered how Ian Markham, the notorious Duke of Edgeware, came to be seated between her and Dillie. And might have wondered why Dillie felt so comfortable beside him when everyone knew that the dangerously handsome duke was not to be let near their unmarried daughters.

Lily hurried into the garden when the recital ended. Her head was pounding and her heart ached. Dillie followed her outside. "They're merely friends," she said, trying her best to be supportive.

"I have a headache, that's all. I wasn't thinking of Ewan's friends."

Dillie nudged her. "Yes, you were. Who could miss the way Miss Corkstopper was clinging to Ewan's arm? I'll put a laxative in her wine. That ought to keep her occupied for the duration of this party."

"Don't you dare!" Despite her desire to wallow in pity, Lily laughed. She knew her sister was capable of doing just such a thing. "I'll be fine, Dillie. You needn't poison Ewan's sweetheart."

"Who said she was his sweetheart? Did he say so? I'll poison his wine too, if he's so foolish as to be taken in by her outward appearance. I saw her eyes narrow when she looked at you. She's a cat with claws bared and that merry politeness is just an act."

Lily wished the evening would end. She'd lost the Royal Society. Never had Ewan to lose, that point made painfully clear by the arrival of the beautiful Callie. She wasn't used to all this turmoil in her heart. How did others bear it?

"Seems Ewan's smarter than you give him credit for. Here he comes. See, he's looking for you and not that wicked Corky MacCorkstopper."

"She isn't wicked. And her name's Callie MacCorkindale."

"That's what I said. I'll leave you in his capable hands." She slipped away.

Lily held her breath as Ewan approached. She pretended not to notice him, instead busying herself by gazing at the stars. It was a beautiful night. She would have noticed sooner if not for fretting over Ewan. The bright silver moon shone like a diamond amid a tapestry of sparkling stars. It was a perfect night for moonlight kisses.

A cool breeze ruffled across her cheeks and through the loose curls of her hair. However, Lily could only feel the warmth of Ewan's body, so close to hers as he came up beside her and crossed his arms over his chest. "You shouldn't be out here on your own, lass."

"I'm not." She glanced up at him and smiled, aching to touch those broad, flexed muscles. "You're with me."

He wasn't smiling as he said, "That's even more dangerous."

"Why?" Was he going to kiss her? *Yes. Please.* But he did not care for her romantically. He merely considered her a friend, even though they'd shared a few spectacular kisses. She'd been the one to initiate each one. He had merely gone along.

"Lass, it's dark. You're alone. Who knows what evil is lurking out here?"

"We're in the Simmingtons' garden. There are sixty people close by in the music room."

"None of whom would notice if someone came up from behind, clamped a hand over your mouth, and dragged you into the shadows."

Lily's smile faded. "My, you're morbid this evening. Have you discovered something about those villains who attacked you at the horse auction?"

"No, but I intend to." He stared at her hard, and then ran a hand across the back of his neck, something he tended to do when perplexed about an issue. "They attacked you as well."

"That still troubles you?"

"Of course, lass. I won't stop thinking about it until I figure it out. Why did they come after you?"

"I've also given it thought since we discussed it this morning. I'm certain it was simply a matter of mistaken identity. Those horrid men mistook me for Meggie."

"You're assuming those wharf rats were hired to send me a warning. Problem is, I don't know of anyone who wishes to harm me... now that we've ruled out my own family."

She placed a hand on his arm, unable to resist comforting him. There was pain in his voice when he spoke of his family. "I'm glad they're innocent. Even Despicable Grandfather, so Meggie ought to be safe now. No one will dare approach her while she's in his company. And he always travels with a contingent of footmen. They'd stop any stranger who got near her. When she isn't with your grandfather, she's with you."

"Then there's you."

Lily shook her head. "Since that incident with Desmond, your grandfather's footmen have been with us wherever we go. To the shops. To the park."

"Only when you're with Meggie. Whenever you're *not* with Meggie, there's no one protecting you."

"But I've assured you that I'll be more careful. Oh, I see." He was pointing out that he did not plan to protect her, that he couldn't protect her since he was going to be busy with Corky MacCorkstopper now that she was in town. "You needn't worry about me." She reached into the fashionably styled sash that was designed into her gown and circled just beneath her breasts. "I have this." She held up a hat pin.

"A meager weapon, and of no use if you're attacked from behind. The first thing any self-respecting assailant would do is grab your hands."

Lily sighed, wishing he would grab her hands and drag her into his embrace. She wouldn't struggle. Indeed, she was leaning so close, her body was more than halfway there. "Consider me duly warned. May we please speak of something else? Did you know that your grandfather and Meggie joined us for supper? He's been wonderful to Meggie all evening."

Ewan's expression darkened, and though his arms were still stiffly crossed over his chest, she saw that he'd curled his hands into fists. Was standing in a moonlit garden with her such a chore? "Bastard. He only did it to torture Desmond and Evangeline. They couldn't attend because

I broke Desmond's nose. But they'll hear all about the musicale, particularly how the old duke fawned over Meggie."

"That's horrid." Lily hadn't thought of that possibility. She'd been so easily taken in by Ewan's grandfather, so delighted by the courtesy and attention he was giving to Meggie. Of course, horrid old men didn't turn into gentle lambs overnight.

Ewan eased his stance and turned to face her. Silvery starlight shone on his hair and broad shoulders. He looked like a Highlands warrior. Brave. Strong. Fearless. "Don't be taken in by his games, Lily. His cruelty is all the more venomous because of its subtlety."

Which explained why Ewan had worn the kilt. Deliberately. As she'd first thought. He meant to stick his thumb in the duke's eye, meant to let the old man know that he wasn't fooled by the outward show of kindness. Also, Ewan was a Scot through and through. The second part of his message was a declaration—Ewan was not going to bend to the duke's English ways.

Ewan tucked a finger under her chin and drew her gaze upward once more to meet his. She melted at the soft grin on his face. "Seems a shame to waste a perfect night," he said in a husky murmur.

Lily smiled back. "Would be criminal to waste it."

He lowered his head and was about to fulfill her every fantasy when Callie called to him from the terrace. "Ewan! There you are." Had she noticed Ewan about to kiss her? She'd brought along reinforcements, dragging Archie behind her, and her long, catlike fingernails were clamped onto his arm as she pulled him down the small row of stairs onto the soft, dewy grass. "Who's this? A friend of yours, darling?"

Darling?

Ewan introduced her to Callie again.

"Of course! You must forgive my oversight. But I've met so many Farthingales this evening, can't seem to get any of you straight. It's most confusing. Didn't I see you dancing in the arms of the Duke of Edgeware a short while ago? You seemed quite transported, not that any woman wouldn't be while in his arms."

"You're mistaken. I've been out here."

"I saw you with him." She appeared indignant.

"It must have been my sister you saw dancing."

Callie beaded her eyes. "I know what I saw."

Lily sighed and glanced at Ewan. The Duke of Edgeware had no interest in her. No man did. Ewan winked at her, obviously finding humor in Callie's confusion. He knew the notion was ridiculous. After the way she'd gawked at him this morning, how could he doubt she was attracted to him? Like a bee to honey. She supposed Ewan was used to women flitting around him. Probably had them by the hundreds, while she'd never even had a beau.

Men didn't like her in that capture-a-man's-soul way. Ashton had paid attention to her because of her research. He'd stopped coming around now that she was banned from the Royal Society. Where was he, come to think of it? Was he purposely avoiding her? She understood Ashton's concerns. He didn't want the duke to be reminded of their connection and decide to ban him as well. Still, he should have been here this evening.

"Oh, you're the one," Callie said, interrupting Lily's thoughts. "I recall now. Ewan told me about you. You're the bluestocking he hired to ease Meggie's introduction into London society. You needn't worry. We'll take her and Ewan off your hands. Darling, did you hear? Lord and Lady Abercrombie have also come to town. They've invited all of us to their estate this weekend. It's just outside London. Uncle Archie has a splendid new carriage. Plenty of room for you and Meggie. The four of us can travel together. Won't that be fun?"

Ewan ignored her, turning to Lily instead. "You look cold, lass. Come, I'll escort you inside."

"Please don't. I'm fine. Stay and chat with your friends. I promised to ride home with Eloise. You know how she tires easily. I'm sure she's ready to leave now."

Callie grabbed his arm as he attempted to follow her. "Do stay with me, Ewan. Miss Farthingale doesn't want our company. Isn't it obvious?" She said something in Gaelic that Lily didn't understand, but it drew a gale of laughter from her uncle and a Gaelic response from Ewan. Though Lily didn't understand Ewan's response either, she knew he wouldn't indulge in a jest at her expense. Nevertheless, she was made to feel like the outsider.

What had she thought? That he'd magically kiss her in a scented garden under a silver moon?

She turned on her heels and started up the terrace steps to return to the music room, and then realized Archie was following just steps behind her. Which meant Ewan and Callie were alone in the cool breeze and carpet of shimmering stars. Great. Just perfect. Ewan was going to kiss that Scottish predator in the moonlight. *My moonlight.*

It wasn't fair.

It was an English moon. *My moon.* Not Callie's.

Chapter 13

EWAN PAUSED OUTSIDE of Desmond's townhouse in Kensington the following afternoon. It seemed elegant on the surface, but a closer inspection revealed early signs of wear around the window frames and paint beginning to peel around the lintels. Were his cousins hurting for funds? He had no doubt that their grandfather kept tight control of the purse strings, providing just enough to allow them to maintain the appearance of comfort, but never enough to grant them any freedom from his domination.

The door opened as he approached. An elderly butler ushered him in, his steps achingly slow as he settled Ewan in the salon, and then inched across the room, back into the entry hall, and up the staircase with the speed of a snail to see if his master was home to visitors. Ewan, never a patient man on his best days, wanted to haul the old man over his shoulder and carry him upstairs himself. It was the only way he'd have the answers he desired before nightfall.

Evangeline returned home while he waited, obviously having come from a shopping trip. He was never happier to see his younger cousin. Though only a year or two older than Meggie, the strain in her eyes made her appear substantially older. She was still a beautiful girl— or would be, if she ever learned to smile. "Let me help you with those packages," he said, startling her.

She glowered at him, her cheeks pink from a mix of the cool outdoors and anger on finding him standing in her home. "What are you doing here?"

"I've come to sort things out between us, and to correct any idle gossip you may have heard about last night."

"To correct it? Or to gloat?" She drew away when he reached for her packages. One appeared to hold dishes and the other was shaped like a teapot. No personal items, just the functional sort that would be set out in a cupboard display.

He sighed and took them from her anyway. "Where do they go?"

"In the dining room." Her lips began to quiver and she was obviously about to cry.

He sighed again. "Summon your brother down here. I think your butler died along the way. Not sure he made it up the stairs." He drew aside one of the dining room chairs and settled into it. "I'll wait here, Evie."

That use of her name drew him back fifteen years. It surprised her as well. "What do you want with us? You've won, Ewan. Why can't you leave us alone?"

"I haven't won anything. Nor do I wish for anything from our grandfather. By the way, I'm sorry I broke Desmond's nose."

Evangline nodded. "He shouldn't have struck your friend. Lily. Is that her name? He didn't mean to, but she stepped between him and Meggie... it just happened. And he told me he'd seen you at Tattersalls. I know he stood by while those villains punched the stuffing out of you. He didn't know they wielded knives. He would have helped you had he realized you were in serious danger."

Ewan doubted it.

"Bring him down here, Evie. We're even now. Here's our chance to start over."

"I wish I could believe you." However, she turned and left the room, her step light on the stairs as she scrambled up them to fetch her brother.

Desmond wasn't nearly as hopeful or polite. "Get the hell out of here, Ewan."

"Sit down," Ewan ordered as though this were his home and they were the guests. He wasn't trying to belittle his cousins, but he'd come here to talk and *damn it*, that's precisely what he was going to do. "You ought to know Grandfather better than anyone. When have you ever seen him be kind or gracious to his kinfolk? To anyone, for that matter. He never is, unless he has an ulterior motive."

"He has a motive." Desmond grabbed a chair, swung it out and settled into it. Though his movements were tense and angry, Ewan took his decision to sit as a good sign. "He wants to make you duke and leave me to rot."

"I doubt it."

"He's had years in which to make me his heir and hasn't done it," Desmond insisted. "Not when my father died. Not after your father died. I've helped him with the Lotheil affairs for years. I've worked hard and done a damn good job, but nothing I do is ever quite good enough for him."

"I think he's trying to manipulate both of us. Even if he does offer, I won't accept. He knows it."

"Hah! Am I supposed to believe you? Am I to ignore the gossip now spreading like a wildfire about town? He doted on Meggie at the Simmington musicale, showered her with attention and every courtesy. He introduced her as his granddaughter."

"She is his granddaughter."

Desmond pounded his fist on the table. "So is Evie, but he didn't invite her to join you, or send a carriage around to deliver her to the Simmingtons."

Ewan felt badly about that. Not even he had thought to call on Evie and bring her along, nor had he bothered to make arrangements for Eloise to pick her up. He couldn't have asked Lily, not after what Desmond did to her. But had he asked, she would have agreed. Unlike his grandfather, Lily was sweet-natured and loving. She would have helped him win back his family, whether she liked them or not. "You're right, Des. To my shame, I didn't think beyond getting myself over there before the blasted party ended. It won't happen again. I promise you. Until you're healed, I'll take care of Evie."

He noticed the flicker of surprise in Evangeline's eyes, perhaps a ray of hope in their sad depths. Damn it. Why hadn't his father interceded sooner?

Desmond's expression darkened. "We don't need your charity."

"I'm not offering any. We're family. If Evie needs an escort, let her send word to me and I'll provide it." Ewan turned to her. "Truly, Evie. You're welcome to join—"

"She's *my* sister." Desmond was now out of his chair and rounding the table toward him, hands curled into fists at his sides. "I'll take care of her. Do you think I'd ever trust her in your care? You who wish to disgrace us in the eyes of our grandfather?"

Ewan hadn't expected it to be easy, so he was prepared for his cousin's accusations. "I know it will take time to heal our family."

"Time?" He shook his head and let out a sad laugh. "It will never happen."

Ewan rose to face him, trying not to wince at how truly pathetic Desmond looked with that stark white bandage across his nose and the deep purple and yellow bruises under his eyes. "It will. I don't blame you for doubting me. My father ought to have stepped in after your own father died, but he didn't. He allowed the old man to take you in, knowing all the while the damage he might cause. I know what that old bastard has done to you and I'm trying to fix it. Give me the chance."

"There's nothing to fix." Desmond's hands were still balled into fists, but his tone was strained and revealed his desperation despite his best efforts to maintain that angry facade.

Ewan's heart twisted into knots. His cousins were suffering, yet too proud to admit it. Not that he blamed them. Were he in their position, the sky could have collapsed on his head and he wouldn't have uttered a word. "Evie, I'm at your service whenever you need it. Have you made arrangements to attend Lady Dayne's dinner party? I know you were on the guest list."

"I won't be going." She nibbled her lip. "I'll send word to Eloise right now."

"Don't. Come with us. Please." Ewan wondered if she had a proper gown to wear, but he didn't have the heart to ask. The mere question would have utterly destroyed her. In any event, she'd been fashionably dressed in their prior encounters. Clothes weren't the problem. Their grandfather and his cruel manipulations were. "Don't let Grandfather win, Evie. Meggie and I will come round at seven to pick you up."

Desmond glanced at his sister, his jaw in a spasm as he sought to contain himself, but his love for Evie was obvious. He didn't wish to deprive her of anything, and they both knew Evie wanted to go to the party. "Go with him, Evie. I don't give a damn. I'll be here for you when you come home in tears."

*   *   *

The ride to Eloise's was an unexpected torture for Ewan. He'd done the right thing in bringing his cousin along, but hadn't expected the flood of tears from Meggie and Evangeline the moment the two of them were settled in his carriage. Both girls were shy and sensitive, and though Meggie had overcome her fears recently, this unexpectedly poignant family reunion—if one could call it that—had set off her waterworks. Then Evangeline had started crying.

The only saving grace was that they were crying for... he wasn't exactly sure what they were crying about, but they seemed pleased to be together and neither one was angry or tossing daggers at him. Progress.

He'd hired his own conveyance for the remainder of their stay in London, preferring to move about London independent of the duke. The old bastard could come and go as he pleased in his own glossy black carriage with the imposing Lotheil crest emblazoned on it. Ewan was not going to beg the old man for its use. He had no doubt the old man would have denied it to him once he learned Evangeline was to join them. That's how the bastard operated. Control and separate. Dominate and scare.

They turned onto Chipping Way and slowed behind the row of carriages stacked up to let their guests off in front of the Dayne townhouse. Lily and her family lived next door. He looked forward to seeing her. She'd be a great help to him in calming the girls. Not that Lily was much more than a girl herself, but she had that adorably logical way of dealing with matters. He stifled a grin at the thought of her. It wouldn't do for Meggie and Evie to realize just how badly he ached for Lily.

The thought of Lily also gave rise to unpleasant thoughts of Callie. Damn. Callie didn't like competition, and Lily—whether the little bluestocking realized it or not—was competition in her eyes. Callie didn't have Lily's warmth or kindness. She'd bare her claws and scratch at Lily's confidence until only shreds were left.

Ewan ran a hand through his hair, uncertain what to do. He couldn't handle one girl. How was he to handle all four? No, if Callie was there, he'd have to stay close to her to keep her from causing mischief. Afterward, first thing tomorrow, he'd pay a call on Lily and apologize for any rudeness on his part or Callie's. She'd understand once he explained.

"Evie, please stop crying," Meggie said—she of the torrent of tears flowing down her own cheeks. "Lady Dayne is the loveliest person. You know that, of course. So are the Farthingales. They won't hold the earlier unpleasantness against you or your brother. Not after Ewan explains the misunderstanding to them. You'll adore Lily. We both do."

Evie blew into the handkerchief Ewan had offered her earlier. "Why would she be nice to me? She has every reason to hate me."

"She isn't like that," Ewan found himself saying. "She believes in close family ties and will be pleased we've taken steps toward reconciliation." That's what made Lily so different from Callie. Though beautiful on the outside, Callie wouldn't hesitate to destroy anyone who got in her way. She was much like his grandfather. Why hadn't he noticed the similarity before? More troubling, he'd actually considered offering for her. Had his father not taken ill and died, he might very well be married to her now.

Ewan shuddered.

The thought made his skin crawl. No. Callie was a momentary lapse in his good judgment, a lapse he'd quickly correct, perhaps this evening if the opportunity presented itself. Having met Lily, he now understood the qualities to look for in a wife. He wanted a Highlands girl with all of Lily's good qualities.

In truth, he wanted Lily.

But marriage to the little bluestocking wouldn't work, though for entirely different reasons. They'd suit in bed. Lily was passionate about everything. She'd respond exquisitely to his guiding touch. However, as much as her passion would work for them in bed—Lord, he ached to get her naked under him—it would work against them in every other aspect of their marriage. She couldn't be happy in Scotland, so far away from her beloved family. So far away from her beloved halls of science.

Seeing Lily sad—knowing he was the cause of it—would destroy him.

Yet, not to see her. Not to hold her in his arms. That felt wrong, too.

Ewan helped his sister and Evangeline down from the carriage and escorted them into Eloise's home, relieved as they were quickly announced and now free to mingle. Eloise's townhouse was filled with well-dressed lords and ladies. Music wafted through the crowded salons, and butlers eased through the sea of bodies, silver trays laden with glasses of champagne held out in front of them. Ewan grabbed a glass for each girl. He didn't bother taking one for himself. He had other things on his mind.

His first thought was to find Lily. Where was she? He'd escorted Meggie and Evie from room to room—Farthingales everywhere—but no Lily. He finally spied Lily's twin standing beside the French doors leading out onto Eloise's terrace. He frowned. She was wearing spectacles, which meant she was trying to cover up Lily's absence.

Since his sister and Evie were engaged in conversation with other guests who seemed quite friendly, Ewan left their side and made his way toward Dillie. "Where is she?" he asked, more annoyed with himself for the disappointment he felt at Lily's absence.

"Home. She didn't wish to see you."

He arched an eyebrow in surprise. It was one thing for him to decide not to see Lily, which was not at all what he'd decided. He'd merely decided not to marry her. Quite another thing for *her* to decide not to see *him*. "Why not?"

Dillie frowned at him. "I'm not at liberty to tell you. However, if you gave it a moment's thought, you might figure it out on your own."

Bollix. He would never understand women. "Have I done something to offend her?" He glanced at Evangeline, wondering whether bringing his cousin to Eloise's gathering had displeased her. Not that he would blame Lily for resenting Evangeline. She and her brother hadn't been nice to her.

"It isn't about Evangeline," Dillie said, following his gaze and understanding the path of his thoughts. "She'll be pleased when I tell her that you escorted her to the party. She was hoping you'd reconcile. How is it going?"

"It's a first step." If that wasn't the cause of Lily's disappointment, then what was? "Will you give me a clue?"

"No. I'm sworn to twin secrecy."

"Then I'll have to get it out of her, won't I?"

She shot him a grin. "I was hoping you would. Do you plan to confront her now?"

He nodded. "It's as good a time as any."

"I suggest you make your way through the garden to avoid the crowd. Hop over the brick wall. That's what we often do. Lily's likely to be in the parlor playing marbles with Charles and Harry. Our butler, Pruitt, will let you in. He likes you."

Ewan arched an eyebrow in surprise. "He doesn't know me that well."

"You've come to our home once or twice. Anyway, Lily's told him all about you. Though I'm still sworn to secrecy, I can say that Pruitt likes what he's heard about you."

Great, just what he needed. A snooping butler.

He slipped out of the salon, into the garden, and over the wall with ease. He landed in the Farthingale's side garden and immediately realized their parlor overlooked it. Conveniently, there were two large windows dominating the room. It would have been easy to creep to one of those windows and peer in, but he didn't wish to frighten the children if they were still playing in there.

Instead, he avoided the windows and went around to the front. He didn't have long to wait before Pruitt opened the door to let him in.

The thin, gray-haired man with kindly eyes cracked the tiniest smile, so small one might not have noticed it unless carefully watching. "You've caused quite a stir, m'lord. Miss Lily's in the parlor. Tread carefully," he said, and Ewan wasn't certain if the warning was for the marbles likely littering the floor, or for Lily's heart.

Probably both.

The sconces were brightly lit, allowing him to easily make out the contents of the elegant room. Blue silk fabric covered the chairs and settees that stood upon a carpet of Oriental design. Blue silk drapes were drawn back to frame the windows. The soft blue matched the color of Lily's eyes.

At first he saw no one, but then noticed Lily's dark curls bobbing just above the back support of the settee that faced the large fireplace. He heard her sweet voice as she read a story to her young cousins, just finishing it as he entered. "Lily," he said quietly, not wishing to disturb her or the boys who were nestled beside her and appeared to have fallen asleep on her lap.

She gasped, and then gently shifted the boys so she could rise to face him. "What are you doing here? You startled me." She wore a casual, tea rose gown and her hair was loosely drawn back with a matching ribbon of tea rose velvet. Her dark hair fell below her waist and the ends curled becomingly about her slender hips. She wasn't wearing her spectacles since her twin had them.

His breath caught at the sparkling beauty of her blue eyes. "Sorry. Didn't mean to."

She glanced toward the windows. "Was that you I saw watching me from the garden earlier? Why didn't you come in sooner? You startled me," she repeated, as though she had been quite spooked by a face in the window. Except he hadn't gone close to the window. His shadow must have swept across it.

"Sorry, lass. Truly, it wasn't my intent to frighten you. Your sister suggested I hop over the wall, so I did."

She frowned. "What else did she say?"

"Nothing. You've sworn her to that sacred, double secret oath that applies between twins, though I don't know what secret is so important that it must be kept from me. Have I offended you in any way?"

"No. You've been wonderful." She forced a smile, and his heart tightened at the pain so obviously reflected in her eyes. "You look wonderful, too. Quite fashionable in your very proper evening clothes."

He arched an eyebrow. "Every bit the London dandy."

"Not at all." She moved a little closer. "The black jacket emphasizes your broad shoulders, and the cut of it perfectly tapers at your waist. You've cut your hair and shaved off your beard, but you still have the bold look of a Highlander. Stubborn. Defiant. Proud."

"Stubborn to a fault," he admitted.

She glanced at the angelic, sleeping boys before turning back to him. "We all have a little bit of that in my family. Stubborn, impulsive, and a host of other faults, but none so terrible as to cause any serious rift among our loved ones. I had better take the boys upstairs to bed. Well, thank you for stopping by. I'm sure you'll be missed at the party. Simply everyone is bound to be there."

"I won't be dismissed quite that easily, lass. Besides, you can't carry them up on your own. Where are their nannies?"

"Two quit this morning. It happens fairly often in this upside-down household. Only one remains, though we'll hire more tomorrow. In the meantime, the lone surviving nanny is exhausted and roundly snoring in her bed. I don't have the heart to wake her."

He made up the remaining distance between them. "I'll take the boys." He lifted the oldest child into his arms first, settled him over one shoulder, and then scooped up little Harry in his free arm and rested his pink-cheeked face on his other shoulder. They were so small and trusting, not even stirring as he picked them up. Harry's pudgy fingers curled on the lapel of his evening jacket, and though he merely tugged at the lapel, Ewan also felt a sweet tug at his heart.

This is how it could be with his own children. Someday. "Where to?"

She cast him the softest smile, but the pain reflected in her eyes seemed to intensify. "Three flights up. Can you manage?"

"They weigh no more than feathers. Show me the way."

Lily walked ahead of him, her hips lightly swaying as she climbed the stairs. He liked the view, but her tense silence bothered him. She wasn't angry, but he sensed that she was deeply hurt and determined to hide it. What had he done to cause her this anguish?

He deposited the boys in their beds, his gaze lingering on Lily as she tucked them in and kissed each on the forehead. "Love you," she whispered.

The girl had so much love inside her. She'd make a wonderful mother someday, tender and protective of her children. He wanted her to whisper those words to him—*love you*—but he knew it would raise a host of other problems. He'd be leaving England in two months. Why start something that could only end badly? She'd be miserable in the Highlands, so far away from her family.

As soon as the boys were settled, Lily hurried out of the room ahead of him. He stopped her halfway down the first flight of stairs. Obviously wary of him, she edged back against the wall. Her breaths were uneven and he noticed the slight heave of her perfect breasts with each intake of air. Her gaze remained on him, questioning his reason for being here. Questioning his reason for stopping her on the steps. Questioning the hunger in his eyes.

He placed his hands on each side of her shoulders, neatly trapping her against the wall. They needed to talk. Just talk. He wanted to ask so many things about her. First and foremost, why did she wish to avoid him?

"Oh, hell," he said instead, lifting her into his arms and crushing his mouth to her generous lips. Passion and frustration had built within him for weeks, sensations he was unable to control when it came to Lily. He didn't want to kiss her. More precisely, he desperately wanted to kiss her, but knew he shouldn't. So what the hell was he doing with his tongue sliding across her teeth, possessively delving inside her velvet-warm mouth?

He tried to gentle the kiss.

She clutched his lapels and drew him closer, tilted her face upward to give him better access to her warm, lightly parted lips. She didn't want gentle.

She wanted him. She wanted him hungry for her.

A good thing. He couldn't manage gentle just now, not while he held her glorious body in his arms. Not while his own body ignited in flames at her mere touch. Hell, his body blazed hot at the mere thought of the girl. He was worse than Jasper.

She arched into him, drawing him over the edge as her breasts came in contact with his chest and her taut nipples teased against his body. He wasn't just on fire. He was wild, out of control, walls-of-Jericho-toppling ablaze. All cannons firing ablaze. He wanted to strip her out of her confining clothes, touch her warm, silken skin, lick the molten core between her thighs and taste its flowing nectar. He wanted skin to skin contact. He wanted to be inside her. He wanted to ignore his intense need for her, pretend she didn't matter.

He wanted answers. He wanted *her*.

"Ewan, I can't bear it," she whispered against his deepening kiss. "You have to let me go. You're with Callie."

"Never."

He felt a tear stream down her cheek. Her hands, no longer pinned by his, slipped upward to circle his neck. "What do you mean by 'never'? That you'll never let me go? That you'll never be with Callie? Because it seems to me you've made your decision, told your grandfather and the entire world quite clearly that you'll never take an English wife. Not that I even want you to want me. I don't. We're friends, nothing more."

So that was it? She was jealous of Callie? "Lily—"

"No. I have work to do. Lots of research work."

"You've finished your monograph on the structure of baboon colonies. Swampland baboons, to be precise. I've read it. Thought it was brilliant."

"You have? I thought your grandfather burned it."

"He didn't." Ewan kissed her again, loving the sweet eagerness with which she kissed him back.

She broke away with a slight moan. "I'm helping Ashton with his Madagascar lemurs. He's desperate. He can't finish it without me and doesn't dare let your grandfather know. I promised to help him out. Go back to your party. Callie must be wondering where you are."

"You're doing this for Ashton?" He frowned. "Your family forbade you to work on the report. The Royal Society won't publish it if they suspect you wrote it."

"Are you through listing all the reasons why I hate my life at this moment?"

"Lily—"

"I was fine until you came along. I need you to go away. Forever."

He'd been thinking the same, but hearing it from her was like a kick in the teeth. She was right. Neither one of them wanted the involvement. Why couldn't he leave it at that and walk away? "Put on one of your pretty silk gowns. Come to Eloise's party."

"So your Scottish sweetheart can make fun of me in Gaelic?"

"She won't make fun of you. I won't allow it."

"How thoughtful of you." Her tone was laced with sarcasm. "I look forward to the announcement of your betrothal. You deserve each other. Your grandfather will be apoplectic. That should delight you." She darted under his arms and hurried downstairs to the front door, where Pruitt was standing, trying to mind his own business and at the moment obviously wishing he were anyplace but by the door.

Lily marched past him and threw it open, her pert chin raised in indignation. "Ewan, go back to your sweetheart. And don't you dare spy on me through the window again!"

No one could out-stubborn a Scot. "Pruitt, talk sense into the girl." Turning back to Lily, he felt his frustration mounting and knew he was about to make a Scottish ass out of himself. Why did he care that Lily wasn't at the party? Why did he care that she was jealous of Callie? Unnecessarily so. He felt his gut churning. "I'll stand outside your door and wait for you."

"Make yourself comfortable. You'll have a long wait."

"Make no mistake, ye're coming to that party with me, lass. Ye canno' hide behind yerr baboons and yerr books." He winced at his rolling r's and thickening brogue, a sign of his mounting frustration. "If you're not out here in five minutes, I'll haul ye over my shoulder and carry you there myself!"

Complete ass of himself.

Instead of fury, he saw genuine confusion in Lily's eyes. "Why?"

A simple question. One of the many he'd been asking himself. Why the party? Why the kiss? Why did he need Lily? He needed her desperately. He hated needing anyone. "No one makes up my mind for me. Not my grandfather. Not Callie. Not you. If I've a mind to marry a bluestocking *Sassenach*, then that's what I'll do." He walked out, slamming the door behind him.

He was a complete and utter baboon's ass.

CHAPTER 14

LILY STOOD GAPING at the front door for a long moment before finally turning to her butler. "Pruitt, what did he mean by that?"

"I'm not sure, Miss Lily. I think he just proposed to you."

She shook her head and laughed. "No. No... that's not... oh, crumpets. Do you really think so? He can't have meant it. He's going to marry Caledonia MacCorkindale. She called him *darling*."

"But he kissed you."

She winced. "You saw that? Never mind. Don't answer. Truly, Pruitt. What do you think? Should I go?"

"Do you love him?"

She winced again. "Isn't it painfully obvious?"

"Yes, Miss Lily. It is."

"What would you do if you were in my shoes?"

"It isn't for me to say, but I've never known a Farthingale to back down from a challenge."

She nodded. "Thank you, Pruitt. You've been immensely helpful."

It didn't take Lily very long to slip out of her day gown and into the ivory silk with pale blue sash already set out on her bed. Ashton would simply have to wait another day for his lemur papers. She'd finish the report in the morning and somehow slip it to him tomorrow afternoon, no one the wiser.

To her surprise, Ewan was still standing by the front steps. She hadn't really expected him to be there. He gazed at her with a surprised but satisfied smile that reached into his dark eyes. "Lass, you look beautiful."

Prettier than Caledonia MacCorkindale? In truth, she wasn't the most worrisome challenge. The Duke of Lotheil was the man to fear. He wanted an English wife of noble blood for Ewan. Lily hadn't a drop of *blue* blood in her. No, the only things blue were her eyes. The men in her family were tradesmen. Successful ones, but still commoners. Plain red blood. "Ewan—" She didn't know what to ask. She sensed that he didn't know what he wanted. He'd tell her once he worked it out.

He straightened to his full height, looking ruggedly handsome and dangerous while standing under the moon's glow. He reached out to take her hand. "Let's go to a party, lass."

He escorted her to Eloise's familiar residence and led her inside, but he paused beside the music room. "Lily, will you allow me to introduce you to Evangeline? Properly this time. I know it's asking much of you. I'll understand if you prefer to avoid her."

"I know how important this family reconciliation is to you and Meggie." She nibbled her lip, giving his request serious consideration. "If it will help Evangeline and Desmond overcome their fear of you, accept you not only as one of the family but as their friend... of course, I'll do it."

"Thank you, lass." Ewan's tension noticeably eased. "There they are, standing beside your uncle George. Ah, his son is talking to Meggie. The lad seems to be around her quite a bit these days."

Lily nodded. "You needn't worry about him. He has a good heart."

"He had better," Ewan grumbled.

Lily couldn't help but grin. "You men are the oddest creatures."

Ewan arched an eyebrow. "Why do I think you're about to compare us to your swamp baboons?"

"Perhaps because you're acting just like them. They're quite territorial and protective of their females. Male baboons bare their teeth to show their aggression. If that doesn't deter a young male upstart, the dominant baboon will go after him, threatening to tear him to pieces with his sharp teeth if the upstart doesn't back away. Just as William is now backing away from Meggie. Oh, and he's looking straight at you. In fear." She turned to stare at Ewan. "What did you just do?"

"Nothing," he replied, but his expression revealed he was anything but innocent. Perhaps it was that Scottish mix of arrogance, pride, and stubborn sense of honor that made him seem so appealingly dangerous.

She shook her head and sighed. "Yes, you did. William is shaking in his boots."

"Perhaps. Come on, they've all seen us now."

Evangeline turned ashen as she approached. If Lily felt any trepidation, Evangeline obviously felt it tenfold. She saw that Evangeline's eyes were now glistening. Were those unshed tears? Ewan had warned her of his cousin's sensitive nature.

Lily sighed. She wanted to despise Ewan's cousin but simply couldn't. She'd seen that same look of fright and loneliness in her little cousin Harry's eyes when Harry's beloved father had died. "I'm delighted to meet you, Miss Cameron."

Evangeline responded by launching into a sincere and humble apology, obviously so remorseful that Lily found herself feeling desperately sorry for the girl. Lily had to remind herself that she, and not Evangeline, had been the one struck by Desmond's cane. However, as Evangeline poured out her regrets, Lily saw the extent of the damage caused by her grandfather. He hadn't taken a cane to the girl, but he might as well have, for he'd surely struck wounding blows to her confidence with his sly and manipulative words.

"Apology accepted," Lily said, managing a word in edgewise. The girl seemed truly distressed, and Lily never could stand to see anyone suffering. "Shall we make our way to the dining room? Lady Dayne's parties are known for their excellent food. I don't know about you, but I'm famished."

Evangeline's eyes rounded in obvious surprise. "You're asking me to join you?"

Lily nodded. "I hope you will."

George held out his arm to Meggie and Evangeline. "I'll escort you ladies, if you don't mind having this old man around." It was true that her uncle was a little over forty years old, but he'd retained his youthful good looks, and there was no denying that he was a very handsome man. Evangeline appeared delighted, relieved, and ready to cling to his arm the entire evening if he'd let her. Since George had a soft spot in his heart for the downtrodden, Lily knew he wouldn't mind at all. In any event, Evangeline was a beautiful young woman. Truly, he wouldn't mind at all.

Meggie also seemed to be fond of Farthingale men. George's son, William, in particular. At the moment, William was keeping a safe distance, as any young, upstart baboon would when faced with hostility from the older, dominant male. Ewan being the dominant male. Though only a few years older, Ewan was far stronger... tall, broad-chested, muscled thighs... muscled everywhere.

Lily watched in fascination as William circled around them, waiting for Ewan to leave before daring to approach Meggie again. She cast her poor cousin a hopeful smile, knowing he was miserable and pining for Meggie. He could not happily pass the evening until she and Ewan walked away. Well, she needed to retrieve her spectacles from Dillie. That was as good an excuse as any to draw Ewan away.

She made quick apologies and hurried off to find her twin. Reclaiming her spectacles was not the only reason to seek out Dillie. She wanted to confide all that had happened, especially Ewan's kiss and what he'd said in front of Pruitt, but that would have to wait until she'd lost Ewan in the crowd.

Ewan clamped a hand on her elbow. "Lily, slow down."

She gazed at him, uncertain what he intended, for he now had a worried look in his eyes. His grandfather was in attendance. So were the MacCorkindales.

"Lass," he said in a husky voice, suddenly casting her a hot, tender smile that melted her heart. "You were brilliant in there." He paused a moment, as though struggling to find the right words. "You went beyond merely accepting Evie's apology. You forgave her, offered her your friendship, and made her feel valued."

She'd been referred to as brilliant before, but usually with disdain. Women weren't supposed to be brilliant. They were supposed to smile and simper, and look as though they needed help to manage the easiest chores. But Ewan wasn't like others. He admired her for who she was, a bluestocking who frightened away most men and understood very little about social etiquette, but did understand the importance of love and family.

She returned his smile with a warm one of her own. "Will you help me find Dillie?"

He laughed. "Ah, the spectacles switch." He craned his neck and scanned the room, his height a decided advantage. "There she is, in the corner speaking to the Duke of Edgeware."

Him again?

"Him again," Ewan said, frowning as he echoed her thought. "I wonder if he thinks he's speaking to you? I noticed him seated beside you at the Simmingtons' musicale."

Holy crumpets! Was he jealous? He couldn't be. But a subtle change had come over him, a slight tension in his stance, and he'd puffed out his chest as a baboon would have done when preparing to challenge an interloper.

Fascinating!

He still held her possessively by the elbow, a sure sign he was marking his territory. "I'll walk you over there."

Dominant males within the animal kingdom would establish the boundaries of their territory by lifting their leg and emitting a spray at each corner. It not only warned away interlopers but also attracted females willing to mate.

No wonder she found him so appealing. He had all the characteristics of the dominant male. Good looks, arrogance, and a fiercely protective nature. He was a rugged Highlander who refused to be civilized, who looked dangerous even when wearing fashionable clothes, and who refused to bend to his grandfather's wishes.

His gaze shot to hers as they made their way through the elegant crowd. "Lily, why are you looking at me that way?"

She blushed. "No reason."

"I'm not one of your male baboons." He arched an eyebrow, as though waiting for her to agree, and then chuckled when she didn't. "Come on, let's get you to your sister."

Lily approached her twin carefully, even though she sensed that Edgeware had not been fooled by the spectacles. Not wishing to give away their ruse, she decided to take her cues from Dillie on the chance that she had guessed wrong.

"We're safe. He knows and won't tell," Dillie said, making quick introductions. She took off the spectacles and handed them to Lily. "Thank goodness, I can see again. Do I look cross-eyed?"

"No, you look perfect," she and Edgeware answered at the same moment.

Lily stared at him. Edgeware stared at Ewan. Ewan once again arched an eyebrow as he stared back. In the animal kingdom, two males staring each other down was extremely aggressive behavior. Would they spray their territories next? Apparently, it was not necessary. Edgeware realized that Ewan had no amorous intentions toward Dillie. At the same time, Ewan was satisfied that Edgeware had no such intentions toward her.

Crumpets! This was most interesting.

Edgeware and Dillie? Though not nearly old enough to be considered a confirmed bachelor, the duke had made no secret of his intention never to marry.

And what of Ewan? Despite Pruitt's assessment, Lily doubted that Ewan had marriage in mind. He had to settle his family matters before considering a bride. Hopefully, he'd dismiss Callie as a prospect. She knew he would if his head were clear, but at the moment it was crammed with deathbed promises and a general dislike for all things English. He was proud and stubborn and on terrible terms with his grandfather, and his grandfather was just as proud and stubborn. She hoped he would not goad Ewan into making a stupid decision, but she knew the old duke was just the sort to goad and poke at festering family wounds.

How would Ewan respond? By poking back at his grandfather and marrying Callie MacCorkindale to spite him?

Ewan tipped a finger under her chin and forced her gaze to his. "Lass, I'm not one of your baboons."

"What?"

"Your head's in the clouds again. Have you heard a word we've said?"

"Sorry. I didn't."

He grinned. "I have a few matters that require my attention. I'll escort you to your uncle. He's still entertaining Meggie and Evangeline."

"I think I can keep my head out of the clouds long enough to make my own way into the dining room." She turned to the crush of guests merrily chatting in the overheated room. "I know a shortcut across the terrace. I'll avoid the crowd entirely."

* * *

Ewan was about to insist on accompanying Lily, but his grandfather was making his way toward him with a scowl as dark as thunderclouds.

Callie, also scowling and with claws bared, was approaching from the other direction. "Go straight to your uncle. Promise me, Lily."

She eyed him curiously. "I will. Are you always this demanding?"

"No. Sorry, lass." He didn't know why he had such a bad feeling about letting her out of his sight. The little hairs at the nape of his neck were on end and stiff as iron spikes. No doubt because he was about to face his grandfather—who would be furious that he'd brought Evangeline to the party, and furious that she was having a nice time with the Farthingales. No doubt because he was also about to tell Callie to find someone else to marry (and make miserable)—and she'd be furious and ready to lash out at anyone who got in her way. Couldn't have Lily standing beside him when that happened. "I'll meet you in the dining room. I won't be long."

He was about to ask Dillie and Edgeware to accompany her, but the pair were now distracted by Rupert Farthingale, one of the many Farthingale uncles, who was decidedly in his cups and mistaking Dillie for her twin, although Dillie had already handed off the spectacles. Edgeware was helping to steady the man, who seemed about to tip over.

Ewan stepped away, knowing Edgeware and Dillie had the matter well in hand. He started toward the terrace, then stopped himself. He was being overly protective. And hadn't Homer Barrow, the Bow Street runner he'd retained, put a man on to watch Lily?

So why were those little hairs still on end?

Callie reached him first, the old duke having been delayed by Eloise, who'd called him over for more questions about his birthday party. He'd have to thank her afterward, for Eloise had surely done it on purpose, drummed up some excuse to divert the old bastard from spewing his venom at Ewan during her party. Ewan knew him better than that. The appearance of civility and proper English manners was too important to his grandfather. Likely all he would have done this evening was quietly threaten Ewan. He'd proceed to the task of destroying him, Meggie, and Evangeline once the party was over. Lovable old fellow.

Callie clamped a cold, bony hand on his forearm to gain his attention. "Who do you think you are? You can't make a fool of me. We had an understanding."

"We've been friends a long time, Callie. But you and I know we never had any such arrangement. If there had been one, I would have honored it." He doubted she would have, though. When looking back, Callie had never been a sappy, moon-eyed girl. She used people, treating most as though they were some small, inconsequential trinket such as a comb or hair ribbon to be used until something newer and shinier came along. Then the old trinket would be tossed into the dustbin and forgotten. She was that way with men as well, tossing over one suitor when bored for the next who happened to catch her fancy.

"We're alike, Ewan. We suit each other."

He hoped not. "I'm not that same man I was a year ago. However, I value our friendship and am sorry if I ever gave you hope it might turn into something more." He met her gaze, looking for a spark of anything other than the anger that now marred her beautiful face. Nothing. No pain of lost love, no gleam of hopefulness, no trace of affection. Had she ever cared for anyone other than herself?

Lily was so different, a delightful mix of logic and warmth. She genuinely cared for others. He'd seen the pain, the ache of love in her eyes, and cursed himself a fool for failing to appreciate how important she'd become to him. She could add meaning and wonder to his life. So why was he desperate to keep her out of his heart? Instead of reciting reasons why he and Lily could never work, he should have been counting his blessings. To be sure, there were problems to overcome, but Lily was worth the effort.

"I know what's troubling you." Callie's voice was now a kittenish purr that he found surprisingly unappealing for its lack of sincerity. "You're hurt that we never shared that bit of *something* more. I was willing. You were always such a prude about it, Ewan."

"It was never my style to seduce virgins."

"You worried needlessly. I was never the sweet, innocent sort. I can prove it to you now, if you'll let me."

He arched an eyebrow, not particularly eager to indulge in the sexual pleasures she was offering. "This isn't the time or place to speak of such matters."

"Join me in the garden and I'll show you what you've been missing." Her hand still felt like a clamp about his forearm, not soft or caressing as Lily's had been. She leaned close and brushed her breasts against his tense body. Her nipples were hard, and her skin lightly pink with arousal. "I know how to please a man. I'm wet for you, Ewan. So hot and wet, aching to take you inside of me." She gazed at his crotch as she ran her tongue slowly across her lips. "I'll make you forget the *Sassenach* virgin. Wait a few minutes and then follow me into the garden. I'll meet you beside the lilac trees."

She licked her lips again. Looked at his crotch again. Then was gone.

All he felt was relief. However, no sooner had Callie left his side than his grandfather approached. "You brought Evangeline." That was it, just three words, but they were laden with menace.

He wanted to curl his hands into fists and pummel the old man. "It seemed the right thing to do."

"She ought to have known better than to accept a ride from you."

"Why? You weren't going to offer. She's your granddaughter, yet you treat her worse than a pair of old boots. All she wants is for you to love her. She has only you and Desmond. She'd give you her heart if you opened up yours just a crack, but you'll never do it. Your only desire is to control and manipulate. You treat her worse than the old rag that's used to clean your old boots."

"Don't you talk to me that way. I'm still your grandfather."

"As well as Evie's and Desmond's. Start acting like it. They're your family, not some marionettes to be pulled by your strings."

His grandfather's eyes were now blazing and his hands, like Ewan's, were flexing at his sides to fight the temptation to curl them into fists. "You're quick to defend them, yet you haven't any notion of their true natures. You've been here less than a month. What do you know about them? You haven't experienced firsthand the extent of their greed."

"What have they done to make you think they only covet your wealth?" He didn't necessarily disagree with the statement, for he didn't know his cousins at all, but the little he'd seen of them and of their home did not give him that impression.

He'd seen desolation, not avarice, in Evie's eyes. Not that he was an expert with women. Quite the opposite, they confounded him at every turn. Lily especially. He still didn't understand why his heart leapt into his throat and his blood turned fiery whenever he saw her. It just did.

He missed her, even though they'd only been apart a short while.

"You'll find out for yourself," his grandfather said, answering his question after a long moment's pause. "They'll pretend to like you, but don't be fooled. They'll hate you as they hate me. They blame me for the death of their father."

"Do they have reason?"

"No. Damn you, Ewan. I loved my sons, both of them. I'm no monster."

He'd humiliated Evie and banned Lily from the thing she loved most. If he wasn't a monster, he came fairly close. But this wasn't a discussion to be pursued amid a party. Though he and his grandfather were on their own in a corner, they were drawing notice. Ewan resolved to renew their conversation later at Lotheil Court.

Right now, he was eager to see Lily again. He'd find her with Evie and Meggie, no doubt putting both of them at ease, because it was her nature to calm and comfort. Not that he was ever comfortable around Lily. He wasn't. But it was a good discomfort. A hot, melt-the-butter-on-your-biscuits desire that he always felt around her.

He noticed Callie walking in from the garden and felt her presence like a splash of cold water. Bollix. He'd forgotten about her, kept her waiting by the damned lilacs. He had no intention of taking her up on her offer of sex. She wasn't remotely tempting.

Still, he shouldn't have dismissed her from his thoughts the moment she'd walked away. An angry, ignored woman was always trouble.

To his surprise, instead of casting daggers at him, she tossed him a look of smug triumph. Like a cat who had swallowed a bird.

What had she done?

Suddenly concerned that she might have said something to hurt Lily, Ewan made his way to the dining room. He spotted George, Meggie, and Evie. All three were smiling and engaged in lively conversation. He interrupted them. "Where's Lily?"

George appeared confused. "Isn't she with you?"

"No, she left me a while ago to join you. She cut through the garden to avoid the crowd."

The smile on George's face faltered. "We haven't seen her. She never made it here."

Meggie rolled her eyes and laughed. "You know how easily Lily can be distracted. Someone must have caught her attention. I'm sure you'll find her in the music room discussing her theories on baboon colonies with one of Eloise's professor friends."

Ewan's heart began to pound a little faster. Meggie was probably right. Still, Lily was missing and Callie had a smug look on her face. Those hairs at the nape of his neck were iron-hard spikes again. But Callie couldn't have seen her. She'd gone into the garden long after Lily had been there. "I'll be right back."

"I'll help you look for her." Though George kept his tone light, Ewan knew he was worried too. "Perhaps she went home. After all, we live right next door."

Ewan nodded. "I'll search the music room, then the rest of Eloise's house."

Meggie began to wring her hands. "What's going on? Do you think something's happened to Lily?"

He assured her that he didn't, but he spoke with little conviction. His instincts were on alert. Lily was in trouble. "As you said, she becomes so lost in her thoughts that she forgets what's going on around her. I'm sure she's chatting with one of her scholarly acquaintances, or hiding in Eloise's library reading a musty book."

However, a quick inspection of every room, including the library, turned up nothing. Dillie hadn't seen her either. Ewan's heart was now firmly lodged in his throat.

The garden? He'd already looked out there. But she wasn't anywhere else. She had to be there. Had Callie encountered her and said something to make Lily run off to a quiet corner in tears? He blamed himself for insisting that Lily attend the party, and fervently hoped George would find her at home.

But he didn't. "She isn't there, Ewan. Pruitt hasn't seen her since she left the house with you. I don't like this. We all know she occasionally walks with her head in the clouds, but never like this. She wouldn't simply wander off."

Ewan ran a hand across the nape of his neck. Lily had a way of perplexing him. If he wasn't careful, he'd rub his neck raw worrying about the girl. "I think Callie might have seen her."

He went in search of the cold beauty and found her in the entry hall standing beside her uncle. They had on their capes and were waiting for their carriage to draw up. "Leaving early?"

Callie shot him another smug look.

"Callie wasn't feeling well," said Archie MacCorkindale. "In truth, she's homesick and has decided to join me when I return to Scotland in a few days' time. I have business to attend to up there, so we're cutting short our London stay."

"Awfully sudden, isn't it, Callie? I thought you'd come down here for the season."

She tipped her chin up and shot him an indignant glare. "A woman has the right to change her mind. Not that I wouldn't mind staying around to see you humiliated."

Archie frowned. "What do you mean? What's going on here?"

"His precious Lily." She shrugged her shoulders. "I suppose you'll find out soon enough, Ewan. She doesn't love you. You stupid fool. I saw her in the garden in the arms of another man."

"I don't believe you."

"As I said, men are stupid. She's obviously taken on a lover. They were intimately wrapped in each other's arms, then he lifted her into his arms and carried her away. She made no protest."

"Show me." He grabbed Callie by the arm and led her to the garden, darting and weaving through the crowd, which thankfully paid them little notice. George and Archie followed close behind. The four of them were alone once outdoors since the night had turned chill, and Eloise had sumptuous food and elegant entertainments to keep her guests enjoyably occupied indoors. "Where did you see them, Callie?"

"I don't recall."

He was too angry and frustrated to be politely accepting of her lies. "Where! I vow I'll wring your neck if you don't tell me now."

"Ouch! You're squeezing my arm."

"I'll do worse if you continue to play games with me. Tell me!"

"Now, see here Ewan. I—"

"Shut up, Archie." He turned his glower back on Callie, realizing in that moment just how capable he was of murder.

Callie must have sensed it as well, for she suddenly didn't seem quite so certain of herself. "All right, I'll tell you. It was over there, by the hedgerows."

Ewan and George raced over to where she'd pointed, Archie close on their heels. "Och, Ewan. What's that odd smell?"

Ewan picked up a damp handkerchief lying on the ground. It was a man's handkerchief, plain, no initials or crest embroidered on it. He held it a good distance from his nose, yet still coughed and felt its foul, potent reach when his head began to lightly spin. "Lily's been drugged."

Callie, now beside them, cast him a malicious smile.

He was incredulous. "Damn it, you knew she was struggling. Didn't you? Yet you left her to fend on her own. You knew she was in danger and did nothing to help her."

"You can't prove it. If asked, I'll say I didn't notice anything out of the ordinary."

George let out a low growl. "There's a special place in hell for people like you. That's my niece in trouble. If anything happens to her—"

"You ought to have watched her more closely. She isn't my problem." She turned away from Lily's uncle. "Come on, Archie. This party is a crushing bore. Take me home."

"Not on your life, lass. We dinna leave here until ye've told them all you know. The girl's life could be at stake. I'll not have that on my conscience. Tell them everything you saw."

But Callie was of little help. She refused to describe Lily's assailant or tell them in which direction he was headed, claiming she was too overset to recall. Ewan knew she was lying, that her distress and tears were all a pretense. And he had once considered marrying this witch!

They were wasting precious time here. He cursed inwardly, blaming himself for Lily's peril. Still, none of this made sense. If he had an enemy, why was his enemy so intent on harming Lily? No one knew how deeply he felt about her. Hell, he hadn't realized it until tonight. The flurry of gossip several weeks ago about him and Lily being an "item" had quickly been dismissed once word got out that he'd only been protecting her from Jasper. While everyone believed Lily capable of attracting men, no one actually believed her capable of holding on to one for very long. She scared most men with her talk of fluxions and swamp baboons. "Get her out of my sight, Archie."

He nodded. "I'll let you know if she remembers anything. Sorry, Ewan. I'll pray for the lass."

As they left, Ewan turned to George. "After the incident at Tattersalls, I hired a Bow Street runner by the name of Homer Barrow to investigate on my behalf. I also had him put a man to watch over Lily. He must be around here someplace. Perhaps he's following them."

"Let's hope so. These runners are clever. He might have left word with one of the coachmen. There are dozens of carriages lining the street. Let's start asking questions. Even if they didn't see the Bow Street runner, they might have seen something else helpful. The blackguard couldn't have walked down the street carrying Lily in his arms without anyone noticing. Come to think of it, he must have had a carriage. It's a small circle. These coachmen know each other, so even if the carriage had no markings, someone might have recognized the driver."

But to Ewan's frustration, none of them had seen or heard anything.

"There's a mews behind Chipping Way," George said. "That's where he must have left his conveyance. One can slip unnoticed from the garden to the mews if one keeps to the shadows."

"Lead the way."

It took little time to reach the isolated structures that housed the horses, riding equipment, and carriages for the residents of Chipping Way. All was dark and silent. Since George was familiar with these structures, he lost no time in finding a lantern and lighting it. "Look, Ewan! Over there. What is it?"

There was a man sprawled unconscious on the hay-strewn floor. "Do you recognize him, George?"

"No, not one of our groomsmen. Perhaps one of the blackguard's men."

"Not likely. They wouldn't have left one of their own behind to be questioned by the authorities. He could be the runner assigned to guard Lily. Damn. He's out cold." Ewan rose and quickly looked around for clues. Any clue. "Stay with him. Get as much information as you can from him when he rouses."

George nodded. "Where are you going?"

"To talk to Charles and Harry." Earlier, Lily had complained of him spying through their parlor window. He hadn't been, but someone obviously had, and Lily and her young cousins had seen the man. He knew he was grasping at the thinnest ray of hope. If Lily hadn't been able to make out the lurker's face, the boys likely hadn't either. Still, it was worth a try.

He raced to the Farthingale home and tore up the stairs as soon as Pruitt opened the door to let him in. "My lord! You can't just—"

"Not now, Pruitt. Lily's in trouble," he shouted, already at the third floor landing. He entered the boys' quarters and shook Charles awake first, trying not to alarm him but desperate to make up the lost time. "Son," he said in his gentlest voice, "did you recognize the face you saw in the window this evening?"

The boy's eyes drifted closed again. "Charles, wake up. It's important."

He heard a sniffle behind him. He turned and saw Dillie standing in the doorway, tears streaming down her cheeks. "Meggie said you were looking for Lily. I know something's wrong. I feel it in my heart." She knelt beside him. "Let me try." She turned her attention to Charles. "Who did you see, sweetheart? Come on. Wake up."

"The baboon man," the boy mumbled, falling back asleep.

Ewan stared at Dillie. "Who the hell is that?"

"He can't mean Ashton. It makes no sense. He and Lily have been friends forever. He relies on Lily to write his papers."

"Ashton. Are you sure?"

Dillie began to sob. Soft, gut-wrenching cries that broke his heart. "Yes... no... I don't know. Ewan, *please*. Find her."

CHAPTER 15

LILY AWOKE FEELING cold and ill. That nauseating scent still filled her nostrils and her head wouldn't stop spinning. She tried to orient herself, but couldn't. All was pitch black. She tried to move her hands. With senses dulled, it took her a moment to realize they were tied behind her back. Fortunately, her legs were unbound. Her abductors hadn't bothered to tie them, most likely figuring she couldn't get far in her fancy, silk evening slippers.

She tried to move her legs. They were painfully stiff and too weak to support her at the moment, but she knew they'd strengthen as the effects of the drug wore off.

What's happening? Where am I?

Her last memory was of encountering Ashton in the garden. Where was he now? Had he managed to escape? Or was he held captive along with her? She refused to consider that he might have been killed by her abductors. Why had she used the plural? Yes, there had been more than one man. She vaguely recalled being caught from behind by one of those fiends and then handed over to another. She couldn't remember anything beyond that detail.

"Ashton," she called out softly.

No answer.

She feared to raise her voice above a whisper, for her captors might hear and know she had revived. Her chances of escaping would then decrease dramatically. But what of Ashton? She couldn't leave without him, assuming he'd been taken as well. She had to find out if he was held captive, needed time to formulate a plan to save both of them.

First, she had to figure out where she was. It seemed an impossible task at the moment, for her eyes had yet to adjust to the darkness. She guessed that she was alone in some sort of storage room. But was she in a house? A shop? A prison? She didn't know what this place was.

She could hear footsteps and muffled voices on the opposite side of the door, but no sound other than her own breathing in this room. If Ashton was here, they were holding him in another part of this structure.

She heard a dog bark in the distance and thought of Jasper, but the yelp was too high-pitched and sharp. Jasper's howl was longer and deeper. She missed that clumsy dog. She shook out of the thought and concentrated on more important matters. Did anyone realize she was missing? Ewan would eventually. He'd alert her family. Ewan and every Farthingale in London might be on her trail by now, but they wouldn't know where to search. There were dozens of roads out of Mayfair and they all branched out into dozens more. It was a geometrical improbability. There weren't enough Farthingales in London to cover every road leading out, assuming she'd even been taken out of London.

She thought of her parents. They'd be worried, desperate to find her. She knew they were feeling helpless just now, unable to do anything but pray for her safe return. Tears welled in her eyes. She ought to have been a better daughter, attended more of those society functions that her mother thought were so important.

"I'll make it home safe," she muttered to herself. She'd use her wits to stay alive until her loved ones found her. She could manage it. After all, these villains must have grabbed her for a purpose. Likely they were after ransom. Why else take her?

Ashton's family had resources as well. Though not as wealthy as hers, they still had enough to make his abduction worthwhile. Perhaps they would be released together. A chill ran up her spine. She ought to be remembering something. She couldn't quite place what was so important. It didn't matter. It would come back to her as the fog lifted from her brain.

How long had she been unconscious? No more than three or four hours, for she wasn't hungry yet. Which meant they couldn't be all that far from London. Perhaps still in London. Could she smell the Thames? She took a deep breath, but all that surrounded her was the nauseatingly sweet scent of the drug used on her in Eloise's garden. It hadn't worn off yet. How long would such a thing take to leave her body? Mere hours? Days? She didn't know.

Concentrate on what you do know. If they were in London, she'd hear the peal of church bells. There were hundreds of churches throughout the town and they rang their bells at regular intervals. She'd hear something, no matter on which side of the Thames she was hidden.

Hours seemed to pass. No church bells. No scent of a river. No sounds at all, other than the rush of wind and intermittent, pelting rain. She wasn't in London—something about the air and her surroundings felt different. How far away were they?

The lock on her door suddenly clicked and the door slowly groaned open. Someone stepped into the room holding a lantern. She tried to make out who it was, but the brightness of the light blinded her. "M'lord, she's awake," the villain called to someone standing just outside the room. "What shall I do?"

"Put her back to sleep." The voice had an odd, deep quality, as though the man behind it did not wish to be recognized.

"No! No!" She tried to resist, but her struggles were useless against the burly fellow. He shoved a damp cloth against her face and pressed tight until she could no longer hold her breath. The disgusting fumes overwhelmed her senses.

Her head began to spin.

Within seconds, she'd be unconscious. However, all was not lost. She'd recognized the voice outside the room, even though the man had tried to mask it. She now knew who'd abducted her.

And now she was really worried.

*   *   *

Ewan's heart was in knots. Lily's life depended upon the sleepy rambling of a little boy. With only that unreliable clue to work on, he knew they were in trouble.

"What if he's wrong?" Dillie asked, echoing his concerns.

As they hurried downstairs, George strode in. "The Bow Street runner's still unconscious." He glanced around and then motioned for them to join him in the parlor.

Ewan was eager to tell him what they'd learned, but waited for George to shut the parlor doors. The fewer people who knew about Lily's abduction, the better. Even though she was the innocent victim, Ewan knew her reputation would be irrevocably tarnished if word got out.

"I left the runner in the care of the Duke of Edgeware," George continued. "He's offered to do all in his power to help."

"Edgeware? How did he find out?" This was bad. If the duke knew, then how many others did as well? Ewan began to pace a hole in the elegant carpet. Though eager to ride off in search of Ashton, he needed to hear the rest of what George had to report.

Dillie, who had just fallen into a seat on the settee, shot back up. "Ian's helping? I certainly didn't tell him. He must have seen me fretting and figured out something was wrong."

"Ian, is it? Quite friendly with him. Too friendly, I'd say. I already have one niece in trouble. I don't need another."

Dillie shot her uncle an indignant frown. "Rest assured, I have no intention of losing my heart to that man."

"I hope you're right. No matter, we'll discuss it later." He turned back to Ewan. "Edgeware will inform us as soon as the Bow Street man comes around. He also knows Homer Barrow. Said he's the best at what he does. He sent one of Eloise's servants off to summon him with instructions to report to him at the Farthingale residence. Mr. Barrow will come straight here."

"You can wait for him. I won't." Ewan quickly told George what they'd learned from Charles. "I intend to bang down every door in London, turn over every slimy stone until I find that wretched bastard."

George let out a short, mirthless laugh. "Ashton? No, I don't believe it. Charles is just a boy. Who knows what goes on in his childish mind? He must be mistaken. Let's wait for Mr. Barrow. Running off on that flimsy lead without a well thought out plan will be a waste of precious time."

"Perhaps, but it's the only lead we have to go on. Staying here, doing nothing is worse."

George sighed as he nodded. "You're right. I'll go with you. I know where he lives. Let's start there."

Dillie put a hand on her uncle's arm. "What about me? I can help."

"We need someone here to act as our field general, to instruct Mr. Barrow when he arrives, to know where each of us is at all times and send word if there's a breakthrough," Ewan said.

George patted her hand, his voice laced with pain as he said, "Your parents will have to be told about what's happened."

Dillie's eyes rounded in alarm the moment the import of his words struck her. "And you want me to do it? I can't! I don't know how. The news will destroy them."

Ewan wished he could be more encouraging, but he was in quiet agony as well. "Do your best, Dillie. Be strong for your sister. For your parents. Don't let them give up hope. Whoever did this can't have more than a fifteen-minute head start on us. If he meant to harm Lily, he would have simply done it in the garden. She was drugged and carried off. This was planned. He wanted her alive." The fear in her eyes mirrored his own, though he hoped he hid his better. "Tell Mr. Barrow where we've gone. Have him catch up to us at Ashton's residence."

In truth, he was relieved George had agreed to join him. Besides being a cool and steady hand, he was a capable doctor. Though Ewan didn't want to think of the ominous possibilities, he knew George would be needed if Lily was hurt.

No. Lily was strong. Smart. She was damned perfect.

He'd get her back safely.

He issued final instructions to Dillie though she didn't really need them. George hugged his niece. "Do your best to keep the Farthingale clan under control. If Ashton is behind Lily's disappearance, I'd rather he isn't alerted. For that matter, I'd rather no one but the immediate family be alerted right now. Your sisters and their husbands will want to help. Ask them to stay close. We may need their muscle or their useful contacts if the search leads us out of London."

"I'll do whatever I can," Dillie assured, even as more tears welled in her eyes. "Please find her."

The Mortimer townhouse was directly across the park, so cutting through it on foot was faster than taking a carriage. The night was dark despite the full moon, but gathering storm clouds partially hid its silvery glow. If not for the occasional lit torch, the park would have been plunged in darkness. A swift, damp wind was at their backs and Ewan noticed a sudden wintery crispness to the air. Damn. Lily's thin silk gown wouldn't keep her halfway warm.

"What if Ashton isn't there?" George asked. They'd cleared the park and were turning onto the fashionable Belgrave Square where he resided.

"I don't expect him to be. If he's involved in Lily's abduction, then he's likely with her. I'm more interested in talking to his father, hoping he'll point us in the right direction. I'm no expert in matters of abduction, but Lily wasn't taken on a mere lark. Ashton, if he's our villain, planned it over the course of several weeks. Perhaps months. I'm starting to think the attack on Lily at Tattersalls was a kidnap attempt that failed. That planning must have included a suitable place to hide her. We needn't reveal our true purpose. A few, well-phrased questions should get him to tell us where his son has been spending his time lately."

George let out a shaky breath. "I hope you're right."

"If he won't talk, we'll try his servants." Though he doubted they'd get much information out of them. Servants were often wary of those whom they believed were above their station.

Homer Barrow caught up to Ewan as he was about to knock on the door of the Mortimer residence. "M'lord," he said breathlessly, the jowls on his face wobbling as he shook his head. "Good thing I happened to be checking on my man tonight."

"Indeed, we sent a footman off to fetch you, but I feared he'd never find you in time." He gave silent thanks for this small stroke of good fortune.

"So I gathered. I came upon His Grace, the Duke of Edgeware, who was helping my injured man. He sent me over to the Farthingale home and Miss Dillie told me what's happened. 'Tis a nasty business, but I'll put my best runners on it. No charge, sir. Though I'm sure that's the least of your concerns. I feel responsible. Ye trusted me and my men to protect the lass and we failed."

"As did I, Mr. Barrow. I'm glad you're here."

"So am I, m'lord. I'll talk to the servants while ye're talkin' to the father. Don't think he'll be of much help. But them servants notice everything. They'll open up to the likes of me."

He watched Homer scurry to the servant's entrance with surprising speed for a portly man. He was pleased to know his Bow Street runners would be doggedly on the case. These were skilled, determined men and he needed their assistance.

A little less than half an hour had passed since Lily's abduction. Why hadn't he figured it out sooner? All the while, he'd thought the enemy was his. But Lily was the one in peril all along. He'd hired a man to shadow her. He ought to have put an army to the task.

He knocked at the front door. The Mortimer butler led them in and settled them in the parlor. "You'd better ask the questions, George. He doesn't know me."

George nodded.

It seemed an eternity before Ashton's father deigned to come down, though it couldn't have been more than a few minutes. They'd probably roused the old man from his bed. "Dr. Farthingale, I'm surprised to see you at this hour. Fields said it was important. Is something wrong? Has something happened to Ashton?"

"No, my lord. Well, perhaps. We're not sure. You see, he and my niece, Lily, are missing." He introduced Ewan as a friend, not mentioning his name since it would have revealed his connection to the Duke of Lotheil. Ewan thought it wise. His grandfather had come down hard on Ashton, and Lord Mortimer may not have been too pleased about it.

"What are you suggesting? An elopement?" His ancient eyes brightened. "He's been talking about her quite a bit lately. I thought something was afoot."

Ewan exchanged a glance with George.

"Yes, children can be quite impulsive these days," George said, trying to sound casual, though Ewan heard the tension in his voice. "Did he mention where he might have taken her? You see, she's underage and still requires her parents' consent to marry. She's such a clever little thing, we often forget how young she is. Perhaps Ashton's forgotten as well."

"I wouldn't be surprised. Youngsters in love rarely think of practical matters."

"Of course, the Farthingales would be delighted by a union of our families. We'd like to make certain it is properly done, no embarrassing oversights. You understand."

Lord Mortimer nodded. "I certainly do. Lily's a fine girl. I wish I could be of help, but my son isn't one to confide in me."

"Think, sir. Any hint of where they might have gone? No matter how trivial."

The old man shrugged his shoulders. "No, but I'll summon you if something comes to mind." With that, he dismissed them and rang for Fields to help him up the stairs.

Ewan sensed the old bastard was lying. He wanted to ask more questions, but decided against it. He'd caught an urgent look in the butler's eyes.

"We're sorry to have bothered you," George said, his disappointment obvious.

They both rose, but instead of heading for the door, Ewan held George back. "The butler knows something. I think he's willing to talk. Let's wait."

It didn't take long for the man to return. Whispering, he drew them aside and turned to George, his expression clearly troubled. "You say your niece is missing?"

George nodded. "Tell us what you know. *Please.*"

"The Mortimers have a house in Maidstone. Sparrow Hall's the name. Haven't used it much lately. It was in Lady Mortimer's family and Lord Ashton inherited it upon her death last year. A drafty old place. Never cared for it m'self, but he was there just last week stocking supplies for the house. When Mrs. Fields asked him about it, he muttered something about hunting on the grounds with friends. She's my wife and is housekeeper here. We're a small staff, only five of us in service."

"Did he mention to your wife who these friends were?"

"No, m'lord. But that bit of nonsense about hunting struck me as odd at the time. Lord Ashton's no hunter. Never has been. I suspected he was planning something unsavory, the way he's talked about Miss Farthingale recently. She's a cheerful girl. Always had a kind word for me and my wife. I would never forgive myself if something happened to her. I won't have her murder on my soul."

George turned pale.

Ewan caught his arm, understanding his despair. He was just as shaken. It was one thing to fear the worst, and quite another to have it spoken aloud. "Maidstone, you say?"

"Aye, I can't think he'd be anyplace else. But there's more. My wife found a box hidden beneath Lord Ashton's bed. She opened it and saw a collection of feminine trinkets. Handkerchiefs with the initials LF, hair ribbons, that sort of thing."

Ewan exchanged another glance with George. Lily hadn't been misplacing her belongings. Ashton had been stealing them.

"I thought it odd, but harmless," Fields continued, "until that nasty business with the Duke of Lotheil and the Royal Society occurred. Lord Ashton was quite distressed. Began talking about how Miss Farthingale had betrayed him."

After a few hasty questions to confirm Ashton's movements over the past month, Ewan and George left. Homer was waiting for them at the corner. "Maidstone, m'lord," Homer said, confirming what they'd just learned. "That's where he is. I'll wager m'life on it. 'Tis a bit of good news. The girl's sure to be alive. He wouldn't have bothered replenishing the larder and gathering supplies if he only meant to... you know."

Ewan wasn't familiar with England's southern countryside. "How far is it from here?"

"Depends on how fast we ride, m'lord. Can't ride too fast at night. I'd say about four hours. Less on that stallion of yours," he said. "But I wouldn't advise taking off on yer own. It isn't safe. The fancy lord surely had others helping him."

Nor did Ewan know the way. He couldn't afford to ride off on his own and get lost. Even if he did find his way, he wasn't so foolish as to believe he could capture Ashton, defeat the rats he'd hired, and rescue Lily all on his own. He might be able to fight off four or five of them with the element of surprise on his side, but it only took one of those rats to slip away and harm a defenseless Lily.

Damn. He figured they were almost an hour behind Ashton now, assuming he was the culprit, and assuming he'd taken Lily to Maidstone.

"We'll need a couple more men to ride with us," Homer said, "just to be safe. I know the men I want. M'pals, Mick and Bert, are experienced runners. They'll be of help in these delicate situations. Might I suggest that I round 'em up and we regroup at the Farthingale home within the hour? M'lord, we'll need horses. Ain't much use for good ones here in London. The nags we usually ride won't make it across the Thames at a trot, much less at a gallop."

"We have a supply of good horses," George said.

More precious time lost. But Ewan knew Homer was right. He returned to Lotheil Court, immediately ordered Hades saddled, quickly changed out of his formal attire, and collected Jasper. The hairy lump could track better than any dog he'd ever owned. He'd be of use in finding Lily, especially if Ashton held her in a hidden room. Or off the grounds of the Maidstone house. He packed weapons and filled a saddlebag with a few useful supplies.

When he arrived at the Farthingale residence, Dillie and her mother were seated on the settee in the parlor, their hands clasped together in a death grip. The mother, Sophie, was a beautiful woman for her age, dark hair sprinkled with strands of white, a soft, pink complexion, and blue eyes that at the moment held no sparkle. Lines of worry were etched into a face that held such profound sadness, Ewan couldn't bear it.

Dillie glanced up at him. "What time is it? After midnight already? Lily and I are scheduled to give a recital at Lady Finchley's home this evening. In the excitement, I'd forgotten all about it."

"We'll have to let Lady Finchley know as soon as possible," Sophie said, casting him a pleading gaze. "I'll tell her that Lily suddenly fell ill. She'll suspect something is amiss. Soon, all of London will realize she's missing. I don't care what any of them think. I just want my daughter back." She took a deep, raspy breath. "I should have told her that I loved her."

"You did," Dillie insisted.

"Not often enough. I was always after her about one thing or another, about her books and that stodgy Royal Society. I'm so sorry! And now it's come to this!"

Dillie looked as lost and anguished as her mother, even as she tried to comfort her. "Lily knows you love her. She's smart. She knows everything."

Ewan knelt beside the ladies. "I'll find her, Mrs. Farthingale. I promise you. Don't send word to anyone just yet. No need to say anything until the last possible moment."

"The recital isn't until eight o'clock tonight," Dillie added, her lips quivering despite her best efforts to remain composed. "That gives Ewan almost twenty hours to get her back to us." She turned to him and cast him a trembling smile. "She plays the harp. Surprisingly, not very well, but she tries hard, and I'm sure she'll master it someday. I play the piano and sing. We haven't rehearsed the pieces yet. Lily's always finding excuses to avoid practice. She hates that harp." She cast him another weak smile. "Please make this recital happen. We'll stink worse than a basket of fish left sitting in the sun. The audience will cringe. Lily's harp playing will offend their ears. I'll consider it the best recital ever."

"So will I. Can't wait to have my ears assaulted." Ewan rose and turned to the men. George had also changed into riding clothes, and he and Lily's father were standing on the opposite side of the room speaking quietly, no doubt of the darker possibilities, of what to do if matters did not turn out as well as hoped. Ewan refused to lose faith. Lily was alive. He'd find her. All would be well.

George had his medical bag beside him. Ewan hoped they wouldn't have need of it. Dillie had packed a change of clothes for Lily, handing the small bundle to him with a murmured, "I have faith in you." He hoped it wasn't misplaced.

To Ewan's surprise, the Duke of Edgeware strode in, appearing slightly out of breath. "The Bow Street man is awake. He identified Lord Mortimer's son, Ashton, as the fiend who took Lily."

"Now we know we're on the right track." Ewan quickly filled him in on all they had learned and then listened to the rest of Edgeware's report.

"The runner says he counted four men with Ashton. Not gentlemen. More like dockside ruffians. There could be others, but that's all he saw." Edgeware glanced at Dillie and her mother before turning back to Ewan. "What can I do to help?"

Ewan also glanced at the pair. They looked pale and scared. They looked as though their hearts had been ripped from their chests. "I appreciate all you're doing for Lily and her family. I don't think they'll hold up much longer. Will you stay here and take care of things? They're all about to fall apart."

Edgeware nodded. "Of course. I'll stay for as long as I'm needed. I have my own men making discreet inquiries throughout the seedier parts of London. I'll let you know if they come up with any more news. Who else has heard about Lily's abduction?"

"Only a handful. If we find her in time, I think we can keep it quiet. My sister, Meggie, and my cousin, Evangeline, suspect something is wrong, but they don't yet know what's happened. I'd rather keep it that way." He ran a hand through his hair. "Eloise's party will break up soon. They'll expect me to escort them home."

"I'll take care of it," Edgeware said, stepping away from the ladies to quietly explain. "A word to your grandfather that you and I are off to

Regent Street for another sort of party and would he mind escorting his granddaughters home should do it. Having a bad reputation has its advantages. Who else knows?"

Ewan nodded. "We questioned the coachmen outside of Eloise's home, but only asked if they'd seen a man. They don't know we're looking for Lily. However, the MacCorkindales know. Archie can be trusted to keep his mouth shut. I don't know about Callie. She'll keep silent only if she thinks it will work to her benefit."

Edgeware frowned. "Unfortunately, I've met too many such women."

Ewan agreed.

The Bow Street runners arrived, three of them including Homer Barrow. "M'best men," he assured Lily's father, who wanted to join them but had been convinced by Ewan to remain behind. He had no doubt that Lily's father was clever and competent, but this was his daughter at risk. Lily was his little girl. Any father would be beyond mad with worry, and a crazed man couldn't be counted on to remain calm during their search... or afterward, if things didn't work out as well as hoped.

In truth, Ewan was in no better shape than Lily's father. Though he'd tried his best to appear calm, he was filled with dread and anger. Scots had tempers, and Highlanders had the worst tempers of all. Rage would get him nowhere, probably get him and his companions killed. He had to keep his wits about him. For Lily's sake.

His gut was now twisted in a Gordian knot. Almost two hours had passed since her abduction. Another four hours to reach Maidstone, possibly longer. They'd be riding the entire time in darkness, an ink-black darkness that matched the raging darkness within his heart.

* * *

Lily wasn't certain how much time had elapsed since the blackguard drugged her that second time. However, this time she awoke hungry. Cold and hungry. No one had bothered to provide her a cloak or blanket for protection against the night's chill. The room was still dark, though rays of gray light appeared to stream in between the cracks of a shuttered window above her on the right.

Of course, it could be mere illusion. Her head was still in a foggy spin and she'd lost all sense of place and time. However, she hadn't forgotten that disembodied voice she'd heard earlier. It was Ashton's. He'd tried to disguise it, but she knew him too well to be fooled. She recalled what had struck her as odd in the garden. While she'd struggled and tried to scream, he'd just been standing there. He wasn't a victim. He was the mastermind behind her abduction. But why?

His actions didn't make any sense, but she wasn't going to sit quietly and wait to find out. She had to escape. Her hands were still tied to the chair. First order of business was to slip out of her bindings. How to do it was the problem.

She was good at solving problems.

As her eyes adjusted to the unrelenting dark, she began to make out shadows. Large squares that resembled crates were piled against one of the walls, but otherwise the room was bare of furniture save her chair and a small table underneath the window. The crates likely contained food supplies. She caught the slightly pungent scent of onions and the rank scent of raw meat. No wonder her stomach had been growling. Even stale bread would taste heavenly just now.

She also caught the scent of gunpowder, and realized some of those crates must contain weapons. Was she locked in an armory? She didn't think so, for the door appeared to be made of wood, not iron, and this store room was small. She didn't have much experience with gunpowder, but knew enough to understand the damage it would cause if it went off. She needed to get out of here. Fast.

As her eyes continued to adjust to her dark surroundings, she noticed something odd about the shuttered window. It was situated just beneath the ceiling, unusually high for any ordinary window. This store room was a cellar. That would explain the crates and the numbing cold. Likely the cellar in someone's house. Would the window have iron bars on it? There was no way to tell while it remained shuttered.

One problem at a time. She had to slip out of her bindings first. After that she'd worry about any iron bars. She'd find a way out, no matter the obstacles.

She wiggled her chair, trying to break its spindled back. If she broke it apart, her wrists might slip out of their bindings. She tried. It was too sturdy. She'd have to slam it against something hard to crack it apart. Her captors would hear and come running in. *That won't work.*

Were they stupid enough to leave tools lying about? She scanned the room again. Unfortunately, no. She looked for a sharp piece of metal or rock jutting out from the walls. Nothing.

Rubbing her bindings against the side of one of those wood crates might work, she decided. She managed to quietly move herself to the crates and began to run the taut ropes at her wrists up and down, then side to side, in a sawing motion. The scratch of the ropes against the crates sounded deafening to her ears, but logically she knew it wasn't. No one on the other side of the closed door would hear what she was doing unless they had the sensitive ears of a bat.

After what felt like an eternity, she managed to free one of her hands. It took another few moments to untie the other. Her arms were numb and she had nasty scrapes along both wrists. She tested her legs. Stiff and wobbling, but she was able to walk. She hurried to the table, climbed on it to reach the window, and quickly drew the shutters aside.

As she did so, a flash of lightning caught her by surprise and left stars blindly twinkling in her eyes long after its glow had faded. She didn't care. She'd made it this far without any light.

The rain started again, a heavy, pelting rain that worked in her favor to muffle any noise she was making. More luck, there were no bars on the window. She tried to push it open, but it wouldn't budge. She tried several times, pushing up, down, in and out. The blasted thing was sealed.

She'd have to break it.

She scooted off the table, found the chair, and quickly set up a simple fulcrum and lever system. Using her weight as leverage, she cracked the back of the chair and removed one of the sturdy spindles. Another burst of lightning. One, two, three, four. Then came the roll of thunder. She'd use the spindle to smash the glass pane. All she had to do was wait for the lightning's flare and strike at the thunder's roar.

Luck was on her side. The storm gained in intensity as it rolled over them, a fast-moving torrent that she feared could end within minutes. She didn't have any time to spare.

She timed the first strike perfectly.

And the next.

The glass cracked on the third strike. She cleared away as much of the jagged edges as she could, especially clearing the fragments stuck to the lower sash. The drenching rain and howling wind quickly washed most of the glass away from the opening. She heaved herself through the window, not caring that her gown was ripped, or that splinters dug into her hands, or that glass cut into her knees. She was cold and soaking wet. Her knees were scraped and bleeding. She was lost, had no idea in which direction to run.

She was free!

She breathed in the fresh outdoors, and then she ran for her life.

CHAPTER 16

THE VIOLENT WIND and rain slowed Ewan and his companions. The dirt roads were now flowing rivers of mud. Their horses were spooked by the distant rolls of thunder and sharp bolts of lightning, and Ewan wanted to shout his frustration each time they had to stop to calm the temperamental beasts. All were cold and soaking wet, and progress was achingly slow. It was as though the forces of nature were conspiring against them, but Ewan refused to give up hope. Each step, no matter how slow, drew them closer to Lily.

She was with Ashton in Maidstone, and held at Sparrow Hall.

Lord, help Lily if we're wrong.

The rain stopped as they reached the crest of a hill. Sprawled out before them was the town of Maidstone. Though a vibrant market town, it appeared eerily quiet just now. A gray mist covered the roads leading in, and the menacing, red dawn cast a disquieting hue over the houses, as though their roofs and walls were tinged with blood. Ewan wasn't superstitious by nature and refused to take it as a bad omen.

Any sailor knew that a red dawn breaking over the horizon meant more storms were on the way. While dangerous at sea, on land it was a nuisance. Nothing more. A cock crowed in the distance, signaling another problem. Damn. He'd hoped to reach Sparrow Hall under cover of darkness. "How are you holding up, Jasper?"

The loyal lump of a dog gave a weak *woof* in reply.

"Not far now," he assured, looking down into his trusting chocolate eyes. Jasper was used to romping and chasing sheep over the Highlands cliffs and dales for hours at a time, but this trek was a bit too much even for his boundless stamina.

Homer drew ahead to take the lead. "I know the area well, m'lord. My wife's family lives in these parts. Sparrow Hall is just beyond the next hill. A bleak place it is. I doubt any of its residents were ever happy there. Not surprised young Lord Mortimer," he said, referring to Ashton, "turned out as he did. There was always a darkness to this house. M'wife always thought so."

They rode over the hill and across a soggy meadow that ended at the edge of the woods. "We'd better leave our horses here, m'lord. Sparrow Hall is just on the other side of those trees. Unfortunately, they've cleared much of the grounds around the house, so any guards posted by the windows will see us once we reach the clearing."

Ewan nodded. "We'll have to create a diversion. Mr. Barrow, you and your runners must somehow distract them while George and I break into the house."

"Aye, m'lord. Leave it to us."

But as they approached, Ashton and his men suddenly ran out the front door as though the devil were on their tails. Ashton appeared furious, cursing at his men as he pointed in various directions. He shoved one of them toward the house. "What are they doing?" George whispered.

For the first time in what felt like a century, Ewan cracked a smile. "Searching for Lily. She's outsmarted them all. She's escaped." And he meant to find her before Ashton got his hands on her again. He turned to Homer. "Start your diversion. Jasper and I are going to track her down."

"With pleasure, m'lord. Don't ye worry, we'll round up these louts. Stay back, Dr. Farthingale. Wouldn't want you hurt. Those men are armed and dangerous, so it's best ye leave the dirty work to us."

As Homer created his diversion, Ewan took off at a run through the woods, Jasper lumbering at his heels. He heard shouts and gunshots behind him, but stopped as soon as he was moderately clear of the action to withdraw a pair of Lily's gloves from his breast pocket and hold them out to Jasper to sniff. "Find Lily." He hoped the torrential rain hadn't wiped away all trace of her.

Jasper let out a howl and began to lope straight toward the house. "Bollix," Ewan muttered, realizing his dog had picked up an old scent. Fortunately, Ashton's men were too busy fending off the Bow Street runners to pay the beast any heed. But where was Ashton? He'd slipped away.

Damn.

Now done sniffing the house, Jasper tore once again into the woods. Ewan raced after him, doing his best to keep up, following the sound of that large, lumbering body crashing through the underbrush whenever he lost sight of him. Jasper howled again. Ewan spotted him at the intersection of three small trails, spinning around as though chasing his own tail. *Damn it.* Jasper had lost her scent or might have caught it in too many directions.

Ewan reached for Lily's gloves again, and was about to kneel beside him when he heard the cock of a pistol. In the next moment, he heard Lily cry out from behind him. A simple "No!" from her lips at the same moment a shot rang out. He felt a fiery sting at his shoulder. Ignoring the sudden explosion of pain throughout his body, he whirled toward Lily. She was alive!

Ashton had her in his grasp, and now that his pistol was useless, he'd thrown it aside and was about to draw a knife to her throat. Ewan lunged at him, knocking Ashton and Lily to the ground. It couldn't be helped. The blackguard still held her. He managed to get between them, digging an elbow into Ashton's wrist so that he yelped in pain and released Lily. She quickly rolled away. At the same time, Ewan grabbed Ashton's other wrist and twisted it. "Drop the knife."

Ashton had a wild gleam in his eyes. "Bastard! She's mine! You can't have her. No one ever will." He fought with the madness of a wounded boar, but Ewan was stronger and barely able to contain his own mad rage. Ewan subdued him with relative ease, and then hauled him to his feet.

"I'll kill you," Ashton hissed at Lily, the venom in his voice startling Ewan. "You meant to ruin me, whispering your lies about me in the Duke of Lotheil's ear."

Lily struggled to her feet, hurt and confusion clearly reflected in her eyes. "I'd never do such a thing!"

Ewan supposed this was why he was so fond of her. She was generous and loving by nature, too innocent ever to feel malice, envy, or hatred toward anyone, even those who wished her ill.

"Ignore him, Lily. He's out of his mind." Ewan wanted to twist Ashton's arm until it broke, anything to shut up the bastard.

"That's right. Ignore me." Ashton let out a crazed laugh. "I'll still come after you. You're mine. You'll never make it out of Sparrow Hall alive."

Ewan silenced him with a punch to the jaw that knocked him out cold. "Guard him, Jasper."

Jasper crouched low and let out a soft, feral growl, ready to lunge at Ashton if he so much as batted an eyelid. The hairy lump had never obeyed so readily before, but he adored Lily and probably meant to show off to her.

With Ashton no longer a threat, Ewan turned to Lily. Was she hurt? How badly? He gazed into the beautiful blue depths of her eyes and saw fear and relief all muddled together. She was exhausted, had been crying. She was shivering. He shoved out of his jacket and wrapped it around her shoulders. "Och, lass. I've never been so glad to see anyone in all my life. It's over. Let's go home."

He swept her into his arms, and as a tidal wave of relief washed over him, he lowered his lips to hers in a long, desperate kiss. She was safe. She was alive! It was a hard, possessive kiss. A Highlander's kiss. Not at all gentle, but filled with ache and yearning. Not at all refined, just hot and roughly tender. His lips crushed against hers, teeth scraping and tongue delving into her soft, inviting mouth. Lord! He'd almost lost her.

She wrapped her arms around his neck and kissed him back just as fiercely. "I knew you'd find me. I never gave up hope." Then she completely fell apart, sobbing against his shoulder, her sweet, perfect body heaving and shuddering with a heart-wrenching ache that tore him to pieces. Tears cascaded down her cheeks, and though she tried to say more, she couldn't. Instead, she took in great gulps of air.

He held her close, kissed her again, gentle and messy, for Lily was crying and finally laughing, and he could taste her salty tears against his mouth. As much as he wished to hold on to this moment, he felt the *whoosh* of air around them, heard the light rain pattering against the leaves above them, and knew they had to get out of here. The trees would offer them some protection from the rain, but not for long. His boots sank into the moist underbrush that was already soaked from the earlier torrent. "Lily," he said gently, though there was nothing gentle about his feelings for this slip of a girl.

She smiled at him, waiting for him to say something more. Her lips were blue, and her nose and ears were red from cold. Despite the warmth of his body against hers, she was still shivering. Her dark hair was damp and curling wildly over her shoulders, the effect enhanced by the leaves and a few twigs caught amid the long strands. She looked spectacular. "Lass, you're a beautiful mess. And you've somehow turned my life upside down. I haven't had a quiet moment since you walked into my life."

She snuggled against his chest. "Oh, Ewan! I'm so sorry."

He kissed her on the forehead. "Don't be. Meeting you was the best thing that ever happened to me."

Jasper let out a howl, a long *wrooolf, wrooolf,* as though to proclaim that meeting Lily was the best thing to ever happen to him as well.

"Quiet, ye looby," Ewan said. "I know you love her. I—"

He stopped himself, realizing what he'd been about to say. Bollix. He couldn't tell her, not here with that insane bastard lying unconscious at his feet and Bow Street runners chasing down the other culprits who'd abducted her.

No, whatever he planned to say to Lily would have to wait. And hell, he wasn't sure what he would say to her. He'd figure it out once she was safely out of Ashton's reach.

"I had Ashton's report at home," Lily said, her voice heartbreakingly soft. "I would have given it to him, let him put his name on it. I was willing to give him all the credit. Why did he take me captive? What could he gain by it?"

The thought of Lily bound in chains for the rest of her life and forced to do Ashton's bidding made him ill. Writing science articles for that madman was the least of it. Lily was a beautiful girl. He refused to think of what else the bastard had planned for her. "I don't know, lass."

Though she was now huddled in his jacket, he doubted it was enough to keep her warm. He had to get her back to London as soon as possible, but she needed food and a change of clothes first. The air was an unappealing mix of cold and damp. He'd noticed a cozy inn about an hour's ride north of here, a good place to stop and allow Lily some time to rest. "The Bow Street men will question him when he awakens."

She nodded, and then her gaze fell upon the sleeve of his shirt. "Oh, Ewan! You're hurt."

He'd forgotten about the blood seeping down his arm, purposely ignored the burning pain. "It's just a flesh wound. I'm fine, lass. More important, you're safe, and I mean to keep you that way. I'll get you out of this bloody place as soon as I can."

"I'm not scared any more. Not with you beside me."

He let out a soft laugh. "I'm the one who should be thanking you. You came out of your hiding spot to save me, didn't you?"

She nodded. "He had the pistol aimed at your back. I didn't think about it, just shoved at him with all my might. He still struck you, though."

"As I said, a mere flesh wound. Thank you, lass. You saved my life."

She burrowed more deeply against him, rested her cheek against his chest. "As you saved mine. And I didn't even need my hat pin." Her fingers fumbled into the stained sash of her gown and drew out the long, thin metal for his inspection. "Look, it's right here."

"Hold on to it. You may still need it. I'm not sure if the Bow Street runners have secured his accomplices."

He needn't have worried. Homer and his men did their jobs, capturing all five accomplices, two of whom were shot and seriously injured. The other three were trussed up like Christmas geese about to be roasted over a fire. Homer had moved their prisoners into the house and George was working on the two wounded culprits as Ewan marched in. "Jasper's guarding Ashton. He's in the woods."

Mick, a burly man with a leathery face that reflected the wear and tear of a hard life, moved to the door. "I'll take care of that fancy cove."

For a moment, Ewan wasn't quite certain what Mick meant to do, but these were trained Bow Street runners and not heartless killers. "Here, take this rope," Homer said. "Tie him up like the others. We'll haul his dismal arse to London along with them other knaves. Don't want to be dealin' with no Maidstone magistrate beholden to the Mortimer family."

Ewan told Mick where to find him, silently praying that Jasper hadn't let the bastard slip away. The dog was a playful beast used to herding harmless sheep, not deranged blackguards.

George shot Lily a smile filled with relief.

Ewan could see that George wanted to drop his medical instruments and swallow his niece in his arms, but he had blood all over his hands and was still working on one of those injured men. "Lily, are you hurt?"

"No, Uncle George. I'm fine. Just a little cold and hungry, that's all."

He nodded. "Can you stand on your own?"

She wrapped her arms securely around Ewan's neck. "Yes, but I'm quite comfortable just where I am."

Ewan laughed. "Good, because I'm not putting you down until I have you safely back with your family."

And he didn't. He held her while Homer and Mick prepared to ride off with Ashton and his knaves, and while he made arrangements for George and Bert to remain behind with the injured men. Holding Lily felt so right, as though she'd become a part of him... as though something important would be missing in his life without her. The feeling went beyond mere physical pleasure, though her body perfectly molded to the planes of his body. It was as though they were two pieces of a puzzle perfectly fitting together to complete it.

Within hours, Homer would report to the Farthingale family and bring reinforcements to assist George and Bert with those injured men. Within hours, he'd be facing the Farthingale family as well. That left him little time to figure out what to do about Lily. She was a forever sort of girl. He wasn't thinking beyond the next two months. She felt perfect and right just now. Would he feel this way forever?

He gazed at Lily. Though she put on a brave face for her uncle, he knew she was still scared and shivering, not to mention exhausted and hungry. She'd never make it to London in her present state even if the weather turned warm and sunny, which it wasn't going to if the red sky at dawn was any indication. Noticing her frown, he told Lily of the inn they'd passed about an hour's ride north of Maidstone.

"A hot meal, warm bath, and a few hours' rest? Sounds heavenly." She let out a breathy sigh that lit him up like a furnace.

He'd be alone with her at the inn. A stupid, dangerous idea. Anything could happen. Something *would* happen, because she was a lit match to his tinder. She set him on fire with a mere glance. She was doing it right now, looking fragile and beautiful, swallowed up in his jacket and her small hand still gripping the hat pin. "Ewan, there's something I must show you before we leave this awful place." Her lips were pursed and her brow adorably furrowed in the way it furrowed whenever she concentrated her attention on something complicated. Never him. He wasn't that complicated for her.

She was one hell of a complication for him.

Reluctantly, he set her down and followed her to the cellar, but made certain to keep hold of her. She was still weak and wobbling on her feet. That he wanted to touch her, *needed* to touch her was of no moment. He was thinking only of her. Not of his damn male urges.

She pointed to a row of crates stacked along one of the cellar walls. "Some of these are filled with gunpowder. What use would Ashton have for such a large store?"

"I don't know." He opened a few of them and let out a long, low whistle. "There's enough powder here to level an entire building."

"Look, there are numbers stamped on each crate. Four, five, six, seven." Her lips pursed again.

"What's troubling you, lass?"

She looked up to meet his gaze. "Where are crates one, two, and three?"

* * *

Ewan wasn't going to think about anything other than getting Lily safely home. After that, he'd deal with the crates of gunpowder. Likely they'd been stolen from a local armory. Those numbered one, two, and three were probably still there, safely under lock and key. "I'll ask Edgeware to investigate the matter once we're back in London. This is the sort of inquiry best left to his discreet efficiency."

"I suppose. Even if Ashton did steal them, he's safely in Mr. Barrow's custody and unable to cause more mischief."

Ewan could see the matter still troubled her despite his assurances that it would be resolved. That's how Lily's brain worked, noticing problems and dwelling on them until she'd worked them out. Not just small problems, but the great unknowns of life. Had she always been this way? Even as a little girl? Would their children be just like Lily?

He took a deep breath. Bloody hell. Marriage and children. He wasn't ready for any of it. Were all dominant male baboons this cowardly? Did baboons think this hard about commitment and procreation? Or did the dominant male just stick his pole wherever he found an opening, giving no thought to the consequences?

He led Lily back upstairs. As he closed the cellar door behind them, Jasper came bounding down the hall, heading straight for Lily in a great, furry ball of excitement, his tongue hanging out of the side of his mouth and tail wagging furiously. Having been relieved of guarding Ashton, the dog's first thought was to find Lily. Not that Ewan blamed him. Lily had a way of getting into one's heart... or under one's fur, in Jasper's case.

Lily let out a squeal of delight and knelt down to greet him. She gave him a fierce hug, burying herself in his damp fur. "My hero! I knew you'd find me. I never doubted for a moment."

"*Wrooolf! Wrawooolf!*"

"Oh, you missed me?" She scratched Jasper behind the ears, and he went from mere dog happiness to dog-in-ecstasy happy. "You were worried about me? Worried that the bad man would hurt me before you reached me? What a good, brave dog!"

Ewan was jealous. Pathetic. Jealous of his own, damn dog. But Lily's hands were all over that furry beast, her breasts pressed against his thick coat, and all Ewan could think of was having Lily's hands all over him, and having his hands all over Lily's breasts. Right. He wasn't complicated.

He wanted Lily.

*　*　*

The two of them left Sparrow Hall the moment George finished patching up his shoulder. The damage turned out to be a flesh wound after all, the bullet merely grazing him so there was nothing to dig out. Within the rain-drenched hour, they reached the inn he'd noticed on his way to Maidstone. It looked cozier and more charming by daylight, or what passed for daylight amid the gloom of rain and black, rolling thunderclouds. The innkeeper ran out to greet them, fussing over them as they hurried inside. "We ran into a little trouble," Ewan said, not quite a lie. "I'm Lord Carnach."

"We're honored to have ye with us, m'lord. Look at ye, all cold and wet. I've got a fire started. Come into the parlor and keep yerselves warm while the maids ready yer chamber. Ye'll have our finest."

"We'll be needing food. And a hot bath for—"

"Aye, poor dear. We'll take good care of yer lovely wife." The innkeeper glanced at Lily, who had her chin up and was doing her best to smile, but her lips were blue and she was noticeably shivering. She had dark circles under her eyes which she had trouble keeping open because she was so obviously exhausted.

Had she heard the innkeeper refer to her as his wife?

Probably not, he decided when she made no move to correct his mistake. All the better. He had no intention of leaving her side, not even for a moment. He carried Lily into the parlor. Jasper settled himself beside the hearth and immediately fell asleep. Ewan didn't have the heart to wake him. He ordered water and a juicy bone for him to chew on once the big lump awoke. That would keep him content for a while. He also arranged for a messenger to deliver a note to Lily's father assuring him of Lily's safety and telling him where they were. Lily was in desperate shape. She needed food, warmth, and sleep. A few hours delay in reaching London wouldn't matter.

The creak of floorboards overhead meant the inn was coming to life. The other guests were beginning to stir, and Ewan didn't want Lily seen. Fortunately, their room was quickly made ready, and he and Lily were settled in before any prying eyes fell upon them. Within moments, the efficient staff had delivered warm bread, jam, tea, additional blankets, a lavender soap, and a tub that they quickly filled with buckets of heated water.

One of the maids asked if she should stay to assist Lily. Ewan was about to accept the offer when Lily shot him a desperate glance. "No, my husband will take care of me."

He thanked the maid, dismissed her, and latched the door before turning to Lily, his body once again on fire at the thought of what would come next. Lily had heard his exchange with the innkeeper after all. Did she understand the import of her words? They'd be alone while she stripped out of her clothes, while she stepped naked into the tub and rubbed soap all over her soft, silken body. He let out a tortured groan. "I'll turn my back while you undress and get into the tub."

She nodded, but didn't move.

"Lass, do you want me to leave the room?"

"No," she said in a ragged whisper. "I need you, Ewan. Right here, with me. I feel safe when I'm with you."

But not safe *from* him. She stirred his blood. She roused his hunger. He wanted to feel her skin against his palms, taste her against his mouth. He turned away. This was a bad idea. He was no gentleman. Lily was every inch a lady. "Lass, I should go."

"Ewan, my hands are shaking. I can't feel my fingers. I can't undress myself. You'll have to do it for me. You don't have to close your eyes. I don't wish to hide anything from you." He heard her sniffle. More tears? "I thought I was going to die in that cellar... or worse, that those men would do something so horrible to me that I'd wish to die."

He turned to face her. In two strides, he had her in his arms. "Come, sweetheart. No nasty thoughts. I'm here for you. I'll take care of you." He held her until her tears subsided, dying a little inside each time she gazed at him with a lingering fear in her eyes. Not of him. It was fear from her ordeal.

When she'd calmed a little, he helped her out of her damp gown. The silk slid softly down her body as she stepped out of it.

He knelt beside her and rolled the stockings off her legs. First the right, then the left, all the while his fingers on her skin. A very bad idea. It took all his control to keep from sliding his hands between her shapely thighs and claiming her with his mouth. All that now stood between him and her naked body was a thin camisole. She didn't stop him as he slipped it off her slender frame.

He understood how she felt, knew what she was feeling. It was as though no one else existed in the world but the two of them. Not two strangers thrown together by circumstance. They were two missing parts of a whole, meant for each other. Unable to exist without each other. "Lily, lass." His voice was a raw, raspy whisper. "You're so beautiful."

"So are you, Ewan." She moved out of his arms. He heard the gentle lap of water as she eased into the tub. "Oh, the soap is on the table."

She was killing him. He let out a ragged breath. "I'll get it for you."

He tried not to look at her naked body. Failed miserably. Couldn't take his eyes off her. He handed her the soap. Still looking at her. Eyeballs practically pasted to her breasts. She didn't reach for the soap. "Will you help me, Ewan?"

She was killing him slowly and painfully. "If you wish."

"I do." She lifted her long, dark curls off her pale, white shoulders. "I like the way you look at me."

Your father won't.

He rolled up his sleeves and slowly began to rub the soap over her hands. Waited for her to take it from him and ask him to turn away. She didn't. She wasn't going to. He was her missing half. He rubbed the soap up her arms. He lathered her shoulders. Lathered her breasts. Was very thorough with her breasts. He cupped one in his hand and slowly slid his thumb across its taut nipple. Lily let out a soft gasp. "Do that again."

He did, this time with his tongue.

"*Crumpets!* I had no idea it could ever be like this." She demanded more, closing her eyes and allowing him access to every inch of her beautiful, pink body, driving him over the edge with her breathy moans and innocence. He lathered her everywhere, rinsed her off, and lathered her again. He licked and tasted, ate about half of that soap lather because men were stupid that way, never stopping to think about anything but sex, and a hot, lavender-scented Lily tasted better than anything he'd ever tasted in his entire life.

He dropped the soap and dipped his finger between the junction of her thighs. "Ewan!" She arched her back and gazed at him in wondrous confusion. He kissed her, parting her lips with his tongue and gently plundering her warm, inviting mouth as his finger plundered her nether lips, gently stroking her swollen essence, encouraging her to move against the pressure, and watching her beautiful face, the graceful arch of her body, the glorious peak of her nipples as her body exploded in pleasure. She clung to his shoulders, called his name in achingly sweet ecstasy. "Ewan. *Ewan.*"

When she'd calmed, she was his Lily again, the beautiful bluestocking with trusting blue eyes and a smile as bright as sunshine. "I never knew baths could be quite so... interesting."

He grinned despite the rock-hard pain between his thighs. "Are you hungry?"

She nodded, her smile so sweet and radiant, he wanted to swallow her up in his arms, haul her to the large, neatly made up bed, and bury himself inside of her again and again, as often as possible before his heart gave out from the intense excitement of repeated ecstasy. Death by sexual frenzy. He wondered how many male baboons died that way.

Lily licked her lips. "In truth, I'm famished. But also curious."

When was she not?

"Do you know any interesting sexual tricks with food?"

He hauled her out of the tub, grabbed a cloth to dry off her perfect, pink body, wrapped the large cloth around her, and carried her to the small table where the maid had set out their food. He kicked out the stool beside it. "Sit down and eat while I wash up. No damn tricks with food."

She looked disappointed.

He set her on the stool more urgently than intended and took a step back. He wasn't merely hot and hard. He was on fire and about to erupt with the force of a volcano. "Lily—"

"Before you lecture me about what we should and should not be doing, I want you to know that I liked it."

"I know, lass. I liked watching you." His throat constricted, an effect of the heat radiating from his loins. "But I'm not made of stone."

She glanced at the hard, throbbing bulge of his groin against his trousers.

"I don't despoil virgins. We've already crossed the line."

"What line?"

"Any line. Though we needed to stop at this inn for your sake, I ought to have taken another room. I shouldn't be in here. With you."

She reached out and took his hand. "Ewan, I'm glad you're with me. Here. Now. I was scared and frantic a few hours ago, and now I feel as though I'm in heaven. You make me feel this way. The whole time I was at Sparrow Hall, I thought of you. I knew you'd come for me, and that knowledge kept me sane and breathing. I loved the touch of your hands on my body as I bathed, the hungry warmth of your lips on mine. You washed away the stench of my ordeal."

"Och, Lily—"

"Ewan, I love you."

His heart shot into his throat. Lord, those words. Simple words. *I love you.* They felt so right and natural, and all the more wonderful because they came from Lily. "You're overwhelmed right now, lass. You only think you do because you believe I saved you. I didn't. You had already escaped on your own."

"You did save me. I wouldn't have made it very far on my own. I know the difference between love and gratitude. I love you. I've felt this way for quite some time."

"We've only known each other a month."

"I know. But these feelings I have for you seem eternal. They're powerful and deep, as though existing since the beginning of time. I don't know how else to explain it." She cast him a poignantly hesitant smile. "They're not always good feelings. When I saw you with Callie—"

"She means nothing to me. Not anymore."

"But she did once," she said quietly. "I'd never experienced jealousy before. It's such an ugly sensation. I didn't want her to have you. I wanted you all to myself, no sharing with anyone else. My feelings were little different from what Ashton screamed out. *You're mine. No one else will ever have you.* Of course, I know that you're free to choose whomever you wish to love. I would never have acted upon my feelings as he did, not in that ugly way."

Her lips began to tremble and tears welled in her eyes. "I'll always love you, Ewan. No matter what happens once we're back in London. I know you'll leave soon. I may never see you again. I wanted this precious time with you. I wanted your hands on my body and your lips on mine... I wanted the magical experience that my married sisters told me about. I want all of it. Now. With you. I can't imagine it being magical with anyone else."

Her words were like arrows shot straight through his heart. She loved him, or so she thought. Lily knew books. She didn't know life. He'd taken advantage. He'd told the innkeeper she was his wife. Had Lily mistaken it as a declaration of his love? He was a miserable cur. "Lass, get some rest. We'll speak of it later."

She shook her head and frowned. "Oh, I see. You feel responsible for me. You think I don't know my own mind and will regret it later. You think I'll blame you and expect you to protect me from my own mistakes. You mustn't feel any obligation on your part. None whatsoever." A tear slid down her cheek.

Thwack! Not just an arrow through his heart. A damned harpoon. The sort that brought down whales. "Those are your terms? I'm to show you a good time without facing any of the consequences?"

She nodded.

He wasn't a London gentleman, but Highlanders had their rules of honor. She was his, whether or not she realized it yet. He'd sealed their fates the moment he'd called her his wife and asked for a single room. He'd said it out of a need to protect her. He'd said it because he couldn't bear to have her out of his sight. The damn, rotten thing about it was that calling her his wife had felt great. Felt right. He'd talk to her father. No question about it, they'd have to set a wedding date. "We have a deal."

"We do?" She didn't seem quite so sure of herself now.

"But I'm adding one requirement to this arrangement. You can say no at any time and I'll back off. *At any time, Lily.* You're safe with me. I'm not taking you against your will." He wanted her now, was on-hands-and-knees-begging desperate to have her. But he'd wait until their wedding night if he had to. He wanted to make Lily happy. Seeing her shed tears of regret would kill him.

She pursed her lips, obviously contemplating his proposal as though negotiating a contract. The girl couldn't see the forest for the trees. She didn't realize that he was negotiating for her heart. "Seems only fair to agree to reciprocal terms, Ewan. You can say no as well and I'll stop whatever it is I'm supposed to stop."

He let out a groaning laugh. "No, lass. I'll no' wish to stop." He knelt beside her to caress her cheek. "It's you who must be free of doubts."

She leaned forward, her damp hair spilling over her shoulders in glorious disarray, and kissed him lightly on the mouth. She drew back smiling. "I'm sure. You're giving this far too much thought. I suppose it's what makes human males different from baboon males. When the male baboon feels the urge, he relieves it. Did you know that female baboons have their own tricks to attract a male and heighten his pleasure?"

He gulped. "No, Lily. I didn't."

"If you ever get me into that big, comfortable-looking bed, I'll show you."

CHAPTER 17

LILY DIDN'T KNOW how to make it any clearer to Ewan that she wanted him, wanted his arms around her, his lips on her mouth and breasts and any other place on her body he thought appropriate... or highly inappropriate. She'd leave this business of lovemaking to him since he seemed to know what he was about. She liked what he'd done to her in the tub.

She swallowed hard, recalling the heat of his tongue teasing her nipple, and the sudden, hot rush of sensation caused her to almost choke on her biscuit. *Cough! Gag!* And if that wasn't humiliating enough, she topped it off with a sneeze. Well, that was attractive.

Ewan turned to her, his expression worried at first, and then he realized what she'd done. He laughed, still watching her as he stripped out of his clothes. *Blessed saints and burnt crumpets.* It wasn't just that he was stripping out of them, but the manly, Highlander way he grabbed his shirt and raised it up and over his broad shoulders, the way his tall, lean body flexed and strained to accentuate his rock-hard muscles. Goodness, the man had muscles.

If she were the sort of girl to swoon, she'd be sprawled on the floor in a faint, spittle drooling from the corner of her mouth.

He strode to the fireplace and set his shirt beside her damp clothes. His back was to her, allowing her to study him as long as she wished. The lively fire cast a delicious glow across his lightly bronzed skin, the delicate firelight washing over his back as he bent to remove his boots. Handsome didn't begin to describe Ewan.

The bandage wrapped over his shoulder enhanced his good looks. There was something strong and primal about men with wounds. It would make for interesting research.

He glanced at her as he began to unbutton his trousers, and then stopped. Grinning, he shook his head. "I'd better keep these on for now."

"Why?"

"Because you're looking at me as though I'm a laboratory specimen and you can't wait to dissect me."

She blushed. "There's nothing wrong with curiosity. You were staring me quite avidly a few moments ago. Do you dare deny it?"

He shook his head and let out a soft chuckle. "Nay, lass. Finish your tea. Have another biscuit. Try not to choke on it." He glanced at the large four-poster. "Once I have you in that bed, I'm not letting you out of it for a good, long while." He came to her side and set his hands on each side of her body. Still grinning that sexy, dangerous grin of his, he leaned forward and gave her a possessively tender kiss that curled her toes. Then his dangerous grin faded and his eyes turned to hot, green embers. *Crumpets!* She was going to miss him when he returned to Scotland.

He left her side to wash away the dirt and sweat of the night's ride. He rubbed the lavender soap over his chest, shoulders, and hair, and then rinsed himself off in that carelessly manly way, allowing the water to slowly stream in droplets down his neck and across his broad chest. The droplets gleamed against the firelight, and all Lily could think of as they glistened against his bronzed skin was that being alone in a cozy inn with a hot, wet, almost naked Ewan beside her was the best thing on earth. Even better than membership in the Royal Society.

He returned to her side with the look of promise in his eyes and lifted her into his arms. He smelled of lavender and clean, male heat.

"Finally," she whispered, circling her arms around his neck. His hair was damp and curling at his nape. Then she was on the bed, naked and curling her fingers in his damp hair as he settled over her, his big body covering hers and his mouth slanted across hers in a kiss that put sparkles in her eyes. Not that she could see her eyes, but the sparkles were there. Shining as bright as diamonds.

His gaze locked on hers as he unbuttoned his trousers and slipped them off to reveal his long, muscled legs. Lily's eyes widened at the sight of his male hardness. She wanted to reach out and touch him, but he had a glint in his eye that warned he wasn't quite under control, and she decided not to test him. She wasn't certain of the consequences.

Then all further thought flew out of her head, for he was atop her again, his long, lean body pressing her down against the mattress, the exquisitely intimate weight of him so arousing against her skin. He eased her thighs apart and shifted himself between them. "My fair Lily," he whispered, lowering his mouth to hers and kissing her with a tenderness that stole her breath away. Then his lips moved lower... down the arch of her throat, to her breast. His tongue began to work its magic, flicking across her engorged nipple. She groaned, felt a hot pulse at the junction of her thighs, and almost shot off the bed as he moved lower. He closed his mouth over that hot pulse, teasing and licking the swollen nub between her thighs, evoking sensations she'd never dreamed possible.

She felt herself floating upward to the stars, lifted so high she could touch the silvery ball of the moon. And floating higher, beyond the moon and stars. Her heart thudded to a rampant beat. Her skin felt hot. She was mindless. She was a coiled ball of heat about to explode. Then it happened, that same magical sensation she'd experienced in the tub, but this time the wave of ecstasy was even stronger, like a shower of meteors striking the ground, sending shocks and ripples through her body, exquisitely hot and pulsing, exquisitely and endlessly magical.

"Lily, what you do to me," he whispered, shifting himself upward so that his erect member was now between her thighs, poised and throbbing. Then he slid inside her, filling her, gently thrusting in and out, his body taut as he struggled not to hurt her. He guided her legs so that they wrapped around his hips, murmuring his pleasure as her hands caressed his skin. He watched her even as he lost control. She knew the moment he'd crossed into mindless instinct, for his eyes turned dark with molten desire. But even then, there was a gentleness in the way he held her, the way he looked at her. He'd never hurt her. That need to protect her was so much a part of who he was and why she loved him.

As he moved inside her, her body became a liquid pool of heat, steaming and bubbling, eager to take him in. All of him. He thrust into her intimate depths, taking her with him as though they were one. He kissed her throat, her lips, called her name in that deep, moaning brogue of his that ignited another shower of meteors within her body. His thrusts became urgent, and his body suddenly tensed.

He grunted her name. *"Lily. Lily!"* And groaned as meteoric explosions took place within his own body, his powerful muscles rippling and straining, his cry ecstatic as his male essence spilled into her, marking her forever as his. She was his. Heart, body, and soul. *Ewan, please be mine too.*

After several climactic shudders, he collapsed atop her, his skin hot and glistening, his breaths deep and groaning. She reveled in the weight of him, still connected to him for he hadn't pulled out of her yet. She felt a twinge of disappointment when he did ease out of her, but he didn't let her go. Instead, he shifted their positions in one easy motion so that she lay atop him, wrapped in his protective arms. She made no protest. After all, he couldn't stay inside her forever. This was nice, too.

He cast her a smug, supremely satisfied smile.

She grinned back at him. "Well, what did you think?"

He caressed her cheek. "Not bad for a beginner."

"That's all? Oh," she said, suddenly feeling disappointed. He'd had her so hot and mindless she'd forgotten about using that female baboon trick to arouse him. In truth, he hadn't seemed to need it.

He laughed and drew her closer for a quick, tender kiss. "No, sweetheart. You were brilliant. Spectacular. You were Lily. My fair Lily. Innocent and trusting and honest. I've never felt more content with anyone than with you at this moment." Then he turned serious. "Lily, I understand the consequences of what we've just done. Do you?"

She frowned lightly. "I assured you that I wouldn't hold you responsible."

"And what if you find you're with child? My child." He let out a heavy breath. "Lass, I'm willing to take responsibility. I wouldn't have touched you if I weren't. Your family will demand it of me, perhaps not immediately, but once the joy of your safe return wears off, they'll realize you and I spent the morning here, just the two of us alone in this chamber. They'll expect me to marry you."

She paled. "Did you seduce me on purpose, Ewan? Out of a misguided sense of duty to protect me?" She shoved off him and tried to draw away, but he wouldn't allow her off the bed. He held her in the circle of his arms and turned her to face him, but she spoke first. "Is that all I am to you? Some baboon female to take into your colony, an attractive vessel upon which to breed your offspring?"

She rolled to her knees and glowered at him, hurt and aching for the words she realized he never meant to say to her. "Why mark me as your mate?" And he had marked her, spilling his seed into her and leaving his scent upon her to warn all other males away.

"Bollix, lass. We're not baboons. I've asked you to marry me."

"That's the problem. You haven't. You've given me excuses why you'll reluctantly sacrifice your freedom. I don't need your noble sacrifice. I can take care of myself." She tried to hold back her tears, but felt them welling in her eyes despite her determination to stay strong. *Crumpets!* What had she just done?

What if she were with child? She wasn't worried about the consequences to herself. In truth, there would be none. She was wealthy in her own right, or would be in a few years when she came of age. Unlike Ewan, she had a loving and loyal family. They'd never shun her or cast her out. However, the consequences to the child would be devastating.

"Lass, you're overset by all that's happened. We'll discuss it once you're well rested." Then his voice gentled. "We belong together. We fit right together. You're not forcing me to do anything I don't wish to do."

Did that mean he loved her? If so, why didn't he just say it? Or were all men incapable of admitting their feelings? Her sisters often joked about it, but she'd never believed they were serious. Perhaps Ewan was right. She'd sleep on it and hope the answers would be obvious once her head was clear.

"Come under the covers, Lily." He waited for her reluctant nod, and then drew her against his warm body, spooning her so that her back was to his chest. His arms closed around her, and he drew her legs between his, enveloping her in his heat. She didn't feel trapped, for he held her loosely, as though wanting her to understand how it would always be between them... together because they wanted to be together, not because one had forced the other.

He brushed her hair back gently, the gentle caress of his fingers wonderful against her skin. This felt perfect. Almost perfect.

He didn't love her.

* * *

Ewan awoke several hours later, for a moment forgetting he was wrapped around Lily's luscious body. He caught himself in time and carefully slipped his arm out from under her, hoping the movement wouldn't wake her, but she was exhausted and sleeping so deeply, he doubted anything, not even the blast of a foghorn, would rouse a response from her.

He studied her as she slept, watched the gentle rise and fall of her breasts with each soft breath. Lord, she was beautiful. Sweet and angelic.

He ran his fingers along her skin, relieved to find her warm. Her hair had dried and the dark, silky strands were now splayed across the white pillows and her pink shoulders in glorious disarray. He bent to kiss her cheek, inhaled the sweet scent of lavender that lingered on her body.

I'm a monumental ass.

Lily loved him. She had told him so in every way possible. Her actions, her words. Her honest heart. Why couldn't he tell her how he felt? Showing her had been easy, but saying the words aloud, revealing how completely she'd conquered his heart, was a frightening proposition for a man so used to being in control.

He rolled from the bed, made sure Lily stayed warm by tucking the covers around her, and crossed to the fireplace. He felt cold air on his skin. The fire was low and about to die out, so he added several more logs and watched as they took flame. He didn't want Lily to be cold when she rose.

He'd earlier laid out their clothes beside the hearth and now checked to see if they were dry. His shirt and trousers were. Lily's gown was still damp, but her sister had packed a fresh one for her. He drew it out of his pouch, annoyed with himself for not thinking to take it out earlier. Fortunately, Dillie had packed it carefully and he easily smoothed out the few wrinkles.

He set the gown across the back of a chair and did the same with the other items Dillie had supplied, the simple chore feeling intimate and *right*. Everything he did with Lily felt perfect. "You're definitely an ass," he muttered to himself. Three simple words. *I love you.* Lily deserved no less from him.

He quickly dressed and donned his boots, and then went downstairs to wait for the chaotic mob that was Lily's family to arrive. He didn't have long to wait. He was still nursing his coffee, Jasper still sound asleep and sprawled beside him, when the Farthingale carriage drew up.

Jasper's ears perked. He scrambled on all fours and let out a cheerful *woof*. "Right. Fun's about to start." The abduction would be quickly forgotten once the Farthingales realized he and Lily had shared that bedchamber.

Lily's father and sister sprang out of the carriage and hurried in. They weren't alone. Riding alongside the conveyance were Lily's three brothers-in-law. "Bollix," Ewan muttered under his breath, realizing he couldn't take them all on. They were too big. Too strong. Perhaps not as strong as he was, but too strong to take on all at once. They'd pound the stuffing out of him. They'd do worse once they found out what he'd done to Lily.

"Ewan!" Dillie threw herself into his arms and began to tearfully babble. "I prayed you'd find her. Is she hurt? Where is she? I must see her. What happened? Tell me everything. But take me to Lily first. Father's been frantic. So have I. So have we all."

He gave her a quick hug in response. "She's well. She's resting. I know you want to see her, but it's best if she comes down here on her own. One of the maids will wake her."

He quickly fetched the innkeeper, ordering not only the maid to rouse Lily but also ordering refreshments to be brought into one of the private salons. "We can talk in there," he said, leading the Farthingales and the brothers-in-law into the salon, praying that none of them had overheard the innkeeper refer to Lily as his wife. Otherwise, he'd be carved into little pieces before he drew his next breath.

John Farthingale approached, his face pale and haggard. "I can't thank you enough for all you've done. We're eternally in your debt."

"No, sir. Don't be. All I did was notice she was gone." *Then I found her and ruined her. No thanks necessary.*

The private room was cozy, furnished with an oak table finer than those in the common hall, several long benches, and several large chairs. The innkeeper started a fire in the hearth, and then closed the door behind him as he left. Ewan drew out a chair for Dillie and motioned for the others to take a seat. He quickly told them all that had happened, mentioning Lily's escape and how she'd managed it on her own. He knew that would somehow give her father and sister comfort. This was their beloved Lily. Brave, clever, able to outwit a gang of very nasty men.

He'd just finished his story when the door slammed open and Lily flew into the room. Without so much as a glance at Ewan, she threw herself in the arms of her father, then Dillie. Then all three of them were hugging and laughing and crying.

"Lily, my sweet angel! Your mother and I were frantic with worry, but it's over. You're safe. You're—" His joy and relief obviously overwhelming, he began to sob.

"It feels so good to be in your arms," Lily said, now the one to comfort her father. "And yours too, Dillie! I missed you all. I never want to be parted from you again!"

Dillie hugged her fiercely. "Same here. I promise never to complain about sharing a room with you, or having to put up with your abominable harp playing, or those odd scientific objects you're constantly sneaking into our room."

Lily laughed. "I won't hold you to that promise. I want us back to normal as fast as possible."

"So do we," Graelem Dayne said.

Ewan glanced at the brawny brothers-in-law, all of them the sort he would not like to meet in a dark alley. Their eyes were moist as well.

Then Lily took a moment to look at him, one brief, open-hearted glance before returning her attention to her father and sister. Graelem stepped forward and clamped a hand on his shoulder. Big hand. Painful on his shoulder. His good shoulder. He would have been on his knees in agony had he touched the injured one. Gabriel and Julian took positions on each side of him. *Bollix.* They knew.

How? Lily had barely looked at him. "I've already asked her to marry me." Not that they deserved an explanation, but he had asked her, and it seemed pointless—and would be needlessly painful—to allow them to think otherwise.

Graelem lightened his grip. Still strong. "It'll be a quick wedding."

Ewan sighed. "I've asked Lily, but she hasn't given me an answer yet. She isn't keen to be parted from her family, as you've just heard her say. I'm not sure she'll accept." In truth, he hadn't considered that she might decline his offer. She loved him. She'd told him so in a delightfully breathy way.

Graelem scowled at him. "She had better accept."

"Are you threatening me or her? Because if you set a hand on Lily, I'll cut out your heart and stuff it—"

He was stopped short by Gabriel's groaning laugh. "Let him go, Graelem. He isn't the problem. She is. Daisy will speak to her, find out what she really wants."

Julian nodded. "They'll all speak to her. I'll ask Rose to call one of their sisters meetings and talk it out." He slapped Ewan on the shoulder, and though his smile was amiable, his next words were not. "You'd better hope she accepts your proposal. We'll have to cut out *your* heart if she doesn't."

Ewan nodded.

He'd done the deed. He was willing to face the consequences. Did she wish to remain with her family? Or return to the Highlands with him? He'd heard her heartfelt words to her father a few moments ago. *I never want to be parted from you again.*

A sick feeling rose in Ewan's gut.

Was he going to lose Lily?

CHAPTER 18

"LILY, ARE YOU CERTAIN?" her sister asked once they were safely back home and her mother assured that she had not been harmed. The gentle warmth of her mother's embrace, soon followed by her usual fluttering and fussing, lightened Lily's heart. While her mother had gone off in her usual dither to order tea and Lily's favorite lemon cake, she and Dillie had returned to the bed-chamber they'd shared for most of their lives. "We can beg out of tonight's recital."

Lily flopped onto her bed, wishing her arms were large enough to embrace their entire townhouse and all its inhabitants, even all the inhabitants of Chipping Way, her favorite street in all of London. Not only was it beautifully quaint, but their neighbors were generous and charming. Lady Eloise Dayne had been a wonderful friend to all the Farthingales ever since they'd moved here. Even General Allworthy had been kind to them in his own curmudgeonly way. "No, it's important that you and I appear together, Dillie. You heard what Mother said about the rumors circulating."

Dillie frowned. "That you'd eloped with Ashton! I know who started that ugly rumor, and mark my words, if Corky MacCorkstopper dares to rear her ugly head at Lady Finchley's recital, I'll knock it clean off her shoulders."

Lily couldn't help but laugh. "You needn't do anything so drastic. I'll appear, play my harp abominably, and that's the best way to halt the rumor." As their moment of merriment died down, she yawned.

Dillie sat on the bed beside her. "I'm so thoughtless! You must be exhausted and I'm keeping you up with needless chatter. Here, let me tuck you in. Do you need anything? Other than for me to stop talking and leave you alone to rest?"

Lily laughed. "Just a hug. And if you dare tell anyone I asked it of you, I'll deny it and accuse you of being a fiend. Everyone knows you're the evil twin, anyway."

Her sister did as asked. "I love you. My heart ripped in half when I thought you were lost to us. It was as though the most important part of me was suddenly gone. And if you dare tell anyone I said this, I'll deny it and accuse *you* of being a fiend."

"You're the best sister ever."

Dillie rolled her eyes. "It's about time you figured that out." But after a moment, she sobered. "Ewan was so worried about you. If he hadn't noticed your disappearance when he did, who knows what might have happened? He tried to play down the importance of his rescue, but I know he would have followed you into the bowels of hell to get you back. I think he's fallen in love with you. Did he say anything to you at the inn?"

Lily felt the jolt of heat to her cheeks, and turned her face toward her pillow to hide her blush. "He didn't say he loved me."

"Well, his actions showed it."

He'd made love to her. Not said he loved her. Then he'd puffed out his chest and said he'd marry her, as though he were doing her a favor. She didn't need anything from him. Not his delicious kisses. Not his strong, protective arms to hold her. Not his dangerous smile to melt her heart. "Dillie, we'll talk about it later." She rolled away and buried herself in the comfort of her covers.

Her sister sighed. "Of course. I'll wake you in time for the recital."

* * *

Ewan reached Lotheil Court in the late afternoon, his body sore and his heart aching. He'd settled Lily in the Farthingale carriage and stuffed Jasper beside her for the ride back to London earlier this morning. The hairy beastie, delighted to ride in comfort, had rested his head on Lily's lap and promptly gone back to sleep. Lily's father and sister had been forced to share the seats opposite Lily and the big lump beside her. "We'll take care of Jasper," Dillie promised, though Ewan hadn't been worried about him. Lily was his concern. "The children will love him. He'll be in good hands until you return."

After seeing them off, he'd led her brothers-in-law to the Mortimer residence in Maidstone, left them under George Farthingale's capable direction, and then returned to London on his own. Hades made swift time, and he was glad of it. He needed sleep. He needed time to think about Lily... not that she was ever *off* his mind. He needed to court her, somehow convince her that he truly loved her.

His grandfather was waiting for him when he strode into the house. "How is the girl?"

"I don't know who you mean." How much did his grandfather know of Lily's disappearance?

"Edgeware told me all that's happened. In confidence, of course. You can count on me to keep it to myself. I'm asking after Lily Farthingale. How is she?" The old man appeared tired, and looked somehow different, as though beaten down by life.

"She's fine."

"Truly? Ewan, I must know."

"She's perfect." And he was an idiot for not telling her so.

"No thanks to me," his grandfather said with an ache Ewan never expected to hear. "Come into my study. There's something I must tell you."

He meant to decline, but he had never seen his grandfather so openly distraught. He followed him in as requested, hesitating a moment when the old man gestured toward the two oversized chairs beside the fireplace. Ordinarily, Ewan would have remained standing like a proud, stubborn Scot and probably tossed an insulting comment at the old man. It was time he behaved himself as his father would have wished. He settled into one of the chairs without protest. His grandfather settled into the other and slowly rubbed a hand across his aged brow and let out a heavy sigh. "Ewan, I'm to blame for what happened to the girl."

He leaned forward, his body tense. "How?"

"She's been a thorn in the Royal Society's side for years now. We all knew she'd been working on that baboon monograph of hers, comparing us to a colony of monkeys. We're scholars, men of science, and considered it thoroughly insulting. She wanted to send the monograph to Sir William Maitland."

"I know. She told me." Ewan felt his anger rising, for he recalled the sparkle in Lily's eyes when she spoke of her research. The very scholars who should have been cheering her on were the ones plotting to undermine her good work.

His grandfather shook his head. "Needless to say, we on the board of directors were furious. We resolved to do all in our power to discourage the little upstart."

Ewan opened his mouth, preparing to insult the unworthy lot of them, but his grandfather held him off. "I know what you must think of us. What you must think of me. We were wrong to dismiss her talent, but that isn't all I did. You see, I learned a few days ago that Ashton Mortimer intended to quietly circumvent the ban I'd placed on Lily and the presentation of any of her work. I knew they had collaborated on several papers, and in my heart I knew she'd done most of the brilliant work. Ashton doesn't have the intellect. He's a dullard, and he couldn't have obtained membership in the Royal Society without her help."

"Which Lily readily gave. She's generous that way."

His grandfather paused a moment and shook his head. "I was furious that he'd disobeyed my instructions, so I dismissed him from the Royal Society yesterday afternoon. He was devastated, begged me to reconsider, for he'd secured funding for an expedition to Madagascar and feared he'd lose it once word got out. I refused, and that must have sent him over the edge."

Ewan ran a hand raggedly through his hair. He wanted to wrap his fingers around his grandfather's neck and choke the life out of him, but in truth, the old man could not have known what Ashton intended. "He had Lily's abduction planned long before you dismissed him. I'm sure now that the attack on her at Tattersalls was his first attempt at it. As for his expedition, I don't think it ever existed other than in his distorted imagination."

His grandfather gazed at him, silent for a long moment as he considered Ewan's words. "I'm still to blame. I was so intent on breaking the girl's spirit that I gave no thought to who else I damaged along the way. Ewan, you must believe I never intended any harm to befall her."

His grandfather was referring to physical harm and still had no understanding of the many other ways a person could be damaged. Looking at his grandfather, he suddenly wondered about his youth and the treatment he'd received while growing up. It didn't absolve him of the harm he'd done to Evie and Desmond, or the attempted harm to Lily, but the old man did appear genuinely sincere. Ewan didn't know him well enough to tell for sure, but his instincts rarely guided him wrong. "There's a way to make matters right. You banned her from the thing she loves most in the world. You broke her heart." *As I did.* "Allow her to attend the Royal Society lectures. Publish her monograph. Make her your first female member."

"She can attend the lectures, but as for the rest of it, she's just a girl and will soon have much to distract her attention. A husband, children." He shook his head and sighed. "You ask for more than I can give, Ewan. She'll be satisfied to be allowed back in."

Ewan rose, his fists curled in anger, though it was mostly aimed at himself. He'd treated her no better than those old fossils. They'd merely wanted to control her ideas. Ewan had wanted to control all of her, expecting her to give him everything while he held himself back. He must have sounded as dismissive as his grandfather sounded now. "Just a girl? She's Lily. There isn't another like her in all of England."

The old man eyed him speculatively, then let out a bark of laughter. "You're in love with a *Sassenach*. What are you going to do about it?"

"The right thing. The best thing. I've asked her to marry me."

Whatever he expected from his grandfather, it certainly wasn't to see the old man break down and weep. "Thank goodness," he said in a ragged whisper, unashamed of the tears welling in his eyes and suddenly spilling down his cheeks.

"Grandfather?"

"I'm proud of you, Ewan. You didn't make the same mistakes I did. I've always been an arrogant bastard, and when you first came to Lotheil Court, I thought you were just like me. But you're not. You're able to bend, to admit you were wrong and move on."

"Grandfather—"

"I almost killed the woman you love because of my arrogance! After all these years, I still haven't learned a single, damn lesson in life. I've made everyone around me miserable, Evangeline and Desmond most of all. Lily's right. I deserve to die alone in this mausoleum."

"She didn't mean it. She isn't the sort to wish ill on anyone."

He brushed a tear off his cheek as he nodded. "I tried to bribe her. Did she tell you that?"

Ewan frowned. "No."

"I demanded her help in making us a family again. I couldn't just ask her, couldn't imagine the girl would do it as a favor to me, for I'd never done a blasted thing to help her out. So I offered to make her the first female member of the Royal Society as reward if she succeeded. She looked at me as though I'd grown two heads. Never responded to my offer."

Despite his turmoil, Ewan grinned. This was so like Lily, the good-hearted girl who didn't understand about the underbelly of life and its base, human temptations. Her natural instinct was to nurture and encourage. She must have been so confused by the illogic of the offer that she'd simply ignored it.

"The worst part about it is that I lied. I had no intention of ever making her a member. In truth, I can't do it. Neither my rank nor my influence on the board will ever break the fear and animosity in the hearts of our members. They'll never accept a woman as their equal." His shoulders sagged and he buried his face in his hands. "Ewan, I'm sorry."

He never thought to hear those words from his grandfather. Not ever in this lifetime. In return, he did something he never thought he'd do in this lifetime. He reached over and hugged his grandfather.

* * *

Lily's heart was in her throat as she and Dillie entered Lady Finchley's salon and directed the butlers to set her harp (that horrid instrument of torture she'd tried to break at least a dozen times without success) beside the piano. Dillie placed her sheets of music on the piano, so obviously eager to play that Lily felt deeply sorry for her. They hadn't rehearsed nearly as much as they ought to have this afternoon after she'd awoken from her nap. Not that Dillie needed to work on the pieces. She knew them by memory, didn't need a sheet of notes to guide her nimble fingers over the ivory keys.

"The guests are strolling in," Dillie said with annoying glee. "I don't see Ewan yet."

Lily pursed her lips to hide her dismay. "I doubt he'll come." After all, he'd offered to marry her and she'd kicked him to the curb. He was a proud man and her words must have bruised him.

"And I'm sure he will." She nudged her toward the harp. "Do your best."

"I'll try." It wasn't only that she had no musicality in her bones— which she didn't—but her hands were sore, and if it weren't for the gloves she wore, everyone would have noticed the little cuts on her palms. She'd have to take the gloves off when she played, but her injuries would be sufficiently hidden from everyone's view while she ran her fingers across the harp strings. In any event, most guests would be turned away and wincing as she played.

"Uh-oh. There's Corky MacCorkstopper," Dillie whispered. "Bet she's surprised to find you here."

Lily tried to tamp down her alarm. Goodness, she'd managed to hold her own against some nasty-looking blackguards. But none of them was the woman Ewan had almost married. "Crumpets, what shall I do? She's coming straight toward us."

"Straight toward you, to be precise, with Lady Finchley on her heels. Now everyone's gawking. They've all heard the rumors, of course." Dillie grinned. "When she stops in front of you, punch her in the nose. Draw blood. If you won't do it, I will."

"No wonder you're the evil twin. You're not helping." Though the idea had merit. She had a better one, an idea that would take care of two problems. She would smash the harp over Caledonia's head, hopefully breaking it—the harp, that is, not Caledonia's head. She wasn't that bloodthirsty.

"You leave that harp alone." Dillie put a hand on her elbow. "I know what you're thinking, and you can put it from your mind immediately. We're going through with this recital."

"What trick is this?" Caledonia said with a hiss, or so it sounded to Lily. The girl was a viper, after all. A wicked Scottish viper.

Lily drew in a breath, trying to remain as calm as possible in this awkward situation. "Good evening, Lady Finchley. I'm sorry, but I don't know what *trick* your friend is referring to."

"Of course you don't, you sweet girl. The rumors of your ruination at the hands of Lord Mortimer's son are a bit of malicious gossip obviously started by a callow, calculating individual who's simply jealous of you." She stared pointedly at Caledonia as she spoke. "I was assured you would not appear. Yet here you are, looking quite lovely."

"Why, thank you." Lily tossed her an innocent smile, relieved that Callie had made such a monumental mistake, a novice debater's mistake. It was one thing to claim she'd been ruined—that juicy tidbit was readily devoured by the elite of society. But to also predict she would miss this evening, clearly proved false by her presence here, undermined all of Callie's previous assertions.

"I never believed those ridiculous rumors," Lady Finchley continued. "No doubt, this callow person will soon be leaving London, hopefully never to be heard from again. Don't you heartily agree, Miss MacCorkindale?"

"I do not. She was taken. Abducted and ruined! I don't know how she got back here, but I'll get to the bottom of it."

"I don't think so," a stern voice said from behind Caledonia.

Lily had been too distraught to notice Ewan's appearance, but there he was, as magnificent as ever, freshly shaven and impeccably attired in black tie and tails. The perfect, proper English gentleman, except for that gleam in his eyes and the Scottish swagger in his stance. He was better than an English gentleman. He was Ewan. "Good evening, Miss Farthingale. I look forward to your harp recital. I hear your talent is quite... er, unusual." Lily melted at his smile.

Their brief but intimate exchange only served to rile Callie. "You're trying to protect her. It won't work. I'll make sure everyone learns the truth."

"Enough, Callie," he said, the ice in his tone obvious to all. "I can assure you, if there ever was a scheme afoot to ruin Lily's reputation, and you were involved in any way, the consequences will be severe."

Lady Finchley thought it important to express her opinion as well. "The Farthingales have close connections to the Prince Regent. I'm sure he'd personally mete out the punishment."

"Can't you see he's lying? They're all lying!"

Caledonia's uncle joined them. "Enough, Callie. You're only getting yourself into deeper trouble. As Laird Carnach said, anyone involved in such a scheme will have their heads hung on Traitor's Gate for the ravens to scavenge. I wouldn't like to see yours up there, and it will most certainly end up there if you persist."

Caledonia blanched.

He cast Lily a tender glance. "Glad to see the rumors are completely unfounded, lass." Then he led his niece away.

Lily let out the breath she'd been holding.

"Horrid creature," Lady Finchley whispered once the pair were out of earshot.

"Indeed," Ewan muttered. "I wonder that we were ever friends. Archie's a good chap, though."

"The best," Lily said with enthusiasm, for he'd obviously known the truth and kept it to himself.

Ewan arched an eyebrow. "Not better than me, I hope."

"What do you mean?" Lily was uncertain what he wished to hear from her. At the inn, she had told him that she loved him, and he'd said nothing in return. She wasn't going to say it again in front of others. No, she'd had enough public humiliation for one evening. She wanted to run to Lady Finchley's library and hide out there all evening. Those musty books were looking better and better. Lady Finchley had hundreds in her library.

Dillie squealed. "He's trying to tell you that he loves you."

"But he doesn't." She let out a pained laugh. "Ewan, stop this now. Tell my sister that you don't love me."

All eyes turned to him. Lady Finchley's were as wide as eyes could possibly be without popping out of one's head.

One. Two. Three. Four. Ewan said nothing, just grinned.

Lady Finchley gasped and took off at a sprint, neither her advanced age nor impractical evening slippers holding her back.

"No! He's jesting. Please don't—" But it was too late. Their hostess was busy spreading this latest embarrassing rumor through the crowd. "You see, this is why I hate these functions." She frowned at Ewan. "Why didn't you deny it?"

"Because it's time I stopped acting like a Scottish baboon. Lass, I'd like a private word with you after the recital. Afterward, if you've found it in your heart to forgive me for what I did to you at the inn—or rather, what I failed to *say* to you at the inn—I'd like a word with your parents." He kissed her softly on the cheek, and then turned and walked away to take a seat beside his grandfather in the front row.

"Holy crumpets," Dillie muttered, "what happened at the inn?"

Something magical. They had never held back secrets from each other, but she couldn't reveal this one yet, not even to Dillie. "Never mind. The guests are taking their seats. Let's just muddle through this evening."

CHAPTER 19

EWAN SAT BESIDE his grandfather and Meggie, eager for the recital to begin. Not that he wished to hear the insipid pieces that passed for music in refined society. He didn't. Nor was he eager to hear Lily's harp playing since everyone had warned him she was execrable. William Farthingale sat on the other side of Meggie, leaning too close to her for Ewan's liking, but he said nothing. Who was he to admonish the Farthingale lad for sitting too close to Meggie?

He, arrogant Scot that he was, had ruined Lily.

William leaned over to grin at him. "To think, a cat gave up its guts for those harp strings."

Meggie giggled. "That's an awful thing to say about your cousin."

William shrugged. "Lily knows I'm only teasing. She's perfect in every other way."

Ewan had been warned, but he wasn't prepared for how truly awful her playing was. Dillie deserved a medal for her patience. In truth, Dillie seemed not in the least perturbed by her sister's missteps. She smiled at every missed note. Ewan never realized there were so many notes to miss.

He didn't care. Lily was alive. Lily was back to her cringe worthy, imperfect harp-playing form. All was right with the world... he hoped. She hadn't agreed yet to marry him. He'd work on that problem tonight.

When she'd finished and taken a bow to polite applause, Ewan drew her aside. She smiled at him, that warm, open-hearted smile he didn't deserve. "I was horrid, wasn't I? Are your ears bleeding?"

"Numb and bleeding," he replied with a feigned shudder. "I'm not complaining. Your sister's quite accomplished."

"I know, but she hates to perform on her own. She's a coward at heart."

So was he, but not anymore. He led her past the crowd and was about to draw her into Lady Finchley's library when the Duke of Edgeware intercepted them. He looked worried. "Those crates of gunpowder are missing," he said, following them into the library where they could all speak without being overheard.

Ewan would have sorely liked to have had this time alone with Lily, but knew Edgeware's news was important. "The ones numbered one, two, and three?"

Edgeware nodded. "They were stolen with the others. I stopped by Lord Mortimer's house to question him further, and—"

Ewan's arm tightened around Lily's waist, not liking that pause one bit. "And?"

"Ashton's father is also missing."

Lily gasped, took a step back to burrow against Ewan's chest. "Has he been abducted? Your Grace, what's happened to him?"

"I think he ran off on his own. His staff appears to be genuinely concerned about his disappearance, but they don't suspect foul play. They say he was distraught and raging about Lily and the Royal Society. How was he when you and George spoke to him yesterday?"

Ewan shook his head. "Odd. He acted as if he thought Lily had eloped with Ashton, but he was eager to end our discussion and go back to bed. I haven't spoken to him since. No one has. George and the Bow Street runners only made it back to London a short while ago. They're making arrangements to hand Ashton and his villains over to the authorities as we speak."

"Somehow, the old man got wind of what was happening. The truth about what his son has done must have set him off." Edgeware ran a hand through his hair. "Or perhaps he isn't as innocent as we first believed."

Lily glanced at Ewan. "He's a frail, old man. What harm can he do?"

Ewan could think of a dozen dangerous possibilities, but didn't wish to alarm Lily any more than she was already. Every way he figured it, Lily ended up the one in danger. "I don't know, but I'm not leaving your side until he's found."

"I'll watch Dillie," Edgeware said. "She's your identical twin, easily mistaken for you. In truth, I think Ashton must have been shadowing her the other night. She was wearing your spectacles, pretending to be you. When I approached, she seemed relieved." He winced. "She's never happy to see me. She thinks I'm an idiot. However, she asked me to stay close because she had an uneasy feeling that someone was watching her. It went away once you appeared and made the spectacles switch."

Lily put a hand to her throat. "I put Dillie at risk."

Ewan let out a soft growl. "You didn't. Ashton's to blame. He's deranged, and so it seems, is his father. I mean it, Lily. I'm not letting you out of my sight. Not ever."

"Is that your arrogant way of asking me to marry you?"

She was frowning again. At him. "I've already asked you. I've been waiting for your answer."

"You never asked. You simply assumed."

Edgeware's eyes widened. He began to back out of the room. "I've heard more of this conversation than I ought to have. In any event, your family must be warned of the continuing danger. I'll take care of it." He left the library, closing the door behind him.

"Damn it, Lily." Ewan raked a hand through his hair.

She held him back when he started to turn away, but he only meant to peer out the window to see if the old bastard was lurking outside. "Honestly, Ewan. You can't expect him to be hiding among Lady Finchley's bluebells and primroses. He's old and frail, and moves with the speed of a snail. You're using him as an excuse to avoid facing the truth about us. I need my answers. You never asked me to marry you."

His collar suddenly felt as if it had grown too tight. What was wrong with him? This was Lily, the woman who'd conquered his heart. "You know how I feel about you."

"You're right. I do. But perhaps you don't. You're still afraid to admit it."

"This isn't the conversation I planned to have with you."

She took a deep breath and sighed. "Then tell me what you intended to say."

He thought of his grandfather, that old man crying in his arms, afraid he was going to die sad and alone. Ewan was much like him, and about to make the same prideful mistake that would cost him Lily. No, not if he could help it. He drew her into his arms. "What I wished to say to you is that I want to spend the rest of my days with you. I can't imagine my days without you in my life, or my nights without you in my arms. I know our marriage won't be easy for you, for I'll be taking you far from your family. But we'll work it out. I promise. Your family is welcome to visit us whenever they like, and welcome to stay as long as they wish."

"Heaven forbid," she said with a jovial grimace. "That's the longest speech I've ever heard you give."

"There's more. We have scientific societies, geographical societies, a slew of historical societies in Scotland, mainly in Edinburgh, but you can start as many as you like in the Highlands. I'll sponsor every damn one of them." Smiling, he tipped a finger under her chin and drew her gaze to his. The soft blue of her eyes met the determined green of his. "Lily, lass. My sweet lass. My fair Lily. Will you marry me?"

"Of course I will. I love you so much, Ewan. I'm so relieved. I thought you'd never ask me straight out. I was afraid you'd return to Scotland and leave me behind."

"Och, I'd never do that." He kissed her on the mouth, determined to take gentle possession of her heart and soul. He didn't hold back either, needing Lily to know that he was hers forever, that he treasured her and couldn't exist without her.

"Am I dreaming? Or did I just feel the earth move?" Lily whispered, her eyes closed and lips swollen with passion.

"Bollix, I felt it too." The windows began to rattle. "Those missing crates of explosives!"

Lily gasped, and her gaze turned anguished. His arms were still around her, so he felt the violent shudder that ran through her body. "Lass, it's all right."

"No, it isn't. The Royal Society!" She let out a heaving sob. "He's destroyed it."

* * *

Ewan was in his unrepentant, dominant Scottish male baboon temper once again, holding Lily back when she sought to leave Lady Finchley's townhouse. "You don't understand! The Society's library—"

"Lass, ye're to stay close to your-r-r par-r-rents." Though he was spouting orders in full Highlander brogue and rolling his r's, Lily knew by his expression that he was exasperated and concerned. He wasn't angry with her. After all, he couldn't be angry with her for wanting to save the precious books and artifacts on display within the Royal Society's imposing halls.

Or had Ashton's father blown up only the building's new wing, the one to be named after Ewan's grandfather? His grandfather's birthday celebration had been scheduled to take place there next week. "Don't leave yer-r-r father's side. I'll see what's happened."

She shot him an indignant scowl. "You just promised never to leave my side."

"I'm only trying to protect you." He kissed her on the lips with hot determination, one of those divine Ewan kisses filled with hunger and longing that spoke to her heart and turned her legs to jelly. No doubt, he'd kissed her to stop her protests.

Well, it wasn't going to work. "I'm going with you."

He clenched his teeth. "No, the place may be on fire. Ashton's father—"

"All the more reason why I should be with you. More important, I know which books and artifacts are valuable. We may yet be able to save some of them. There's a private room filled with ancient maps and manuscripts."

"Where?"

"Hidden behind one of the bookshelves. You'll never find it on your own. I'll have to show you." She tried to shove out of his arms. He wouldn't let her go.

"Och, lass. Don't look at me that way."

She didn't mean to be angry with him, but so much time had already been lost standing here arguing. "How am I looking at you?"

"There's so much pain in your eyes, as though a precious part of you were trapped inside that building, buried under all that marble. It's just a building. The artifacts are just objects, no matter how important you think they are. They're not living, breathing things. But you are. I almost lost you once. I won't lose you again."

"So you'll break your promise to me, just like that?"

He clenched his teeth again. "I said it and I meant it. I want you by my side. In my bed. In my arms. Not ripping my heart to tatters worrying about you while battling a raging fire."

"You're wonderful, Ewan. I sincerely mean it. But you know you've lost this argument. I'm safer with you than without you. And your grandfather will need you to go with him to the Royal Society. He's probably looking for you as we speak."

He sighed and dropped his hands to his sides. "So help me, if you take a step from my side, I'll—"

"As you've promised never to leave my side, I promise never to leave yours." She smiled at him. "Still eager to marry a *Sassenach* bluestocking?"

He ran a finger lovingly across her cheek and groaned. "Never more eager for anything in my life."

They hurried out of the library in search of Ewan's grandfather and found him in the entry hall, donning his cloak. Relief washed over him as he spotted them. "There you are! I thought you might have gone off without me. I don't know what the hell just happened, but the rafters shook and now there's a red glow in the distance. It's the Royal Society, isn't it?"

Ewan put a hand on his shoulder. "Possibly. We don't know for sure."

"But I do. This is my fault. I've brought this destruction down on all of us." His gaze softened as he looked at Lily. "Lass, I owe you an apology. You'll have it properly from me, in writing, so that all will know that I was in the wrong."

She stopped him, for there was such desolation in his eyes she felt as though he were punishing himself worse than she ever could. "It isn't necessary. We have a building to salvage. And a birthday party to plan for you. We mustn't let a case of explosives get in our way."

Actually, it was three cases of explosives.

She turned to Ewan and saw that his brow was furrowed. He was thinking the same thought... had Lord Mortimer used all three cases? Or were more buildings about to crumble? Two possible targets came to mind, Lotheil Court and the Farthingale residence.

They had to stop Lord Mortimer.

The duke's carriage rattled through the London streets with all the speed his horses, bred for power and endurance, could muster. The carriage drew to a halt about a block away from their destination. "Ain't safe to proceed further, Your Grace," the driver said. "Looks like 'alf the building toppled onto the street and it's blockin' our passage."

Lily, Ewan, and his grandfather climbed down from the carriage and hurried the rest of the way on foot, pushing through the crowd already gathered. Ewan kept hold of Lily's hand, his not so subtle way of assuring she'd remain by his side. Finally, they broke through the barrier of spectators and approached the building. Ewan held her back a moment while he surveyed the damage. Lily followed his gaze as it wandered from the street and upward to the imposing structure that rivaled the British Museum for grandeur.

Her heart shot into her throat. She'd never seen so much destruction in her entire life. She'd read about battles between ancient civilizations. She'd even read accounts of recent wars. Nothing had prepared her for the ruin that stood before her very eyes. The roof of the Royal Society's new wing had fallen onto the street. The Roman statuary meant to decorate its cornices were shattered chunks of rock now partially blocking the street. The massive stone wall facing the street had completely crumbled and a red glow was visible from inside.

"Stand back, lass. It isn't safe," Ewan said as a gust of wind carried the smoky stench of fire toward them. A mix of sadness and the physical effect of stinging heat from the flames brought tears to her eyes. The air was too hot to breathe.

Ewan drew her back, for she was too distraught to consider obeying him. The new wing had been enormous, and now it was reduced to rubble. Fortunately, it had been left empty of exhibits, for none were to be brought in until after the duke's party.

She turned to Ewan. "Do you think he used all of it up?"

His expression was grim. "No, lass. Two cases at most. The fire will destroy the rest of the building."

"But it hasn't spread to the original structure yet. That's where all the important artifacts and documents are stored. We can still save them." A brigade of men carrying buckets were forming a line from the building down to the Thames. She didn't think their small buckets would defeat the fire, but they could delay its spread long enough to save the precious contents.

Ewan clamped his hand on her arm. "Lily, you're not going into that building."

At that moment, Evangeline, Meggie, and Desmond reached her side. "Of course not," Desmond said, glancing from Ewan to his grandfather. "Not alone. We're going in with you. Grandfather, do you have the key?"

Evangeline and Meggie grabbed a wheelbarrow that was sitting near a small side entrance beside an array of workmen's tools. "Well? Are we Camerons going to just stand here and allow this building to burn?" Meggie demanded.

Ewan let out a strangled oath as Lily attempted to take a step toward that side entrance. "You're coming with me. Remember your promise to stay close."

She grinned at him and turned to his grandfather. "Your Grace, where's that key?"

He withdrew it from the inner pocket of his jacket. Ewan gaped at him. His grandfather sniffed. "Always carry it with me. It's an honor granted to the highest ranking member on the board. I take my responsibilities seriously." He turned to Lily. "Unfortunately, I don't always execute them properly. In truth, we old fossils seem to have lost our way these past few years. But things will change going forward. I do care deeply about the Royal Society and the great work it undertakes for the betterment of society."

Lily shot him an indulgent smile. "I know, Your Grace. I never doubted your love for this place."

"As I never should have doubted yours."

Ewan took the key out of his grandfather's hands. "Are we done with these mawkish displays of affection?"

"Quite," Lily said with a soft laugh. "Let's save some books."

*   *   *

Within the hour, not only the ancient texts but masks, weaponry, utensils, maps, journals, and all manner of items displayed within the halls had been taken to safety. A regiment of soldiers housed in the Somerset Court barracks around the corner from the Royal Society had helped with the task. Half of those soldiers had worked with Ewan and Desmond to extinguish the fire, while the other half had assisted Lily, Evangeline, Meggie, and the duke in protecting and cataloguing the precious items that were then taken to their barracks for safekeeping.

As the night wore on, Lily realized that the Camerons, working together as a family, had saved almost everything precious. She felt a well of pride and satisfaction. As though reading her mind, Ewan came up beside her and drew her into his arms. She was covered in soot and smelled hideous, but he didn't seem to care. He hadn't come out of the past few hours unmarked either. He was sweating, and his crisp, white lawn shirt was badly stained, but Ewan—being Ewan—looked incredibly handsome, better than any man she'd ever set eyes upon. Ever. "Well done, lass."

He'd rolled up his sleeves, and she felt the solid muscles of his forearms as he wrapped them about her. She snuggled against his chest. "An excellent night's work. We work well together, don't you think?"

"That we do."

She smiled and gazed up at him. "You were spectacular in the way you organized all the men, those fighting the fire and the others who were helping us. It would have been chaos otherwise."

He laughed and shook his head. "You have it backwards, lass. The Continental forces would have defeated Napoleon years earlier if they'd had *you* for a general. The Camerons can't take credit for any of this. You're the one who saved the Royal Society. You alone."

She took comfort in the solid warmth of his chest. She had worked hard. Very hard. But she hadn't managed the salvage operation on her own. Ewan and Desmond had meted out the tasks, had coordinated the fire brigade, and had made sure none of the men who'd gone into the dark, smoke-filled halls of the older building stole any valuables. The duke had been watching them as well, strutting back and forth, his aristocratic gaze sharp and assessing.

No one would dare cross the old duke.

Evangeline and Meggie had been just as busy assisting with the enormous task of cataloguing every saved artifact. They'd done a brilliant job of it.

By the time dawn broke over London to signal the start of a new day, most of the board of directors of the Royal Society had arrived and were now gathered in the regimental barracks. Lord Guilfoil was the last to arrive. Lily stiffened as he scowled at her. "What's she doing here?"

The duke stepped forward. "Saving our sorry souls. If it hadn't been for the girl, we'd have lost everything. Where were you? It hasn't escaped my notice that you took your sweet time in getting here."

Lord Guilfoil began to sputter a lame excuse, but the duke cut him off. "Save it, Guilfoil. You weren't here when it mattered, so the board proceeded without you. We're going to rebuild and improve the Royal Society. All applicants for membership will be welcomed and seriously considered on their merits. I'll be sponsoring Lily Farthingale's application." He turned to Lily. "If you'll allow me, lass. I've been an old fool and wish to make it up to you."

Lily felt overwhelmed. She smiled at him and knew that smile must look ridiculous, for she was grinning from ear to ear, probably crying too. Her heart was about to burst with joy, and she was shaking. "I'd be honored."

"Lily, you're a miracle worker," Evangeline said softly.

Lily wiped away a stray tear and stared at the Camerons, who were now lined up in a row in front of her. Evangeline and Meggie were clasping hands and smiling at her. The three Cameron men stood tall before her, their arms folded across their arrogantly puffed chests. Also smiling at her. The duke cleared his throat and turned to his granddaughters. "You both did a splendid job. I'm so pleased. Evie, I'm particularly proud of you. I've treated you miserably all these years, yet you responded without hesitation in this, my darkest hour."

She blushed. "Thank you, Grandfather."

"I'm going to need your help putting everything back in order. Will you work with me? You'll have a title, of course. Curator of Antiquities. Will that do? Or would you prefer Director of Expeditions? You'll require funds, of course. We'll decide upon a budget, and if it isn't enough, the board will approve more." He turned to the other directors. "Isn't that so?"

They all voiced their approval, stumbling over each other in their haste to agree.

The duke appeared content. He turned to Desmond. "Since the Royal Society will take up most of my time from here on in, I'll need your help in running the Cameron shipping line. I know you're familiar with the business. Will you take it over for me, Des?"

Desmond appeared wary at first, his gaze darting from Ewan to his grandfather, as though believing it was a trick. But Lily saw the hopefulness in his eyes and knew this was what he'd dreamed of. Ewan gave him an encouraging nod. There must have been a silent exchange between the two cousins, because Desmond's wariness quickly disappeared. He turned to the old duke. "I'll make you proud of me, Grandfather. I'll start today. Right now. I won't let you down."

"I trust you, Des. I know the enterprise is in good hands. I've always been proud of you and Evie. Forgive me for not telling you sooner. Forgive me for all I've put you through. Things will change. Starting now."

Though Desmond held back, Evie felt none of his reserve. She threw her arms around her grandfather and hugged him fiercely. "You've made us so happy. I love you, Grandfather."

The duke hugged her back. Lily thought she detected a sniffle in his voice as he said, "I love you too, my sweet Evie."

Ewan drew her back as his cousins and grandfather enjoyed their moment. "Lily, you've singlehandedly saved the Cameron family. We Cameron men are a bad mix of pride, arrogance, and stubbornness, but you managed to overcome all our defenses. I don't know how to thank you." He shook his head and put a hand to her lips before she had the chance to respond. "I take it back. Yes, I do."

She gazed at him in confusion. "You do? How?"

"I'm going to ask you again to marry me." He took her into his arms. She always liked the feel of his solid arms around her.

She continued to stare at him. "But you've already asked and I've accepted."

A gleam sprang into his eyes. A wicked Highlander gleam. "I didn't do it right." He leaned forward and kissed her lightly on the lips. "I didn't explain why I desperately wish you to marry me."

She nodded. "Go on." Her heart was in her throat. Butterflies were fluttering in her stomach. Her legs had turned to butter.

She thought he was going to tell her that he loved her, so she wasn't prepared when Ewan suddenly drew her behind him, muttering something that sounded like "Mortimer" before turning to lunge at his grandfather. Seemingly in the same motion, he grabbed the old man and shoved him to his knees just as a shot rang out. Desmond did the same with her, Evie, and Meggie, hauling them down and shielding them with his body.

Everything happened all at once. The echo of that shot still resounded in her ears as Lily turned to Ewan. Her eyes widened in horror at the crimson spurt of blood now spewing from his body. He tried to move, but grunted in pain and collapsed against his grandfather.

"No! Ewan!" She surged to her feet and started toward him, as did his family and the Royal Society board members. Then she noticed Lord Mortimer withdrawing a pouch from his cloak and moving toward a lit torch. The gunpowder! He meant to kill them all!

Lily lunged toward him, at the same time fumbling for the hat pin she carried within the folds of her sash. She tackled Lord Mortimer and stuck his hand with the hat pin. He yelped and dropped the pouch. She kicked it away and grabbed the torch to keep it out of his grasp.

"Jezebel! Witch! Ashton loved you and you betrayed him!" The soldiers of the Somerset barracks now burst through the door and quickly took Lord Mortimer into their custody.

"We'll keep him locked up and under guard. Don't you worry, Miss Farthingale," said their captain.

"Search him. Search his coach. Look for gunpowder." The captain nodded and issued more orders to his men. Four of them secured Lord Mortimer in their custody. The others hurried off to search his belongings.

As the last of them left, Lily turned to Ewan. Meggie was in tears, kneeling beside him. "Oh, no." Lily's heart began to pound through her ears. He wasn't dead. He couldn't be. He was too proud and stubborn to die.

She heard him groan. Oh, thank goodness! "Ewan, where are you hit?"

"Just my shoulder. Solid shot this time. That hot metal lodged deep between the muscle. Hurts like blazes."

Evie was first to her feet. "Come on, Desmond. We have to find Lily's uncle. He's a doctor. The best in London."

Lily carefully removed Ewan's jacket and shirt and then, with the assistance of several soldiers, settled him on one of the freshly made up cots in their barracks. While she gathered clean cloths and ordered water boiled, Meggie and her grandfather remained by Ewan's side. She had watched her uncle tend to the injured, but had never seen him operate on anyone who had been shot. After thoroughly washing the soot and grime off her hands, she returned to Ewan's side and busied herself by cleansing his wound, doing her best to stem the flow of blood. She didn't know what else to do.

Despite her protests, Ewan eased himself into a sitting position on the cot. "Lily, lass. It's just my shoulder. Nothing fatal."

Though he tried to hide it, she heard the strain of agony in his voice. "I know," she said in a shaky whisper, not quite believing his assurances.

He took her hand and held onto it until her uncle arrived. This was so like Ewan, determined to comfort her even though he was the injured party. George finally arrived after what seemed like forever and quickly set to work on Ewan's shoulder. The others were herded out of the room, but Lily remained to assist him. She promptly and carefully followed each instruction. There was so much blood! Ewan was in so much pain.

* * *

"Sweetheart," Ewan said softly, several hours later. The last of the metal fragments had been dug out of his shoulder and the wound properly bound. He was now safely back at Lotheil Court, his every comfort attended to by the Lotheil servants. George had ordered him to stay in bed and rest.

Ewan was already ignoring those orders, Lily noted with frustration. He'd bathed, put on clean clothes, and had a tempting array of plum cakes and raisin biscuits set out on a table by the hearth in the library. He was seated in one of the fat cushioned chairs in front of the hearth, his long legs stretched before him. Jasper was sprawled beside him, eyeing the raisin biscuits and whimpering. "Be quiet, ye bloody looby. I have something important to say to Lily."

He stood up, giving no hint of discomfort as he rose, though he moved a little more slowly than usual and his injured shoulder was slightly stooped. He took her hand again, squeezing it lightly but with firm determination, as though to prove he wasn't going to die. They were alone in the library. She had come straight here with him, not taken the time to return home to bathe or change into clean clothes. She was a disheveled mess and suddenly felt quite awkward standing beside him.

He looked spectacular. Of course, he did. He was strong, proud Ewan.

She was a bluestocking who'd spent the past hours crying in the carriage on the ride to Lotheil because she thought he was going to die each time they hit a bump in the road, and crying some more in the Lotheil garden while the duke's staff tended to Ewan upstairs. "I ought to go home to wash and change."

"Stay. Please."

She began to fuss and fidget. She couldn't help it. She'd almost lost him. She was green and nauseated and still frightened out of her wits. Yet, he seemed so calm. "Sweetheart," he repeated to gain her attention. "I've been stabbed and shot twice since coming to London."

"Oh, Ewan! I know. It's all my fault."

He gave her hand another gentle squeeze. "No, lass. That isn't my point. As I said, stabbed and shot twice."

"And almost blown to pieces."

"Right. I don't think this town agrees with me."

She shook her head and sighed. "I suppose not."

"What I'm trying to tell you is that I don't belong here. Lass, my place is in the Highlands."

She held her breath in sudden panic. Had he reconsidered? Decided not to marry her after all? She did look a sooty mess. "Ewan, what are you saying?"

"I'll be leaving here when my three months are up. Perhaps sooner, since I think I've accomplished what this visit was meant to bring about. With your help, of course."

She nodded, now wishing she'd taken a moment to tend to herself. If he was going to rescind his marriage proposal, she wished to be properly dressed to receive the bad news. Not that it mattered how she looked or what she wore while her heart was being ripped to pieces. She continued to hold her breath as he resumed the conversation. "Desmond is more than capable of running the dukedom of Lotheil. He's been raised to the task. He wants it, but most of all, he's earned it."

"You're just as capable. Why are we speaking of Desmond?" Lily tipped her gaze upward to study his expression. She let out a small gasp. "Has your grandfather offered the dukedom to you?"

He nodded. "The old man believes I'm a natural leader."

"You are."

"He claims I've shown more wisdom in dealing with problems than he ever has."

"You have. He's right to be impressed with you. You're smart and honest and caring, and everyone respects you."

He teasingly tweaked her nose. "Enough, lass. You'll swell my head with such compliments. But as I said, my heart is in the Highlands." He gazed at her, cast her a boyishly hopeful smile that tugged at her own heart. "Rather, my heart will be in the Highlands if you'll come back there with me. I haven't given Grandfather my answer yet, but I know what I'd like to say."

Her eyes rounded in amazement. "You intend to refuse him."

"I wanted to talk it over with you first. If I refuse, I won't be a duke. Can't make you my duchess. But I'm Laird Carnach in my own right and I can't think of anyone who'd make a better Lady Carnach than you. Life won't be as comfortable for you up there as it is down here. But we have beautiful hills and lochs, and you'll never want for anything. I mean it, Lily. All I have is yours. I need you, lass. I can't be happy without you. I love you."

She grinned. "More than Jasper loves me?"

He laughed. "Never thought I'd have a dog for competition. That clumsy oaf fell in love with you at first sight. I suppose I did too. Tongue-dragging, heart-thumping, baboon-stomping, head over heels in love with you. But I'm dumber than that big looby. Dumber than a baboon, too. It took me longer to admit that you'd captured my heart. So what do you say? Can you love me if I remain a mere laird?"

She threw her arms around him, careful to avoid his injured shoulder. "I can't help but love you. I'd love you even if you were a baboon. If you don't want the dukedom of Lotheil, then I don't want it either. In truth, I'd make a terrible duchess. All those stuffy affairs. All that time away from my research."

"About that," he said, groaning as he drew her even closer, "I've written to Sir William Maitland about you. I sent a letter off to him shortly after Lord Guilfoil's lecture, and received his response about an hour ago."

She gasped.

"He's settled in Scotland and has invited us to visit him on our way back to the Highlands."

"You're taking me to meet him?" She kissed him with all the joy and passion residing in her heart.

He kissed her back, this time more urgently, his good arm sliding across her shoulders to draw her close. Jasper nuzzled his big head between them. His ears were perked and tail was wagging. "Stay put, ye looby. I'll no' have you interfering while I properly kiss the lass."

Jasper snorted in obvious disdain.

Ewan kept his attention on Lily. "You claimed my heart that first day we met, the moment I pulled you out of that puddle. I should have admitted my feelings to you then, but I was too arrogant to give up control of my heart. I've finally come to my senses."

She laughed softly. "Stabbings, shootings, and buildings blown up. I'd say it took a bit of doing to make you come to your senses."

"As I said, I'm an uncivilized baboon. But I love you, Lily. I need you."

"I've always loved baboons. Especially big, handsome Scottish baboons. I love you too, Ewan. Forever."

"Aye, lass. Forever." He kissed her again and it was magical. Lily knew her life would always be joyful and fulfilling with Ewan.

She couldn't wait to practice those sexual tricks on him that baboon females used to rouse their mates into a monkey frenzy. She wondered whether they would work on Ewan.

She was eager to find out.

THE END

Dear Reader,

I hope you enjoyed reading about Lily and Ewan! I've always had a soft spot in my heart for men in kilts, and although my husband has never worn one, he is of Scottish descent and remains the man of my dreams. I'm a twin, but hadn't planned on having twins in any stories. Lily Farthingale had other ideas. As soon as I started writing *My Fair Lily*, she stopped me in Chapter 1 and told me that I had to give her a twin. An identical twin, no less! So look for Daffodil's story next. Dillie, as Daffodil is known to her friends and family, is about to meet Ian Markham, a rakehell duke and London's most notorious bachelor. He is determined never to marry, but we know that the tougher they are, the harder they fall—and Ian Markham, the tough and sexy Duke of Edgeware, is about to fall hard. Read on for a sneak peek at Daffodil's story, the second in the FARTHINGALE SERIES.

SNEAK PEEK OF THE UPCOMING BOOK:
THE DUKE I'M GOING TO MARRY
By MEARA PLATT

London is never the same after the boisterous Farthingales move into their new townhouse on Chipping Way, one of the loveliest streets in fashionable Mayfair. With five beautiful daughters in residence, the street quickly becomes known for its so-called bachelor's curse. The youngest daughter, Daffodil, is horrified to learn the man she has just rescued from ruffians outside her townhouse is none other than the notorious Duke of Edgeware. If the Chipping Way curse holds true, she's doomed to marry the wretched rakehell. Determined to break the curse, she hastily leaves town, little knowing that the duke, equally determined to remain a bachelor, has just left town as well. With the Farthingale family and the duke's assailants on their trail, the pair find themselves trapped in the same charming inn during a torrential rainstorm… and wind up falling in love.

CHAPTER 1

Mayfair District, London
November 1818

WHEN DILLIE FARTHINGALE crossed to her bedroom window to draw the draperies before retiring to bed, she never expected to wind up in front of the Farthingale townhouse, elephant gun in hand, worried that she'd just shot the Duke of Edgeware. Not that this season's most eligible bachelor and dangerously handsome rakehell didn't deserve shooting. He most certainly did, but not by her.

"Crumpets!" She fell backward after getting off a shot that merely startled the duke's assailants. She aimed lower, getting off a second shot that almost ripped her shoulder out of its socket with its recoil. Scrambling to her feet, she reloaded and hurried out of the townhouse, shoving open the front gate that led onto Chipping Way, eager to inspect the damage and dreading what she might find.

Her street was one of those charming, quiet streets, a most desired location in London. Eligible dukes did not die on such streets. "Ian, you idiot! Are you hurt? Who were those awful men, and why were they attacking you?"

She knelt beside him, her heart firmly lodged in her throat. Her nightgown and thin wool shawl offered little protection from the midnight chill. Had his eyes been open, he would have been ogling her, for that's what rakehells did best. Ian Markham, as the duke was known, was as rakish as they came, but he would never dare more with her. She was related to his best friend, and as disreputable as Ian was, he did have a code of honor. Of a sort.

She had never considered Ian more than a mere nuisance deserving of a frown or indignant tip of her chin. Certainly not worth shooting, except for that one instance when he'd thoroughly surprised her by kissing her with enough passion to curl her toes. It was their first and only kiss, a case of mistaken identity in a moonlit garden, for he'd expected another lady to be standing beside the lilac tree where Dillie happened to be hiding while she innocently spied on her neighbor's dinner party.

Dillie had been trying to forget that kiss for the past two years. No doubt the duke had put it out of his mind immediately.

"Ian?" He appeared to be unconscious, his large, muscled body sprawled beneath the tree she'd practically splintered in half with the force of the elephant shot.

She set down the gun and shook him lightly when he failed to respond. "Oh, please wake up."

He opened his eyes with noticeable difficulty, his gaze decidedly fuzzy as he cast her a pained grin. "Bloody blazes, it's you. What are you doing here?"

"I live here. You're the one who's out of place."

His eyes were still unfocused. He blinked them slowly in an attempt to regain his vision. "Oh. Right. Then I ought to be going." But he made no attempt to rise. "I'll be off now. Good evening, Daffy."

Dillie ground her teeth in irritation. "Don't call me that." In a moment of madness, her parents had named her Daffodil, but she'd managed to sail through most of her nineteen years avoiding that hideous appellation. Everyone called her Dillie. Everyone but Ian Markham, the arrogant, infuriating Duke of Edgeware, who took every opportunity to torture her with the use of her given name and every ridiculous variation of it that came to his fiendish mind. "The name is Miss Farthingale to you."

"And I'm a duke. That's *Your Grace* to you."

She fisted her hands, wanting to pound the feathers out of him, but those two blackguards who'd attacked him seemed to have done a wickedly good job of it already. They were hired ruffians, certainly paid by someone angry enough to want him dead. "Very well. *Your Grace*, you idiot! Whose wife did you seduce this time?"

"That's better. About time you showed proper respect for my title." He tried to sit up, but he couldn't and fell back with a gasped oath, struggling for breath as he clutched his side.

Dillie shivered, not only from the wintery chill in the midnight air but also from her concern that she truly might have shot him. She had been aiming for those awful men. To be precise, aiming a warning blast above their heads to frighten them off. She was sure she'd hit one of the larger branches of the sturdy oak tree standing by the front gate. It now lay splintered on the ground near Ian.

She glanced around. His attackers had run off, frightened but unharmed. So why was Ian still on the ground, fumbling to rise and determined to hide his obvious agony? "Let me help you up."

He brushed her hand away when she reached out to steady him. "No, I can manage."

"Are you sure? Because you seem to be doing a spectacularly dismal job of it." She couldn't see him very well. The only light available was from the moon's glow, a full, silver moon that shone brightly against the crisp, starry sky.

"Are you still here, Daffy? Why don't you go away and leave me to my misery?" He sank onto the cool grass with another pained gasp, his head thumping against the hard trunk of the oak tree as he fell back.

"I'm having far too much fun watching you struggle," she said, though her heart was still in her throat and she was now seriously worried about him. Another shattered tree branch dangled precariously overhead, held up only by a small scrap of bark. It was in danger of falling atop him.

She reached out again, determined to move him out of its path, but as she touched his jacket she felt something warm and liquid seep through her fingers. "Ian, you clunch! You're bleeding. Oh, my goodness! Did I hit you?"

She let out a sob, now worried that she truly had done him damage. The air released from her lips cooled and formed a vapor that swirled about her face. It was too cold for Ian to be left out here for very long, and he wasn't in any condition to get up and walk on his own. "I didn't mean to shoot you."

He took hold of her hand, gently stroking his thumb along her palm to calm her down. "You didn't. I've been stabbed."

Dillie gasped. Was that supposed to calm her? "I'll get help. Don't move." Even in the dim light, she could see the crimson stain now oozing through his fancy silk vest. As she scrambled to her feet, the Farthingale butler came running through the gate. "Oh, Pruitt! Thank goodness! Fetch Uncle George. He must come right away, and tell him to bring his medical bag."

Pruitt's eyes rounded as wide as saucers the moment his gaze fell on Ian. "At once, Miss Dillie." He hurried back into the house as fast as his old legs would carry him. She heard him shouting up the stairs for her uncle, something the staid butler had never, ever done before, even when faced with an army of boisterous Farthingale relatives and their unruly children. Pruitt never lost his composure. His voice never rose above an ordinary, conversational tone. *Never.*

Until tonight.

Dillie sank back to her knees beside Ian. His hands were now pressed against a spot just above the left side of his waist. "That's it. Use your palms to press down hard on the wound," she instructed while quickly removing her shawl. The clunch was bleeding everywhere, and that meant he'd been stabbed more than once. She folded her shawl and then, nudging his hands aside, firmly pressed it to his waist and secured it by tightly tying the ends about his body. Big body. More solid strength than she'd realized. "Where else hurts?"

"Right thigh, just above my knee."

She ran her hand along his thigh, careful to avoid the hole in the fabric where he'd obviously been stabbed. He tensed and let out a laughing groan. "Better not touch me there."

No doubt to hide his extreme pain. She grabbed the velvet ribbon from her hair, ignoring the sudden cascade of long, dark strands about her shoulders and down her back. She used the ribbon to form a makeshift tourniquet around his thigh, hoping it was tight enough to stem the flow of blood from his leg until her uncle arrived to properly treat him.

Her hands were beginning to numb. It was freezing outside, the grass hard and crunching beneath her knees. A cloud of vapor formed with her every breath. She'd given up her shawl and was definitely underdressed. "Where else?"

"My forearms are sliced up, but not too badly. My jacket sleeves absorbed most of the damage." He studied her, as though noticing her for the first time. Really noticing her, a sign that he'd finally regained his full vision. He cast her a wickedly seductive grin. "There's a hard ache between my legs."

More injuries? All her fault. "Oh, dear! How bad? Show me."

"Did I say that aloud?" He let out a deep, rumbling laugh. "Gad, you're innocent. Don't look so stricken. The ache will disappear once you put on some clothes. Maybe."

"What?" She was in a panic, her heart pounding through her ears, and he was tossing jests?

"Your nightgown hides very little," he continued, as though needing to explain the meaning of his jest. "If you lean any closer, I'll have a clear view down your—"

She smacked him. Then smacked him again for good measure.

"Bloody hell! Wounded duke here. Show a little mercy."

She wanted to smack him again, but as he said, he was seriously injured. The folded shawl she'd applied to his waist was already stained through with his blood. He took hold of her hand, no longer smiling. She stilled, unable to draw a breath, for the first time realizing that he might not survive into the morning. "I'm so sorry, Ian. Just keep your mouth shut and I'll stop hitting you. Much as I hate to admit it, I don't wish you to die."

He gave her hand a light squeeze. "Much as I hate to admit it, I'm glad it's you by my side if I am to die." He paused, the effort of speaking too much to manage. "I thought you'd returned... to Coniston with the rest of your family... all five thousand of them." Those last words were spoken through shuddering pain.

Oh, God! Not you, Ian. You're invincible. She shook her head and tried to keep her voice steady. "They went on ahead." But her voice faltered as she tried to hold back tears. "All five thousand of them, traveling north like a great horde of locusts, eating everything in their path. I stayed behind with Uncle George to help him close up the house and enjoy the blessed quiet."

"Guess I've foiled your plans." He sounded weak, his words even more strained.

She melted at his soft gaze. Ian, with his gorgeous gray-green eyes, had a way of melting female hearts. Good thing it was dark and she couldn't clearly see the beautiful green of his eyes. That soft glance was devastating enough. "We were supposed to leave yesterday, but my uncle was called to a medical emergency. We had to delay our departure."

"Must thank the poor, sick blighter." His voice was weaker still. "I mean it, Dillie. If I'm to die tonight, I can't think of anyone I'd rather have beside me than you."

There were times when Ian rankled her.

In truth, he always rankled her.

But not tonight.

"Keep breathing, you clunch," she said in a ragged whisper, keeping tight hold of his big, cold hand.

*   *   *

Ian awoke in an unfamiliar room, uncertain how much time had elapsed since he'd been attacked. At least eight hours he guessed, for the morning sun was streaming in through the unshuttered window and glistening against the peach silk counterpane that covered the bed in which he lay. He recalled Dillie asking him about his assailants, but he didn't know who had sent them, only that they'd done a good job of carving him up with their knives.

Where was he? Somewhere safe, of that he was certain.

He had to get word to the Prince Regent. He suspected those men were disgruntled agents of the now exiled Napoleon, seeking retribution for his dismantling of the French spy network that had flourished in England until recently. Ian and his friends, both of whom now happened to be married to Dillie's sisters, had crushed the web of spies and exposed its leaders, some of whom had held prominent positions in the English government. Was this attack an act of revenge?

Or part of a more sinister scheme?

He tried to move his hand and realized someone was holding it. Someone with a soft, gentle touch. He glanced down and groaned. Dillie, primly dressed in a morning gown that hid all her good parts from view, was perched on a chair beside his bed, her slender body slumped over so that her head and shoulders rested on the mattress beside his thigh. Her dark hair was loosely bound, flowing down her back in a waterfall of waves. Her lips were partly open and she snored lightly.

Hell. She looked adorable.

What was she doing here? He glanced around and realized he must be in her bedchamber, the one she'd shared with her twin until last month. There were two beds, two bureaus. Matching sets of everything. *Bloody hell.* He had to get out of here fast. But how? His arms and legs felt as though they were weighed down by blocks of granite. He'd lost a lot of blood and knew he was as weak as a damn kitten.

"Dillie," he said in a whisper.

She responded with a snore.

"How long have I been here?"

Not wishing to wake Dillie when she failed to answer, he tried to move his free arm. A mistake, he realized at once, suppressing a yelp as a lightning bolt of pain shot from his waist, straight up his arm, and into his head. His temples began to throb and his heart began to thunderously pound against his chest.

It wasn't only pain making his heart pound. Dillie was temptingly close. He had only to reach out and… *better not.*

Why had he been settled in Dillie's quarters? He recalled being carried into the Farthingale townhouse and up the stairs by a team of footmen. What had Dillie said shortly before he'd blacked out? "Put him in my room, Uncle George," she'd insisted, explaining that the rest of the house had been closed up for the winter, the beds stripped of their linens and the mattresses put out to air.

Her uncle would never have agreed to the arrangement otherwise.

Ian let out a breath as the pain to his temples began to fade and then looked around the room again. The feminine, peach silk bedcovers and peach and white drapery suited Dillie. Sweet summer peaches was her scent, refreshingly light and fragrant.

The furniture seemed a little young for a girl her age. Dillie was nineteen or twenty years old by now, and of marriageable age. He frowned. No doubt the family expected her to marry soon and leave the household. The other four Farthingale daughters were already wed and several had children. Dillie's identical twin, Lily, had married only last month. Dillie wouldn't last another season. She was too beautiful to remain unattached for very long. And clever. She'd marry well.

Just not him.

That was for damn sure.

He wasn't the marrying sort, didn't want a woman in his life making demands on him. Cheating on him.

Dillie let out another soft snore, revealing she was still soundly asleep. How long had she been sitting by his side? Clinging sweetly to his hand? He liked the gentle warmth of her hand and the way her fingers protectively curled about his.

Felt nice. Too nice.

He carefully slid out from her grasp, but instead of drawing away from the dangerous innocent, he allowed his fingers to drift over the glistening waves of her dark hair. So soft. Unable to resist, he buried his hand in her silken curls, caressing the long, thick strands that fell over her shoulders and down her back. Bloody hell, she felt nice.

Too nice, he reminded himself again.

He stopped, desperate to climb out of bed before he did something spectacularly foolish, such as pulling her down atop him and kissing her rosy, lightly parted lips into tomorrow. No, not just into tomorrow. Into next week. Perhaps into next month. No woman had ever held his interest longer than that. He preferred it that way. Easier to remain unattached. Easier to remain free of messy obligations.

Perhaps that was why Dillie always referred to him as an idiot.

He was one, but not for the reasons Dillie imagined. He was an idiot because he couldn't seem to get *her* out of his thoughts. Going on two years now. No doubt because she, unlike all other women, found him completely unappealing. Where others would shamelessly proposition him, would flirt, swoon, scheme, or find any reason to gain his attention, Dillie usually cringed when she saw him coming.

She was a challenge, a beautiful, dark-haired, blue-eyed challenge. Where others succumbed, she resisted. But he knew better than to take up the gauntlet against Dillie. He wasn't certain he could win. She was different. She was dangerous. One look at the girl and all blood drained from his head to amass in a hot pool between his thighs.

He couldn't think straight when his loins were on fire. Could any man?

Unfortunately, Dillie managed to set him ablaze every time she looked at him. Didn't have to be much of a look, just a glimpse was enough. Sometimes the mere sound of her voice got him hot. He even knew her scent, that refreshingly sweet trace of peach blossoms wafting in the air.

When it came to Dillie, he was like a damn bloodhound able to recognize her presence even amid the heavily perfumed odors that permeated a room. He didn't know why the girl had that effect on him, for she wasn't the sort of woman who usually gained his notice. He liked elegant, more worldly women. He usually sought out the married ones who were bored with their husbands, for such women were interested in mere dalliances and expected no promises.

Dillie required faithfulness and heartfelt promises.

Dillie demanded everlasting love.

She disapproved of his scoundrel ways and never hesitated to tell him so. She didn't give a fig that he was a rich-as-Croesus duke. She wasn't impressed by his wealth or title.

She wasn't impressed by him.

Ian moaned.

Dillie must have heard him, for her eyes fluttered open. Those big, soft blue eyes that stole his breath away every time she looked at him.

"Ian, you're awake. Thank goodness." She cast him a beautiful, openhearted smile.

He closed his eyes and sank back against his pillow, drawing his hand away before she noticed that it had been buried in her luscious hair. "I feel like hell."

She laughed lightly. "You look like it, too."

"Ah, I knew I could count on you for compliments." He opened one eye.

Her smile faded and she began to nibble her lip. "You've been unconscious for three days." As though to prove her point, she leaned forward and ran her knuckles along his chin, gently scraping them against his three-day growth of beard. "If it's any consolation, you look wonderful for a man who's spent that much time fighting at death's door."

"Was I that bad?"

She nodded. "Let me feel your forehead. You were running a very high fever." She placed that same hand across his brow. "Oh, thank goodness. No longer hot."

He was hot. She wasn't looking low enough.

"Have you been by my side all this time?" Both his eyes were now open and trained on Dillie. Her morning gown was a simple gown of gray wool, its only adornment a velvet ribbon of a slightly darker gray trim at the sleeves. Her hair was long and loose—as he well knew since he'd just run his feverish fingers through it. She had a sleepy look in her eyes, slightly tousled hair, and a smile as beautiful as a moonbeam.

She was the most beautiful girl he'd ever set eyes upon.

He wanted her badly... naked and in his bed.

It was one thing to have those desires, but another thing altogether to act on them.

"Yes, I've been beside you most of the time," she replied, unaware of the depraved path of his thoughts. "Uncle George had to tend to that important patient of his, so he hasn't been around much. He left me in charge of you. Fortunately, the stab wound to your side was the worst of it. And it was bad, if you wish to know the truth. The blade missed your vital organs by a hair's breadth. You wouldn't have pulled through otherwise."

The notion seemed to distress her. It felt odd that she should care whether he lived or died. No one in his family did.

In truth, he didn't either.

"I never lost faith that you would survive. You're strong. And Uncle George is the best doctor in all of England," she said with noticeable pride. "He cleansed your wounds thoroughly and stitched you up. Your arms weren't slashed as badly as we'd feared, and the stab wound to your leg wasn't very deep."

She sounded efficient, as though she were taking inventory. Suddenly, she paused and there were tears glistening in her eyes.

Surprised, he reached out to run his thumb along the thin trail of water now sliding down her cheek. He winced as a painful jolt shot from his fingers to his brow. He'd braced himself against the expected pain, but it hurt like blazes anyway. One of those assailants must have sliced through muscle. Perhaps cracked one of his ribs. The mere raising of his arm would not have caused him agony otherwise.

No matter. Dillie was worth it.

"How silly of me." She shook her head and let out a delicate laugh. "I don't know why I'm crying now that you're better."

He arched an eyebrow. "Disappointment?"

Her smile faded. "How could you even think such a horrid thought? Of course I'm not disappointed. I would have been shattered if you'd died. In my bed, no less!"

"Right. Nobody likes a dead duke in their bed."

She was frowning now, but she made no move to remove his hand that was once more caressing her cheek. Her blue eyes still shimmered with tears. "It would be especially difficult to explain to the authorities."

He nodded. "Or to the patronesses at Almack's. My death would have been quite the scandal, and certainly the ruination of you."

She tipped her head, turning into his hand so that he now cupped her chin. She didn't notice, obviously distressed by his words. "Surely not my ruination."

"Dillie, nobody would have cared that you'd worked tirelessly to save my sorry life. All they would have noticed is that I'd departed this world in Dillie Farthingale's bed."

"You're simply being your cynical self, thinking the worst of your fellow man."

"And you're thinking like a wide-eyed innocent. People will always disappoint you. The sooner you realize it, the better."

Her gaze turned tender. "Ian, who hurt you so badly to make you feel that way?"

He laughed and then winced as the effort sent more shooting pains up and down his body. "No one." *Everyone.* "I was born this way."

"No you weren't. Children aren't born cynical."

"I'm a man now. I'm as manly as they come."

She rolled her eyes. "I suppose all the women you seduce tell you that."

"Breathlessly and often." Damn, she had beautiful eyes. A soft, sky blue.

"You aren't as manly as you think." She slipped away from him and rose to grab one of the clean cloths from a stack beside the basin of water on her night stand. Grinning mischievously, she dipped it in the water and wrung it out. "I had to hold you down while Uncle George treated your wounds. You cried like an infant the entire time. *Waah, waah,* just like a baby," she teased, making a pretense of rubbing her eyes and sniffling like a child who'd fallen and scraped a knee. "Amos, our strongest footman, had to help me hold you down."

He laughed again, then winced again. "Good try, but not possible."

"How do you know?" She arched a delicate eyebrow. "You were barely conscious most of the time."

His merriment faded. "Dillie, you saw my body. These aren't my first scars, and they're not likely to be my last."

She returned to his side and set the cool, damp cloth over his forehead. She didn't sit down but remained standing and slightly turned away, as though suddenly troubled. "Very well. You didn't cry out. Not even once," she said in a whisper.

"I know." He'd shed his last tears at the age of four, spent every last one of them wishing... no matter, his life had been changed forever that day and he'd learned to endure.

Were her eyes watering again? He didn't want her to cry over him or feel anything for him beyond her usual disdain. "Where are my clothes? I have to get out of here."

She whirled to face him, her eyes wide in surprise. "The ones you wore are ruined. Your valet brought over several outfits. Choose whichever you like, but you're not leaving here until Uncle George gives his approval."

"Nonsense. I'm fine." He sat up and swallowed a howl as he tossed off his covers, swung around to other side of the bed, and rose to his wobbly feet. Damn! That hurt!

Dillie let out a gasp and clamped her hands over her eyes. "Ian, you idiot! Get back in bed. You're naked!" Her cheeks were a hot, bright pink.

"What?" He glanced down. No wonder he'd felt a sudden rush of cold air against his chest...and other parts. He was too unsteady to walk and too angry at his infirmity to get back into bed. He wasn't a doddering old fool who needed porridge and bed rest. He was young, strong. He refused to think of himself as dazed and stupid, but that's precisely what he was. He hadn't meant to shock Dillie. She was a decent girl.

Luscious and decent.

Now that she'd seen his naked backside, for one crazed moment he considered turning around and—

No, that would be an incredibly stupid move.

Finding a pebble of sense, which happened to be the only thing rattling around in his foggy brain at the moment, he wrapped the peach coverlet securely around his waist and turned to face her.

As he did so, he saw her fashion a peephole between her fingers. So the girl wasn't a paragon of virtue after all. She wanted to see him naked. He grinned. "Like what you see?"

She gasped and looked away. "I wasn't staring at you. Not in that way. My only concern is to keep you from falling and slashing open your healing wounds. You're an idiot. I hate you. Why can't you behave?"

Good question. One for which he had no answer. Well, he did have an answer, just not one she wanted to hear.

"Find me my clothes." He sank back onto the bed, ever careful to keep the covers about his waist. He was loathe to admit he was dizzy and had almost fallen, just as she'd feared. He resolved to eat as hearty a meal as he could manage and then get dressed. Once he had regained his balance, he'd walk out on his own. No, not just walk. Run. His damn blood was pooling around his loins again. In another moment he'd be conspicuously hard and throbbing. "Why aren't you married yet?"

She let out a choking laugh. "I'd hit you if you weren't already bruised over your entire body. None of your business. Why aren't *you* married?"

"Bachelorhood suits me fine."

"Good, because I have no intention of marrying you."

"I don't recall asking you."

"You raised it. What made you think of marriage?" Suddenly, she gasped. "It's that Chipping Way bachelor curse. No, no, no. It can't be true!" She sounded pained. And scared.

Not as scared as he suddenly was. What if the curse did prove true? "I don't believe in it either."

"But you ran down my street. And now you're worried that you inadvertently fell into the Chipping Way trap." She sounded horrified. "For pity's sake, why did you do it? There are a thousand streets in London. You could have chosen any of them. Why mine?"

"It wasn't intentional. I was running for my life, and you should have been back in Coniston. Don't tell me you're the superstitious sort. You can't believe in that silly curse. Your sisters would have met and married their husbands no matter what. They fell in love. I'm not loveable. I'm a dissolute who intends to stay that way."

She paused to study him, her expression a little too thoughtful for his liking. "Why did you just say that?"

"Say what? That your sisters would have met and married—"

"No, about your not being loveable."

He laughed and shook his head. "No one on this earth cares about me. No one ever did. Not even me."

*   *   *

Dillie came around the bed to face Ian, wanting to be angry with him and at the same time wanting to throw her arms around him to assure him that someone cared. Someone must have loved Ian at some point in his life. His parents. His siblings. A sweetheart?

She felt a pang in her heart. It wasn't jealousy. She'd have to care for Ian in that way to feel such a thing. She didn't care for him and never would. Absolutely not. "I'll fetch your clothes." It was of no moment that looking at his broad, lightly tanned chest and the soft gold hairs that lined its rippling planes was making her lightheaded. She glanced away from his dangerously gleaming gray-green eyes.

Ian knew how to make women swoon.

Fortunately, she never swooned. She was too practical for such nonsense.

Nor did his muscled arms make her body tingle. She was merely responding to the ugly red gashes crisscrossed on them.

He wasn't in the least attractive. Not after three days of sweating out a high fever. Besides his ragged growth of beard, he had a large cowlick sticking up from his matted honey-gold hair. It didn't matter that some of those gold curls had looped about his neck and ears in a manner that made her fingers itch to brush them back. The cowlick made him look ridiculous.

Ridiculously handsome.

No! She refused to find him attractive. Absolutely not. Not in the least. Yet, the casual way he dismissed his wounds tugged at her heart. He was used to pain, used to hiding deep, ugly scars. The horrible sort, the unseen ones capable of destroying one's spirit.

Who had done such a thing to Ian? The elephant gun was still loaded. She wanted to hunt down those wicked people and shoot them with both barrels.

END

Daffodil, or Dillie as she is known to her friends and family, is not your ordinary debutante. She has a history with Ian, as you may have guessed from reading this first chapter, but it will take all of Dillie's strength, confidence, and love to break through the considerable barriers Ian has erected around his heart. Ian is a wounded soul who harbors a terrible secret. Can Dillie break through those barriers and teach him not only to trust her, but to love her as well?

Interested in learning more about the Farthingale sisters? Join me on Facebook! Additionally, we'll be giving away lots of FARTHINGALE swag and prizes during the launches. If you would like to join the fun, you can subscribe to my newsletter and also connect with me on Twitter.

If you enjoyed this book, I would really appreciate if you could post a quick review, even a few sentences, on what you thought about the book. It would be most helpful! You can write one for Goodreads. If you do leave a review, send me a message on Facebook because I would love to thank you personally! Please also consider telling your friends about the FARTHINGALE series and recommending it to your book clubs.

ABOUT THE AUTHOR

Meara Platt is married to her Russell Crowe look-alike husband and they have two terrific children. She lives on Long Island, New York, and loves it, except for the traffic. She has traveled the world, occasionally lectures, and always finds time to write. Her favorite place in all the world is England's Lake District, which may not come as a surprise since many of her stories are set in that idyllic landscape, including her Romance Writers of America Golden Heart–winning story to be released as Book 3 in her paranormal romance Garden series set to debut in 2015.

MORE GREAT READS
FROM BOOKTROPE

Paradigm Shift by **Bill Ellis** (Historical Fiction) A rich blend of social history, drama, love, passion and determination, Ellis delivers a powerful page-turner about the struggles and perseverance to overcome all odds.

Revontuli by **Andrew Eddy** (Historical Fiction) Inspired by true events, Revontuli depicts one of the last untold stories of World War II: the burning of the Finnmark. Marit, a strong-willed Sami, comes of age and shares a forbidden romance with the German soldier occupying her home.

Sweet Song by **Terry Persun** (Historical Fiction) This tale of a mixed-race man passing as white in post-Civil-War America speaks from the heart about where we've come from and who we are.

The Duel for Conseulo by **Claudia Long** (Historical Fiction) The second novel of the Castillo family, a gripping, passionate story of a woman struggling to balance love, family, and faith in early 1700's Mexico—a world still darkened by the Inquisition.

The Old Cape House by **Barbara Eppich Struna** (Historical Fiction) A Cape Cod secret is discovered after being hidden for 300 years. Two women, centuries apart, weave this historical tale of mystery, love and adventure.

The Secrets of Casanova by **Greg Michaels** (Historical Fiction) Loosely inspired by Casanova's life, this novel thrusts the reader into an adventure overflowing with intrigue, peril, and passion.

Discover more books and learn about our
new approach to publishing at **booktrope.com**.